Books by Joseph Souza

THE NEIGHBOR

PRAY FOR THE GIRL

THE PERFECT DAUGHTER

Published by Kensington Publishing Corporation

PRAY FOR THE GIRL

JOSEPH SOUZA

KENSINGTON BOOKS
www.kensingtonbooks.com

KENSINGTON BOOKS are published by

Kensington Publishing Corp.
119 West 40th Street
New York, NY 10018

All Kensington titles, imprints, and distributed lines are available at special quantity discounts for bulk purchases for sales promotion, premiums, fund-raising, educational, or institutional use. Special book excerpts or customized printings can also be created to fit specific needs. For details, write or phone the office of the Kensington Special Sales Manager: Attn. Special Sales Department. Kensington Publishing Corp., 119 West 40th Street, New York, NY 10018. Phone: 1-800-221-2647.

Kensington and the K logo Reg. U.S. Pat. & TM Off.

ISBN-13: 978-1-4967-2553-0
ISBN-10: 1-4967-2553-0
First Kensington Hardcover Edition: May 2019
First Kensington Mass Market Edition: March 2020

ISBN-13: 978-1-4967-1625-5 (e-book)
ISBN-10: 1-4967-1625-6 (e-book)

10 9 8 7 6 5 4 3 2 1

Printed in the United States of America

BOOK ONE

1

*T*HE GIRL'S BODY WAS FOUND AFTER A DAYLONG SEARCH, her frail corpse discovered not far from the banks of the Alamoosa River. She was nestled between two unmovable boulders rising up out of the ground. I heard my sister say that a kayaker paddling down the river saw what looked to be a body protruding from the ground and called the police. The girl, later identified as a refugee from Afghanistan, was fifteen at the time of her death. Rumor had it that she'd been buried up to her chest and then stoned. Wendy said that the trauma to her face was so devastating that she was almost unrecognizable to her family and friends.

The news of the girl's death startled me when I first heard it. Things like this didn't happen in Fawn Grove. Or at least they didn't happen when I grew up here. Then again, I left this place fifteen years ago—and I've seen a lot of bad since.

I'd roused myself from a long bout of self-imposed hibernation when I heard the news. My sister and her husband were discussing it at the dining table over lunch, although it could have been breakfast for all I knew. I was standing upstairs and holding on to the railing for support, unsteady and fighting off a stubborn case of vertigo. Time had lost all meaning to me. It seemed not to exist in the sorry state I had gotten myself into.

To say that I was in a bad frame of mind during this conversation was an understatement. My current woes included PTSD, anxiety, and depression, and they were all acting in unison to cloud my thinking. I hadn't experienced such helplessness in a long time. As much as I tried to disassociate myself from the conversation my sister was having with her husband, I ended up hearing every last word of it.

I stumbled back to my room, numb, narcoleptic, not wanting to hear any more of this. Depressing news seemed to be all I ever heard while living in New York City. Murders, rapes, greedy Wall Street types ripping off investors, stabbings, shootings, terrorist attacks, to name just a few of the heinous crimes that occurred there. The sound of police sirens became like elevator music to my ears. But now that I was back home in Fawn Grove, I just didn't care. Hope seemed like some long-lost campaign slogan from a bygone era. I'd lost track of my med schedule and started taking whatever pills lay in front of me that day. Sometimes the shape or size appealed to me. Other times a certain color reflected my ever-changing mood.

Whatever I took, it wasn't helping the situation.

On the bureau sat a vial and next to it a syringe

wrapped in plastic. I was supposed to administer a shot to myself every day. I ripped the syringe package open with my teeth and gazed at the troubled woman staring back at me in the mirror. The eyes were accusatory and judgmental. In another time I would have run from this red-haired witch, but instead I drew the liquid into the syringe and stared back at her with an adversarial snarl.

It infuriated me that my mirror image couldn't or wouldn't share in the emotional pain I was feeling. But the shell she wore that day was certainly beautiful. Or had been beautiful at one time. Maybe she still had the capacity to be beautiful under the right conditions. I pulled out the bottom drawer, rested my toes on the wooden lip, lifted the robe up to my waist, and plunged the needle into my scarred thigh. The quick burst of pain never failed to thrill me, and I shivered with excitement as the juice wormed its way into my system. It was the one time each day that I felt alive, and it made me envious of the addict's ritual.

But back to the girl's murder. I'd allowed a girl to die while serving as a combat medic in Afghanistan, and I vowed never to let that happen again. Not on my watch, anyway. It still weighs on my conscience. It's part of the reason I left New York City and returned to Fawn Grove. The pain of that memory lingers long after I left the battlefield. Healing both body and mind takes time as well as effort. I thought if I could only confront my past and let it go, everything would be better. But I found that I couldn't. It was too painful. There's a toxic hostility seeping through me that I can't quite cast out.

Something *has to* give.

Here's the deal. That Afghani girl is a part of me

now. Forgetting her death, as well as the voices that continue to cry out in my head, would destroy me far sooner than coming to grips with their existence, especially now that a girl has been killed in my hometown. I feel compelled to act, or it'll eat away at me until whoever committed this crime is caught.

They say everything happens for a reason. This must be the reason I wigged out one night in my bug-sized efficiency and returned to Fawn Grove: the veritable armpit of Maine. I feel I was brought back here for a reason.

To find out who killed this girl.

2

*W*HEN I LEFT NEW YORK CITY, I LEFT WITH A SUIT-case filled with my best clothes (admittedly, not many), some personal stuff, a canvas roll of professional knives, and my ego in splinters. Heather was not exactly a happy camper when I gave my notice, which took effect immediately after saying "I quit." She was eight months pregnant at the time but looked ten, and most of her line cooks were junkies, alkies, or whack jobs. I felt bad about leaving like that. But shit happens in this business. I tried not to stare down at her pumpkin belly as I said the dreaded phrase. I tried not to dwell on the fact that her body would soon burst with life, something mine would never do. She was already short-staffed on the line, and the restaurant was packed to the gills night after night.

Heather was a victim of her own success. If I could have stayed and helped her until she found a replacement, I would have. But in the fragile state I'd descended into, I knew I wouldn't last another minute in that place. Dropping the ball in that fashion was a terrible thing to do, and considered one of the worst offenses in our profession. But what choice did I have? When the inner demons awaken from their deep slumber, there's not much one can do but let fate run its course.

So I returned home to Fawn Grove, a town best known for two things: its paper mill and the plane crash that occurred there in 1975, which took the life of hard-partying rock star Angus Gibbons and all his band members. They were on their way to Bangor for a concert when the Convair they were flying in ran out of fuel. Sensing a financial opportunity, the town quickly erected a memorial at the sight of the crash, and just like that, a small cottage industry was created, celebrating the life of a guitar god taken too soon.

Returning to Fawn Grove was never in the cards for me. Then again, not much in my life has gone as planned. It's been a little over fifteen years since I've been back here, and every day that went by I missed this town a little bit less, until one day I forgot it ever existed.

I stare at myself in the bureau mirror, under the soft light of a faux Tiffany lamp my sister has a fondness for collecting. The skin over my face appears remarkably smooth, considering all that I've been through. I lift the brush and dust a light smattering of rouge over my cheekbones. Putting on makeup is something I've become quite adept at. I pencil in black eyeliner, apply a swathe of lavender across my lids, and then draw a thin sheen of glossy pink over my lips. A quick pucker and I'm ready to go.

But go where?

It's three-twenty in the morning when I look up. The old Victorian is deathly quiet at this hour. I swear it groans under the considerable weight of my family's history. I move gingerly through the room, the floor-boards warped and weathered with wear. Being nocturnal has its advantages. It also has its downside, and considering that I've barely left my room in the last few weeks, I'd say everything's evenly matched.

I'm all skin and bones. Lying in bed for over a week tends to do that to a girl. Still, most women would kill to have my svelte figure and razor-sharp features. I know this because many women have come up to me on the street and said as much. I'm not trying to brag by saying this. In fact I've never had much in my life to boast about. But women definitely yearn for the smooth skin along my cheeks; my long, thin legs; and my perfectly shaped nails. If they only knew what I had to do each day to look this beautiful, maybe they wouldn't feel so envious. If they only knew about the capricious panic attacks that strike out of nowhere. The constant anxiety I experience over my weight. Or the fact that I eat like a hummingbird on an Atkins diet, despite being an accomplished sous-chef in New York City. But worst of all is the insomnia.

The main reason I can't sleep is because of the voices. They fill my head when I least expect it, be-seeching me for help. They cry out for me to do something. *Anything*. They plead for me to save them from the terrible fate that awaits them. But I don't know how to help them. I'm forced to listen to their high-pitched pleas with a hopelessness bordering on resignation. I hear chains scraping and pulling from their mooring. I hear men's stern voices. And screams. It's one of the reasons I became a chef, so I could avoid them by working late into the night. Then stay up until dawn when the light rectifies the anxiety and puts the voices to bed. I'm a vampire infected by my own past.

But today I'm up and about, casually outfitted in a sleeveless white sundress imprinted with a pretty floral pattern. It's the first day since I've arrived that I feel good enough to leave the house. It's time I do something productive. Like find out more about that dead girl.

I unfurl the canvas bag and run my hand across the collection of knives I've amassed throughout the years. After caressing the black walnut handles, I slide a finger over a razor-sharp blade until a papery layer of skin splits apart like a white rose in bloom.

I traipse down the stairs, trying not to make the floorboards groan. Holding the polished rail for support, my eyes struggle to adjust to the dark. I see photographs of my family on the wall as I descend. Near the bottom, there's a portrait of Jaxon taken in his high school days. In it he looks serious and reflective, which is completely different from the Jaxon I remember. The sight of him hiding behind that long mane makes me want to cry. Despite all the years that have passed, and my conflicted feelings about him, I still miss that boy.

I make my way into the kitchen and see the keys to the '94 pickup hanging by the light switch. Before grabbing them off the hook, I slip into my sweater, checking to make sure my sunglasses are still in my pocket. Then I make my way into the darkness.

Not a week after I'd arrived in Fawn Grove, the girl was found dead. At the time, I was in no condition to reflect on this crime. I had my own problems to deal with, and it took all my energy just to care for myself. I buried my head under the covers, hiding out from the world, and stayed in that state for over a week. During this period of self-imposed isolation, time ceased to have any meaning. Two weeks could have been two days. I staggered out of bed for minutes at a time to nibble on stale toast left over from the previous day's breakfast. I ignored whatever dish happened to be brought up to my room. All I could stomach was toast, charred and tasteless, in nibbles that fooled my stomach into believing it was full. And sips of water. Or else plain tea, in order to swallow the random pill I had chosen that day.

But today I feel more like myself. Not 100 percent, but better.

I leave the house and climb inside the pickup my sister has allowed me to use during my extended stay here. It starts without hesitation, and the engine has a nice rumble to it that travels up my spine and warms me with a nostalgic glow. A chill hangs in the air this morning, my breath visible like powdered sugar flung haphazardly in the air. I let the engine idle. After a few minutes, the steady stream of defrosted air clears the fogged windshield and allows me to see the road ahead. The inside of the cab is warm and cozy as I punch the clutch and shift into first. The truck jerks forward, tossing my head back.

Now to see what's become of my old hometown.

It never occurred to me that I would in any way miss Fawn Grove, or accept the fact that it had changed during the fifteen years I'd been away. There's the paper mill on the north side of town, still hanging on by a thread. At one time, the mill employed half the town, providing good wages for the people who lived here. Not so much anymore, as their line has shrunk down to producing one specific product: catch-and-release papers. On the south side of town, up on the hill, sits Dunham College for the Deaf. The school is, without a doubt, the quietest forty acres in Fawn Grove. In the event one ever needs a bit of solitude, Dunham is the place to go. On the western part of town, by way of the grubby train terminal, is the development of townhouses where the Afghani immigrants have settled. This is where the murdered girl lived.

I drive past the mill, smoke billowing out the tall brick stack. Even with the windows up, I can still detect the sour stench of rotten eggs, a natural by-product of the papermaking process. My grandfather always said that smell was a good thing. The smell of money, he'd announce with pride. A skeletal crew works around the clock struggling to produce these catch-and-release papers, which are used to create synthetic textured finishes for certain manufactured goods. These skeletal crews keep the plant afloat one ream at a time. I try not to stare at the plant as I pass, but the smokestack has become somewhat of a landmark in these parts. Mention Fawn Grove to anyone outside of the town, and depending on who you ask, they'll either mention Angus Gibbons or the paper mill.

The mill has taken up a good chunk of real estate in my mind. Even when it's not in sight, it looms large in my consciousness. My dad worked there for over ten years, as did his dad, overseeing the lines of print news, when print news was the shits. Newspapers put a roof over our heads and food on our table. These days no one my age reads newspapers.

I turn off Mill Road and head back to the main artery that cuts through town. Past the grimy strip mall with the sad bowling alley, the Bennie's Original Steak Burger, and the town's lone movie theater. Taking a right on to Beardsley Road, I drive toward the townhouses where the new arrivals have settled. Even in the dark, I can see that they're poorly constructed. Officially, they call this neighborhood Blueberry Hill, but I heard from my sister that some people in town refer to it as Mecca. The rows of drab gray townhouses run up and down and along the back side of the hill. An aerial view might mistake it for a series of Marine barracks. At one time this area was populated with trees and brooks and places for townie kids to play. Everyone came here to pick the wild blueberries that grew naturally. We used to race bikes up and down the dirt paths, making ramps out of discarded plywood boards, and cutting trails through the woods so that we could get from here to there. We'd play Relievio, hide-and-seek, and any other adventurous game that could occupy us until dinner.

I cruise slowly through the narrow streets, mindful of the speed bumps, eying the broken-down cars and porches littered with junk, wondering which unit the missing girl had once lived in. The shabbiness of it all depresses me. It makes me wish they'd just kept it the way it was. It's a reminder that not all change is for the best.

But who am I to say what's best? To the refugees

who've settled here, this town might seem like paradise. Or hell. I can't imagine escaping from some shitty war-torn parcel of dust only to be moved halfway across the world to Fawn Grove. To arrive upon our frigid Maine shores and realize that in many ways America is a more dangerous and depressing country than the one they left. A place where children die for no good reason.

Not a soul is out at this ungodly hour, and so I cut short the tour and head back to the center of town. Surprisingly, I discover that I'm famished, which is a good sign. I haven't been this hungry in weeks. Maybe such hunger pangs are a sign that I'm finally getting better and will soon be able to face my sister and her family.

I glance at the clock and notice that it's almost four A.M. I've been driving for nearly forty minutes. It's way too early to return home and start chopping potatoes, frying bacon, and scraping sweet cream butter across slightly charred squares of toast. My only hope is that The Galaxy is open at this hour.

Back in the day, when the mill was going full steam, The Galaxy used to be open twenty-four seven. You could find people in there at all times, especially on weekend nights after the local bars and pubs let out. It was a place for workers to go after a long night toiling in the mill. At one time it boasted about having the best corned beef hash in Maine. Come fall, there would be lots of burly, bearded men dressed in camouflage, oftentimes a freshly killed moose or deer lying bloodied in the bed of their pickup.

The road I travel on is dark and surrounded on either side by woods and gentle hills. As I speed past, I see a police cruiser hiding between a grouping of trees. A quick glance at the speedometer tells me I'm doing nearly seventy in a forty-five mph zone. Lights flash and the siren blips. I peek in the rearview and see a cop car racing in my direction. I pull over and watch as the cruiser comes to a stop behind me. The officer steps out of his car and ambles toward the truck, one hand on his holster (this never used to happen here). I place both hands on the steering wheel and pray that I've never crossed paths with this cop. My long blue nails tap nervously on the hard plastic. I admire their shape and hue as he approaches, but I try not to focus on the many scars and burns dotting the back of my hands. Women who make their careers in kitchens rarely have smooth skin.

A knock on the window and I roll it down by hand.

"Good morning, ma'am. Out for a drive?" he asks in a low voice that sounds vaguely familiar. He leans forward so that his face can be seen through the open window. I continue to look straight ahead. A distrust for authority once ran strong through these veins.

"Something wrong, Officer?"

"You tell me."

"I couldn't sleep, so I went for a drive." I turn and notice that it's Rick Dalton. How could I forget those magnetic blue eyes and butt cheek chin. Or the barest trace of acne scars over the lower half of his face. Pinned to the breast of his uniform is an American flag. Underneath it, it says AMERICA FOR AMERICANS.

"Going a little fast in this old truck, wouldn't you say?"

"Honestly, I didn't realize I was going so fast." I stare nervously at the road ahead, praying he doesn't recognize me. I've changed since those days. I'm not the same dorky kid he once bullied.

"What's your name?" He breathes a cloud of smoke.

"Lucy."

"Well, Lucy, I'm going to need to see your license and registration."

I pull the registration out of the glove compartment, pluck my New York City license out of my purse, and hand them to him.

"Wow! All the way from New York City." He stares at my license before breaking into his most charming smile. "Now, don't go away, Lucy. I'll be right back."

I'm a wreck and can barely hold myself together. As I wait patiently for him to return, I pray he doesn't make the connection between my current and former self. But how could he? I'd changed my name and my appearance since moving away. After a few minutes pass, he gets out of his car and walks toward me. I apply another shade of gloss over my lips, pop a breath mint into my mouth, and toss my hair back over my shoulder. I can't help but notice that he's aged well since I last saw him.

"Well, Lucy Abbott, it appears you have a very clean driving record."

"Do I get a sticker for that?"

He laughs. "Not quite."

"I'm sorry if I went over the speed limit, Officer. Honestly, I didn't intend to."

"No one ever intends to. But the law is the law."

"I'll make sure to pay attention to the road signs from now on."

"Probably not the best idea to be driving around here at this time in the morning. Especially the way this town is changing."

"Changing?"

He leans in a bit closer. "You haven't heard?"

I shake my head.

"Just passing through town, are we?"

I laugh. "Something like that."

"Where're you staying?" He leans on my door a bit too close for comfort.

"Is this an official interrogation?"

"Just making polite conversation."

"Good, because for a moment there I thought I might need to call my attorney."

"This used to be a good, law-abiding town. Unfortunately, a girl was recently kidnapped and killed here. I'm concerned for your safety."

"Don't go worrying your pretty face, Officer. I know how to take care of myself."

"Didn't you hear what I said? A girl was murdered."

"Girls are murdered all the time in New York City. That doesn't stop me from going out and living my life."

"Fawn Grove is definitely not New York City," he says, laughing. "I've always wanted to visit that place."

"You definitely should. The restaurants there are to die for."

"Listen to me, Lucy. This girl's murder was different than most murders you hear about."

"Are you trying to purposefully scare me? Just because I went over the speed limit?"

Dalton stares at me for a few seconds before breaking into laughter. "Maybe I am."

"What's so funny?"

"You."

"Me?"

"Big-city girl like you cracks me up." He reaches

for something down by his pocket. "You plan on staying long in Fawn Grove?"

"I'm not sure just yet."

"Well, whatever you decide, I hope you have a pleasant stay here." He rips off a pink sheet and hands it to me. "Today's your lucky day. I'm letting you off with a warning. So take it easy on the gas, okay?"

"Trust me, you won't catch this girl speeding through town again." I laugh in spite of myself.

"Maybe I'll see you around."

"Not if we're meeting in this fashion."

"Something tells me that with a lead foot like yours, this speeding thing could be habitual."

"Habitual," I say. "Good word."

"Never underestimate the intelligence of a Mainer." He raps his knuckles against his temple.

"I would never."

"Maybe we can grab a coffee sometime."

"Did you become a police officer to spice up your love life?"

"A guy like me doesn't need a badge to get a date in this town."

"Maybe we'll run into each other one of these days."

"I'd like that," he says. I start to roll the window up, but he stops it with his fingers. "My friends call me Rick."

"You have friends?"

"I have one now." He winks at me. "Have a great day, Lucy."

I watch as he walks back to his car. The headlights in the rearview flash in my eyes, momentarily blinding me. I sit quietly, overcome with emotion, trying to keep my hands from shaking. A fine line exists between police work and criminality, and Rick Dalton is no exception to the rule. I half expected to learn that he was behind bars or out on bail. Or that maybe someone had killed him in a fit of rage. Nothing would have pleased me more than to have spit in his face and sped away.

His car does a U-turn and heads back down the long, dark road. Thankfully, he won't be following me back into town. He'll be setting a trap for some other poor sap.

By the time I get to the diner, I'm in a much better space. My stomach growls for pancakes, sausages, and bacon. Or maybe a cheese omelette as plump as a princess's pillow. There's only a few cars parked in the lot. I pull up in front of the stainless steel caboose, remembering all the times I spent here in my youth. A dilapidated sign over the caboose says THE GALAXY DINER in neon pink lights. It's the same sign from my youth.

I walk inside the brightly lit dining room, slipping on my sunglasses as I make my way to the counter. My heels click loudly against the chipped and moldy tiles, announcing my presence. The sun will soon start to rise, which will cause me to retreat back to the safety of darkness. If I fail to return to my room by then, the headaches might return with a vengeance. Then I'll be right back where I started when I first arrived here.

3

I FOLD MY DRESS UNDER MYSELF AS I SIT AT THE COUNTER.
Apart from an elderly man sitting in one of the tattered
leather booths, I'm the only person inside the place.
The Galaxy looks almost the same as when I left, just
rattier and more run-down. Hung on the wall are dusty
photographs of Angus Gibbons despite the fact that he
never set foot in The Galaxy. Those are new and probably put there to attract the occasional tourist who
wanders in. Water stains are splattered across the drop-
down ceiling like a Pollock canvas. Tiles along the
floor are chipped and dirty. The smell of grease and
mold is quite strong. It's a scent any chef worth a damn
can detect. Working in a pit like this would send me
over the edge, which is why I was always fanatical
about keeping my kitchens clean.

In my floral sundress and gradient cat-eye sunglasses, I feel completely overdressed for this place. My unease will become more profound in an hour when the mill's shift workers storm in ordering pancakes, bacon, sausage, and eggs.

I grab the weekly rag sitting on the counter and begin to read about the dead girl. She was fifteen when she was killed and lived in this country less than two years. There's a black-and-white photo of her wearing a hijab and staring into the foreground. Her face is placid, and there's virtually no expression over it. I wonder how her family is dealing with this tragedy. They'd barely escaped the devastation in their own country only to come to America and experience the senseless murder of their daughter.

"Coffee?" the girl behind the counter asks. Her splotched nameplate says STEF and she has the complexion of a Mediterranean princess.

"I'd love some," I say, folding the paper in half. She pours me a cup as I glance at the plastic menu spattered with grease and dried food. "I'll have the Western omelette while you're here."

Frowning, she snatches the menu out of my hand and goes back to the kitchen. She shouts my order to the cook and then returns to the breakfast bar. "I've never seen you in here before. Passing through town?"

"I suppose you could say that." I pour cream and sugar into my coffee. Yellowing grains of salt ball up near the middle of the dispenser.

"You don't look like anyone from these parts."

"Why do you say that?"

"The flowery dress and fancy sunglasses at four in the morning. Who in their right mind does that?"

"I like to look my best when I go out." I sip this dreadful coffee and try not to show my displeasure. "And the glasses are for light sensitivity."

"For real?"

"Would I lie about something like that?"

"How would I know? I don't even know you."

"Trust me, I wouldn't."

"I noticed you were reading about the murder of that immigrant girl."

I stare in irritation at this busybody. "Shouldn't you be in school or something?"

"School doesn't start for a few more hours."

I look around the near-empty diner, not in the mood for conversation right now, especially with a moody teen asking me a lot of useless questions. Ripped leather stools to the left of me. Empty stools to the right. Where's all the paying customers?

"Where's Harry?" I ask.

"Who?"

"Harry Baker. The old guy who used to run this place?"

"So you do know something about The Galaxy." She looks surprised by this. "He died and his kids sold it to my papou. He's been running it for the last eleven years now."

I push the paper aside as an elderly couple settles into a back booth. Stef shrugs so that her black hair cascades down around her shoulders.

"You can't be much older than this dead girl."

"She was in a few of my classes, but I didn't know her very well." She walks away as if that's all she's going to say on the matter.

The girl is limber and quick, and moves gracefully

around the counter with coffeepot in hand. She reminds me of someone I once knew but can't quite place. I hear her take the elderly couple's order. When she returns to the counter, she stares at me wearing a goofy smile.

"Why are you smiling like that?"

"Those two old-timers asked about you."

"Why would they do that?"

She rolls her eyes and laughs. "Are you that clueless? Someone like you stands out in this town. They think you're famous."

"Me?"

"With your fancy hair, sunglasses, and dress. And wearing all that goopy makeup." She laughs. "Of course I told them you weren't anybody worth staring at."

"Gee, thanks."

Despite the obvious sarcasm in her voice, I find her rather amusing. The irony is that she's likely more striking than any other girl in town. If she looks this way now, how will she look in five or six years? Back in New York City, no one raised an eyebrow at me on the streets, especially after I'd spent twelve hours toiling in a hot kitchen, my grease-laden hair up in a bun, sweat dripping down my oven-blasted face. In the city, I was a nobody, a drone worker like everyone else. A lesser species of tuna in a sea constantly swimming with grade A bluefin. And that's exactly how I wanted it. To fit seamlessly into the teeming masses and live my life the way I saw fit.

"So, how do you know about Harry?" she asks.

"I spent a little time here back in the day," I say. "So what about this girl? How well did you know her?"

"What's it matter whether I knew her or not? She's dead."

"Just trying to make polite conversation."

The girl shrugs. "She's one of the immigrants who settled here. Not sure which country she came from and don't really care. I have my own life to live."

"Come on, now. Working here in this diner, you must hear all the scuttlebutt around town."

"You don't stop with the questions, do you?"

"It's been a long time since I've been back in Fawn Grove. I'm just trying to catch up on what's going on here."

The girl sighs as if she's annoyed with me. "Some people think they're sponging off the system. Free housing, free food, driving around town in brand-new vans. Blah, blah, blah." She flips her hair back as if to make a statement. "I heard customers complain that a few of them might even be terrorists."

"What about the girl? How was she killed?"

"How should I know?" She refills my cup. "All I know is that there's a lot of people who aren't happy about them being here."

"What do you think about it?"

"I'm fifteen. What does it matter what I think? No one listens to kids in this town, anyway."

"You must have an opinion about these people."

"Everyone deserves a chance as long as they follow the rules and obey our laws," she says as if reciting the line from a class on diversity.

I'm about to reply when a burly chef dressed in soiled whites drops my omelette on the counter in front of me. I can tell right off that he's overcooked it, and judging by its bright orange color, I'm certain it was made with liquid eggs. The two of them begin to argue in a foreign tongue, and it makes me slightly uncomfortable. I readjust my sunglasses and study the chef closely. His hair is much grayer than I remember, and he's gained a few pounds, but I recognize him immediately. Yanni Doulos. His family immigrated here twenty-plus years ago and landed in Fawn Grove. I know this because I used to date his oldest child.

The chef throws up his hands and storms back to the kitchen. I scan the plastic menu and read the lunch offerings. Spanakopita, grape leaves, moussaka, and keftedes. He's added Greek fare to Harry's classic diner menu. The girl rests her elbows on the counter and smiles at me. The steaming pile of shit on my plate looks so unappetizing that I've now lost my appetite.

"What were you two fighting about?" I ask.

"I told my papou to stay out of the dining room, but he never listens to me. Customers don't want to see a fat, old Greek guy when they're eating."

"Good advice," I say. "Do you have any other family members who work here?"

"My uncle sometimes, and my mom helps out from time to time whenever we're short staffed. And there's Billie, who's practically useless, although she's not family."

"What does your mom do beside working here?"

"She's a social worker. Helps the refugees get housing and benefits once they arrive in town."

"Did she know the missing girl?"

"We never talk about that kind of stuff." She stares down at my omelette. "Aren't you going to eat that?"

I hold it up and inspect it. "Would you?"

"No, but then again I hate eggs." She snaps a wad of gum between her teeth. "You're the paying customer."

"I think I'd pay *not* to eat it."

"Try it before you knock my papou's food. You might like it."

I fork a rubbery cube into my mouth, along with some fries, and it takes all my might not to toss it up. The home fries taste bland and undercooked. The old Galaxy used to at least serve decent food back in the day.

"So?" Stef asks.

"You want the truth?"

"Sure."

"It's disgusting."

"You think you're too good for us? Because you wear a fancy dress and are from out of town?"

"You wanted the truth, I gave it to you."

"I think you came in here determined not to like anything."

"Hate to burst your bubble, kid, but this is one of the worst omelettes I've ever had the misfortune to eat." I hold a rubbery piece of the orange protein up to the light.

"Look, lady, we're an old-fashioned diner. We don't make all that fancy food you're probably used to eating."

"I'm used to eating?" I laugh. "Don't give me that bullshit. I know for a fact that your beloved papou didn't crack any real eggs to make this."

She glares at me for a few seconds. "My mother and I have told him a million times to use fresh eggs, but he's always trying to cut costs."

I drop a twenty on the counter and turn to leave.

"Where you going?"

"Home, to make a real omelette."

"Ha! You don't strike me as someone who knows how to cook, never mind turn on a microwave."

I laugh as she clears my plate and pockets the twenty. "Then you obviously don't know me."

"You staying in town long?"

"What's it to you?"

"Just trying to make *polite* conversation."

"Now that's a first in this place."

"I dare you to come back tomorrow morning and try the omelette I'll make you."

"You mean a smart-ass kid like you knows how to cook?"

"You may think you're funny, lady, but you're really not."

"At least I know how to make an omelette." I open the door. "Tell your mother Moo Moo was here."

"Moo Moo?" The girl looks perplexed. "My mother knows you?"

"Just tell her I was here."

I grab my purse and head out the front door. Moo Moo was the pet name her mother used to secretly call me back in junior high. Supposedly, it was a Greek term that translated to *lover*. As I saunter to the truck, two burly lumberjacks turn their heads at me and whistle. I smile at them, toss my hair back, and then flip them the bird. Being whistled at flatters me, but it also feels good to express myself in such a forceful manner. Attention like this rarely happens to me back in the city, and for once it feels good to bathe in the admiration of complete strangers.

4

*I*T'S JUST PAST FIVE A.M., AND I CAN ALREADY FEEL MY-self reentering that wobbly state of mental fragility. In roughly thirty minutes the sun will come up over the horizon. I hope I'll be in my room by then, buried under an avalanche of covers. Despite the hunger pains rolling through my gut, my appetite has gone to shit. There's little time left for me to get reacquainted with my hometown, and I fear what might happen when the light of day strikes.

I cruise through Fawn Grove's deserted business district. It's gotten seedier in the years since I've been away. The ghostly silhouettes of the brick buildings rise up in shadowy forms. Hidden behind the darkness looms an abandoned shoe mill from the last century, pregnant with forgotten memories of its glory days. I pass an Asian nail shop, a drab dollar store, Fawn Grove House of Pizza, and a convenience store with a sign in the window that says WE ACCEPT EBT CARDS. Toward the end of the street I notice a block of stores with foreign lettering: butchers, a halal market, a kebab take-out joint, and a tandoori bakery. Is this representative of a town's happy equilibrium? Of diversity and tolerance? Or simply an act of white-knuckled coexistence?

I'd spent many days in my youth hanging out in this downtown area, searching for comic books and CDs, or buying donuts at Ida Mae's while skipping Sunday Mass. Ida Mae's no longer exists; another casualty of the mill's downturn. It's been taken over by a used clothing store called Hadassah's. I remember hot donuts fresh out of the fryer slathered in sugary icing and chocolate frosting.

The sight of all this depresses me, and so I hit the gas. There's a rest stop on the outskirts of town that offers a nice view of the downtown area. It's where Nadia and I would sneak away, listening to rock music as we cuddled in the front seat. It's not far from where the Convair famously crashed, and where they found Angus Gibbons's burnt and smoldering corpse. However, his signature red Stratocaster was discovered not thirty feet from his body with not a scratch on it. It hangs prominently in the Rock & Roll Hall of Fame.

I stop and look down upon the town's twinkling lights. Nadia was the love of my life back then, or what I believed passed for love. For obvious reasons we were forced to keep our relationship secret. Small-town life doomed us, and since I left Fawn Grove after my eighteenth birthday, I'd been trying to put that part of my life behind me. Although I haven't spoken to her since leaving, I've never stopped thinking about her.

The first rays of the sun begin to sneak up over the horizon. My father's house sits just up the road a ways, but I haven't yet worked up the nerve to see him. It's been ages since we've talked or laid eyes on one another. Maybe one of these days I'll sit down and ask him why he abandoned us. But I have more important things to do right now.

Because of my past, I've developed this powerful urge to learn more about this dead girl. Like why did she have to die and who killed her? It's this restless nature of mine that compels me to seek answers. I regret my inaction in Afghanistan and letting that poor girl from the fruit market die. It's the reason I still hear voices at night, no matter how hard I try to shut them out.

The Victorian sits back from the street and is fronted by toothpicks of maples and elms. I park up the driveway so I can access the back door. Wendy is waiting for me in the kitchen as soon as I enter, her hydraulic wheelchair elevated so that she can see the laptop sitting on the counter. She turns and stares at me, a cigarette smoldering in her long, nicotine-stained fingers.

"Look what the cat brought in," she says, moving around strips of bacon in a grease-filled frying pan. "Thought you'd never come out of that room."

"Thanks for putting up with me these last few weeks, sis."

She puffs on her cigarette. "Feeling any better?"

"A bit." I fan the smoke out of my face, both bacon and cigarette.

"You've barely left that room since you've been here."

"I know. This healing process really sucks."

"You're not the only person around here trying to get better." She blows smoke up into the exhaust fan and regards me with something other than sisterly love. "I'm sorry, Lucy. That was a shitty thing to say."

"Forget it."

"No, I was being petty. You've been through quite a lot in your life," she says. "Sit down and have some breakfast. You're all skin and bones."

"Mind if I take a rain check?"

"At least take a plate up to your room in case you get hungry," she says, stubbing her cigarette out in an emerald-colored ashtray. She grabs a plate and loads it with bacon, scrambled eggs, and a buttered slice of toast. "So, where'd you go this morning?"

"I wanted to see Fawn Grove when it's nice and quiet."

"You mean when no one could see you?"

I laugh. "That too."

"They wouldn't recognize you, anyway."

"Probably not. It's been a long time since I've been back."

"Fourteen years?"

"Give or take."

"Been a lot of changes in this town." She holds the plate out to me and I take it, although I know I'm not going to eat a bite of it. "I suppose the more Fawn Grove changes, the more it stays the same."

"In what way?"

"If you haven't noticed, we have all these new immigrants in town."

"Is that why this dead girl is creating such a stir?"

"Where did you hear about that?"

"I was standing at the railing one day when I overheard you and Russ talking about it."

"It's insane what people in this town are saying. I suppose I should have expected as much from these small-town minds."

"They say it might have been an honor killing."

"Those jackals will say anything to sell papers." She waves her hand in the air as if to dismiss the notion. "When I was healthier than I am now, a few years ago, I used to volunteer my time helping those Afghanis, and I can tell you from experience that most of them are wonderful people."

"So you don't believe it was an honor killing?" The powerful stench of smoked pork is beginning to make me nauseated.

"No, I don't. There's always a few bad apples in every barrel, but I worry more about the bigots in this town than I do these refugees."

I thank Wendy for breakfast and stagger up to my room. As I pass, I see Brynn sitting at the dining room table with Wendy's husband, Big Russ. He lowers the newspaper and eyes me suspiciously. Russ is a burly, taciturn guy with a thick mustache and an intimidating glare. He's been on permanent disability ever since injuring his back while working at the mill. Brynn is a freshman at Fawn Grove High. We met last week for the first time but have yet to get fully acquainted because of my condition. I wonder how well she knew the dead girl. She stares at me with those moon-shaped eyes that will one day drive the boys crazy, if they don't already.

"Hello, everybody," I say.

Big Russ and Brynn grumble something under their breaths. I can't say I blame them for their ambivalence toward me. I'm a stranger in their midst. Although we're related by blood, we barely know each other. I hope to sit down with them at some point and get better acquainted. But now's not the time. Not until I can work myself into the right frame of mind.

I climb the stairs, burst into my old room, and collapse onto the bed in exhaustion. Driving through Fawn Grove took everything out of me, and it'll take at least a day for me to recover. I look at the pile of food on my plate and debate whether I should dump it out the window. My olfactory sense can't handle such an awful stench. My appetite has completely abandoned me after that trip down memory lane. I set the plate down on the nightstand, close my eyes, and pray that the voices in my head will allow me at least a few hours of sleep. That's all I need right now. Just a little rest.

The voices start to grumble, which stirs me awake. It's rather comforting to know that my trusty set of knives sits nearby on the dresser. They've become an important part of me and an extension of who I am. But what would I use them for now that I'm no longer working as a chef? They're more a crutch than anything else. A reminder of who I am and what I've accomplished in life despite all that has happened.

The voices today are not the usual ones I hear. In fact, they're not even voices, but more like sounds from my past. It's the sounds I heard while working in that cramped East Village kitchen. Orders being shouted out at the top of one's lungs. Pissed-off waitresses cussing out line staff. Steaks and chops sizzling on flaming grills. Heavy metal music blaring over speakers. Exhaust fans whirring nonstop. Pans smashing against one another in symphonic disharmony. The skin of a Chilean sea bass ripping away from its filet.

Why am I remembering all this? And why now? Do I miss being a sous-chef? I don't miss the long hours on my feet or the oppressive heat bearing down on me on a humid summer day. I don't miss falling behind on dinner orders and working madly to keep up. Nor do I miss the relatively shitty pay and the accumulation of scrapes, burns, and bruises I'd collect during a frantic dinner service. Individually, I don't miss any one of these things. But as a whole, I very much miss working in that busy kitchen.

More than anything, I miss the anonymity of the city. New York allows you to be whomever you want to be. There's no judgment or shame living there. This observation has never been more apparent as when I returned home. In the city, my past didn't matter like it does here. In the city, there's a thousand things to do at all times. In the city, I could work at being the person I always aspired to be. I miss the camaraderie with other chefs, getting off shift and drinking cocktails in Soho till sunrise. I miss passing out from exhaustion once back in my overpriced broom closet. At least once a day, staff and cooks would join together for our nightly dinners. It was the closest thing I had to a family meal. We laughed and joked before the storm. Then the doors opened and the mad rush of diners turned us into raving, homicidal lunatics wielding sharp knives and pointing them at anyone who looked at us the wrong way. Or failed to keep up with the pace.

There's no use trying to sleep. I look over at the clock and see that it's nearly two A.M. It's hard for me to believe that I've been lounging in this bed for over twenty hours. It's too early to go to The Galaxy and sample the omelette that girl threatened to cook for me. At least I feel better than a few weeks ago—less depressed and without the crippling anxiety that caused me to scamper back to my old haunts. I'm under no illusion that my life has returned to anything resembling normalcy. Being able to face the world is a reward unto itself.

I move to the bureau and take in the vast collection of unguents, elixirs, pill bottles, and liquid prescriptions. They await me like toy soldiers at parade rest. I grab a random handful, swallow them, and then retreat to the bed with bottle and syringe. It suddenly occurs to me that I've not bathed or showered since arriving here. I draw the liquid into the tube, flick the needle point with my finger, lift my sundress up to my blistered thigh, and plunge the tip into my awaiting flesh. Injecting myself has become like second nature to me, as easy as boning out a chicken or breaking down a young pig.

I run a hot bath and undress before sitting down on the toilet. My skin feels dry and prickly as I gently remove the first prosthetic from below my left knee. I remove the other and place it next to the first one. The flesh at the bottom of my stumps appears red and swollen, but they've looked worse. Nothing a little ointment rubbed into the folds can't fix.

Slowly I lower myself from the toilet until my entire

body is enveloped in hot, soapy water. I rest my head back until I'm floating lightly on the surface. Free of prosthetics, my body fits perfectly inside the tub. I tie my hair up into a bun and look down toward the faucet, where I see my two stubs emerging from the water.

5

I FEEL LIKE A NEW WOMAN AS I WALK INTO THE GALAXY,
dressed in A pair of crisp blue jeans, a pink button-
down shirt, and quilted white sneakers. The doors have
just opened, and I can see that I'm the only one here.
My stomach is a vast pit of emptiness that often leads
me astray in times of crisis. But as a chef I've learned
to trust my gut. The self-induced fasting I've endured
leaves me weak and fatigued, and my hungry heart
howls like a wolf inside my chest. The message is
clear: Eat something, Lucy.

It feels warm and safe inside this brightly lit diner.
Despite it being in disrepair, it still feels familiar to me.
I breathe in the nostalgic ambience of the past, recalling all the ghosts who once sat on these stools. The
confines seem to envelope me in a loving embrace, as
if we've reconnected after a long split. Maybe that's a
vestige of all the stored-up memories I have. Or maybe

it's simply my preference for all things culinary, dating back to my childhood.

"Look who it is: Miss Fancy-Pants," Stef says, pulling up behind the counter dressed in chef's whites.

"I'm back for that amazing omelette you promised."

"You mean a glamorous woman like you hasn't gotten sick of this town yet?" She leans on one elbow, her perfectly white teeth contrasting gloriously against her olive-toned skin.

"How about going into the kitchen and making me that omelette?"

"Get ready for a party in your mouth."

"Humble, aren't we?"

She disappears into the kitchen, leaving me sitting alone at the counter. I hop off the stool and make my way behind it. Grabbing a mug off the shelf, I help myself to some of their bland coffee. The door opens, and I turn to see the second customer of the day walk through the door. It's Dalton. A look of surprise comes over his face upon seeing me. That's followed by a knowing smile. He takes off his cap, places it on the counter, and grabs a stool two removed from mine.

"Taking a part-time job here?" he says.

I place a mug down in front of him. "Care for some coffee? It appears to be Help Yourself Day."

"Coffee's the only reason I come here."

I fill his cup. "Where's the old Greek?"

"Yanni comes in late a few days a week," he says. "Usually Nadia comes in, but I guess she's busy today."

"Catch any speeders as of late?"

"Just one pretty lady with a chunk of lead in her foot. Lucky for her, I was feeling generous that day."

"Lucky lead foot, then." I rest the pot back on the

warmer and stand across from him. "Learn anything more about this murder?"

"I thought you were going to take my breakfast order?"

"Unfortunately, pouring coffee's the extent of my generosity."

"Why so interested in this dead girl? You got a thing for Afghani refugees?" He sips his coffee.

"Let's just say that old lead foot here has taken an interest in the case since you told me about it."

"I shouldn't have been talking to you about such things."

"Official business, huh?"

"On a need-to-know basis."

"What could you know, anyway? You're too busy chasing speeders and pulling cats out of trees."

"I stop only the pretty ones."

"Here's a tip, Officer Dalton. Try not coming off so strong and you might do better with the ladies."

"Don't flatter yourself, Miss Abbott," he says. "And for your information, it's Detective Dalton."

"How sweet that you remembered my name."

"Not every day I stop a speeder dressed to the nines at four in the morning."

"Detective Dalton. That's got a nice ring to it." I lower myself so that I'm eye to eye with this man from my past. "Is that *detective*, as in charge of this murder investigation?"

"Actually, I'm the lead detective assisting the state police on the case."

"Your department isn't able to handle the murder investigation on its own?"

"The state police are the lead agency on most homicide investigations in Maine, but I'm their go-to guy in town."

"A lawman like you wouldn't lie to impress a big-city girl, would he?"

"If I knew stripes got you so hot and bothered, I would have told you I was chief of police," he says.

I shoot him a smile. "So what can you tell me about the case?"

"What are you willing to do for it?"

"Hopefully, not what you're thinking." It pains me to beg this asshole for information.

"I'm offended that you think I'm so crass."

"How about making me an offer and we'll see how crass you truly are."

Stef dashes out into the dining room with a broken, misshapen omelette smoking on the plate. What a complete mess. She's failed miserably at presentation, but at least she's used real eggs to make it. Although I've developed a strong antipathy toward her, I admire her spunk and determination. I have to remind myself that she's a fifteen-year-old girl forced to work at four in the morning in a crappy diner run by her grandfather. She places it down on the counter and stabs a fork at me. I cut into it, blow on the chunk, and ease it gently into my mouth.

"Pretty damn good, right?" she says proudly.

Dalton reaches over with his fork, cuts off a piece, and takes a bite. "Not bad for a kid."

"I'm no kid, Dalton."

"It's Detective to you. Show some respect for the law."

The girl rolls her eyes.

"Besides, I was paying you a compliment," Dalton says. "That's a damn good omelette."

"I'm more interested in what Miss Universe has to say," she says.

"I've had better." I push it away as if disappointed, but in actuality it's a big improvement from the one I sampled yesterday.

"There's nothing wrong with that omelette." She glares at me.

"If you say."

"Okay, Miss Fancy-Pants, tell me what you don't like about it."

"For starters, you didn't whip the eggs long enough. See the discolored strands of yoke running through it?" I point out the striations in the egg. "And you added milk. That's the worst thing you can do to an omelette."

Stef crosses her arms as a vein pulses on her forehead.

"And you let the pan get too hot. See the brown spots on the bottom?" I lift it up and show her.

"Okay, I heard you. I'd like to see you do better," she says defiantly.

I turn to the cop. "How do you like your omelette, Dalton?"

"Love a good Western."

"How about we make a trade. I make you an omelette and in exchange you give me some information about the girl?"

"Okay, but only if it's the greatest omelette I've ever tasted."

"Trust me, you'll think you went to omelette heaven after I'm through with it." I turn to Stef. "Okay if I use the kitchen?"

"Knock yourself out. And I mean that literally, b . . ." Did she just mutter *bitch* under her breath?

I dash back to the kitchen and am horrified by what I see. It's in such woeful condition that it makes me think twice about cooking here. Without a doubt, it's the dirtiest, grossest kitchen I've ever come across. I debate turning and leaving, but the chance to learn something new about this murdered girl prevents me from doing so. I grab a dented frying pan, add a dollop of butter, and heat it up. After finding the whisk, I gently break four eggs into a bowl and then beat them until everything blends perfectly together. When the pan is sufficiently warm, but not too hot, I pour in the eggs. Using a wooden stick to agitate the curds, I work the pan until the omelette starts to set. Then I add ham, chopped onion, red and green bell pepper, salt, and pepper. I fold it over, give it a gentle flip, count to ten, and then plate it. Two slices of toast, buttered and cut diagonally, get placed on either side of the plate. After garnishing it with a twig of parsley, I walk back into the dining room and drop the plate on the counter so that it makes a loud clatter. The omelette is shaped perfectly and resembles a crescent moon. Whorls of steam coil gently upward the water-stained ceiling.

"Holy shit!" Dalton says.

"*You* made that?" Stef says, staring at it in awe.

"With my own hands," I say. "Making an omelette isn't exactly rocket science."

"Better taste it, Dalton, before you start getting all lovey-dovey," she says.

"How many times I got to tell you, Stef? It's Detective Dalton to you."

"Stop bickering, you two, and dig in," I say.

"Oh my God! This tastes like a pillow in my mouth," Dalton says. "It's so light and airy."

"Beginner's luck," Stef says bitterly before slinking back to the kitchen.

"Where'd you learn to cook like this?" Dalton asks.

"Just shut up and enjoy your omelette."

He takes a bite and then another.

"You ready to make good on your promise now?" I say.

"What is it you want again?"

"How about taking me down to where the girl was murdered?"

He stops chewing and stares at me. "Really?" He takes another bite with a piece of toast and appears to mull it over. "Okay, I don't see why not."

"When can we go?"

"How about this morning around eight? I have a few things to do beforehand."

I open my mouth to answer when the door opens and Stef's mother walks in. Despite it being a long time since we've seen each other, I recognize her instantly. She's even lovelier than when I saw her last. She looks in my direction, but I can tell she doesn't recognize me. It's only when she approaches the counter and sees the miniature tattoo of Hercules Knot on my inner wrist, that her face turns ashen and our eyes lock.

She knows who I am.

6

NADIA TIES AN APRON AROUND HER WAIST WHILE keeping her eyes glued to me. After downing the dregs of his coffee, Dalton introduces me to her before heading out to his cruiser to resume catching speeders and saving cats. We agree to meet back here in the parking lot and then take his cruiser down to the crime scene.

"What are you doing back here, *Lucy*?" Nadia whispers. Her Greek accent is barely noticeable.

"It's complicated," I say. "I'm amazed that you recognized me."

"We dated for three years and have known each other a lot longer. And how could I forget the secret tattoos we got on our wrists?"

"Symbolizing our undying love and commitment?"

"Exactly. And look how that turned out."

"Do you know how much it bothered me that we had to keep our relationship secret?"

"It was a different time. This town wasn't ready for a couple of misfits like us." She smiles in that girlish manner I've always loved.

"It's one of the reasons I left."

"My family was right off the boat from Greece, and you know how traditional my parents were."

"They wanted you to marry a nice Greek boy."

"And you were the furthest thing from a nice Greek boy."

"Seriously, Nadia, you look wonderful."

"Not as good as you. You look absolutely ravishing." She stands back to take me in, grabbing a few strands of my hair. "When did this happen?"

"After I got out of the army."

"No one here will even know you."

"That's what I'm hoping."

"I can't tell you how much I've missed you all these years."

"I missed you too."

"It broke my heart when you upped and left without even a good-bye."

"I had no choice. Fawn Grove was suffocating me," I whisper. "Besides, we both knew we had no future together."

She shrugs and leans into me. "Look at you, girl. I can't believe you've returned home after all these years."

"Temporarily."

"How does it feel to be back?"

"Weird." I notice the diamond ring on her finger. "I really missed certain things about this place while I was away. Like The Galaxy's double cheeseburger."

"How about we sit in one of the booths and catch up on things."

I suddenly feel like crying for no apparent reason. "I can't right now."

"That's all right, sweetie. We can do it some other time."

"I'd appreciate it if you didn't bring up Jaxon while I'm home."

"Of course. He's in the past now. Just know that I'm here for you if you ever want to talk about him."

"I have all these confused feelings swirling inside me now that I'm back. It might take a while to get adjusted."

"Most people in town believe you were killed over in Afghanistan."

"They're partially right."

"How bad were you hurt?"

"Lost both legs below the knee."

Tears fall from her eyes, and she grabs a napkin and dabs them away. "I'm so sorry."

"I suffered a breakdown while living in New York City and couldn't work anymore. That's why I returned to Fawn Grove. To get my shit back together."

"Is there any chance you might stay longer?"

"Don't really know just yet."

"You must think about that attack every day of your life."

"Three soldiers were killed and two others were badly wounded. But that wasn't the cause of my breakdown."

A customer walks through the door and sits at the counter.

"Can we talk about this later?" she asks, grabbing a

mug and the pot of coffee. She pours the man a cup before returning to where I'm sitting.

"As long as we don't bring up the past. That's my only rule."

"Of course." She pauses a few seconds before saying, "I overheard you saying that you're going somewhere with Dalton."

"He's taking me down to the spot where that girl was murdered."

"But why?" She looks startled.

"I'll tell you about it later."

"Dalton's not really changed since you left, except now he's a cop. I don't trust him, and neither should you."

"I despise Dalton, but I can handle him." I stand to leave. "I have to go home and change before I meet up with him."

"I'm warning you, Lucy. He's still a snake."

I laugh. "And snakes never change their stripes, right?"

"Right. And don't let him fool you into thinking he's sympathetic to the plight of these immigrants. He's totally against them settling here and will tell anyone who will listen to him."

"Then why is he assisting the state police on this case?"

"Supposedly, he's the only cop in the department who received homicide training at the academy," she says. "I just want you to watch yourself around him."

"Don't worry, Nadia, I'm a big girl."

"I worry about you. I have ever since you left town without even a good-bye."

"What you should really be worrying about is the

state of this diner. It used to be so wonderful. How could your father let it get in such a sorry condition?"

She glances around. "I agree that it needs some freshening up, but my father's a stubborn man. If only he made a few changes here and there he'd be able to attract more customers."

"I hate to be the bearer of bad news, Nadia, but this place needs more than just a good freshening up. This diner needs a complete overhaul."

"I've got to get back to work," she says as two old women file into the diner. "We'll talk later, okay?"

The sky is still dark when I go outside, stars twinkling in their murky tar sheets, the crescent moon hanging low enough to touch. I rest my head against the steering wheel and try hard not to cry. I never anticipated feeling such powerful emotions upon seeing Nadia. Whether it's my fragile mental state or the possibility that I still love her, I don't really know. But seeing her after so many years apart has affected me in unforeseen ways.

After a few minutes, I glance in the rearview mirror and notice that my mascara is streaking down my cheeks. I'm like a goth girl caught out in the rain. I speed away from The Galaxy. Surprisingly, I feel like I have a renewed sense of purpose now that I'm back in Fawn Grove.

7

WHAT HAVE I GOTTEN MYSELF INTO? I THINK AS I PULL the L.L. Bean boots up over my prosthetic feet. Will I be able to survive the morning light without suffering from an anxiety attack? Breaking down in front of Dalton is the last thing I want to do. I don't want him to write me off as a silly, frivolous woman not deserving of his attention. Another pretty face in town who thinks she's better than everyone else. I need to project strength and confidence in his presence. I can't let on that I suffer from a variety of ailments or that I'm totally repulsed by the mere sight of him.

Big Russ is sitting in his plaid recliner when I arrive downstairs. He's listening to the radio and reading the local newspaper, his thick legs covered in corduroys and stretching horizontally over the footrest. With his thick mustache and full head of auburn hair, he looks like an alpha walrus at rest. He lowers the paper and seems to study me at length. As long as I've known him, he's been a man of few words.

"Heading out?" he asks in his familiar low growl.

"Yeah. I've got a few things to do."

He stares at me with a pensive look.

"Thanks for letting me stay here, Russ. I know it's been an imposition having me."

"No imposition at all. You're family."

"I know it must be weird."

"I can deal with weird," he says. "Besides, I should be the one thanking you."

"Thanking me?" I laugh. "For what?"

"For your service to this country. You're a true-blue patriot and an American hero. They don't give Purple Hearts to cowards."

His words of praise both surprise and embarrass me. I never heard as much in New York City because no one ever knew about that part of my life, and I was happy that way.

"If you ever want to talk about what happened since you left here—"

"Trust me, I don't!"

"Well, if you change your mind, you know where to find me," he says.

"Thanks, but I won't change my mind."

"If you say."

"If you want what's best for me, you'll also not bring up Jaxon in my presence."

"Mum's the word, then," he says, lifting the paper so that it hides his square face.

"Can I ask you a question, Russ?"

He lowers the paper, this time so that only his eyes can be seen.

"Do you think that Afghani girl was killed by one of her own?"

"Of all the crazy questions."

"I can't help it. It's all I've been thinking about as of late."

"Why in the world would you think about that?"

"I don't know. Maybe coming home and seeing how much everything has changed here has made me curious."

"My belief is that that girl was killed thousands of years ago when they started fighting in that region." He lifts the paper back up, signaling that this discussion is over. Clean and simple: classic Russ. The sound of a piano concerto wafts out of his radio and fills my ears.

I head back upstairs to my room to grab the keys to the truck. In the hallway I hear voices coming from inside Brynn's room. Although I know I shouldn't be spying, I can't seem to help myself. I move quietly until I'm standing just outside her room. The door is slightly ajar, allowing me to overhear Wendy and Brynn's conversation. Maybe this will be a way for me to learn something about Brynn.

"I know it's been hard having her here, but you need to try to be nice to Lucy," Wendy says.

"How can I be nice to her when she spends all of her time in her room?"

"Lucy's family. Besides, she has some issues she's trying to work out."

"What about our issues? Everyone in this family has problems they're trying to fix."

"It's just that I haven't seen her in some time," Wendy says. "I used to send her photographs of you when you were little, and letters describing how wonderful you were."

"Were? As in the past tense? Really, Mom?"

"I didn't mean it like that. Of course you're still wonderful. You mean the world to us, honey. Your father and I would do anything for you."

"I know."

"So just do me this one favor and be nice to her."

Brynn laughs. "What makes you think I'd be mean?"

"You do have your mood swings. I know that you're a teenager and all, but sometimes I worry about you."

"Well, don't worry yourself over me. You've got enough to deal with, with your own health problems. And if it makes you feel any better, I'll treat Lucy as if she's a queen."

"Thank you, honey. I love you so much."

"Love you too, Mom."

"Your father and I are so proud of the way you're handling everything."

"I try my best," Brynn says. "Here's what I'll do. I'll wait until Lucy feels better before I start making conversation with her."

"That's my girl. I have to go downstairs now and fold laundry."

Wendy begins to wheel herself toward the door. I tiptoe toward my room and quietly slip inside, keeping the door open so I can make sure to see when she leaves. At the top of the stairs, she positions her wheelchair onto the lift. When the chair is secured, she pushes the button and the lift slowly descends. I grab the keys to the pickup and wait a few minutes so they don't suspect me of listening in on their conversation. Then I head out so I can meet up with Dalton.

8

*D*ALTON PULLS UP NEXT TO MY PICKUP FIVE MINUTES before we're supposed to meet. I'm wearing jeans tucked into boots and a black peacoat with thermally insulated gloves. My hair is tied into a ponytail and I'm donning my best diva sunglasses. Fortunately, the light has yet to bother me, but it's still early. I slip into his cruiser and do a double take upon seeing him. He's dressed in a suit coat and tie and looks far too GQ for a small-town cop. Is he doing this to impress me? So why, to my chagrin, do I feel so thoroughly impressed?

"Do you take all your dates to violent crime scenes?" I instantly scold myself for using the word *date*.

"So this is a date?" He caught it.

"No. This was part of our deal."

"That *was* a great omelette."

"It was an *amazing* omelette," I say. "So what's up with the prom tux?"

"For your information, sweetheart, these are my detective clothes, so don't flatter yourself. I have to appear in court later today."

"Did you just call me sweetheart?"

"Yup, but I'll deny it if you cry sexual harassment or some other politically correct bullshit."

He starts the car and drives for about ten minutes before turning onto a dirt road that cuts into the woods. It's a road that I recognize from my youth. He slows the vehicle down, and we rock along the bumpy surface, branches sweeping against the side of the cruiser. We go about a mile before the road abruptly ends. He turns the ignition off and gets out without saying anything. Then he starts down a narrow trail leading to the Alamoosa River.

I try to follow him, but I realize I'm not in the best of shape. This depresses me because at one time I could run and hike for miles on end, and through the most difficult terrain. Thankfully, I've worn my boots today, but they're loose fitting and cause me to occasionally trip over the rocky trail. It's been a long time since I've made my way along this path. Branches whip back into me and block my view, making it difficult to tell how far Dalton has gone ahead of me. I stop for a second and pick a stick up off the trail to use for balance. Then I walk until I come to a clearing. Upon looking up, I see Dalton shuffling sideways down the steep bank that winds its way toward the river. I notice he's tucked the bottom of his trousers into the boots he's wearing. Using the walking stick, I carefully make my way down as the sound of the river gurgles in my ears.

A heavy rain season has led to a surging river. Upon

reaching the bottom of the hill, I limp painfully over to where Dalton stands. Despite wearing his suit, he jumps onto one of the bigger rocks and stares down at me. By the time I reach him, I can see the slight depression located between the two boulders, and I can only assume that that's where the girl was buried. This hike has taken a toll on my legs. They feel irritated and sore, and are clearly not cut out for this type of travel. Using the stick, I prop myself up onto the opposite rock so as not to be at a height disadvantage.

"Is this where she was murdered?"

"The Muslim bastards buried her up to her chest. Then threw rocks at her."

So there's where his bias lies; he assumes one of the immigrants did it. Still, the thought of the girl dying in this manner causes me to bristle, and try as I might, I can't get the disturbing image out of my head. What had she done to deserve such punishment? I know from personal experience that in some parts of Afghanistan the sentence of stoning is handed out to women accused of adultery.

"The state police collected as many of the rocks as they could and sent them to the lab for prints. But nothing has hit so far."

"What about shoe prints?"

"Unfortunately, the rains that evening washed them away."

"So there's no evidence whatsoever?"

"Nothing that we could find. The way she died makes it difficult to do a forensic investigation, and there's more than a few of those Afghani bastards who could have committed this crime."

Despite his harsh words echoing in my brain, I stare

out at the flowing river and see black whirlpools and violent eddies. A swimmer wouldn't last long in that fast-moving water. It's cold and unforgiving. Beyond the river are thick groves of trees, and on the south side there's a field of some sort. It's too beautiful a spot to contemplate such a violent murder, but it wasn't always beautiful in this way. Growing up, these waters were infested with toxic, life-sucking mill waste. It was a river dying a slow death.

I remember my father taking us down here when we were kids, before our family started to disintegrate. He taught us how to fish and tie flies despite the pollution choking the life out of it. And when we caught a rare brookie, he showed us how to crack it over the head and fillet it on the nearby rocks. Of course this was all for show, as he'd never let us eat the diseased flesh, believing he was doing the poor fish a favor by killing it. Only when we fished way up in the northern regions of Maine would we then fry them in a cast-iron pan sizzling with oil. In the fall, he would lead us into the woods with his Browning and teach us how to shoot. Then we wouldn't leave those woods until he bagged a deer or moose.

The image I have of this dead girl brings back painful memories of the girl I failed to save. I was stationed in Afghanistan when two weeks into my tour a rumor started to spread that a woman in town had been caught having sex outside of marriage. The local soldiers our troops were training typically shared all the local gossip with us. When we heard that she was to stand trial, we knew what that meant: The woman had most likely been raped or had rejected a prominent suitor. The crime of rape was a serious offense in Afghani culture, and the woman was typically assigned the blame. Such an accusation dishonored the family and brought shame to everyone involved, including the rapist. Days went by before I got word that she'd been convicted and sentenced to be stoned in front of family and friends.

When they told me who the woman was, I became enraged. She was a beautiful young girl who used to sell fruit at one of the nearby markets. She couldn't have been more than fifteen at the time. I used to make it a point to go to her stand to pick out some fruit. There was nothing unusual about our interactions. In fact we barely talked except to conduct our transaction. But I remember how wonderful her smile was and the way she brightened my day whenever I saw her working behind that stand. I also knew she was beautiful beyond words and likely the object of many village men's desires.

It infuriated me that they would put this beautiful girl to death for such bullshit. I had no doubt that she was innocent of whatever they'd accused her of doing and that some spurned suitor was trying to exact his revenge against her. Another female soldier and I reported what we heard to our superiors, but they ordered us in no uncertain terms to stay clear of local customs. I was young and at the time, couldn't believe such an injustice could be committed in the name of religion. Why were American troops there if not to promote decency and justice and to protect the local citizens from abuse? I wanted to go down there, armed to the teeth with my unit, and rescue that poor kid from those monsters. But I knew that would be impossible. My cynicism embittered me and made me as distrustful of my own government as it did these savages carrying out this brutal death sentence. When I eventually learned that the villagers had carried out the punishment, I vowed to never again sit back and do nothing. Next time I would take action.

"Is there anything else you need to know?" Dalton asks, startling me back to reality.

"Did they use a shovel?"

"We found no evidence of that. But I can't see how else they dug that hole." He jumps off the rock and walks toward me with his hand out.

"Did you talk to anyone over at the hardware store?"

He laughs. "Yeah, we asked Ernie if any Afghanis had come in and bought a shovel. Seems that our Afghani brethren don't shop at Ernie's for their tools. Or use them for gainful employment to support their lazy asses."

Why is he so hostile to these unfortunate immigrants? I grab his hand and carefully make my way down to the bank. It's a good thing, too, because my legs are burning and inflamed. I wonder if I'll be able to make it back to the car in this condition. A particular memory returns of Dalton as a young boy, finding me down by the river one day with some friends. We were goofing around and throwing stones into the foamy swirls. For whatever reason, he chose me to pick on that day. He snuck up behind me as I was standing ankle deep in the sickly green water. I remember his hands wringing my neck under my long mane of hair. Then I remember as my head plunged into the frigid river. I couldn't breathe and began to swallow the acidic water, thinking I was going to drown. I was about to pass out when he jerked my head up and shoved me down onto the mud. He stood over me, laughing in that cruel way of his, reveling in my utter humiliation. I couldn't get that taste of polluted river water out of my mouth for weeks.

The breeze picks up and I can feel my cheeks turning rosy. I glare at Dalton, the memory of that day filling me with hate for the boy who did that to me. My hand remains in his and he's not letting go. He moves toward me, stopping inches from my body. It's all I can do not to spit in his face. The sunglasses mask the anger growing within me like a raging typhoon. And yet part of me wants to forgive him and be a better person than when I left. To believe that we've all matured over time and transitioned into caring, responsible adults.

"Why the hell are you so interested in this case?" he asks.

"Tell me something, Dalton. Have you ever done things in life you regret?"

"Huh?" He looks at me as if I'm nuts. "Of course I've done things I regret, but what's that got to do with anything?"

"I don't know. I was just thinking out loud."

He laughs. "Why? Have you done something you regret? Maybe murdered someone with that killer smile of yours?"

"For me to know and you to find out."

"I love a mysterious woman."

I stare at him through my sunglasses, trying hard to contain my anger and resentment. And yet there's a flicker of something else tingling inside me. Something foreign and completely unexpected. Excitement? Attraction?

"You're an enigma, Lucy." He leans over and tries to kiss me, but I put a hand up. All at once I feel repulsed and attracted to him at the same time. But why?

"Whoa!"

"You don't like me?"

"It has nothing to do with liking you."

"Then what is it?"

"Come on, Dalton. This isn't the time or place. A girl was murdered here and now you want to kiss me?"

"I got the impression you wanted to be alone with me."

I laugh. "What in the world gave you that idea?"

"Are you like one of those groupies who gets off on murder?"

"Of course not. I just wanted to see where the girl was killed."

He shakes his head. "I'm heading back to the car."

He walks up the steep riverbank and quickly disappears into the woods. There's no sense trying to keep up with him, and I couldn't even if I wanted to. I stroll around the crime scene a bit longer, looking for anything remotely related to the girl's murder. The cops have no doubt combed the area for evidence. I poke the stick in the mud, making a series of holes so that they form a dotted triangle.

Something about this crime scene seems off to me, but I can't quite figure out what it is. I close my eyes and envision rocks flying through the air and hitting the helpless girl in the face and chest. Her arms and legs are useless to her, and there's no escape. I pray to God that she experienced a quick and painless death, but I know that the punishment of stoning is meant to be slow and deliberate.

The voices in my head cry out to be heard. I fall to my knees, covering my ears in an attempt to block them. But they're coming from inside my head. I can't take this anymore. At least Dalton's not here to see me knuckling under the weight of my troubled past. My connection to this small Maine town sickens me, harkening back to a sadder time in life. Strangely enough, I also feel protective of this place, nostalgic in a way that defies explanation. I'd been desperately trying to forget Fawn Grove existed all those years, but maybe embracing it will prove more conducive to my healing process.

With the help of the walking stick, I struggle to my feet and start back toward the car. The pain in my legs shoots into my lower back and ascends my vertebrae. The ground is soft and pliant, and it makes the going slow. At the base of the bank, maybe ten pitched feet, I stop and stare up at the top. Reaching it will be a near impossibility the way I'm struggling. Turning my body sideways, I edge slowly upward like a cross-country skier climbing a terraced ice ridge, digging the heel of my boots into the dirt as I ascend.

Upon reaching the top, I rest my hands on my sore knees and catch my breath. But something in the brush hits the sun and catches my eye. What is it? I reach through the branches and feel around until I pull out an earring. Is it just a random find, or does it belong to the person involved in this murder? I know that many people wander down here to fish, hike, or drop their kayak into the water. I stick it in my coat pocket and hobble down the narrow path toward the police cruiser. I'm sweating profusely by the time I reach it. Dalton's sitting inside the idling car and staring down at something on the dashboard. The sight of him pisses me off, and I realize I hate the bastard for leaving me like that. I'm almost too angry to be in the same car with him, but it's cold and I'm tired, and I know I can't trudge home on foot.

"Fine way to treat a girl," I say once I'm seated next to him.

"Consider yourself lucky I waited for you. I have a court hearing to attend in twenty minutes." He's staring coldly at his cell phone.

"Take me back to the diner, please."

"With pleasure."

"What's your problem, Dalton?" I turn and stare at him.

"Who says I have a problem?"

"You can't expect me to kiss you at the scene of a violent crime. That's gross."

He laughs. "Who says I was going to kiss you?"

"You saying you weren't?"

"Get over yourself." He peels down the road faster than I care to go.

"What's the big rush? Got another hot date?"

"You think you're so witty and clever," he says, eyes on the road. "You're really no better than anyone else in this town."

"I never said I was."

"Stef's right. You act like you're some fancy big shot."

"That girl needs a serious attitude readjustment," I say. "And so do you if you believe that crap."

"You really think I'm interested in a woman like

you? A gingerbread from the big city? Hell, I can get any girl in this town."

"Then why haven't you?"

"Who's to say I haven't?"

"So now you're a gigolo?" I laugh.

"You're so clueless."

"Whoa! What's with the attitude, mister? You're supposed to serve and protect. Remember?"

"A girl has been murdered in the most despicable way and all you can think to do is crack jokes and make light of the situation. You think this is a game, Lucy? You think I'm here to entertain you?"

"Trust me, seeing that crime scene was not entertaining in the least."

"Then why are you so hot and bothered about this dead Muslim girl? And why are you here in Fawn Grove in the first place?" He turns into The Galaxy's parking lot and pulls up next to my pickup.

"It's really none of your business why I'm in town. I have my reasons."

He leans over me and opens my door. "Have a great day."

"Fawn Grove seems like a really nice place. Maybe I will stick around a bit longer."

"Good luck with that," he says. "Because Fawn Grove will break you like it's broken everyone else in town."

"Excuse me?"

"Let's just say that this place has a way of humbling people. Sure, you could stay for a while, but eventually someone else will come along and you'll stop being the prettiest face in town. Then you'll grow old and bitter before your time, and that's when you'll know you're finally one of us."

"Speaking from experience, are we?"

"Go back to New York City, Lucy. For your own good."

"Is that a threat?"

He smiles wearily. "Just the truth, sweetheart. Consider it my advice to you."

"Thanks, *sweetheart*, but advice is like assholes. Everyone's got one, and your mother had two."

I slam the door shut and watch him speed recklessly out of the parking lot. There's only a few cars parked here. Years ago this place would have been jammed with customers, and parking spaces would have been at a minimum. But not anymore. I stand at the door to my pickup, debating whether to go inside. What I really should be doing is heading home and rubbing medicated ointment over my bloody stumps. I'm exhausted and hungry, but if I walk into that house now I'll be the object of Big Russ's withering glare. At least Stef will be in school at this hour and not serving up wisecracks.

I decide to go inside and see if there's anything edible on that greasy menu.

9

I WALK INSIDE AND NOTICE THAT THERE ARE TWO WAIT-resses on shift. One is Nadia and the other is a mousy-looking woman I've never seen before. As soon as Nadia sees me, she rushes over to the counter before I can sit down, holding a greasy pot of that unbearably bland coffee. It pains me to watch her pour my cup, knowing I'll barely touch it. She promises to be right back, and as she leaves, she unties her apron and disappears into the kitchen.

The pain in my legs radiates outward, and it's all I can do not to cry. My foot snags on something and I almost fall face-first to the floor. One of the tiles is cracked and uneven. I collapse onto the stool as my hands land on the unwashed counter. Something sticky dampens my palm, and I realize that no one has cleaned the surface. So unprofessional. After pulling three napkins out of the dispenser, I wipe the funk off my hand, but it still feels gross.

My phone buzzes. It's a text from my former boss. She wants to know if I'll reconsider coming back to work for her when I return to New York. Sitting here in this shitty diner, the offer seems more appealing than ever. I'm tempted to blow this town and return to my old job, the job that at one time consumed my entire existence. The relative anonymity of the city is something I badly miss. But I can't deny the visceral pull Fawn Grove now has over me. Or the mystery of this girl's murder. It's a more powerful draw than I thought. It's rooted in my deep connection to this place. There's a voice within that's whispering for me to stick around and see how this all plays out. To see how much things have really changed in this town, and how willing people will be to accept someone like me. A woman with considerable baggage and many hard miles logged on her engine.

It doesn't bother me that I'm using Dalton to get what I want. Maybe that's the real reason I'm so gung ho about finding the killer; I'm an incredibly selfish person. I have this urgent need to free myself from the voices enslaving me. It's about forgiving myself and accepting the fact that there are certain things in wartime that were beyond my control.

The problem is that I'm a mess, emotionally and physically. Broken and imperfect, too. And as much as I try denying it, Dalton's aborted kiss did not entirely offend my sensibilities. It's been a long time since anyone's tried to kiss me in that way, and I yearn for such intimacy. He's always been strikingly good looking, even as a kid, which made his cruel acts seem that much crueler. Something deep inside me wants to experience what it would be like to kiss my former tormentor. I know this sounds crazy, but in my twisted mind Dalton feels like the personification of everything that's right and wrong with Fawn Grove. It's like being intimate with my past; it repels me as much as it makes me desirous for something more.

I'd run myself ragged in New York City, doing all I could to escape the inevitable question about whether I would find someone to love. I worked so hard as a chef that I kept pushing this desire further back in the recesses of my mind. Drinking, working, and exhaustion filled the gaps that might have composed my romantic life. Because of that, nothing ever materialized. Maybe I feared getting close to someone. The emotional turmoil hadn't helped either. I kept thinking, What person in their right mind would want to be with a woman like me? A tortured mind to go along with a tortured body. Two prosthetics that hid my sorry past, although they were the least of my secrets. Then so close to a dishonorable discharge before the incident that cost me my legs. I spent two brutal years recovering at Walter Reed. Who in their right mind would want someone like me sleeping next to them at night?

As I consider why I'm sitting here, in my hometown diner, Nadia grabs my arm and leads me to a booth in the back. I inhale sharply from the pain, not wanting her to know how badly I'm hurting. She sits across from me and smiles, almost as if the world had stopped spinning since I left. The ensuing years have only made Nadia more beautiful, despite the spiderwebs forming at the corners of her eyes and lips. There's tinsels of gray in her short black hair, which she repeatedly swipes over her ears.

"I don't have long," Nadia whispers, hands folded over the table. "Fortunately, my full-time job allows me some flexibility."

"Your other job?"

"Yes."

"Social work, I believe your daughter said?"

"I fill in here to help out my father. Stef hates working at the diner, but she loves the money. Without her help, my father would not be able to keep this place running. He can barely afford to pay Billie her fifteen hours a week."

"It's no secret why the diner's failing."

"There's so much competition in town after Denny's opened up last year."

"Don't lie to yourself, Nadia. Everything about this place screams for a makeover, including the menu."

"Don't you think you're being a bit harsh?"

"Harsh is an understatement."

"Come now, Lucy. Try something else on the menu before you make such a rash statement. The spanakopita is delicious and from my great-grandmother's recipe."

"Nadia, look around the place. There's no one here. If the food was any good, don't you think it would be packed at this hour?"

"People in this town are narrow-minded and struggle with anything remotely ethnic. It's the same reason these Afghanis are having such a difficult time integrating into the community."

"I could cook sheep's head stew and get more people through that door."

"You know how to cook?"

"It's how I've been supporting myself all these years. Can't live in Manhattan off my disability check alone."

"Then you should go in there and talk to him. Maybe he'll listen to someone like you."

"Stef says you help these immigrants get settled into town," I say, purposefully changing the subject.

"That's part of my responsibility."

"What about your husband?" I nod at her wedding ring.

"My husband and I have been going through the motions for the last three years. Our marriage is all but over."

"Why do you stay married to him, then?"

"We pretend everything is normal for Stef's sake. Our parents are old-school Greeks, and they'd be very upset if they knew the truth about us. Maybe they already do know and are not saying anything. Once Stef graduates and goes away to college, we'll make it official."

"I did the math and noticed that you had Stef soon after I left."

"You broke my heart, Lucy. I was so distraught that I ran into the arms of the first man who would make my family happy. Niko Petras."

"You married Niko?" This surprises and disappoints me.

"I had no choice. Our families were pressuring us after they found out I was pregnant."

"So you had a big, fat Greek wedding?"

She laughs. "I guess you could say that."

Niko Petras was one of the most vain assholes in high school, and it surprises me that Nadia married him. He was brash, handsome, and a womanizer who sported a gold earring when it was still risky in this town to wear one. Girls loved him. Guys wanted to be like Niko. With his muscular physique and flowing Greek hair, he was the object of many of my schoolmates' desires.

"We started dating after you left. One night we were drinking over at his parents' house. One thing led to another, and before I knew it I was pregnant with Stef. Getting married made sense. Our parents went to the same Orthodox Church, and there weren't many other Greeks in town. It was the easiest way out after you left."

"I'm sorry."

"You should be. You could have told me you were leaving. I would have been heartbroken, but at least I would have known what happened and that you were all right."

"I'm sorry. I should have told you."

"It's obvious to me now that you had issues at the time, things I couldn't even begin to understand. The good news is that you're back."

"Temporarily, remember?"

"Maybe Fawn Grove can be more understanding this time around, especially when everyone learns that you're a decorated veteran." She looks around, and when she's convinced it's safe to do so, she cups my hands.

"I don't know, Nadia. It's too early for that kind of talk."

"I loved you once, Lucy. I can certainly love you again."

"But I'm not sure how I feel anymore. About anything."

"Take your time. There's no rush."

"I'm broken in so many ways and still struggling with my issues," I say, squeezing her hand. "I beg you, do not tell anyone about my injuries."

"You're a hero, Lucy, whether you want to believe it or not."

"I can't believe getting my legs blown off makes me heroic. Unlucky maybe, but certainly not a hero."

"That can't be the real reason you came back. So you could recover from the trauma you experienced."

"When I first arrived in town a few weeks ago, I couldn't even get out of bed I was such a mess. Once I started to feel better, I realized I needed a reason to stay. A purpose for being here. That's probably why I'm so interested in this girl's murder."

"And so you're going to take it upon yourself to find the killer?"

"I never said that." Admittedly, it does sound rather silly coming from her lips. I glance around the diner, hoping the sunglasses mask my embarrassment.

"Then what, Lucy? When the case gets solved, are you going to run away like you did those many years ago?" She shakes her head in frustration and begins to slide out of the booth.

"Wait," I say, holding onto her hand.

"You can't repeatedly run away from yourself and think you're escaping your past. At some point you need to come to grips with who you are, Lucy, and whatever it is you've done to warrant such self-doubt.

Maybe the people here won't be as dismissive as you think. They might even *accept* you."

"But what if they don't?"

"They will because you're one of us. And if anyone has a problem with that, they can come see me."

Nadia picks up one of the greasy plastic menus and flicks it in my direction. It whacks my chest and flutters down onto the table in front of me.

"Give the spanakopita a try while you're trying to find yourself. Maybe by the time you order, you'll figure out who the hell you are."

I ordered the moussaka, believing it to be more reflective of authentic Greek fare. It sits in front of me waiting to be sampled. I can manage only a few bites because it's so terribly offensive to my taste buds. A puddle of grease has formed at the bottom of my plate, and the eggplant has a distinctly sour taste. The whipped potato topping is dry and came prepackaged. I wish the dish were edible so I'd at last have one good thing to say. It blows my mind that Yanni couldn't be bothered to drain the grease before adding burger to the moussaka. No wonder no one eats here.

I pull the earring out of my pocket and place it next to my mug of coffee, studying it closely. It's slightly curved with gold and white colors. A series of inverted Ls have been cut into the metal that runs the length of the piece. It's an interesting design, one I'd never seen before. Had it belonged to the dead girl? Or someone involved in her murder? Maybe there's no connection at all but the one I'm fictionalizing in my head, a head yearning to connect the dots and find a rationale for this terrible crime.

I wish I'd asked Nadia if she knew the dead girl or the girl's family. I think about her broken marriage to Niko and how she has to keep working in order to help raise Stef. I hope she didn't put any of her own money into this dump. I wonder if she and Niko are still on good terms. Nadia said little about Niko, and I wasn't going to push the matter. What about Stef? All this turmoil must be hard on her. No wonder she displays such a bad attitude. She's home alone most nights and being forced to work at this shitty diner.

Knowing what I know about The Galaxy, and its connection to my past, I can't help but be protective of its place in Fawn Grove's history and to want to save it from dying a slow death. Feeling sorry for myself won't bring in new customers, nor will criticizing the food every chance I get. But something inside me is saying that I have to come up with answers before I can be useful to anyone or anything, including myself.

Or maybe it's something else that's keeping me tethered here. Something that's not even obvious to me. Is it possible that I'm operating under the deluded notion that I can do some good here? Prove my worthiness to the citizens of Fawn Grove? I fled a long time ago, certain that I'd never return. Certain I'd never fit in and be accepted for who I am. But at the age of eighteen, confidence can be a false emotion. Things are different now, I keep telling myself. I'm a better person than the one who left. And this is a better town.

Here's what I know for sure: There's a murderer loose, and this poses a threat to the well-being of the people living here, the people I grew up admiring and resenting. It's natural for them to fear change, and to fear those who are different from themselves. And yet fear is a survival mechanism with the goal of keeping us safe. It's an evolutionary tool we've used to perpetuate the species and divide and conquer. My own fears run deep, and I often believe it's the reason I'm still alive. It's the reason I survived that bomb blast and the pressures of a Manhattan kitchen. But I don't have time to philosophize about such matters. And neither do the immigrants who've moved here, trying to fit in in their newly adopted land.

10

I'D REACHED A POINT IN MY CAREER WHERE I HAD TO make a decision. Do I continue working as a well-regarded sous-chef in a busy East Village restaurant, or do I take the leap and accept a head chef job somewhere else? Maybe even take the plunge and open my own restaurant? My skill set was on par with all but a few top chefs working in the city. The owner of the restaurant where I worked kept asking when I would move on and start my own establishment. Advancement was the norm in that world. It's not that she wanted to lose me; she needed enough time to find a worthy replacement. Chefs of my caliber didn't stay mired in the same miserable conditions for very long. Chefs like me, who worked long and ridiculous hours for shitty pay, usually ended up working long and ridiculous hours for themselves.

But I kept deferring all offers to open my own place

or become someone else's head chef. I actually liked my job. Cooking became my obsession only because the vacuum created in its absence frightened the hell out of me. I was respected by those in the industry, and I'd reached an obscene level of comfort. The thought of leaving terrified me and was something I didn't want to consider. So I kept my head down, put in my hundred-hour weeks, collected my human scrapbook of scrapes and burns, and took solace in the small and insignificant place I occupied in the universe.

I probably would have stayed had I not awoken one day in an absolute panic. Sweat dripped from every pore in my body, and I experienced a sense of dread so visceral that it was all I could do to climb out of bed. *Why now?* I thought. The next day would be better, I kept telling myself. Then the next day came and nothing changed. Neither did the day after that and the day after that. One week turned into three. My sudden and unexplainable bout of depression settled into abject melancholy. Ensconced in that dark cloud, and with no end in sight, it felt like an eternity of gloom sprawled across the universe. The illness had texture and permanence. It felt as if bubble wrap had formed around my body, and I believed at the time that I'd never escape from its formidable grip.

That's when I decided to leave New York. What did I have to lose? The city was my savior, and yet at the same time it spit me out like the whale that coughed up Jonah. It's a volatile and unpredictable place, and it will steamroll you if you don't keep up with its frenetic pace. I stopped and watched as the city left me in its wake, like a person cast overboard in the middle of the ocean, watching helplessly as the cruise ship motored away.

I faltered in that stilted environment, decrying the state of my pathetic life. Little did I know that fate had determined I return home and make my peace with it.

Yanni emerges from the kitchen into the dining room, his tangled gray weave placed carelessly over his seborrheic scalp. His chef's whites are soiled and wrinkled, and I can't for the life of me see how they got that way. Based on the number of customers walking through the door, his stained apron baffles me. He barks something unintelligible to the young waitress, and she jumps at his command. The poor woman is merely a sounding board for his rash of complaints. The bitch session turns into a tongue lashing, and it appears all too apparent that he's using her as the scapegoat for his many failures.

I move to the counter and watch his red-faced theatrics with barely controlled rage. His yelling would be an embarrassment had there been any other customers inside, but since there aren't any, it doesn't really matter. Yanni stops midsentence and sees that I'm watching. I've dealt with assholes like him all my life, and I don't take such fools lightly, especially when they're as incompetent as him. Men like Yanni believe they possess the culinary skills of Thomas Keller and the business acumen of Steve Jobs and thus can treat their employees however they please.

"You want something?" he shouts at me in a condescending tone.

"How about making some decent food for once and stop cussing out the help."

"She's been delivering orders to the wrong table all morning," he says, eyeing me warily, unsure of what to make of a strong woman standing so close to him.

"Maybe if this diner actually had some paying customers you could blame her."

"It's all right," the woman named Billie says, "I deserve it."

I turn angrily to her. "The hell you do! I could make puppy chow taste better than the crap he cooks here."

Yanni's impenetrable demeanor cracks, and he lashes out at me. "I been at this a long time, lady. You think *you* can cook better than me?"

"I think that stool could cook better than you."

"You don't know what you're talking about. The people in this town love my food."

"Name one."

"Did you try the moussaka? It's from my nonni's recipe and a big hit with the locals."

"May she rest in peace, but your nonni would probably turn in her grave if she knew you made it the way you do."

"There's nothing wrong with the moussaka." He seems taken aback by my honesty. Bullies always do when confronted.

"Not if you like extra grease and instant potatoes as toppings."

"You don't know that," he shouts.

"Oh, yes, I do," I say. "I've tried your moussaka, and it sucks."

"You think you can do better?"

"In my sleep—and I have insomnia."

"Tell you what, honey. How about you come back in a few days and show me what you got?"

"Oh, hell no, *honey*!"

Yanni stares at the mousy waitress named Billie. "Did she just say no?"

The waitress nods. "She said, 'Oh, hell no, honey.'"

Yanni turns back to me. "You afraid your food won't be as good as mine?"

"Hardly. I'm not cooking with all that frozen meat and powdered crap you use back there," I say.

"How do you know what I cook with?"

"I'm not stupid, Yanni. I can taste it in your food," I say. "Besides, your granddaughter showed me the kitchen the other day."

"Stefania let you in my kitchen?" His face scrunches up, and his meaty hands ball into fists. "I taught that girl everything she knows and she betrays me like that?"

"Even your granddaughter knows better than to use liquid eggs when making an omelette." I stare at him. "Seriously, are you that stupid? Or just plain cheap?"

"If you were a man I'd punch you in the face."

"So what's stopping you?" I offer up my chin, and he backs off.

"Bah! People love my food," he says not so convincingly. He picks up the spatula on the counter and holds it aloft.

I laugh at this silly gesture. "I drove by the Denny's yesterday, and it was packed."

"Who the hell do you think you are, anyway, coming in here and criticizing me?"

"I'm someone who appreciates good food and knows how to cook it."

"Then come back and cook for me, and we'll see

who's the better chef. I'll even give you some money to buy what you need."

"When?"

"Two days from now."

"Okay, I accept your challenge."

"Good." He peels off two twenties and hands them to me. "You don't get paid a dime until I get results."

"Results?" I laugh, looking around the room. "Could I do much worse than this?"

I remove my sunglasses once I'm out in the parking lot, wondering how long it will take until I go blind. The sun irritates but doesn't necessarily hurt my eyes. I'd visited so many dark places in my life that the light now seems like a foreign entity. And yet here I stand under the September sun, no worse for the wear, feeling more stable than I have in weeks. The feeling won't last long, although I wish it would. I'll eventually need to return to that dark place in order to confront my demons. I need to be strong, because there's no turning back now. I need to follow my gut.

The dead girl's name was Sulafi. According to the paper, she was a month shy of turning sixteen when her body was discovered buried along the river. Of course no one can be sure, because the refugees didn't take paperwork with them when they fled from their war-torn country. Paperwork was the least of their worries. They were brought to these shores unknown and unheralded, then resettled in Fawn Grove.

I sit in the Fawn Grove Library, reading as many accounts of the murder as I can find. But the facts are scant, and there's not much written about the girl. No one knew much about Sulafi's past, and the people in her community aren't talking to the police or news reporters. The few articles about her showed the same black-and-white photo of her staring blankly into space. In the picture she's wearing a hijab. I can't really tell whether she was an attractive girl. I've always found it difficult to judge a woman's appearance when her head is covered with a scarf. Maybe it's the sheer uniformity of the hijab that blinds me to a woman's looks. More likely, it's my own personal bias.

And yet I clearly remember that beautiful young girl from many years ago, smiling brightly beneath a hijab as she arranged the fruit on her stall.

After an hour I stop researching because there's nothing left to read. Somehow I need to dig deeper if I'm to find something more substantial about the girl's death. How I'll do that I have no idea.

My legs hurt from that long trek down to the Alamoosa, and I worry how my stamina will hold up at the diner. What have I gotten myself into? Will I be able to stand all day after taking more than a month off from cooking? Looking back on my career as a chef, I can't believe I lasted as long as I did with these sawed-off legs of mine. The key was keeping my movements economical and efficient and not making extra work for myself. I got to the point where I could work my mise en place blindfolded, every pan and utensil seeming to rise to my hand as I reached for it. My knives were an extension of my body, like Harry Potter reaching for his wand. I even had a specially made rubber mat underfoot that helped absorb the impact on my stumps.

But I'll have none of that at The Galaxy.

* * *

I walk past Big Russ, barely stopping to look at him. He's reclining in his easy chair, boots resting on the footrest, eyes glued to the flat screen. He's watching a documentary on World War II, and the low level hum of B-24 bombers makes it seem as if they're flying overhead. Bombs fall and strafe the European landscape, and for a brief moment it harkens me back to my tour overseas.

Shaken, I quickly climb the stairs before he tries to engage me in conversation. Once safely in my room, I collapse on the bed and burst into tears. This is so silly. I have no idea why I'm crying. Must be the hormones zipping through my system. Maybe exhaustion is finally setting in, having accomplished far more than I should have in one day. I need to rest up and take it easy lest I fall back into the same funk that brought me here in the first place.

It's a relief to take off the sunglasses and gaze mindlessly up at the black void. If this is what death feels like, then there's no reason to fear it. Sometimes I welcome death as an escape from this crazy life. A way out of the pain and suffering I've been forced to endure.

But my emotions snowball and I start to feel worse. At some point I sit up on the bed and sob uncontrollably, unable to rein in this vague feeling of dread. I wriggle out of my jeans and remove the prosthetics, laying them gently on the floor. The medicated tube of cream sits on the nightstand, but I'm too tired to apply it. I lay my head down on the pillow, tears dampening the floral casing my sister makes Big Russ change on a daily basis. I don't want to sleep for fear of stirring the voices. And yet I don't want to stay awake and think about my crazy life.

There's a knock at the door. After a few seconds it opens a crack. Light streams into the room and temporarily blinds me. I don't ask who it is, because I don't really care at this point. I pray it's not Russ, and I *know* it's not my wheelchair-bound sister; I would have heard the mechanical whir of her chairlift. Whoever this person is sits on my bed and whispers sweetly to me. Their sudden and unannounced proximity makes me feel helpless. I reach out, despite my reservations, and grab their hand. It's soft and small, like a child's. It takes me a few seconds to realize that Brynn is sitting next to me. We've hardly talked since I've arrived.

"Are you okay?"

"Not really."

"What's wrong?"

"How much has your mother told you about me?"

"Not much except that you two were cousins back in the day and that you practically lived here because your mom was never around for you."

I nod knowingly, wondering how much of the truth I should fill her in on.

"She said that you called this place home and that my grandmother was more of a mother to you than your own drug-addicted mom. My mom said you were dying to leave this town when the time came."

"This house really was my home growing up." I squeeze her hand tenderly. "I'm sorry we had to meet like this, especially in the condition I'm in."

"No, it's perfectly all right."

"Would you place the comforter over me?"

"Sure." Brynn covers me with it, tucks it under my body, and gasps. "Oh my God!"

"I should have told you."

"You have no legs."

"Not below the knees, anyway."

"What happened?"

"Your mother never told you how I lost them?"

"No. She just said that you were injured in an accident or something. She never told me the details."

"Well, now you know."

"Why didn't you come home and let us help you?"

"I spent the first few years recuperating. Then after that I didn't want to be a burden to anyone, including your mom." Brynn doesn't need to know the entire truth, I realize. Not now. Not here, especially after what her mother has already told her about me.

"Because you didn't want people in town to see you like this?"

"What do you think?"

"I think people would have understood."

"You obviously don't know the people in Fawn Grove."

"Trust me, I know them better than you think," she says. "But times have changed, Cousin Lucy."

"Do me a favor and drop the cousin crap."

"Okay," she says, wringing her hands. "It's just that Dad and Mom wanted me to show you some respect."

"You've already shown me some," I say. "And as for changing times, the more things change in Fawn Grove, the more they stay the same."

"My mom says that you and Jaxon were once close. Do you want to talk about it?"

"No!" I turn away from her.

"What's wrong? Why are you facing away from me?"

"Because I don't feel well."

"Is there anything I can do to help you?"

"Not with what I'm suffering from."

She rests a hand on my hip. "I came here to tell you something because I heard you were interested."

"And what's that?"

"I knew the girl who was murdered. She was in a few of my classes."

I turn to face her.

"I overheard Stef talking to another kid about you. Stef's a bit of a . . ."

"Bee-yotch?"

She giggles at this. "Don't say that about her. She's really nice once you get to know her." She removes her hand. "She said you visited the diner and seemed obsessed with the girl's murder."

"What if it's true? Will you feel any different about me?"

"Of course not." She pauses. "But why do you care? You're not a cop."

"I wish I could give you a reason."

"Does it have anything to do with Jaxon?"

I nod, feeling a tear coming.

"If you want, I can put you in touch with someone who knew her much better than I did."

"Really? Who?"

"She was Sulafi's cousin."

"Why won't she talk to Detective Dalton?"

"Dalton?" She laughs. "That guy's such a tool."

Brynn seems a good judge of character. "But doesn't she want the police to find her cousin's killer?"

"She said it has something to do with her culture. The people in her community refuse to talk to the police because they're afraid of them. Supposedly, they don't trust cops because they remind them of war and the soldiers back home."

"Even a guy like Dalton?"

"Especially him." She holds out her hand and examines her nails. "Did you know that his daughter's in a few of my classes?"

"I didn't know he had a daughter."

"They're not particularly close and haven't been for years," she says. "Brandy feels the same way about him as most people do. And she's totally embarrassed that he leads that ridiculous group in town called AFA."

"AFA?"

"Americans For America," she says. "It embarrasses Brandy that he's so outspoken on this immigrant issue. She feels it reflects badly on her in school and that the teachers and kids judge her unfairly because of her dad's actions."

"Dalton hasn't told me much about his personal life."

"How do you even know him?"

"I met him one morning at the diner," I say, leaving out the speeding part of the story.

"Brandy's parents got divorced when she was little. She lives with her mom now and hardly ever talks to her father. She's always going on and on about what an asshole he is and how she never wants to see his ugly face again. She even changed her last name back to her mother's."

"Who's her mom?"

"I don't know her first name. Last is Millis."

Debbie Millis. In high school she was the drop-dead-gorgeous cheerleader who could have had any guy she wanted. Not a very nice person to those outside her clique. A walking cliché for high school bitches who ruled the roost and excluded everyone else. She was the perfect match for Dalton. Or, as it turns out, the worst match possible.

"Do you want to meet her?"

"Dalton's ex?"

"No, Sulafi's cousin. She might talk to you because you're a woman. Maybe she could tell you what Sulafi was really like."

"You think one of her own people killed her?"

"Who else in town could have done something that evil?"

"Something tells me you know more about all this than you're letting on."

"That's a silly thing to say," she says, averting her eyes from me. "So, do you want to meet her or not?"

"Of course."

"I'll set it up tomorrow, then." Brynn stands and walks toward the door. "Is it true you made a scene at The Galaxy this morning?"

"Made a scene?" I laugh. "Hardly."

"I heard you complained to Stef's grandfather about the food?"

"How do you know that? Did Stefania tell you?"

She shrugs. "You better call her Stef and not Stefania. She hates being called that."

"Have you ever eaten there?" I ask, making a note of that.

She laughs, and it is a girlish laugh—the laugh of a fifteen-year-old who knows she's pretty and more popular than most of the others and can get whatever she wants. It's a laugh that tells me she won't be eating at The Galaxy anytime soon. And who could blame her?

11

*A*NOTHER MORNING AFTER A FITFUL NIGHT OF SLEEP and I'm eager to get to The Galaxy. I wonder if Dalton has the balls to show his face in there after trying to put the moves on me. There's not a car in the parking lot when I pull in. I'm the first one through the door and the only one sitting at the counter. An octogenarian walks in soon after and takes a seat in a back booth. Billie is working this morning, although there's a part of me that misses Stefania's wisecracking energy. It's the only interesting thing in this otherwise depressing place.

Billie pours me a cup of coffee and then skitters off to attend to a customer. A self-admitted snob when it comes to coffee, I've never yearned for a good cup more than I do now. But I need caffeine and so I sip this tepid brew and make do.

I sit quietly reading the paper when Dalton walks in.

He seems to come in here most mornings on the days he's working. I pretend not to notice when he sits three stools from me, giving him the cold shoulder on this cold autumn morning.

"You think you're Jacqueline Onassis wearing those stupid glasses?" he mutters.

"Jackie O was a glamorous and beautiful woman, so I'll take that as a compliment."

"Not so glamorous when she was scooping up her husband's brains off the backseat of that limo."

"Why must you be so crude?"

"At least I'm not being pretentious."

"Do tell. How am I being pretentious?"

"For starters, you wear designer sunglasses inside The Galaxy, and you act like you're better than everyone else in town."

"For your information, I wear sunglasses because I'm sensitive to light." I turn to face him. "Why are you being so mean to me? Was it because of that kiss?"

"What kiss?" He laughs. "I don't remember you trying to kiss me."

"Stop acting like a child."

"A child?" He sips his coffee and stares ahead. "I'm just making an observation. And I was not at all being mean to you."

"You most certainly were being mean to me, Officer Dalton."

"It's Detective Dalton, if you've forgotten."

"Is it because I pose a threat to you?"

He laughs and turns to face me. "Now how in God's name could you possibly pose a threat to me?"

"Because you've made so little progress in this murder investigation."

"I took you down to that crime scene, didn't I? You saw what progress was being made."

"Yes, but I wonder what your motive was for taking me down there."

"You obviously misinterpreted my motive."

"If you say."

He laughs dismissively, and I slide over two stools so that I'm sitting next to him. Our shoulders press lightly together.

"You're frustrated."

"Okay, I'll play along. What am I so frustrated about?"

"You're frustrated because you're not getting any cooperation from the family of that dead girl. You've gone to them, but they refuse to talk to you. They don't trust outsiders, especially a man in uniform carrying a gun. Reminds them of home. This frustrates the hell out of a guy like you because you're used to getting re-sults, and that extends to your romantic life. You need a break in the case and you need it fast because you're the assisting detective on the investigation and the state police are breathing down your neck for answers. The Afghani women who knew Sulafi best act as if they're repulsed by you."

"Don't you worry, they'll talk eventually, even if I have to subpoena them."

"Good luck with that."

"We'll see how they like it when they're being charged with obstruction of justice and then thrown in jail for a few days. They won't like being forced to live without that stupid headscarf of theirs."

"It's called a hijab."

"Whatever. We should have never let so many of those animals in here to ruin our town."

"Have some compassion. They're human beings, not animals," I say, infuriated by his comments. "And their culture dictates that women not talk to strange men."

"I'm so sick of hearing about Muslims and how we need to be so tolerant and kowtow to them. How about we take care of our own citizens first."

"How can you assist on the case when you're so obviously biased?"

"I'm a professional. I can set aside my personal beliefs to do my job."

"Then why am I making more progress than you?"

He laughs. "You should hear how ridiculous you sound."

"Do I?"

His expression quickly turns serious. "I'm warning you to stay out of this murder investigation, Lucy. Do you hear me?"

"You haven't changed one bit, Dalton," I say, instantly regretting the words as soon as they come out of my mouth. He swivels toward me and is about to say something when Yanni walks out of the kitchen, spatula in hand, and surveys the near-empty diner. Upon seeing the two of us sitting side by side, he walks over and stands in front of me. It's laughable the way he thinks he can intimidate me because of his size. The smell he gives off is enough to scare anybody away, but I refuse to budge.

"So you gonna show up tomorrow and show me what you got?" he says.

"Of course I'm going to show up. I never back down from a challenge."

Yanni turns to Dalton. "She thinks she's gonna come here and teach an old dog how to cook."

"*She's* going to be cooking here tomorrow?" Dalton says.

"She thinks she can do better than me. So I give her a chance to prove herself."

"Big spender, this guy. Forty bucks is all I get for groceries," I say to Dalton.

"Take it or leave it. Forty bucks is plenty if you want to cook with me."

"*With* you? I was under the impression that I'd be working by myself."

"Are you crazy? Think I'm going to leave you here alone to screw up my diner?" he says, pinching my cheek in a condescending manner. It's all I can do not to pop this old bastard in the nose. "You may be beautiful, doll, but we'll see if you can really cook."

"I'm beautiful *and* a great cook." I jump off the stool and head for the door. I need to get out of this dump before I say or do something I might regret.

"And be here on time. Doors open at four."

"Don't worry, big guy, I'll be here before you."

I return to the house but can't sleep. Big Russ is parked in his usual spot, watching a Ken Burns documentary about the Civil War. He lifts one eyebrow as I pass, but I don't stop to chat with him. I drag myself upstairs. My bedroom, as usual, has been cleaned to within an inch of its life. The sterile scent of cleaning agents makes it at times feel more like a hospital room than a bedroom—and I know all too well that pungent hospital room smell. The bed is made up like one of those beds you might see at the Ritz Carlton—everything perfectly tucked with hospital corners. My clothes are neatly pressed and folded on the bureau. I suppose I should be happy that all my needs are being met, but for some strange reason the lack of privacy makes me feel vulnerable. Of course I'll never complain. I don't want to appear ungrateful to my sister and her family. If only it were like a hotel room and I could hang a card on the knob, informing everyone to stay the hell out.

I don't want to sleep. Nor do I want to stay in this room for any length of time, pondering my confused existence.

I go into the sitting room, located across the hall. It's sunnier and cheerier than my bedroom, with an oversized window looking down upon the leafy street. I sit in the floral armchair and kick my feet up on the matching footrest, looking around the room for something that might lift my spirits.

Sitting on the bookshelf are the photo albums that my mother collected during our years growing up. I grab a thick binder off the shelf and begin to flip through it. The first picture I see is of Jaxon when he was a little boy, dressed in a Cub Scout uniform, his long hair pouring out of his cap. There's a big smile on his face. The image is so striking that I slam the book shut and melt into a puddle of tears. Poor Jaxon. How I miss that kid.

There's a knock at my bedroom door. I shoot up in panic and look around in the pitch darkness. For a brief second, I'm convinced I'm back in Afghanistan, waiting for the call to head out to the battlefield and tend to the wounded. My left foot is itching like crazy, and when I reach down to scratch it, I remember it's not there. This is a frequent occurrence of mine, and of amputees in general. I sit up and realize that I'm in my old room, in the house that was passed down to Wendy. Was I dreaming?

Another gentle knock and I ask who it is. Brynn answers, and I tell her to come in. She sits down on the bed as I shake the sleep goblins out of my head. It's a good thing she can't see that I've been crying. I'll need to put on my makeup and cover up the blemishes once she leaves. It's a face that needs plenty of TLC and love before it can face the world.

"I'm sorry if I woke you," she says.

"It's okay. I was just lying here."

"Would you like me to turn the lights on?"

"No."

"How can you sleep during the day in total darkness? I'd be, like, totally freaking out."

"The light hurts my eyes."

"You said you wanted to meet Nasreen."

"Yes. Would you give me a few minutes to pull myself together?" I lift myself into a sitting position.

Brynn doesn't move from the bed. "Is it hard taking those things off and on each time?"

"I've gotten pretty good at it."

"So how did it happen?"

"Do you really want to know?"

She nods her head.

"I was driving home one day when this truck went through a red light." Short and sweet lie.

"Did it hurt?"

"Not at first. I went into shock. When I woke up I was in the hospital."

"I get squeamish at the sight of a paper cut."

"Trust me, you wouldn't have felt it." I nudge her with my knee so that she gets off the mattress. "Our bodies possess a remarkable ability to protect us from pain."

"I can't stand the sight of blood. It makes me sick."

"Would you mind?"

"You want me to leave?"

"I need to get ready. Give me just a few minutes."

"Can I watch you put them on?"

"You just said that you're squeamish. Are you sure you can handle it?"

There's a few seconds of silence before she answers. "No, I'm not sure I can, but I still want to watch."

"Turn the lamp on, then. Your mother's Tiffany on the nightstand."

Brynn reaches over and pulls the metal string, and the lamp fills the room with a soft light. I squint until my eyes adjust to it. Swiveling on the bed until my legs dangle over the edge, I instruct her to pass me a prosthetic. Brynn picks it up off the floor and hands it to me. Her face is aglow, highlighting her almond-shaped eyes, which radiate with a youthful naturalness that's breathtaking to behold. What is it with Fawn Grove and these ravishing beauties? There's a particular look over her face when she sees the proliferation of deep red scars zigzagging over my knees and thighs.

"Your legs are all messed up."

"These scars are a constant reminder; always look before you plow through an intersection."

"Do they hurt?"

"Not anywhere near what they used to. The doctors gave me skin grafts."

"What's a skin graft?"

"It's where they take healthy skin from one part of your body and transplant it over the injured areas."

"Oh." Her eyes dart nervously in their sockets. "Can I ask you something else, Lucy?"

"As long as you swear to God not to tell anybody about this."

"I swear."

"To God."

"Okay, I swear to God."

"Ask away then."

"I know I asked you this before, but why are you so interested in Sulafi's death?"

I hate lying, but do it frequently, owing to the strange circumstances of my life's trajectory. It makes things easier that way. "I saw someone die while I was recovering in the hospital. Then I come back to Fawn Grove and see it happen all over again. No person should have to suffer like that."

"I know, right? It's terrible what her own people did to her."

"You sound convinced that one of the immigrants did it."

"Oh, I'm almost certain they did," is all she says. "I have so many questions to ask you, Lucy. I don't even know where to begin."

"Why don't you wait for me downstairs while I get dressed?"

"Then you'll tell me what my mother was like when she was young and not confined to a wheelchair?"

"You don't remember her when you were little?"

"Not as much as I'd like. She started coming down with MS symptoms when I was in first grade."

"That's too bad because your mother was a beautiful woman with lots of energy."

"That's what I heard."

"You look beautiful," Brynn says to me as I steer the pickup away from her house. She'd just arrived home from school and was still carrying her book bag. "I wish I could be like you and escape from here and then go live in an exciting place like New York City."

I turn and stare at this young girl. I don't know what to make of Brynn, having just met her recently for the first time. Is she putting me on? Living in New York City all those years has made me cynical and jaded of most people's attention. I'm certainly not a role model or someone to look up to. Kind words filter through my brain as something foreign and entirely unwelcome. Hardly anyone spoke kindly of me when I grew up here. If they did, it meant they wanted something. So what does Brynn want from me?

In the hot kitchens I slaved in, no one ever had a kind word to say to a fellow coworker. You called them a douchebag or fuckup and it was praise of the highest order. I learned not to trust anyone who was nice to me unless I got to know them better. And there's no better way to know someone than by working side by side with them during an insane dinner service, the kitchen a steaming cauldron of anxiety and hostility. I've always believed that a person's true character comes out in a busy kitchen and that it leads to either lifelong friendships or becoming bitter enemies. Stress brings out people's true nature and reveals them for who they really are. This is not to equate kitchen work with war, but it's not the worst analogy either, having lived through both hells.

"The sunglasses make you look mysterious."

"Thanks, I guess. But I told you they're for light sensitivity."

"I hope I'll grow up one day and be as glamorous and pretty as you."

"Be careful what you wish for," I say, laughing. "Besides, you strike me as a girl who knows her strengths."

"I'm not sure I understand."

I smile at her. "You will someday."

"Whatever."

"I can drop you off back home once we're done talking to her."

"I thought we could hang out for a while. Unless you have something more important you need to do."

"Now that you mention it, I need to go to the market afterward and pick up some groceries. I'm going to cook at The Galaxy tomorrow morning."

"For real?" Her voice breaks as she says the last syllable.

"Yup. I'm hoping to teach Stefania's grandfather a few new tricks in the kitchen."

"Good luck with that. Stef says he's a kind of a dick."

"Brynn!"

"This will work out perfectly, because Nasreen works at an Afghani market. You can shop there for all your stuff. It's in the same building where the old Value Mart used to be."

I turn and smile at her. This is exactly what I want to hear.

"You know that they found the girl's body along the river," I say.

"What happened to her?"

"You don't know?"

"I've heard things." She shakes her head. "Like that someone beat her pretty badly. I heard something about an honor killing, whatever that is. There's all these rumors floating around school, but no one ever said exactly how she died."

"Do you know what an honor killing is?"

She seems to think it over before nodding.

"The rumor is that she was buried up to her chest."

"But she could still breathe, right?"

"She suffered . . . significant trauma to the head."

"What kind of trauma?"

"She was stoned."

"I don't think Sulafi did drugs. It was against her religion or something."

"Stoned, as in someone threw rocks at her."

"Ewww! Who would do something like that?"

"In some Muslim cultures, a woman can be sentenced to death by stoning for certain crimes."

"I wish you hadn't told me that."

"I thought you should know."

"Sulafi was only a kid. She didn't deserve to die like that." Brynn looks visibly shaken.

"Someone must have believed she deserved it."

"But Sulafi was a nice kid who kept mostly to herself. She barely talked to anyone in class because she was so shy."

"Did you ever talk to her?"

"Sure, a few times. We worked together on a group project once. She seemed nice enough."

I turn and see tears streaming down Brynn's face. With my hands on the wheel, there's no way to comfort her. I'm not very good at these sort of things, and in particular dealing with other people's emotions. I turn off Main Street and see the old brick building that once housed the Value Mart. It was at one time the premiere supermarket in Fawn Grove, and our family used to shop there all the time. Two women dressed in full burqas walk toward the entrance, their eyes peering out behind thin slits of fabric.

Brynn is still teary when I park in the lot. I turn to her, wondering what I should do to console her. I'd seen so many cooks suffer nervous breakdowns in my presence that it became second nature to ignore such behavior. But there was never any sympathy in my kitchen. I kicked them off the line until they got their shit together. Deal with it or get out of the way was my manner of handling the situation. Kitchen work was too stressful for crybabies, and I had no patience for those who couldn't handle the fast pace or close attention to detail. It was the same in the army. As a combat medic working long hours dealing with death and trauma, those who didn't pull their weight were quickly dispatched.

I badly want to comfort Brynn and reassure her, but I don't know how. And reassure her of what? Instead, I sit quietly until she's calm. I suppose I could put a hand on her shoulder and say a kind word, but all that feels insincere to me, sitting in this parking lot with a niece I barely know, waiting impatiently to speak to the dead girl's cousin.

She wipes her eyes and tells me she's all right. We get out of the truck and walk inside, and I'm immediately transported to culinary nirvana. The bright colors and exotic smells enthrall me. Back in New York, I'd often spend my rare days off visiting foreign markets in the five boroughs: Italian, Ethiopian, Somali, Iraqi, Kosher, to name just a few.

A man in the back shouts something in his native tongue. The rows of bubbled flatbreads look inviting and smell of pepper and cracked wheat. I gaze around happily. Although we're the only nonforeigners in here, no one pays us any attention. I gaze lovingly upon the fresh produce: bright purple eggplants, fulsome green zucchinis, ruby radishes, tomatoes, and peppers the color of the sun. The smell of freshly ground spices excites me the most. I pick up a bag of za'atar, which is an aromatic mixture of green herbs and spices. Grape leaves beckon as do bowls of freshly made hummus and baba ghanoush. There's Kebab Halali, ground lamb, bulgur, and Mahshi. Bottles of Afghani olive oil. And the coveted and hard to find red tahini.

Brynn sees the girl stocking shelves with apricot paste and begins to walk over to her. The girl is of medium height and weight, unremarkable in appearance, and wearing a bright blue hijab that drapes around her cheeks. She appears startled to see us. She whispers something to Brynn before scampering toward the back of the store.

"What did she say?" I ask.

"She can't talk to us right now. She's on break in a few minutes, and she'll take our bags out to the parking lot when we're done shopping."

"Is it me or did she seem afraid to be seen with you?"

Brynn shrugs.

I grab a cart and walk around, fascinated with all the fresh ingredients available to me. The forty dollars will be gone in no time, despite the fact that everything seems like a bargain. Once I have everything I need, I head to the cash register, where a portly old man with a thick mustache greets us with a toothless smile. Before I can grab the plastic bags from him, Nasreen snatches them out of his hand and leads us toward the door. When we reach the truck, I pull the latch down and lower the tailgate. The girl sets the bags down on the cold, ribbed bed. Then she slams the tailgate shut, pulls out a cigarette, and lights it.

"I've only got a few minutes, so you better hurry," she says in accented English. She's serious and tough, and I find myself liking this girl.

"I'm trying to figure out who killed Sulafi," I say.

"Why? You're not police."

"Let's just say I'm interested in your cousin's murder."

She shrugs and takes a drag on her cigarette. "You should probably forget about it. It's too messed up."

"Are you going to let them get away with killing her?"

"It's a terrible crime, I know, but the girls in my culture know the rules we must live by."

"So what rule did she break?"

Nasreen blows out a ring of smoke and stares at me as if I'm crazy. "I kept warning her, but she didn't listen to me. She wasn't like everyone in school thought she was."

"What was she like?"

"She was very beautiful and wanted to be a model or famous singer. With her hair down, she looked like one of those Kardashian girls on TV. Boys looked at her in ways that are very bad where I come from. In my culture, a girl is not supposed to step out of line."

"What was she doing that was so bad?"

"She wanted to be like American people. I told her she was crazy and that she should be more like Muslim girls, but she didn't listen. I think she was seeing someone too."

"A boy?"

"Yeah, a boy from town." She takes a puff on her cigarette and looks over my shoulder. "She was on her computer all the time, talking to this boy. She watched American TV shows and had big dreams of becoming famous. She would sing songs in her room and dance in a way that made her brother and parents very upset."

"How do you know?"

"I was over at her house one day and walked in on her. She slammed the computer shut as soon as I went in."

"She wouldn't tell you who she was talking to?"

"No, but we were cousins, and she knew I wouldn't tell anyone. Girls who do these things understand the risk."

"How do you feel about living here?" I ask.

She shrugs. "I'm a Muslim girl. I accept the way things are."

"Why won't her parents talk to the police?"

"Because they're embarrassed. They feel she dishonored Allah in some way. It sickens me what they did to her. No one deserves to die like that."

"Do you believe that someone in your community killed her?"

She laughs bitterly. "What do you think?"

"That's why I'm asking."

"Most people here just want to be left alone and be dutiful Muslims. But yes, there are a few trouble-makers among us who think they speak for everyone. They would try to enforce our old laws and traditions if they had their way."

"What would they enforce?"

"To stop selling pork and alcohol. Stuff like that. And they believe all women should dress accordingly." She holds her cigarette aloft. "I don't know much else."

"Nasreen!" a man shouts. His voice echoes through-out the parking lot.

"Oh shit, I gotta go," she says, flicking her cigarette down onto the pavement.

She jogs over to where the man is calling. Then he starts to yell at her about something. His voice grows heated, but she doesn't back down, giving it right back to him.

Brynn and I climb inside the truck and head over to The Galaxy, driving in silence. It's just after four-thirty when we pull into the near-empty parking lot. It still amazes me that someone could run such a successful business into the ground. Despite my intention to cook something new and exciting tomorrow, it's probably too late to save the place. If Yanni's so stuck in his ways that he refuses to change, the end will be sooner than expected.

Stefania frowns upon seeing us walk through the door. She crosses her arms and stares icily as we sit at the counter. I order two chocolate shakes, then move to the kitchen to put away the groceries. Yanni's standing at the table cutting onions when I walk in, although he fails to acknowledge my presence. I go inside the walk-in and place the perishables neatly on the stainless steel shelves. What an unorganized mess. Boxes of spoiled food lie everywhere. Mold tickles my nostrils, and on the floor I notice what appears to be mouse droppings. I can't deal with this right now, so I put the bags on the shelves and head back to the dining room.

"Where's my change?" Yanni says.

I reach into my purse and toss the leftover coins on the table.

"Sixty-two cents is all?"

"You gave me forty dollars to spend and so I spent it."

I laugh at his stupidity. He thinks he's saving money by buying his food off one of those 18-wheelers that delivers vegetables in industrial cans. It's about the worst sin a chef in this business can commit.

"I'm going to show you how to cook an authentic diner meal, Yanni. That's assuming anyone shows up to order it."

"The customers love my food, you'll see." The onions make it look as if he's crying.

"What customers? There's no one out there."

He waves me away, and I leave him to cry over his minced onions. Brynn's whispering something to Stefania when I sit down. I watch them interact, trying to figure out where they stand in the hierarchy of high school cliques. It soon becomes obvious that Stefania is the alpha girl in her pack.

"What are you girls going on about?" I say, slipping in next to Brynn.

"Oh, nothing," Stefania says innocently.

"Mostly school stuff," Brynn says.

"School stuff, huh?" I sip my shake, which to my surprise actually tastes pretty good. "Didn't know you two were so studious."

"We're a lot smarter than you think," Stefania says. "I didn't know you two were related."

"Now you know," I say.

"I feel sorry for you," Stefania says to Brynn.

"Lucy's cool," Brynn replies.

"I'll give you props, kid," I say, holding up my frosted glass. "You make a damn good shake."

"Did you hear that? Miss Fancy-Pants actually likes something in this diner."

"There's a first for everything."

She snaps her gum. "Are you really going to cook here tomorrow?"

"That's the plan," I say, looking around at the empty diner, "although I might not be doing much cooking, judging by the looks of it."

"Why are you always putting us down?" Stefania shifts her weight from one leg to the other. "You think you know what's best for us, but you really have no clue what our customers like."

"Do I have to live in Fawn Grove to know what people here like to eat?"

"I think you're just trying to make a name for yourself at the expense of my papou."

"Listen to me, Stefania. Your grandfather's going to lose this place if he doesn't change his ways."

"First of all, my name is Stef. Second, my grandfather's a talented chef, thank you very much. He doesn't need someone like you coming in here and telling him how to run his business."

"Oh, I beg to differ."

"Did you know he used to have his own restaurant in Greece?" She turns and disappears into the kitchen.

Once Brynn and I finish our shakes, I throw some bills down on the counter before we head back to the truck. I'm surprised at how eager I am to cook here tomorrow. Maybe it's the prospect of returning to the kitchen that's so energizing. Or discovering such a hidden gem as that Afghani grocery. Or the fact that I've learned something about the dead girl that I didn't know before.

I'm feeling upbeat as I walk into the parking lot. Of course my good mood could come crashing down at any moment. I must stay levelheaded and calm, knowing that my life could just as easily fall back into that meaningless state of despair.

Brynn runs up to her room as soon as we go inside the house. Wendy steers her wheelchair to the table in order to prepare a lasagna for dinner.

"Will you be eating with us tonight?"

"I think I will for once," I say brightly.

She spins around and smiles at me. "You seem to be in a better mood today."

"I am," I say. "I must admit, you did a great job raising Brynn."

She lays down the first ribbons of lasagna along the bottom of the pan. "I'm so glad you two are finally getting to know each other after all these years."

"Except she thinks I'm your neglected, orphaned cousin. Why didn't you tell her the truth?"

"Honestly, I wasn't sure she could handle it with all your injuries, and the fact that you've never tried to have a relationship with her. Besides, Brynn's had a rough go of it these last few years."

"How so?"

"She's had some anger and emotional issues in school due to our health issues and has been getting therapy. I didn't want to risk upsetting her good mood by telling her the truth about you."

"So you think lying is a better strategy?"

"At least until she gets to know you better."

I stare down at the ingredients on the table. "Do you need any help making dinner?"

"I'm crippled, not helpless," she says as if offended. "And if you've forgotten, I make the best lasagna in Maine."

"Just trying to be helpful."

"If you really want to help, why don't you go sit with Russ for a few minutes and keep him company. He barely gets off that recliner because of his back."

"I'm not sure Russ likes me."

Wendy laughs. "Of course he likes you. He acts like that with everyone at first. You just need to get to know him better. Now go inside and sit with him."

I walk into the living room and see Big Russ glaring at the television. I sit down in the chair next to him and watch whatever he's put on. He glances at me from time to time out of the corner of his eye. On the nightstand next to him sits a two-liter bottle of diet soda.

"What are you watching?"

"It's a documentary on the Amazon basin and the various creatures that live in its ecosystem."

"Cool."

"Oh, it's *beyond* cool."

"I notice you watch a lot of documentaries."

"Since I rarely leave the house, I like to know what's going on in the world."

"What do you know about these refugees in town?"

He turns and stares at me. "I've heard through the grapevine that you've taken quite an interest in them."

"I guess I'm curious to find out what happened to that poor girl."

"You should be careful where you tread."

"Oh?"

"There's a lot of bad blood in this town over our Middle Eastern brethren."

"How so?"

"Let's just say that their integration into Fawn Grove has been less than smooth."

"So I've heard," I say. "But there are people in town who are happy they're here, right?"

"Plenty that don't."

"Does that include you?"

"Doesn't really matter what I think."

"Okay, I know when to shut up."

He grabs his soda bottle and takes a swig. "The loudest protester of them all is that detective friend of yours."

"Dalton?"

"Who else?"

"Isn't that a conflict of interest, seeing how he's a police officer?"

"I would say so. He and his AFA buddies don't like that the Afghanis settled here. They believe these immigrants want to transform Fawn Grove so it resembles the third world hellhole they left."

"What do you think?"

"Sure, a small minority want to impose their rules on us, but that's not gonna happen. Most of these immigrants are good, hardworking people who just want to live in peace and go about their business."

"When you say transform Fawn Grove, do you mean they want to implement their own laws?"

"Call it whatever you will. There's a small minority that wants to live like they did in their homeland."

"And how do you feel about that?"

"Why come here if you don't like our ways?" He shrugs. "I'm fine with them taking part in the American dream. Just don't try to change the way we do things, because we've been doing them here in Fawn Grove for a long time."

"And the girl. What do you think happened to her?"

"If I knew that, I'd have solved this town's biggest mystery." He turns his attention back to the documentary. Then he takes another sip of his soda and points at the TV. "Look at the size of that damn cobra. Amazing the way people can live side by side with all those poisonous snakes. It'd freak me the hell out if I saw one of those slithering toward me."

I get up, leave Russ's side, and head to my room. I have no desire to watch a show about snakes and reptiles. And his unwitting snake metaphor is not lost on me. All of a sudden I feel weak in the knees. There's no way I can eat dinner with Wendy and her family tonight. I couldn't even fake it. I need sleep and lots of it.

Tomorrow promises to be an interesting day. I'll need to get up early and make myself look pretty before I head over there. If the voices decide to plague me tonight, then so be it. I'll need to deal with them eventually.

12

I GET UP EARLY AFTER A DECENT NIGHT'S SLEEP AND prepare myself for the day. After showering, I apply my makeup with meticulous care. Then I open my suitcase and pull out my crisp chef whites. Just the sight of them puts me in a better mood. The knives sit on the bureau, snug in their canvas bag like a happy family. They're like having a pit bull as a pet—loyal to a fault and yet lethal if necessary. I unfurl it and take in their shiny countenance and beautiful wood handles. They're organized by size and heft and sit neatly in their pockets. I stare lovingly at the gleaming steel angled to razor-sharp perfection. These are my lifeblood and the source of my greatest inspiration. They make me wish I was back in my old kitchen, breaking down a side of beef or coaxing a coho salmon out of its silvery skin. I roll the canvas up, stuff it under my armpit, and head out.

The oak floor creeks underfoot as I tiptoe toward the stairs. It's dark outside, but there's a glow coming from somewhere down the hallway. Upon further notice I see that it's coming from Brynn's room. Why is she up at this hour? A faint light pulses from beneath the door. Has she fallen asleep and left her light on? I twist the handle and open it a crack. Brynn's sitting at her desk, in her robe, and staring intently at her laptop. She's faced away from me and wearing earbuds. I can't see the screen, but it appears as if she's talking to someone on FaceTime. At this hour? Her anger issues come to mind, and I wonder how these issues manifested. Did she get in trouble at school? I gently close the door and make my way down the stairs, decidedly not interested in invading her privacy.

Darkness envelopes me as soon as I make my way outside. It's chilly this morning. I blithely make my way around to the driver's side, in desperate need of caffeine. But when I go to open the door I notice something scrawled over the windshield in red lettering. It's a star inside a crescent moon. Below the image it says *Stop Digging, Infidel Bitch!*

I glance around nervously before checking out the truck's bed. Nothing. The inside of the cab is empty as well. I hop in, tossing my knives on the seat next to me. After unfurling the canvas, I pull a boning knife out of the sheath and slip it into the pocket of my chef's pants for good measure. Then I peel out of there as fast as possible, calling Dalton as I race through the empty streets. By the time I arrive at the diner, the threatening message has become all but unintelligible over my windshield.

* * *

Breakfast and lunch proved to be a huge disappointment. I'm not sure what I was thinking, operating under the deluded belief that my presence here would be an instant success. The old-timers who patronized The Galaxy had long ago lost their appetite for anything fresh and unique. They showed no appreciation for my pillowy omelettes, fresh cheddar/bacon biscuits, and buckwheat pancakes made from scratch. Not one person ordered the lamb burger with tzatziki sauce or the baklava made with locally sourced honey. Instead, they chose the circular brick patties of industrial beef topped with processed yellow cheese, canned limp pickles made bitter from vinegar, and reheated shoestring fries straight from the bag.

It leads me to believe that The Galaxy needs far more help than I can give it. What works in Manhattan doesn't necessarily translate to rural Maine. The place needs a new customer base along with a clever marketing campaign and a fresh design that adds brightness and energy to the decor. It needs a full-time chef who can give it the time and energy needed to turn this dump around. Yanni grinned at me after breakfast service ended, confident that he'd won some hard-fought wager between us. That his customers didn't order my inventive cuisine seemed to validate all that he believed in. As sure as I am of my culinary skills, I've never felt so down about this profession. At least I put away the liquid eggs and cracked fresh ones.

Sadly, I should have known that I'd been set up to fail.

Dalton met me at the diner soon after I informed

him about the threatening note scrawled on my windshield. He wrote up a report and filed it in the police log. None of this made me feel any more secure, but at least the threat was now on record. Dalton sidled up to the counter, despite the fact that we hadn't yet opened our doors, and ordered his usual breakfast. It took a while for Yanni's crappy coffee to brew, so I boiled up some water and made two cups from the private stash I purchased at that Afghani market. I made it using an old press I found in the storage room. I was careful to stir the liquid until a milky froth appeared at the top of each cup. The caffeine kicked in like jet fuel, and I became a tour de force in the kitchen, a force without an opposing force to counter my outsized ambition. A chef without customers is like a lumberjack assigned to cut trees in a clearcut forest.

Now I'm left to clean the kitchen and put all the leftover food back in the walk-in cooler. Yanni gloats as I do this. He watches me with a big smile over his heavily lined face, enjoying a bitter victory that will one day foreshadow his demise. Lovingly, and with care, I slip my knives back into their sheaths and tie the canvas up until it's a sack again. My chef whites are spotless, perfectly creased, and virgin like fresh Maine snow. Their cleanliness is a gentle reminder of my failure here. I'm about to leave when Stefania walks in, eyes rolling and a ticket in hand.

"You're not going to believe this, Miss Fancy-Pants, but someone just ordered one of your lamb burgers," she says.

"For real?"

"Yeah, and it was your boyfriend."

"Stop calling him that. You know he's not my boy-friend."

"Friend with benefits, then."

"Get out of my kitchen, Stefania!"

"It's Stef, not Stefania. How many times do I have to tell you that, *Chef*?"

Although it's Dalton ordering the burger, it's better than nothing. Seizing my opportunity to impress, I grab the ground lamb out of the walk-in, then form it into a ball and then a nice round patty. After it sears on the flattop, I set it down on some split pita bread and add a slice of tomato, lettuce leaves, and some tzatziki sauce. While the burger sets, I fry a batch of hand-cut fries that had already been fried. When they're done, I toss them in a bowl of salt and pepper and then shake them until the seasoning is absorbed. I plate them next to the burger and deliver the plate out to Dalton along with a dollop of truffle-infused chipotle mayo.

"Did you find out who sent me that message?" I ask as I slide the plate in front of him.

"Be patient. I just filed the report this morning." He reaches for the ketchup, but I grab his wrist before he takes hold of it. "What are you doing?"

"I always put ketchup on my burger."

"Not on this one."

"Why not?"

"Because you'll ruin the subtle flavor of the lamb. Besides, it's got tzatziki sauce on it."

"What the hell is Suzuki sauce?"

"It's tzatziki sauce, Dalton. Just open your mind and try it."

He takes a bite.

"It looked like they scribbled the message in red marker," I say.

"This sauce is kinda tangy."

"It's supposed to be tangy," I say. "Did you know that the star inside the crescent moon is the symbol for Islam?"

"Is that so? Well, whoever wrote it did it in red lipstick," he says before taking another bite.

"How can you be sure?"

"Because it was your lipstick. Do you usually leave a tube in your ashtray?"

I nod.

"We need to be discreet about this, Lucy. Some people in town might think you wrote that message in order to attract attention to yourself."

"That's insane. Why would I do that?"

"You're new in town and dress different than most of the women who live here. People in Fawn Grove notice such things."

"Wow, you make it sound as if I'm one of the Afghanis."

"I suppose so, when you put it that way."

Sadly, I know he's right. The people in Fawn Grove are a tight-knit clan, distrusting of most outsiders, and beholden to past traditions. They must feel as if I'm showing them up by strutting around town, dressed like a celebrity, which is the last thing I want to do. If they only knew that I'm an insider, too. But how could they possibly know that unless I told them?

A fresh tube of lipstick sits buried in my purse, and in the ashtray of the truck. I always keep one nearby in case I run out. Maybe it's a result of the trauma I suffered because of that IED. Or the fact that my legs—

what's left of them—are scarred and hideous to the eye. Because of that I always want my lips to look luxurious on a moment's notice.

"Why else would they draw a symbol of Islam on your windshield and call you an infidel if they weren't one of these Muslim thugs?" Dalton says.

"You're the detective. You tell me."

"I can't understand why anyone would want to try to intimidate you like that." He snarfs down a fry dipped in chipotle mayo. "No one knows you went down to the murder scene with me. Or that you're interested in the girl's death."

I bite my thumbnail. "There's something I need to tell you."

"Oh?"

"Brynn and I went to that Afghani grocery yesterday. That lamb burger you're eating is halal."

"Halal?" Dalton drops the burger on his plate as if it's blowfish sushi. "What the hell's halal?"

I try not to laugh for fear of pissing him off. "Easy, Dalton. It's just a method of butchering the animal. It's similar to Kosher."

"It's not goat or horse meat?"

"Of course not. The reason we went down to the market was to talk to a classmate of Brynn's. A girl named Nasreen."

"Why did you want to talk to her?" He holds out his cup. I grab the pot of Yanni's institutionally bland coffee, but he stops me. "Any more of that Turkish stuff you made earlier?"

"You liked that?" This flatters me more than anything else he's said.

"Yeah. That coffee was great."

"Maybe there's hope for you after all."

"I'm not the cretin you think I am, Lucy Abbott. Just because I stand up for the rights of Americans doesn't make me a racist."

"Every American citizen came from immigrants," I say, topping off his cup. He pours cream and sugar into it. "Nasreen and Sulafi were cousins. My theory is that she talked to me because I'm a girl."

"Talked to you about what?"

"About the fact that her cousin was possibly dating one of her classmates and that she was communicating with him over the Internet."

"Sounds harmless enough." He stuffs the last morsel of burger into his mouth. A smear of tzatziki sauce clings to the side of his lips, and I want badly to wipe it away.

"Think she was legit?"

"I have no reason to think otherwise." Two elderly biker types wearing bandanas walk through the door.

"There's another thing I think you should know."

"There's more?"

"She carried our bags out to the truck but then seemed frightened when one of her bosses saw her speaking to us."

"At one of our sensitivity training classes, we were told that Muslim women are reluctant to speak to men or look them in the eye. We're supposed to be aware of this if we ever pull one of them over for a traffic offense."

"The girl seemed eager to keep talking until her boss came out and saw us."

"What did he say?"

"I have no idea, because he was speaking in his

mother tongue. But I did notice that his voice was raised and he was waving his arms in the air."

"Could she have been goofing off instead of working?"

"It's possible."

"You think someone in the Afghani community threatened you because of that conversation? Left a warning on your windshield for you to stop digging into the case?"

"Possibly, but I don't really know."

"So what do you want me to do?" He sticks two fries in his mouth.

"How the hell should I know? You're the cop."

He seems to mull it over. "Okay, I'll go over to the market and have a talk with someone. What's the girl's name again?"

"Nasreen. I don't know her last name."

"That's fine. I don't think there's many Nasreens living in Fawn Grove." He jots the name down in his spiral notebook. Then he closes it and stares up at me. "You said you found the threat scrawled on the passenger side of your windshield?"

"Yes."

"And this was before you went inside the pickup?"

"That's right."

"I never asked you this, Lucy, but where are you staying while in town?"

I hesitate for a second before telling him. "Russ and Wendy Petersen's house." This gets his attention. "Wendy's my cousin."

"Really? Small world."

"So you'll go down there and talk to the manager?" I say, trying to change the subject. I place my hand over his and stare deeply into his eyes, hoping he'll make no mention of Wendy or Russ.

"Sure, although I'm not sure what good it'll do." He puts on his cap. "You do realize they're not going to tell me anything, especially about who threatened you. Or who killed that girl."

"Maybe not, but at least they'll be on notice in case they try to pull that shit again."

"By the way," he says, standing, "that burger you made was off the charts."

"You really liked it?" My spirits soar, and suddenly I want to jump over the counter and hug him.

"I did. And the fries with that spicy mayo were great too."

Flattered beyond belief, I watch as he walks out of the diner. I look down at his plate; he's cleaned it better than any of the Mexican dishwashers I've ever worked with. Even the chipotle mayo and tzatziki sauce are gone. It's my first success at The Galaxy, although it might be my last.

"Looks like you had at least one happy camper," Stefania says, picking up Dalton's plate. "I bet he would have asked for his money back if he wasn't so madly in love with you."

"Dalton's not in love with me, and he wouldn't lie about something like that."

"Wow, you know nothing about that moron. And yes, he is too in love with you, Miss Fancy-Pants."

I grab my packet of knives, except for the boning knife; tuck the sack under my arm; and head for the door.

"You think you're all that because you sold one

lousy burger? Ha! Guess you're not as talented as you think you are."

I turn to her. "I never said I was that talented."

"You should go back there and apologize to my papou for making fun of him, and for saying his cooking sucks."

"I did not make fun of him. And yes, his food does suck."

"Then why don't you just go back to where you came from and leave us alone?"

"Maybe I will. I don't need you or this place."

"No one here likes you or your crappy food. No one but that loser boyfriend of yours."

"I already told you, Stefania. He's not my boyfriend."

"We don't like outsiders like you coming into Fawn Grove and telling us how to run things."

"Are you for real?"

She rolls her head and crosses her arms in defiance. "Do I look like I'm joking?"

"Why do you have so much hostility toward me?"

The girl laughs. "Maybe you should look in the mirror and ask yourself the same question."

What does she mean by that? Does she sense that I loathe myself as much as I loathe this town? Maybe at one time I did, but not so much anymore. Or not to the same degree I once did. I scan the parking lot before making my way out. A lone car sits across from my truck. I hobble toward the pickup, hand in pocket, gripping the boning knife while looking from side to side. If someone wants to come after me, they'd better be prepared. I'm battle-tested and can hold my own in a fight. Many days have passed since that fateful day in Afghanistan, when those voices were conceived, but I pity the asshole who thinks he can take me down.

I walk through the living room, and for once Russ is not in his usual seat. It seems odd, but then again he must have to get up once in a while to snack or go to the bathroom. The odd silence in the room makes me realize that the TV is not on.

I take the opportunity to hobble upstairs and toward my room. My thighs ache from standing all morning. Because of the diner's funky layout, I'd been forced to work in a highly inefficient manner, moving from side to side like Serena Williams playing Wimbledon with a frying pan. It took a toll on my joints and caused my prosthetics to unnecessarily torque beyond what they were designed to do. Yanni's kitchen is disorganized and poorly designed for a chef with my unique disability. It's almost a blessing in disguise that the diner was not busier. Making matters worse, I spent half the morning cleaning out the grease traps, scrubbing that nasty oven, and scraping off burnt food from the flat-top so that I could properly sear my burgers.

My head hurts and my vision remains blurred from the diner's harsh light. Vertigo threatens to derail my brief recovery. I place my bag of knives down on the bureau and collapse on the bed in exhaustion. Something stabs me in the leg, and I shout out in pain. For a moment I think I'm being attacked by a rabid vermin. I jump up, fists clenched as if to defend myself from its hoary fangs. A sharp pain shoots through my leg. Reaching down, I feel a wet spot on my chef's whites.

Blood! I turn on the light and see the stain spreading over the fabric. And then it suddenly hits me—the boning knife in my pocket. I pull down my chef's whites and see a two-inch gash over one of the hideous scars running across my thigh.

There's a knock at the door. I quickly shut off the light and ask who it is.

"It's Nadia. Wendy said I could come up and see you."

"What are you doing here?"

"I wanted to see how you did today."

"Stefania didn't tell you?"

"She texted me that you worked this morning and that a threat had been made against you."

"Someone left a nasty note on the windshield of my truck."

"That's terrible," she says. "Would it be all right if I came in?"

"Sure. But could you go into the bathroom first and get the medical kit out of the top drawer?"

"Are you okay?"

"I cut myself."

"God, no, Lucy!"

I laugh. "Not like that."

"Thank God. Of course, I'll go grab it."

Nadia walks to the bathroom, gets the first aid kit, and enters my room. The blood flows freely from the wound, ruining a good pair of chef's whites. Nadia gasps when she sees the dark stain spreading along my thigh. Or maybe it's the red cicatrices that cause her stunned reaction. Her eyes go from my legs to my eyes, and a profound look of sadness falls over her face. Her pity makes me regret ever inviting her in.

"I'm so sorry."

"Wait a few seconds if you're repulsed, because you ain't seen nothing yet."

She removes some moist wipes from the kit and dabs at the wound. She asks if she can take off my chef's whites, and I nod in approval. Grabbing the trousers by the hems, she slowly pulls them down until they fall to the floor. Her eyes remain glued to my prosthetics as I wait for her to say something.

"Seeing it makes it so real to me." Tears fall from her eyes.

"It's been all too real to me for quite some time now."

"You should have come home and let us help you."

I watch as she cleans the wound. "Did you notice that I'm taller with them on?"

"I didn't, although I probably should have." She laughs and wipes away a tear. "It's been so long since I've seen you that I've forgotten small things like that."

"I've grown in more ways than one."

"How did this happen?"

"Roadside IED."

"I'm so tired of wars and countries fighting each other." She dabs medicated ointment over the two-inch gash using her middle finger. "We're all God's creatures. Why can't everyone just get along?"

"It's what I signed up for when I joined the army."

"Is that how you got all these scars?" She places a bandage over the wound.

"Didn't get them from leaning over hot stoves all day," I say, pushing myself back on the bed. "That cut you see on my thigh was from the boning knife I've been carrying around."

"Why would you do such a thing?"

"Because of the threat made against me this morning."

"What did it say?"

"Someone warned me to stop digging around into the girl's death. They also drew a star and crescent moon above it."

"The symbol for Islam?"

"Yes." I lift my legs and place my hands under my butt. "Thanks, but I can rub in the lotion myself."

"No, let me do it. Just tell me what you'd like me to do."

I instruct her, and with the utmost care she removes the prosthetics and lays them down on the floor. She grabs the tube and gently rubs the medicated ointment into the irritated folds of skin. Her hand moves in slow, circular motions, and I can't begin to show my gratitude for the kindness she's showing me, especially after all these years apart. This is the girl whom I was smitten with so many years ago, when we were teens and on the brink of everything, and hiding our friendship for fear of being found out. It was a forbidden romance in many ways, although in retrospect it now seems kind of silly.

And yet I don't know how I feel about Nadia anymore. I don't know how I feel about anyone in this town. Or anyone in my life. My confusion confuses even me. Things have changed in Fawn Grove and not all for the better. Everything feels situational and fleeting since I lost these limbs, and I can't seem to under-

stand what I like and dislike anymore. I'm not even
sure if I ever actually loved her in the truest sense.

Once Nadia finishes rubbing in the medication, she
places the tube down on the nightstand and lies down
next to me on the bed. She rests her head on my shoulder and squeezes my hand. Her hair smells lovely against
my nose. She leans into me and gently kisses my neck.

"I'm so glad you're back."

"It may only be temporary," I say.

"You never told me how it went this morning."

"Ask Stefania."

She laughs in that girlish way she used to do when
she was sixteen, and we'd be sitting in my car overlooking the site where Angus Gibbons's plane crashed.

"What's so funny?"

"You called her Stefania. I was just thinking how
much she hates being called that."

"I've noticed that too. Why?"

"It was my grandmother's name, and it's so pretty,"
she says, snuggling closer to me. "She's had a rough
go of it these last few years. My faltering marriage hasn't
helped matters, and being forced to work at the diner
has put a strain on her time."

"But why does she hate being called Stefania? It's
such a beautiful name."

"She's embarrassed by her Greek heritage. Maybe
she feels like people in town might mistake her for a
foreigner. She's always wanted to fit in and be one of
the popular kids."

"Like every other kid in this town."

"I told her that our Greek heritage is nothing to be
ashamed of, but she doesn't want to hear that from her
mother. So when she turned eleven she demanded that

everyone call her Stef. She thought it sounded like a normal girl's name."

"Remember how we used to sneak around back in high school because you were afraid your parents might see us together? You dating a townie."

"Being a young Greek immigrant made it hard for a girl like me to fit in here. That is, until I met you. You never cared that I didn't speak perfect English or wasn't from Fawn Grove."

"It seems so silly to think about now. How times have changed."

"Not entirely. Many people here still feel hostile toward immigrants, and that's certainly not progress."

"But I would assume many more are accepting."

"I really want to believe this is a better place to live in than when I grew up, if only for my daughter's sake. I'd do virtually anything to protect Stef and keep her safe. She means the world to me."

"Then you woke up one day and learned that an Afghani girl was murdered, and all your worst fears came flooding back."

"Sadly, yes."

"I really wish Stef liked me," I say.

"She will. I know she's stubborn at times, but she's a great kid with a good heart. Thank you for trying to get along with her and for helping my father out at the diner."

"Unfortunately, there weren't many customers willing to try my food."

"My daughter's a lot like her grandfather. He's hard to get along with and a bit of a bully in the kitchen. But I got the sense, talking to him, that he was excited to have you on board."

"Excited to have me? It felt like he thoroughly enjoyed watching me fail."

"There's something about my father I should tell you, Lucy. He's got a number of serious health issues. I doubt that he'll be able to work there much longer."

"What kind of problems?"

"Diabetes, high blood pressure, coronary disease. Last year he had a mild heart attack, and the doctors warned him to slow down or else he could really hurt himself. He can't go on working seven days a week, ten-hour days, but he refuses to sell the place, assuming he could even find a buyer. And he's so hard to please that he can't keep a line cook for more than a few months at a time before they quit on him."

"Which is why he needs to mellow out."

"That's why he asked for your help. Otherwise he would have never let you in his kitchen."

"He certainly has a funny way of showing his gratitude."

"My father's in a difficult position. The economy here is terrible with the mills closing, and the diner's reputation has taken a big hit in the last few years. The last thing he wants to do is shut The Galaxy down."

"But The Galaxy's an institution here. He can't just let it close."

"Do you really care if it goes under? You'll be heading back to Manhattan anyway."

"I do care. That diner means a lot to me and the people in this town."

"Have patience with him, then. Once he sees that you know how to cook, he might start to trust you. Turning that place around won't happen overnight."

"The Galaxy needs way more help than I can give it."

"Don't give up on him. You might be surprised at what you can accomplish there."

I close my eyes and all I can see is the image of that girl, buried up to her chest and pleading for mercy as the stones rain down on her. As much as I try, I can't vanquish this gory image from my mind's eye. Will it trigger the voices in my head tonight and prevent me from sleeping? At least Nadia's body feels warm and comforting against mine, but I know she can't stay forever.

Rest will not come easy, but rest I must get. Tomorrow is a new day. Tomorrow I will track down Nasreen and persuade her to meet with me in an out-of-the-way place. Then, I hope, she'll tell me all she knows about her dead cousin and the people in her community who might be capable of committing such a hideous crime.

13

*N*ADIA IS GONE WHEN I WAKE UP. I SLEPT SO HARD, I never even noticed her leaving. It's amazing she still cares for me after all these years. We were two gawky teens who thought we were in love, trying desperately to keep it a secret from those around us. I can still see the young coltish girl in her today. She'd just immigrated to Fawn Grove from Greece when I first laid eyes on her in the fourth grade. Her English was stilted and broken but improved greatly with each passing day. At barely over five feet, I'd yet to hit my growth spurt and feared I might never do so. We made an unlikely pair: the Greek and the geek.

I stare at myself in the mirror. Part of me sees a stunning beauty who on the outside appears confident and sassy. A woman who could get most any man in town if she wanted. But hidden beneath the surface is shame and guilt. There's a deep sense of remorse in there too. My eyes see a completely different person at times. I'm getting closer to my ideal, but I'm broken in so many ways that at times it's disheartening, still lost in something I can't quite understand. I see someone looking for meaning and purpose in her life.

There's a text message on my phone. It's from Dalton. Nasreen didn't show up for work yesterday. He'd asked around, but no one admitted to knowing where she lived. People clammed up at the sight of him. It worries me that she's gone missing. My intuition tells me that the girl may be in trouble because of my meddling.

I cruise past The Galaxy and see a familiar sight—a near-empty parking lot. Although this sad state of affairs seems the norm, seeing it over and over saddens me. I have no intention of going inside this morning, although a part of me wants to shake the shit out of Yanni and tell him to wake up before it's too late. Fix this place before it disappears forever. I'd tell him to go home and get some rest, look after your health, and let me take care of the cooking. Given time and buckets of money, I know I could win over the hungry souls in this town. Educate them. Refine their primitive palates. Deep down, they must be yearning for something better than this crap.

The fresh wound on my thigh stings when I move. It doesn't deter me from carrying the boning knife wherever I go. I need to protect myself in case there's a threat against my life. Someone in this town wants to keep me from looking into the death of that poor girl, and I refuse to back down. Unfortunately for them, they have no idea what kind of girl I am. They have no idea what shit I've been through as a combat medic and the debilitating pain I've endured. That threat on my windshield only serves to embolden me.

I glance at the clock on the dashboard and see that it's just past nine A.M.

Who in this town would send me such a nasty threat? Could the crescent and star, and the word *infidel*, have been added to throw me off the scent? Then again, maybe not. Maybe someone in the Afghani community really had seen me talking to Nasreen and decided to warn me off.

Nadia is the only person other than Wendy and Russ who knows the real me. I'm a stranger in my own town, a pretty face from the past that no one recognizes. People I once knew and grew up with now look past me as if I'm a ghost.

I park in the business district of Fawn Grove with its weathered brick buildings and postindustrial ambience. A guardrail is down so that a train can clack its way through the center of town. More than a few of the stores are deserted, graffiti scrawled over the facades. Nostalgia isn't pretty at times, and yet here and there I see nuggets of my past still standing. A reminder of better times when this place was booming and everyone put on a happy face. There's a small, cramped bookstore that's been here since my youth. Bud Whipple's Guitars is still in operation across the street, its windows displaying used Stratocasters and dented old acoustics. Next to Whipple's is Bernie's Deli. Young's Joke Shop is no longer there, which makes me sad. There's the doleful brick pub still in operation. In its heyday, mill workers flooded into Sully's after their shift finished. It has a long, narrow bar that is devoid of light, and one can stand in the middle of the pub and practically touch both of its sticky walls.

Decay has set in, and once that happens it's hard to stop. You can see it in the hardened faces of the juvenile delinquents who skip school to roam these depressing streets. The boys walk with that ape gait, arms hanging and trying to impress the mousy-looking, pink-haired girls they'll one day impregnate. Many depend on welfare, and drug use is rampant, from what I've heard. The older ones barely remember the happier days and know that the kind of affluence their parents once enjoyed will never again return to this town. The younger generation yearns to leave the only place they've ever known.

I remember a time when Fawn Grove was a bustling and vital town. The mill's smokestacks were billowing twenty-four seven. It was near the end of an era of prosperity, and the signs of recession were apparent for all to see. People had good jobs and plenty of cash in their pockets. They say money can't buy happiness, but walking through this run-down section of town, I know that happiness is hard to come by without it.

A cheery coffee shop appears out of nowhere like a beacon of light in the darkness. It resembles any of the hipster coffee shops one might find in the East Village, and its presence brings a smile to my face. Posters line the bottom half of the window advertising local theater shows, concerts, and various community events. One poster is for a protest rally called Love Over Hate. It advertises a march to be held in support of the immigrants.

It's clearly the nicest shop in town. I press my face

up against the cold window and see a group of deaf students sitting at a table and conversing in ASL. Stepping back, I stare at my reflection in the floor-to-ceiling-window. I see a woman hiding behind overpriced sunglasses, dressed in skinny jeans and bundled in a double-breasted pea jacket that's cinched at the waist. How nice this reflected woman would look if she had a plaid scarf to wrap around her neck.

It takes me a few seconds to notice the two women working behind the counter. Pam Price and Jenny Christian. I remember attending Fawn Grove High with them. We'd not been friends, but we knew each other from growing up all those years in the same town. How long has it been since I've seen these two girls? I go inside and sit at the bar, admiring what they've done to the place. If my memory serves me, this used to be a women's shoe store. In the back of the shop sits an elevated stage for musicians and performers. A whir fills the room and, to my delight, I know immediately what it is. They're roasting coffee beans.

"Hi," Pam says cheerfully. "Anything look good to you?"

"How about an Americano?"

"Good choice." She smiles at me, a high-wattage version of the one she used to flash in high school. "You passing through town, hon?"

"I suppose you could say that."

"You look familiar to me for some reason. Do I know you from somewhere?"

"Been to Manhattan in the last fifteen years?"

"Don't I wish? I've always wanted to go there and see one of those Broadway shows." She laughs. "I rarely get to leave Fawn Grove these days because of family and work."

"How's business?"

"Pretty slow, but we just opened a year ago. A coffee shop like ours takes time to grow in a town like Fawn Grove. Thank God for Dunham College. The students there keep us afloat."

"Educating people to appreciate good coffee takes time."

"Especially when you live in a depressed town like this and the coffee is more expensive than Dunkin's," she says, gesturing with a dismissive wave of her hand.

"I think it's so cool that you roast your own beans."

"Thanks, hon. Don't hear that very often. Let me go make you that drink."

She fills the portafilter with finely ground espresso, levels it off, then screws it back into the machine. Pam's hair is shorter and spikier than I remember, but other than carrying a few extra pounds, she looks the same as before. She ran with a group of theater kids who put on the school's musicals and acted in the annual drama production. They were an extremely tight clique and quite active in all the school's activities. I remember Pam singing the lead one year in *Mary Poppins* and how everyone brought her long-stem roses after the show. At the time, she was the closest thing there was in this town to a Broadway star.

She places the mug down on the bar and stares at me.

"Sure I don't know you?"

"Not that I know of." I shrug, wishing I didn't have to lie.

"So what do you think of our little town?"

"It's changed quite a bit since the last time I was here."

"You've been to Fawn Grove before?"

"A long time ago when I was visiting family." I sip the drink and am surprised how good it is. Light-years better than what The Galaxy serves. "Wow! This is an exceptional cup of coffee."

"Thank you so much." Her smile lights up her face as it did when she was singing onstage back in high school. "That's quite a compliment coming from a bona fide New Yorker."

"You from here?"

"Born and raised." She wipes down the spotless granite countertop. "Most of my family worked in the paper mill when the mills were going gangbusters."

"Not so much anymore?"

"They're down to a bare-bones crew. I'm surprised they lasted this long, producing only one product."

"Catch-and-release papers."

"Wow! You know a lot more about our little town than I thought."

"One of my relatives used to work there." I sip my Americano and glance around the place. "I don't remember there being this many immigrants."

She rolls her eyes. "They started moving in a few years ago, thanks to Catholic charities. It's been a hard transition for everyone in town."

"Are you referring to the murder of that girl?"

"No. Well, yes, but that's a terrible tragedy in its own right. The immigrants' arrival here has created lots of other social problems."

"Like what?"

She leans over the bar and whispers, "I try to be tolerant, I really do. But as a mother of three girls, it scares me to death to think what kind of society they'll grow up in if these immigrants ever outnumber us. Whether they'll be forced to wear head scarves and be submissive to men."

"Is that realistic?"

"They tried to get a mosque built in town, which I'm totally okay with, but they wanted to get rid of every restaurant and bar within a thousand feet of it. I'm all for live and let live, but that's not tolerance in my book."

I sip my coffee and try to empathize.

"The rumor around town is that she was stoned to death."

"Do you believe that?"

"It's what I heard, but it could be just a rumor. I did some research on the Internet and learned that they stone girls in their own country as punishment."

"I saw the sign in your window."

"What sign?"

"The one advertising a rally in support of the immigrants."

"We let all the community groups put signs on our window. Most come from the students at Dunham, seeing as how they're our biggest customers. I think they see themselves as an oppressed people just like the Afghanis."

"Don't all college kids these days think of themselves as oppressed?" I laugh.

"I think with them it's a deaf thing," she says. "Honestly, it's not like I'm unsympathetic to the immigrants' cause. We're all immigrants in one form or another, and I know for a fact that many of them are good people who are happy to be here. Fawn Grove really is a nice place to live and raise a family."

"If you can find work."

"True. Many people these days have to get by on government assistance and the local food bank."

"I can't tell you how excited I was to come back and see this town again."

"Excited to see Fawn Grove? Now that's something you don't hear every day." She laughs. "But I'm glad you think so highly of our shop."

"This is one of best cups of coffee I've had in a while," I say.

"Awww! You're such a sweetheart." She reaches out and pats my hand, and the sensation of being touched momentarily repulses me.

"Do any of the immigrants come here?"

She laughs. "Oh, no. They stay to themselves and shop in their own stores. We don't see a dime of their money, and that's fine by me."

"So why do you think the girl was killed?"

"That's the sixty-four thousand dollar question, right?"

"If you had to make an educated guess?"

"I don't know much about their culture, but some people are saying she dishonored herself, whatever that means." She leans down and whispers, "Look, my business partner would freak if she heard me talking about this. We've known each other since kindergarten, but she's one of those bleeding hearts who wants to see the good in everyone. I'm a decent person, but I'm also a realist. Do you really think I want to see my girls wearing a hijab?"

"Of course not."

"My gut is telling me that one of their own killed that poor girl. A radical," she says. "I'm a Christian who believes in forgiveness, so punishing a kid like that is a foreign concept to me. Personally, I hope they find the bastard and kill *him*."

"Has there been a lot of tension in town because of it?"

"It's torn us apart like nothing else. It's caused a lot of pain and suffering among the townspeople who for years have been suffering economic hardship. There've been protests and angry town hall meetings. Neighbors have stopped talking to one another over the issue. Some people have even stopped going to Mass because the Catholic Church dumped them here and made the town pay for their well-being. There's even been a few fights."

"That bad, huh?"

"One day a small group of men marched through town, chanting in their language and making outrageous demands."

"What kind of demands?"

"Not totally sure, because no one couldn't understand them. The newspaper reported the next day that they wanted more welfare benefits and better living conditions," she says. "Sorry, but I didn't catch your name?"

"Lucy Abbott. And yours?"

"Pam Dooley," she says, giving away the fact that

she'd married Easy Ed Dooley, star lineman for the football team and genuinely good guy. It surprises me that of all the guys she could have married, she ended up with the jock. "Are you married, Lucy? Have kids?"

I laugh. "Heavens, no."

"More time and money for yourself then?" She laughs and pats my hand. "Maybe someday, right?"

"If I ever meet the right one."

"I've been married fourteen years now, right out of high school."

"What's your husband do?"

"Ed works at the mill. It's a good job, but I don't know how much longer it's going to stay open. They've been threatening to close that place for years."

"What will you do if that happens?"

"We try not to think about it. Can't live off what I make in the shop right now. I hope things will pick up once people try our coffee." A customer approaches the counter. "Have to run. Nice talking to you, Lucy. If you need anything else, just give a holler."

"Will do."

I take my mug over to a table and stare out the window, enjoying one of the best cups of coffee I've had since moving here. My perception of Pam Price has changed after our brief conversation, and I now feel for her. People grow up and change, mostly for the better, but not always. I wonder if her theater clique was a by-product of growing up in Fawn Grove and trying to rise above being a mill town girl.

I grab a wrinkled copy of the *Standard*, Fawn Grove's weekly newspaper, and begin to flip through it. There are lots of ads and feel-good stories about townspeople trying to make Fawn Grove a better place. But then I stop and fold the paper in half. There's a photo of five high school students receiving awards for exceptional community service. Removing my sunglasses, I stare at the girl standing in the middle of the pack. She's wearing a hijab, and there's the faint hint of a smile over her face. I recognize her immediately.

Nasreen.

14

*A*FTER PURCHASING TWO POUNDS OF COFFEE, I MAKE my way out of the shop and drive over to the Afghani market where Nasreen works. It's bustling with activity this morning. Groups of middle-aged women dressed head to toe in burqas stroll up and down the aisles. Once again I notice that I'm the only American-born person in here. My previous enthusiasm for this place has now been displaced by a sense of fear. Did I put the girl's life in jeopardy by meeting with her? And did she violate some religious code by speaking to us? I walk conspicuously through the narrow grocery aisles, gazing at the various produce while trying to see if Nasreen is on duty. A young man in his twenties kneels on the floor and stocks cans along the bottom shelf. It's a Saturday morning. Shouldn't she be here by now?

Two women in full burqas glance suspiciously at me as I pass, no doubt because I'm dressed provocatively according to their strict standards. I stand out in this market in more ways than one. A wave of anxiety passes over me when I see their dark eyes glaring at me from the end of the aisle. An angry-looking butcher with a thick mustache hacks away at a carcass behind the meat counter, the chopping sounds vibrating through my bones. He stops briefly to see what the fuss is all about before shouting out something. A row of goat heads gaze at me on the counter through lifeless, glassy eyes. The sight of them nearly makes me sick. I pull out the crumpled newspaper and hold it up to him, and he mumbles something unintelligible before waving me away with his bloody knife.

I spot the manager. Was he the man I saw shouting at Nasreen in the parking lot? I ask the man at the cash register if Nasreen is working this afternoon, but he merely lowers his eyes and shakes his head.

I feel terrible about coming here the other day. Had I caused her to lose her job? I pray I didn't put the girl in harm's way. Maybe it's nothing, but I can't shake the sinking feeling that something bad has happened to her. If someone has taken the time and effort to warn me off this case, I can't imagine what they might do to a young school girl caught between two disparate cultures.

I realize I'm wasting my time here. These people won't tell me where Nasreen lives or where I can find her. I drive up to the housing project where most of the immigrants have settled. I don't quite understand why I'm doing this or what it will accomplish, but I need to make an effort. The main road leads up and into the Blueberry Hill development. After parking, I walk up the narrow street until I arrive at the first row of drab townhouses. There's not a soul in sight. Behind the windows I see eyes peering down at me from behind curtains.

My trusty boning knife presses against my thigh. It feels strange to walk alone on these quiet streets, all eyes on me, feeling oddly like a second-class citizen. It doesn't feel as if I'm in Fawn Grove anymore but in some strange foreign land. I know that I'm not supposed to be here, and that it's dangerous and risky, but this is my town; the place where I grew up and played. Besides, someone has to learn something about the dead girl before the case goes cold.

I climb the nearest set of stairs and ring the doorbell. These homes have been poorly built and are breaking down under the weight of their shoddy construction. Shingles splinter apart, and the wood around the window frames looks as if dry rot has begun to set in. I ring the doorbell and wait for someone to answer. A minute passes before the door opens and a pair of eyes appears between slits of black fabric.

"Do you know where I can find this girl?" I ask, holding up the photo of Nasreen.

The woman snaps at me before slamming the door shut. Across the street, I see a tall man and a woman wearing a hijab walking toward me. Gripping the photo, I leap down the stairs, holding the picture up for them to see. The man's eyes widen and a vile expression forms over his face. Before I can show him the photograph, he starts shouting at me and waving his arms in a threatening manner. The man turns to the woman and gestures furiously for her to get in the car parked alongside us.

"Could you please help me? I'm looking for this girl," I say.

"You don't belong here," he shouts in a thick accent. "You dishonor us by coming here dressed like whore."

The force of his insult stuns me. "I can go anywhere I please in this town. Now just tell me where the girl is and I'll leave."

"You're a disgrace. An infidel." He steps toward me and spits at my feet. "Leave before you get hurt."

"I'm not leaving until I find her."

"In my country, they would kill you for talking to me like this."

"I guess we're not in your country now, are we?" I grip the handle of the knife in my pocket.

"This won't be your country for long." He laughs and steps toward me. "Soon we will outnumber you and you'll live under our rules."

"Over my dead body!" I step forward and brace myself for whatever's coming.

He shoves me. The insult of his hands on my body sends a shock wave through my system. I recall all the bullying I put up with when I was a kid and couldn't properly defend myself. It's partly why I fled Fawn Grove and joined the army. I figured that at least I could defend my country if not myself. Then they sent me to medic school, and I ended up saving soldiers' lives. Not all of them, but enough to justify my service. I didn't spend all those years defending this country's freedoms only to return home and be discriminated against because of my gender. Or because I'm an American citizen in my own country, a lone voice standing up for a dead Afghani girl, like the Afghani girl from my past.

I take out the knife and grip the wooden handle. The man steps forward and tries to push me a second time, but I surprise him by stepping out of the way. This pisses him off, and he rushes toward me. I turn slightly and throw a fist filled with boning knife into his face. He falls backward and onto the pavement, crying out in pain. I crouch next to him as he cups his bloody nose. Indignant, I slip the blade into his nostril until I get his full attention.

"Don't you ever put your hands on me again."

He mutters something as I hold the photo up to his hate-filled eyes.

"Now tell me where the girl lives."

His stares up at me in defiance. "I wouldn't tell you even if I knew."

"Nasreen. The girl who works at the Afghani market."

"Go and find her yourself."

I lift the blade higher until he whimpers.

"Where does she live?"

He stares at the photo for a few seconds before laughing. "You stupid whore. You know nothing about my people. We answer only to Allah."

"If you ever put your hands on me again, I'll make sure you get to meet Allah sooner than later."

"Do you realize what might happen to her now? Because of you?" He laughs. "You better pray for the girl."

I retreat down the road, keeping my eyes on him as he stands. The sting of being called a whore reverberates in my head. No one's ever called me that name before. I turn and hobble toward my truck as fast as possible. Glancing back, I see that a group of boys have gathered at the top of the hill. They're shouting in their foreign tongue and waving their arms in a threatening manner.

Rocks begin to pepper my feet. A pebble smacks against my back and takes my breath away. I jump into the truck just as a rock bounces off the hood. Another crash-lands in the bed of the pickup. I do a U-turn and speed down the hill just as a spidery crack appears along the rear window.

What the hell was I thinking by coming here? What a stupid and dangerous thing to do. I accelerate until I'm completely off Blueberry Hill. My back hurts, and I'm trying desperately not to break down in tears. By the time I pull into my sister's driveway, I'm sobbing hysterically.

I'd served in a region of the world where women were treated as inferiors and expected to be obedient to men. To confront a Muslim man in that way is to trap him into a corner and humiliate him. I'm all for tolerance, but how far must we go to honor the customs and traditions that these immigrants have brought with them? Where do our rights conflict? There's no way I'm letting any man put his hands on me and treat me in such a disrespectful way. Or call me a whore. I hope I've taught him a lesson he'll not soon forget. The shock of this encounter furthers my resolve to find out who killed that poor kid. I only hope I didn't put Nasreen's life in jeopardy.

I call Dalton and ask if he'll meet me somewhere.

"Are you okay?" he asks.

"Not entirely, which is why I need to speak with you."

"Did something happen?"

I debate whether to tell him what transpired.

"Lucy? Are you still there?"

"Yeah, I'm here. I may have done something stupid."

"Have you been speeding through town again?" He laughs.

"I went looking for the girl on Blueberry Hill, and one of the Afghani men put his hands on me."

"Jesus! Are you all right?"

"I'm fine."

"Are you crazy? You should have never gone up to Mecca all by yourself."

"You're right, I shouldn't have."

"If you're thinking about pressing charges, you can pretty much forget it. None of those people will testify against him."

"I have no plans to press charges," I say. "But he might consider pressing charges against me."

"For what?"

"He put his hands on me, so I defended myself. That was a mistake he'll not soon forget."

"Damn it, Lucy, you need to get a grip on yourself. You're not in New York City anymore."

"I went up there to find out where the girl lives, but no one would talk to me."

"Of course they wouldn't. Now you know how I feel. Pretty frustrating, isn't it?"

It pains me to realize that he was right all along.

"Just because she wasn't at work these last two days

doesn't mean she went missing. We'll find her. Then we'll work at getting to the bottom of this murder."

"Do you think we can sit down and talk?"

"Would you consider having dinner with me to-night?"

I debate this for a moment, wondering how far I'll go to get answers. "Dinner will work."

"How about I pick you up around seven?"

"Sure," I say, wondering if I'll come to regret having dinner with Dalton.

Wendy is sitting at the table and reading a magazine when I walk inside. It's one of those splashy celebrity magazines that give the reader "the inside scoop." She looks up at me as I close the door. By the expression on her face, I can tell she's been worrying.

"Oh my God, Lucy. You look terrible. Are you okay?"

"I've been better."

"Sit down, and I'll make you a cup of tea."

"Tea sounds nice right about now."

Wendy wheels herself to the counter, fills the kettle with water, and heats it up on the stovetop. She pushes a button on her electronic chair and elevates the seat so that she can reach the cups and tea bags. She places one in each mug and then returns to the table. Once the kettle boils, she pours hot water into the cups and places one in front of me.

"You seem upset," she says.

"I've gotten involved in something I probably shouldn't have by looking into this girl's death."

She laughs. "You go away all these years and now you want to be a member of the Fawn Grove Police Department and solve murders."

"I must admit, I have become a bit obsessed with this case."

"Why in the world would you care about any of that when you have your own issues to care about? Let the police do their job."

"Yes, I suppose you're right."

"You should be working on healing yourself and spending time with your family instead of worrying about all this crazy nonsense."

"Maybe it's because I saw with my own eyes how badly women were treated over in Afghanistan."

"And by finding this girl's murderer you think you can make up for that? Solve all the world's problems?"

"No, I'm not that deluded."

"Then what's wrong with you?"

"Something happened to me over there, Wendy, and it affected me."

"Of course something happened to you. You lost both of your legs."

"No, something else. Two things actually. The last one happened the day before that roadside bombing."

"You want to talk about it?"

"Maybe at some point, thanks, but not now."

"You have two prosthetic legs to show for your service to this country." She places both hands down on the arms of her wheelchair. "At least you don't have to ride around in one of these all day."

"I'm sorry about your illness."

"And for no other reason than MS strikes people randomly and at will." She leans over the table and massages my hand sympathetically. "You know I'm always here for you."

"I know. And I'm here for you too." I place my free hand over hers. "Thank you, sis."

"You're welcome. For your own good, you should just walk away from that girl's death and leave it for the police."

"If only I could."

"This town is changing, and folks here are afraid for their futures. The mill has cut way down, and people have lost jobs and hope. Alcohol and drug use is rampant among our youth, and now we have this influx of immigrants to deal with."

"There's a young girl who works at that Afghani market. I think she might be in trouble because of me."

"Why?"

"I was talking to her about the girl's murder when her boss came out and started yelling at her. Maybe he thought she was ratting out her neighbors."

"So why do you think she's in trouble?"

"Because I can't find her, and no one at the store will tell me where she lives."

"You have to understand, Lucy. These people don't open up to outsiders, especially after the anti-immigrant rally held here a few months ago."

"What happened?"

"It got ugly. Rabble-rousers from outside of town showed up just to stir things up. It's no wonder these immigrants don't feel welcome here. They're constantly being attacked and vilified." She sips her tea.

"It's human nature to circle the wagons."

"If you're so concerned about the girl, why don't you go tell the police what you know?"

"I'm meeting with Dalton tonight."

"Dalton?" She laughs. "You do know that he was one of the loudest protesters that day?"

"Yeah, someone told me he was involved."

"When the mayor heard about his involvement in AFA, he said it was a conflict of interest. The town suspended him without pay and ordered him to take sensitivity classes, and to not take part in any more demonstrations."

"Do you trust Dalton?"

"It's not whether I trust him. The question is, do you?"

"Should I have reason not to?"

"You grew up with him. You know what he's capable of doing. And from what I remember, you weren't one of his biggest fans."

"That was a long time ago when we were young and stupid. People change, Wendy."

"I certainly hope you're right, but I'm not so sure with this guy."

"There's another thing I should tell you." I look down and realize that I haven't touched my tea. "Someone left a threatening message for me yesterday."

"Dear God! Where? Do you have any idea who left it?"

"No. They scrawled it on the windshield of the pickup, warning me to stop digging around in the girl's death."

"I'm really starting to worry about you. You need to step away from all this."

"I wish I could." I walk over and place my tea in the sink. "But that message they left pisses me off even more, and now I feel compelled to get to the bottom of this."

"Then, please be careful. Promise me you will?"

"Yes, I promise."

"I couldn't live with myself if something happened to you after all these years of our living apart."

"Don't worry, sis," I say more confidently. "I can protect myself."

"Brynn tells me you cooked at The Galaxy yesterday."

"I did, and it was a total waste of time. Nadia's father refuses to take any of my advice."

"An accomplished chef like you is out of her league working in that dump."

"I was trying to teach him to be a better cook. He could turn that diner around if he only listened to me."

"Why waste the time and energy? The Galaxy's reputation has been going down the toilet for the last ten years now, and it's not coming back."

"Maybe that's why I'm so involved with this girl's death. I need something to give me purpose and meaning while I'm staying here in Fawn Grove."

"You were always a hyperactive kid. You used to drive Mom crazy because you could never sit still or focus on anything for more than a few seconds at a time."

"That's one of the reasons I joined the army, to keep myself occupied."

"If you're looking for something meaningful to do while you're here, you should go visit your father. He'd really love to see you."

"Has he been asking about me?"

"Every time we talk."

"What does he know about me?"

"I haven't told him anything yet. That's something you should probably discuss with him."

"I will in due time."

"Don't take too long. Time may not be on his side."

"What's wrong?"

"I'll let him tell you."

"You see him regularly?"

"He drives us around to our appointments and helps us run errands when we need it. It's an excuse for me to help him out financially, and spend some time with him."

I walk over and plant a kiss on top of Wendy's head. After grabbing her empty teacup, I wash it out and place it in the kitchen sink next to mine. I leave the kitchen and notice that Russ is reclined in his easy chair and snoring loudly. Not wanting to wake him, I tiptoe past and traipse up the stairs. Instead of going to my room, I enter the sitting room and plop down in the rocking chair. The photo album is in the same place where I left it. I grab the album and flip through the pages, taking solace in my long-ago past. There are photos of Wendy when she was healthy, and I see my mother when she was young and beautiful. A family portrait of all of us. There's my father sporting long hair and a thick mustache. He's holding Jaxon in his wiry arms, and Jaxon's beaming with joy. It's all I can do to keep my composure. Tears fall from my eyes, and I realize I have to stop looking or I'll become an emotional wreck.

There's nothing left for me to do but get some rest before I meet with Dalton tonight. I wonder if he has an ulterior motive for meeting me. He was once a bully, and bullies do what they do because of their own deep insecurities. So what's Dalton's story? What caused him to lash out and treat others so horribly? Had he too been treated badly growing up?

The floorboards creak underfoot, and I fear that I'll wake Russ. But then a door opens and I see Brynn standing there. She looks surprised to see me. Something about her today seems different. She nods for me to come inside, and I follow her into the spacious room. A song is playing in the background, something contemporary and poppy. It's a typical girl's room: boy band posters, dolls on shelves, photos of her and her friends. The room is clean and tastefully decorated. All her clothes are where they should be, books stacked neatly together, and no unnecessary papers or pop cans cluttering things up. I'm impressed and slightly envious of her organization skills. On her desk sits an open laptop. A profusion of multicolored laser beams shoot out from the computer's screen. Brynn falls into her chair and swivels around to face me, a self-satisfied smile over her face.

"Have a seat," she says, gesturing with her hand. "It's just us girls."

"Where?"

"On the bed. It's okay if you wrinkle it."

I lower myself on the bed and cross my legs until I'm sitting comfortably. It's soft and pliable, and the duvet billows with air as I settle onto the mattress. I've not been in this room since returning to Fawn Grove. It looks totally different from what I remember. From when it used to be Wendy's room, littered with toys and stuffed animals.

"How do you like it?" she says, looking around.

"You appear to be a very neat and organized person." I recall Wendy telling me about her emotional issues.

"Yes, I'm like my mother in that regard," she says, smiling with pride. "Any luck finding out who did it?"

"Not yet."

She laughs, which strikes me as odd, considering that we're discussing her classmate's murder. "Nasreen really got her ass chewed out the other day, huh?"

"Have you heard from her?"

"No. Should I have?"

"I was just wondering if she was all right." I don't want to speculate and frighten Brynn.

"Why wouldn't she be?"

"I just don't want her to get fired from her job."

"I can text her if you like."

"Could you?"

"Sure. We text back and forth all the time."

"Tell her I'd like to talk a bit more about her cousin, if she's willing to speak with me."

"Okay," she says. Huge dimples appear over her cheeks when she smiles. "The kids in my school can be such jerks at times. I feel really bad about what happened to Sulafi. Just because she was an immigrant doesn't mean she deserved to be treated like that."

"Treated like what?"

"Teased. Girls my age can be so cruel."

"Something you've seen?"

"Yes, it happened to me in the sixth grade, and I swore to never be a victim again," she says, a hardness in her voice I've not yet detected.

"I'm sorry you were bullied."

"It was humiliating, and I hated myself for letting it happen."

"But you don't hate yourself anymore?"

"Oh, hell no," she says, her tone now upbeat. "I vowed to always stand up for myself and my friends."

"Good for you."

"No, good for you." She smiles and swivels 360 degrees in her chair. "You look so pretty today, Lucy."

"I do?"

She giggles in a girlish manner. "You totally crack me up."

"Why's that?"

"Oh my god," she says, pausing to stare at me. "Maybe I could help you with your makeup some time."

"Too heavy?" I suddenly feel self-conscious about the way I look.

She moves a thumb close to her forefinger. "Maybe just a teensy bit."

"I thought it looked okay when I left."

"It could just be me, then," she says. "How are your . . . legs feeling today?" She covers her mouth as if to keep from laughing.

"What's so funny?"

"I just didn't know how to refer to them."

"Refer to what?"

She reaches down and rubs her hand on the spot where my legs end.

"Oh. Those. I call them stumps."

"Stumps. That's a funny-sounding word."

"Not so funny when they belong to you."

"I'm sorry, Lucy. I wasn't trying to make fun of you."

"It's fine. You didn't know."

She sits up all prim and proper, hands folded over

her lap. "So what's it like being back in Fawn Grove? Is it depressing?"

"Is that how Fawn Grove seems to you?"

"Like, duh! I can't wait to leave this place. Only difference is, I'm never coming back. *Ever.*"

"That's easy to say now. Your hometown always beckons you when you've been away from it for a while."

"This town is so mind-numbingly boring that I'll kill myself if I stay here any longer."

"You shouldn't talk like that."

"Look at my parents and what it's done to them. They say the mills caused a lot of people to get sick and die."

"Your father's injury was a freak accident."

"What about my mother's illness? You don't think all that smoke and pollution caused her MS? Look around this crappy town. Everyone's sick or dying from one thing or another."

"Your parents are doing the best job they can."

"My father sits around on that stupid recliner all day and watches TV. What kind of life is that? At least my mom tries to stay as active as possible."

"I notice she's gotten worse since I'd last seen her."

"The doctors say there's no cure for the kind of MS she has."

"I'm sorry, Brynn."

"I don't need your sympathy," she says, brushing her fingers through her hair. "My only other relative in town is that old pothead who calls himself my grandfather, and he couldn't care less about me."

"Do you see him often?"

"On occasion, although I try not to. I hate going over

to his depressing cabin," she says, making a sour face. "It smells horrible in there."

"What's he like?"

"You wouldn't even recognize him. He looks like one of those homeless bums you see diving in Dumpsters for food. Greasy hair and beard, and his nails are long and yucky. I don't think he ever showers."

"Your mother said he's been doing worse since your grandmother died."

"From what I've heard, he never cared much about her anyway. Gramma was always trying to make excuses for him, but I knew the truth."

"Your mother told you that?"

"No, I overheard my parents talking about him and the way he treated Gramma. He's a total loser."

She's angry, and I realize I need to change the subject before this turns sour. "I hiked down to the river where that girl was killed."

"That's creepy. Why in the world would you do that?"

"Can I show you something?" I say. "Wait right here."

I hobble back to my room and dig out the earring I'd hidden in the drawer. It feels light in my hand. Almost weightless. I don't know why I'm doing this, other than I'm searching for answers any way possible. I return to her room and show it to her. Brynn cranes her neck over my open palm and studies it for a few seconds. The expression on her face changes subtly, and I can tell the earring has caught her attention. Her dimples vanish, and her eyes seem to darken as if reflecting some inner turmoil. She looks up at me and shakes her head. But I sense that she knows something about it.

"I found this in a bush not far from the crime scene," I say.

She stares unblinkingly at me with those large blue eyes.

"You're telling me you don't know anything about it?"

"It's just a stupid earring. Anybody could have left it there."

I can tell she's hiding something. "Who does it belong to?"

She hesitates for a few seconds before heading toward her drawer. She reaches inside and pulls out two earrings exactly like the one in my hand.

"Okay, I wasn't being totally honest. I do recognize it."

"Why did you lie to me?"

"Because I was afraid you might have freaked out and gotten the wrong impression."

"And what impression is that?"

"These earrings are like our secret symbol. They represent the fact that my friends and I have bonded for eternity. A bunch of us got the rings as soon as we entered high school."

"How did it end up in the bushes down by the crime scene?"

She shrugs. "It's obviously been a long time since you've been back in this town. Was it as boring then as it is now?"

"I would imagine even more so back in my day. We didn't have cell phones or social media to keep us busy."

"Lucky you," she says, rolling her eyes. "You've got to promise not to say anything to my parents."

"Okay."

"That place where the girl was killed is a popular spot for kids to party. Triple Bs, everyone calls it."

"Triple Bs? What does that mean?"

"Beers, blunts, and blowjobs," she says, stifling a laugh. "Come on, Lucy. You can't be that much of a prude?"

"Trust me, I'm no prude," I say, slightly taken aback by her bluntness. "You don't go down there, do you?"

"Only when I'm bored." *And I'm bored every second of my life*, her body language conveys to me. "But I don't do *all* that stuff."

"What do you do then?"

"Two out of three, maybe." She giggles.

"But why do you go down there, Brynn? You're only fifteen."

"Dude? There's like nothing else to do in this town except party. Besides, I get decent grades and do all my chores. And there's no way I'm going to sit at home and be the class dork."

"I didn't expect this from you."

"Sorry to disappoint."

"But why?" Sadly, I know why she goes down there.

"Do you know how many kids end up getting stoned or drunk on the weekend? Do you have any idea how many junkies there are in this town because this place is such a dead-end? There's no future here for us kids in Fawn Grove."

"Did you tell the police about what goes on down there?"

"Seriously?" Brynn rolls her eyes and makes an exaggerated show of laughing. "Like Dalton and his band of idiots don't know that kids go down there to party. From what my mother told me, he was the wildest of them all back in the day."

I laugh. "He was."

"You knew him?"

"Some."

"The cops chase us out of there all the time. Then one of the boys got smart and ran a fishing line across the trail. It's attached to a bell so that whenever the cops come after us we have enough time to escape."

"Don't you think it's odd that I found this earring near the crime scene?"

"Hardly," she says, now sitting cross-legged in her chair. "Bet if you look hard enough you'll find a lot more of our stuff down there: bottles, condoms, cigarette butts."

I stand to leave. "You probably shouldn't be partying down there, Brynn. It could be dangerous."

"No offense, Lucy, but you don't get to tell me what to do."

"I understand, but what would your mother say if she knew?"

"My mother was known to party back in the day too. So what's she going to say? I'm just following in a long tradition of Fawn Grove juvenile delinquency."

"But she wants better for you. To get good grades and attend college."

"You're right, but I'm sure you don't want to upset my mother right now, especially with all her health problems."

"Don't worry, I won't say anything."

Brynn seems far older than fifteen at the moment. Then again I was just like her at that age.

"How well did you know Jaxon?"

"Everyone in town knew him."

"What was he like?"

"He's gone now, Brynn. It's still too painful for me to talk about what happened."

"Maybe some other time?"

"Sure." I stand to leave.

"Take care of yourself, Lucy." She smiles.

"You too."

I walk back to my room and bury my head in the pillow, trying not to think about the past. My head is spinning as I reflect on that strange conversation with Brynn. Who is this conflicted girl playing the role of my sweet niece? She doesn't seem so sweet anymore, but then again no one is ever as they seem, especially the more I learn about her. It should come as no surprise that a pretty girl like Brynn would rather hang out with the cool kids in school than be in this house of sickness and impending death. And who am I to talk? I used to be one of the wildest kids in town. I drank, smoked weed, and ran with a crowd that would have shocked most people.

I need to rest before I meet with Dalton this evening. I close my eyes, but all I can think about is that fateful day when my life forever changed, the day before my legs got blown off. Had it not been for that IED, who knows what would have happened to me or how my life might have turned out? I suppose it doesn't really matter at this point. Legs or no legs, the voices in my head would still be there.

Sleep proves difficult, and my mind races like the hands of a clock on steroids. It seems odd how everything has led me back to Fawn Grove. Honestly, I never thought I'd end up back here. Even contemplating a visit seemed far-fetched and ludicrous—until I suffered that nervous breakdown.

The notion that I might be going on a "date" with Dalton terrifies me. Or at least that's how this dinner feels, despite my strong assertion that it's not at all a date. In all my time in Manhattan, I had a total of four dates. There could have been more if I'd wanted, but what's a girl to do when she's working hundred-hour weeks and partying every night in order to survive until sunrise? All I ever wanted was someone to love and love me back. Nadia was the only person in my life who made me feel special, and I left her without even a good-bye.

My eyelids fall gently as I settle into a woozy listlessness. Darkness turns into darkness. It's the one place where all my demons reside. Tonight she visits me, the beautiful girl from the fruit market. She often makes an appearance in my dreams. And although she tells me that she's in a good place now, and that I'm not to blame for what happened, it only serves to intensify my guilt. It's why I will keep searching for this killer.

15

I CHECK MYSELF IN THE MIRROR WHILE WAITING FOR Dalton to arrive. I've not moved from this spot for thirty straight minutes. This is not a date, I keep reminding myself. So why do I care how I look? Or the special way I draw the outline of eyeliner? The long, yellow dress and black stockings tell a different story, although what kind of story I appear not to understand. Ask my subconscious. Ask the black leather boots that come up under my scarred and rebuilt knees, hiding any trace of prosthetic. I can't remember the last time in New York City I wore a dress this nice. To this I add the double-breasted peacoat and flowery black scarf before heading downstairs to wait for him.

Ten minutes pass sitting in silence with Russ and Wendy. Wendy knits a scarf while Russ watches a documentary on the Wright Brothers. Suddenly the doorbell rings. A flock of doves patter in my stomach as if

I'm getting ready for the prom, which I'd never had the pleasure of attending. I open the door and see Dalton standing on the stoop. He's cleaned up nicely and is wearing a shirt and tie. An edgy five o'clock shadow is beginning to form over his chiseled face, and his dark hair has been gelled to look stylishly messy. The black leather jacket over his rugged shoulders reeks of masculine charm, and I can't help but be impressed. I keep reminding myself that I don't want to like him and that he treated me terribly as a child. So why are goose bumps forming along the skin of my arms? I should hate this guy for what he's done. He escorts me down to his car and opens the passenger door like a true gentleman.

"You look fantastic," he says.

"Thanks."

"Look, I'm sorry about what happened the other day at the diner. Are we good?"

I smile at him. "Hell, no, we're not good. Not even close to it. Now start driving before I starve to death."

"You kill me, Lucy Abbott."

The restaurant he takes me to is called Francesca's and it's been here forever. Chefs like to refer to these places as "Tomato Sauce Joints." This is not to demean this style, because if done right it can be a wonderful experience. There's nothing better than a small family restaurant serving old-school classics. In Fawn Grove, however, this type of cuisine is considered fine dining.

A pretty young hostess seats us at a table that is adorned with a checkered linen tablecloth. In the middle of the table sits a burning candle within a wicker basket. Like a perfect gentleman, Dalton holds the chair out for me. Really? It feels kind of nice, though.

Quaint and old-fashioned like in one of those romantic comedies from the forties. In Manhattan no one ever held a chair out for me. It was everyone for themselves and chivalry be damned. A bottle of red wine is brought over and set down next to a mason jar stuffed with breadsticks. They resemble a witches' gnarled fingers reaching for my throat. There's a thimble of olive oil for the bread. I want to laugh so hard that it'll make me run to the bathroom and search for the gun above the toilet.

"Pretty nice place, huh?"

"Lovely," I say, trying hard not to sound sarcastic.

"It might not be as nice as those places in New York City, but the food here is pretty good. The owner serves authentic Italian dishes like the ones his grandmother used to make."

"The chef's Italian?"

"His grandparents emigrated from Sicily in the thirties and were one of the first Italian families to arrive into Fawn Grove."

"More immigrants, huh?"

"Yeah, but like they say, aren't we all the children of immigrants?" he says without irony. "The owner's an old friend of mine."

I nod, trying to keep my sassy opinions to myself, holding out hope that our meal might actually be good. It's not that I don't like this kind of food. Hell, a good tomato sauce joint is what usually cures the common ails in life, including a bad hangover. The simplicity of good food is often what I yearned for after cooking fancy meals night after night, sick of producing purees, reductions, and seafood risottos. But when places like this do it bad, then it's very bad, masking quality with quantity.

A chubby balding man with braids of gold bling around his neck stops at our table. He shakes Dalton's hand and makes small talk. I recognize him immediately as Sal Francesca. He was two years ahead of me in school and a piece of work even then. His face is fatter, shinier, and redder than it was when I knew him. He used to think he was God's gift to women back in the day and would cruise around town in his black Trans Am. He wore T-shirts sporting the colors of the Italian flag, with a cigarette box curled in his shirtsleeve. Sal hung with a group of guys who referred to themselves as the Guidos and who wore their black hair in greasy mullets. The rest of his time was spent working as a line cook in the family restaurant. Now he's reached the zenith of success in town as the owner of Francesca's.

"Sal, this is my friend Lucy."

"Pleasure to meet you, Lucy," he says in a high-pitched voice. "Although I don't know why you're out with this jabroni."

"We're just friends," I say, watching for any sign that he recognizes me.

"With him as your friend, a pretty girl like you don't need no enemies," he says, elbowing Dalton in the shoulder. "Did you know I went to school with this guy?"

"I didn't know that."

"Lucy's quite a chef herself. Works in New York City," Dalton says.

"Is that so?" Sal says happily. "You know Johnny Luisa? I think he lives somewhere in Brooklyn?"

"Afraid not. New York's a pretty big place," I say, laughing.

"You any good? Maybe I put you to work out back making the gravy." He slaps Dalton's back.

"I'm good, but I'm probably no match for your talented chefs," I say.

"It's true, I got the best crew in Maine."

"Go back to the kitchen, Sal, before I call the health inspector," Dalton says.

"Only rat in this place is the one sitting in that chair, Ricky boy." Sal calls over a middle-aged waitress who looks as if she's toiled in the coal mines for decades. "Maria, take good care of these two. Anything they want, you get it for them."

After studying the menu for a few seconds, I order the eggplant parm for shits and grins. I'm guessing it'll be a greasy pile of shit warmed over with sauce and cheese. Or mootz, as we refer to it in the business. Dalton orders the surf and turf before handing the oversized menu back to our waitress.

"Sal's a great guy. I've known him since second grade."

"Seems nice enough."

"Had this black Trans Am back in high school that all the guys were jealous of. He may not look it now, but he was pretty popular with the ladies back then. Then he went bald and put on a few pounds. Now he's got a wife and two kids."

"I bet he was a real lady-killer back in the day, just like you."

"I had a girlfriend off and on throughout high school. Too bad she became my wife."

"What happened?"

"Went from fun-loving party girl to nagging . . ."

"Bee-yotch?"

"You said it, not me." He laughs as he pours me a glass of wine. "Sal took this place over from his dad about five years ago and started adding his own recipes to the menu."

"Is this one of those restaurants where you never leave hungry?"

"So you've heard of this place," he says. "Makes a nice lunch the next day."

"Not to change the subject, Dalton, but have you learned anything new about this murder?"

"Do we have to talk about this now?"

"I thought this was the main point of our coming here?"

"I figured we'd enjoy a nice meal before we started talking about that."

"Can we talk now? Then we can relax and enjoy our dinner."

"Sure." He puts his hand over mine. "I must say, Lucy, you look great tonight."

I sit back and wonder if this is going to be an epic struggle that I'll be forced to endure all evening. But when I look at him I find myself torn between conflicting emotions. Am I attracted to him? What the hell's wrong with me? I must admit, it does feel nice to be desired by someone as handsome as Dalton. Must I continually remind myself that I'm doing this for a specific reason?

"You must have been quite a suave operator back in the day."

He laughs at this, covering his mouth with a napkin.

"What's so funny?"

"You saying how suave I must have been. I find that hilarious."

"Why?" I sip my wine and nearly gag at how sweet it is.

"This may surprise you, but I used to be the biggest a-hole on the planet."

"Really? And you're man enough to admit that?"

"Sometimes I wish I could go back in time and change the way I was. Then I'd apologize to all the kids I . . ."

"Apologize to them for what?"

"Forget about it. Have a piece of my breadstick." He pulls one out of the jar.

"Maybe you've already apologized to them and you don't even know it."

"What's that supposed to mean?" He breaks it in two and hands the other half to me.

"Just saying." I take a small bite and then place it down on my plate. It's like eating a stale, salty cracker.

"What about you?"

"What about me?"

"What were you like in high school? Hot babe with lots of guys hanging around her? Head cheerleader maybe?"

"Oh, hell no." I laugh at the absurdity of this statement as I take the earring out of my pocket and place it on the checkered cloth.

"What's this?"

"This is me bringing something to the table."

"An earring?"

"Perceptive, Dalton. That's what I like about you."

"You gonna tell me the meaning of this?"

"You tell me."

He picks it up and studies it. "What's so special about it?"

"Seems the youth of Fawn Grove like to indulge themselves down by the river."

"How did you know about that?"

"It took me five minutes of asking around town to figure it out."

"The design of this earring is unlike anything I've ever seen before. Do you think it has any significance?"

"It's represents eternal friendship. Some of the girls at Fawn Grove High bought them in order to signify their lifelong bond."

"Where did you find it?"

"In some bushes the day we hiked down to the river. It was the day you took off like a bat out of hell."

"I think we both know why."

"Why deny it? You tried to kiss me at the scene of a murder."

"No, you misinterpreted my good nature."

"Be that as it may," I say, "I'm the only one here producing any results."

"You call this a result?" He laughs. "I call this bull-shit."

"Then why don't you tell me something meaningful about the case."

Our waitress arrives unannounced hefting a huge platter of food fit for an army. How could they have cooked it so fast, unless they precooked it and then zapped it in the microwave? The waitress sets it down on the table and then, with all the enthusiasm of a mortician, proceeds to serve our entrées along with bowls of salad. This troubles me, and I almost say something, because the salad should always be served well before the entrée. My lettuce is drowned in a gloppy white glue that's supposed to pass as bleu cheese dressing. I sample a wedge and struggle not to spit it out. Then I push the bowl aside and stare glumly at my fortress of eggplant. There must be a pound of melted mozzarella bubbling over the top. I cut into it, and red sauce oozes throughout the thin layers. The gorgeous purple skin of the eggplant has been stripped away—such a shame! I fork a column into my mouth and struggle to swallow the mush. It tastes like equal doses of salt and oil.

I ask myself if I'm being too harsh. Has my time spent cooking in Manhattan kitchens turned me into a pretentious food snob? Someone who can't appreciate a good old-fashioned meal?

I look over at Dalton and notice he's wolfing his food down as if it's his final meal. He looks genuinely happy to be cutting into his rare New York strip. Alongside it are three fried shrimp and a medley of soggy vegetables. I suddenly feel bad for hating this place, although I know I can't help it. Working in a high-end restaurant has created this gastro monster within. This trattoria run by a former classmate of mine strives hard to please and doesn't put on airs, and try as I may, I find it difficult to act grateful.

I struggle to work my way through the meal. I'm so put off by the dish that it makes me uncomfortable. A bowling ball settles in the base of my gullet. Most of the pasta and salad I leave untouched. The waitress comes by and boxes everything up at my request. To my surprise, Dalton orders tiramisu for us to share, but I beg off and instead order an espresso.

"Great meal, huh?" he says after they've cleared our plates.

"Very authentic."

"Sal's traveled to Italy and has studied their cuisine."

I look away so I don't break out into a fit of laughter. It would be too cruel for me to pop Dalton's cherry about Francesca's cuisine. If Sal discovered food like this in Italy, they must have sentenced that poor chef to life with no parole.

"There are certain things I haven't told you about the girl's death," he says, taking the bill from the waitress and handing her his credit card.

"Like?"

He smiles at the dour woman and then gives me his full attention. "She recorded videos of herself on her phone and sent them out to her classmates."

"Videos?" I recall Nasreen saying something similar.

"There were only two, and she saved them on her phone. I'm assuming she made more."

"What was she doing on them?"

"She wasn't doing anything you and I might consider crazy. Dancing, singing, and talking into the camera as if she was auditioning for *American Idol*. She bragged that she was going to be rich and famous one day, and leave everyone behind in Fawn Grove."

"Can I see it?"

"Of course not. That phone was confiscated by the state police and is in evidence."

"Was she wearing her hijab?"

"In one she was. In the other she'd let her hair down and seemed like your average teenage girl."

"Was she pretty?"

"Now there's a loaded question."

"Why?"

"It'll make me sound like a perv if I say a fifteen-year-old girl is pretty."

"I see your point."

"But yeah, she was beautiful, especially without her headscarf on. Looked a lot like that Kardashian girl on TV."

"What about her address book?"

"Most of the addresses listed in it were family and friends. But she also had about thirty of her classmates in there too."

"Why would such a shy and reserved girl have so many addresses in her phone?" I say.

"Maybe she was trying to fit in, and maybe she was not as shy as you think."

"That would be a dangerous thing to do living where she does."

"Someone in her community obviously took offense to the fact that she was acclimating so easily to American culture."

"It's possible," I say, trying to process this new information. "Did you try to speak with the girl's parents?"

He shakes his head and laughs. "You already know the answer to that."

"They wouldn't give you or the state police the time of day."

"Exactly. Just like they wouldn't talk to you."

"But what did they say? How did they react when you first told them that their daughter had been murdered?"

"That's the thing I couldn't wrap my head around. They were so calm and collected. No parent reacts like that when told their kid has just been killed, and in that manner. It felt really weird to me."

"And you should know, right? Having a daughter yourself."

"How'd you know about that?" The waitress returns with his receipt.

"It's a small town," I say. "One hears things hanging out at that diner."

"Goddamn Stef!"

"What's the difference who told me, Dalton? I would have found out anyway."

"And that's not a deal killer for you?"

"Deal killer for what?"

"Us."

"Jesus, we're just having a nice dinner. There is no us."

"I'm going to tell you a secret, Lucy. I wish I'd left Fawn Grove a long time ago, like some of my more fortunate classmates. I might have made something of myself had I gotten out of here instead of marrying so early and becoming a father."

"Looks to me like you've done pretty well for yourself."

"By becoming a small-town cop?"

"Nothing wrong with that," I say, letting the moment pass.

"No one respects cops these days, especially in Fawn Grove."

"Were you referring to any classmates in particular who left town?"

"Not really," he says, eyeing me suspiciously. "Not like you'd know them, anyway."

"No, probably not."

"You ever think about having kids someday?"

I laugh. "Hell no!"

"Same here. One moody teenage girl is enough."

"What's your daughter's name?"

"Like you really care."

"I want to know something about you, Dalton."

He sighs. "Brandy."

"What's she like?"

"Used to be a good kid until her mother got into her head."

"How so?"

"Do we really have to talk about my daughter now?"

"Not if you don't want to."

He throws down his napkin in surrender. "I'm stuffed. What do you say we get out of here?"

"Sounds good to me."

We drive in silence back to my sister's house. No music or small talk. Did I hit a nerve by mentioning his daughter? At this stage in the investigation, I don't want to alienate him for fear of being left out of the loop. But I fear I might have unintentionally pissed him off. Or was it because I barely touched my dinner? If so, I have no idea how to make things right. Or if I even want to make things right.

He skids to a stop in front of the house, jumps out, and opens the door for me. I thank him for a wonderful evening as my three-inch heel hits the sidewalk. I head up the walkway clutching my doggy bag, and it takes me a second to realize that he's right behind me. My nerves flutter and leave me confused. I stop and turn to him once I reach the top step.

"Thanks again," I say, holding out my hand.

"You're entirely welcome." He takes it.

"I didn't mean to anger you by mentioning your daughter."

"Don't sweat it. I should warn you, though, that girl's somewhat of a conversational sore spot with me. Her mother's poisoned her against me, and now she wants nothing to do with dear old dad unless it rhymes with honey."

"Don't quit on her just yet. She might still come around."

"It's hard not to at times," he says, still holding my hand. "I try my damnedest to maintain a good relationship with her, but it never seems to pan out. She hates me thanks to her mother. Still, I'll never stop trying to be a positive influence in her life."

"You shouldn't," I say, "because one day she might see the light."

"I hope so, because I'll do anything for that girl," he says. "So how long do you think you'll be staying in Fawn Grove?"

"Not sure. Depends how long my cousin will have me."

"I hope you can stick around for a while. That lamb burger you made the other day was amazing."

"Thanks." Is he saying this just to please me?

"Better not let that pretty head of yours get too swelled, or you'll never squeeze yourself out of that kitchen." He touches my hand.

"I really hope Yanni asks me to cook for him again." I badly want to take my hand back. "I'd love another chance to win his regulars over."

"You definitely should."

"The only problem is, that place needs more than a new cook."

"You have to start somewhere, right?"

"I suppose."

"Once people taste your food, Lucy, word will spread far and wide, and they'll come from all over the county to eat there."

"That would be nice," I say, prepared to go inside. "I gotta run, Dalton. Take care."

Dalton releases my hand and smiles. Is he going to try to kiss me again? We stand there staring awkwardly at each other for a few seconds before he turns and scampers down the stairs. He moves inside his pickup and quickly disappears.

Why do I feel disappointed? Because he didn't try to kiss me? Is that what I really want?

I'm about to go inside when I notice another car parked down the street and idling along the curb. A swirl of exhaust coils out the tailpipe. Is someone watching me, or am I being paranoid? I make my way down the stairs and head toward it, reaching into my purse for the boning knife. But before I reach the curb, the car takes off down the street and disappears around the corner.

16

I SLEEP THROUGH A WHIRLWIND OF MULTICOLORED dreams that segue blissfully from one vision to the next. At times these dreams bring me to a near-conscious state and I feel as if I could reach out and touch the objects and people in front of me. I see Jaxon as a young boy, laughing, and I grab hold of his hand and run through the woods with him. In this dream, he has lots of energy and exudes a happy boyish charm that was rarely seen in his short, troubled life. The dream changes and I find myself in the middle of a busy kitchen, panicked and feeling claustrophobic as the tickets continue to pile up. For some strange reason I can't seem to get the food out in a timely manner—and the orders keep piling up. Exhaust fans thunder like jet planes in my ears, and I find myself transported to Afghanistan, all hell breaking loose around me, the wounded coming in at breakneck speed and in desperate need of medical attention. Everyone's screaming, shouting, or groaning in horrific pain. I watch helplessly as more than a few of them lie dying on tables, their eyes beseeching me to do something. Anything. Then my dream shifts, and I'm asleep. Suddenly I'm awakened by the familiar sound of those voices. I jump out of bed and sprint furiously to the small tent just outside our base. This is the part of the dream that always sickens me. My dream segues, and I find myself buried in a pit down by the Alamoosa, unable to move and listening to the river gurgle past. I'm at the mercy of the people in front of me, although I can't see their faces. But I can hear them laughing and mocking me. Each of them has a stone in hand. A command is given, and the people lift their arms and begin to throw them in my direction. I close my eyes and escape into the void of darkness just before they smash into my face.

A knock on the door startles me awake. I spring up, covered in sweat, wondering who it might be. The sweat is thick and hot and pouring down my face. I'm keenly aware of my surroundings, despite it being pitch black in this room. My stomach growls angrily from that greasy eggplant dish, and it takes me a few moments to realize that I'm actually quite hungry. I recall the thick glob of Italian dressing on my salad. And the stale breadsticks and melted mozzarella that bubbled over the top. There's a second knock on the door, reminding me that someone is outside.

"Come in," I say, adjusting the pillow beneath me.

Light pours into the room as soon as the door opens. I lift my hand to prevent it from reaching my eyes and see Wendy's mechanical wheelchair moving toward me. How did she get upstairs? Then I remember the electronic chair lift on the stairwell.

"Something wrong?" I say.

"Wrong?" She laughs, but she's anything but amused. "Lucy, you've been asleep for two days."

"What?"

"I know you've asked me not to bother you when you are up here, but I was getting worried."

"Two days?" I can't quite believe this. No wonder I'm so famished.

"You scared me."

"I guess I wasn't as ready to face the world as I thought."

"Rick Dalton has called here three times asking about you."

"Why?"

"Could be the date you two went on a few nights ago?"

"It wasn't a date, Wendy."

"Sorry, I shouldn't have assumed," she says, turning away from me. "It's just that something awful has happened while you were asleep."

"What?" I grab her forearm and notice that my hand is shaking.

"They found a boy's body in Garrison's cornfield. He was one of Brynn's classmates."

"Oh my God! What happened?"

"Whoever did it cut a crescent moon and star into the section of cornfield where the boy was discovered. Like one of those crop circles."

"You're kidding?"

"I'm not. A local pilot saw the design from above

and took pictures of it. Then he sent it to the police. They immediately drove over there and found the boy's body."

"Was he Afghani?"

"That's the strange thing. The boy was born and raised in Fawn Grove."

"But that doesn't make sense," I say. "What are the police saying about it?"

"They don't know. I thought I'd come up here and tell you myself, seeing how you've developed such an interest in the case."

"I need to get up," I say groggily, ripping off the blanket.

"Are you okay, Lucy? It's not normal for a person to sleep for two whole days."

"You are aware that I have issues, right? It's why I came back to Fawn Grove in the first place."

"Yes, but two whole days?"

"I'm not entirely sure why I slept that long. Are you still good with me staying here in my condition?"

"You're family, Lucy. You can stay here for as long as you like."

Wendy leans over and hugs me, and as much as this sudden intimacy freaks me out, I don't move. I let her cling to me. It feels as if she needs this hug more than I do. Although she's a bit older, and I haven't seen her for many years, I do love her. Besides Brynn and my estranged father, she's the only blood relative I have left in this town.

The rain batters the windshield as I barrel toward Garrison's cornfield. The eastern handle of Fawn Grove consists primarily of farmland and cow pasture, and it's been like that for years. The only time we ever went there was to pick apples or cut down our annual Christmas trees. We'd get a fresh one every year, and we kids would pile happily into the family wagon for the ride over. Jaxon loved our apple picking outings the most, oftentimes scaling the tallest tree to grab the plumpest, juiciest apple. It's a wonder he never fell and broke his neck. That kid could scale almost anything, including the local quarry's highest peaks, where he would leap off the hundred-foot cliff. Then after we'd finished picking apples, our bags brimming with Red Delicious and plump McIntosh, we'd order a bag of pumpkin donuts straight out of the fryer, along with cups of hot cider. With our goodies in hand, we'd settle at one of the picnic tables and gorge ourselves. Come Halloween, Jaxon would be the first one in the corn maze, sprinting through it as fast as his little legs would take him, always the first to escape.

I pull up to Garrison's and see a police car at the entrance to the farm. It's parked between the split rail fence and the opening where visitors pull in. I leave the truck running and walk toward the officer's car. The frantic sound of the pickup's windshield wipers reminds me that it's pouring outside. The young kid who emerges from the car looks to be in his teens. He's wearing a transparent raincoat over his blue jacket and cap, and the intensity of the rain pounding against it sounds like an assault rifle going off.

"Can I help you, ma'am?" he shouts.

I'm not sure what to say. I stop in front of him, rain dripping off the hood of my rain poncho and battering my ears.

"Ma'am?"

"Where's Detective Dalton?" I shout.

"He's not here right now. If you need to speak with him, you can probably track him down at the station," he shouts back.

I look over his shoulder. "Can I go inside?"

"No, ma'am. It's a crime scene. The state police have instructed me not to let anyone inside the perimeter."

"Would you mind not calling me ma'am, Officer Wilson?" I say, reading his nameplate.

"Yes, ma'am. I mean, sure." He shifts his weight nervously as I look him up and down.

"How old are you?"

"Excuse me, ma . . ."

"I said, how old are you?"

"Twenty-five, but I don't see how that's any of your business."

"You any relation to Steve Wilson?"

"Steve was my-my-my big brother," he stutters.

"I knew Steve back in high school," I say, glad to make a connection that might get me inside. The rain drips down my hair and face, and I hope my mascara's not running too badly.

"You knew my brother?"

"Yeah. We were friends in high school."

He seems hesitant, as if he doesn't want to continue this conversation.

"How's he doing?"

He glances around the farm before saying, "He's d-d-d-dead."

"Dead?" The notion of Steve's passing shocks me. "I'm so sorry. What happened?"

"Overdosed t-t-t-two years ago. H-h-h-heroin." His stutter seems to be getting worse.

"I had no idea."

"It's become a b-b-b-big problem in Fawn Grove these days," the kid says. "A lot of it's laced with f-f-f-fentanyl."

"I don't know what to say."

"Say you want to be part of the s-s-s-solution and not the problem," he says, gesturing toward the cornfield. "Same goes with these towelheads moving into t-t-town. Killed one of our own this time."

"How did it happen?"

He makes a throat-slitting gesture. "Between you and me, I blame those sand niggers! It's about time they go back to their own country."

"Do you really mean that?"

"Of course I-I-I-I do. There's going to be a big protest rally in town. You should go and show your support."

His racist words shock me as much as the news of Steve's death, and I run back to the warmth of my idling truck. The windshield wipers sweep maniacally across the glass as I turn the wheel and gun it back down the road. I put a death squeeze on the steering wheel to keep my hands from shaking. The cop's words about his dead brother haunt me, and I find it hard to believe that my old school friend passed away.

The skies clear by the time I get back into town. A hint of sun can be seen breaking through the clouds. I need to find Dalton. I need to find the missing girl. My stomach rumbles for food as I cruise toward Fawn Grove High. It's the same squat brick building that's been there forever. Tennis courts and a football field sit off to the side. A bell rings, and kids pour out the doors and begin to loiter in the parking lot. A few stop to smoke and chat. I stop the truck across the street to observe them. A circle of students stand conversing behind a row of cars and trucks.

It must be early release day on account of their murdered classmate.

Why have I come here? One of their peers has been killed and the world moves on as if nothing has happened. Maybe they don't yet know about their dead classmate. But I doubt it. Word spreads quickly in this small town, if the past is any indication.

I'm about to speed off when I see Brynn standing in the middle of the circle, her pink book bag sprawled across her delicate shoulder. She's smoking and nodding her head as if in agreement with what's being said. She looks older to me now and not the innocent girl I once thought. She's with Stefania, who is also smoking. Are they friends? Has the murder of their classmate brought these two disparate personalities together? I had no idea Brynn or Stefania even smoked, although nothing surprises me anymore, especially after that conversation I had with Brynn the other day.

I take off down the road and see a logging truck angling toward me. My pickup has veered out of control and slid into the opposite lane. I turn the wheel hard and at the last second swerve out of its path. The sound of the truck's horn blasts in my ears as I accelerate around the truck. The crushing weight of its rear tires churn dangerously close to my left. Once I pass, I pull over to the side of the road and let my heart slow to its normal rhythm. I feel sick. I'd throw up if I had anything in my stomach. But my stomach's an empty pit of despair. If I don't force myself to eat soon, I fear I'll pass out.

I stagger into The Galaxy, light-headed and dizzy, and plop myself down on one of the ripped stools. As usual, the place is empty, except for two blue-hairs sipping coffee in one of the back booths. I know it's usually a slow time in the restaurant business, but the emptiness of the place now seems pathetic and sad. Where is everyone? Years ago there would have been a big crowd in here. I adjust my sunglasses and lean over the counter. It's so quiet, I can hear the clock ticking above the coffeemaker. I get up, go behind the counter, and make my way into the kitchen. The lack of fuel in my system has left me so weak that I must stop and hold the wall to keep from falling.

Yanni's asleep in a chair by the walk-in. For a brief second I fear he's had a heart attack or stroke. But then the violent sound of his snoring rumbles across the room and informs me that he's far from dead. I go over and gently shake his shoulder. It takes him a few seconds before he adjusts to the light. He opens his eyes and sees me standing over him. The shock of being woken causes him to jerk his oversized head up.

"Jesus! You scared the shit out of me."

"You always take a nap this time of day?"

He waves his hand in disgust. "It's a slow time right now."

"Will you make me something to eat?"

"You come here again to make fun of me?" He gets up and walks toward the stainless steel table.

"No." I look around the kitchen. "Where's all your help?"

"Stef will be here soon." He pulls out an industrial-sized can of tomato sauce and begins to open it.

"I'm famished, Yanni. Could you make me a burger and some fries?"

"Go sit down and I'll fix it for you."

He looks at me for a second and then buries his face into his hands and begins to cry. I don't know whether to leave or go over and hug him. Instead, I do what I always do, and that's nothing. I'm so accustomed to seeing people cry in my kitchen that it's almost second nature to ignore them. I know it sounds callous, but the kitchen is a cruel and unforgiving place that will crush you if you let your guard down. My inclination is to tell him to get back to work, but that seems counter-productive now. The weak and unfit always fled from my kitchen, never again to face my wrath. And as far as I was concerned, that was a good thing. Cooking in restaurants is about survival of the fittest.

"My daughter's right. I need lots of help here," he says. "This diner is going to hell, and I can't do nothing about it."

His words surprise me, and I don't know what to say. Saving this diner is more than I can handle at the moment, especially when I can't even take care of myself.

"I've let my family and customers down. I feel so ashamed."

"You can still turn it around, Yanni. It's not too late."

"I'm sixty-six years old and tired. I don't know if I

have the energy to do it anymore." He turns to me. "Tell me what I can do."

"For starters, make me a double cheeseburger with bacon. Fries too. 'The customer is always right' is the first rule of any good restaurant, and I'm your only customer right now."

"Will you help me?"

"Make my burger and we'll talk about it later," I say, barely able to concentrate because of the intense, all-consuming hunger bearing down on me.

I return to the dining room and take a seat at the counter. A rumpled copy of the day's newspaper sits in front of me. I flip through it while Yanni prepares my meal. The top story is about the boy's murder. I see an aerial photo of the cornfield, and the crescent moon and star are displayed prominent in the picture. In the right column is a photograph of the boy. He's smiling and looks like an all-American kid from Anywhere, U.S.A. He was good-looking, and I can tell by his earring, stylish haircut, and bright eyes that he was popular with the girls. Such photogenic smiles, in my opinion, often mask a well of hidden sadness.

I'm about to read the article when I see Stefania walking into the dining room. She ties an apron around her thin waist and grimaces upon seeing me. Not thirty minutes ago she was standing in that high school parking lot with Brynn and the other students, smoking cigarettes. She approaches the counter and stares down at the newspaper in disgust.

"I thought you hated this place," she says.

"You're imagining things." I return to my paper.

"If you don't like it here, why don't you go somewhere else to eat?"

"Why don't you go take a smoke break while your grandfather makes me lunch."

"Smoke break?" She glares at me, the muscles in her jaw flexing. "Why are you making things up about me?"

"Let's cut the bullshit, Stefania."

"I told you a hundred times that my name is Stef. Now how about you stop lying about me?"

"Lying?" I laugh. "I saw you and the rest of your pals smoking in the high school parking lot. Been smoking anything else lately?"

"Were you spying on me?"

"Please. I could give two shits whether you smoke or not. Get lung cancer for all I care."

"Better not tell my mom."

"Why? What's a snotty kid like you going to do about it if I do?"

She stands there fuming, unable to come up with a witty reply.

"I had no idea you and Brynn were such good friends," I say.

"There's a lot about me you don't know." She pokes a finger into the paper and makes a groaning sound. "It makes me sick that they made Taylor look so wholesome and happy. That boy was a total scrub."

"Is that any way to talk about the dead?"

"I just hate that everyone thinks he's a saint now that he's gone."

"No one's ever a saint while they're alive."

"No one but you," she says. "Taylor was such a stoner. That picture isn't even up-to-date."

"He smoked a lot of pot?"

"No, he smoked ribs. Of course he smoked weed," she says while wiping down the counter. "My friend tells me that in Afghanistan they can put you to death for smoking pot."

"So you think that's the reason why he was killed?"

"Who knows what these immigrants are capable of doing?" Yanni rings the bell and slides the burger and fries through the hole. Stefania grabs the plate and drops it in front of me. "Buon appetito."

I laugh. "Do you even know what that means?"

"Yeah. Choke on a bone."

I laugh, my saliva glands loosening at the sight of the burger. Two crispy strips of bacon poke out the sides of the bun. Grease drips onto the plate and puddles up against the fries. I remove the bun, grab the ketchup bottle, and smack it with the heel of my palm as if I'm performing the Heimlich maneuver. Stefania crosses her arms and watches as I press the seeded bun between my fingers and make quick work of it. The burgers are thin and gristly and have that unctuous taste that comes from cheap beef. Grease drips down my wrists and elbows, and I have to occasionally wipe them clean with a napkin. It might be the best burger I've ever eaten. Or the worst. Intense hunger often causes such confused sentiments. I can eat only a few of the fries before a queasy uncomfortableness settles into my rib cage.

"You scarfed that down pretty quick," Stefania says a bit too smugly. "Couldn't have been that bad."

"When you're hungry, anything tastes good." I toss my napkin over the uneaten fries—the white flag of surrender. "So what's the connection between the dead girl and this boy?"

"Who said there was one?"

"Two kids, two murders? There must be something that ties them together."

"I know his father is a preacher in town."

"What church does he belong to?"

"Lighthouse Baptist, I think. His father and Dalton led a protest against the Muslims, calling for them to be thrown out of Fawn Grove."

"So you think they killed his son in retaliation?"

Stefania shrugs. "Either that or because he was a big-time stoner. Whatever theory floats your boat."

"You sound so casual about this."

"Don't come in here and tell me how I'm supposed to feel. You don't know anything about me. I'll still be living in this shithole when you leave."

"Who said I was going anywhere?"

"Oh, you will. A fancy-pants like you won't last long in this town."

A logging truck rumbles past the diner, causing everything to shake. The burger sits like a curling stone in the pit of my stomach as I stagger out the door. Am I suffering from food poisoning? I went from famished to anguished in a matter of minutes.

I badly need to see Dalton and find out the details of this murder. Only now I feel like throwing up. I jump into my truck and head home. My bowels feel as if they're about to explode. I haven't had so many bad meals since being stationed overseas and eating a constant diet of MREs. It doesn't surprise me when the blue lights start to flash behind me. I pull over to the side of the road and glance at myself in the rearview mirror. My skin is flushed and pale, my sorry eyes hidden behind these overpriced sunglasses. I place my hands on the wheel and lower my head, praying it's not *him*. There's no way I want Dalton to see me in such woeful condition. A knock startles me back to reality. I roll down the window and turn in embarrassment to face him.

"Jesus, Lucy, you don't look so good. You been drinking?"

"Worse than that."

"You gonna be okay?"

"Actually, I think I'm going to be sick."

"Better get out of that truck before you make a mess." He opens my door and steps aside.

I stagger down to the line of trees. Falling to my knees, I lean over and heave. Dalton comes over and kneels by my side, lifting my damp hair out of my face. He squeezes my shoulder. It's a gesture of kindness that I appreciate, and yet it feels offensive at the same time. He's making it extremely hard for me to hate him, and I so badly want to despise this guy, the same guy who tormented me as a kid. But it's obvious he's changed. Or maybe he hasn't changed and wants something else from me. Something I'm not ready to give him just yet. Maybe someday, but not now when everything is up in the air.

"Are you okay, Lucy?"

"No."

"What happened?"

"I made the mistake of eating one of Yanni's burgers."

He laughs. "That'll do it every time. Fortunately, I've built up immunity to his shitty cooking."

"I can't stop thinking about these kids' murders."

"There's going to be hell to pay in this town when they find out who did it."

I hesitate before saying, "Will you take me down to the crime scene?"

"You know I can't do that," he says. "Maybe you should just forget about these deaths and enjoy your time here. How about we go out again? There's a great country and western bar a few miles out of town."

"Do you really think I can just go out to dinner with you and forget any of this ever happened?" I stand angrily, walk back to the truck, and lean against the pickup, running my hands through my sweaty hair.

"Best to leave it alone, Lucy."

"Why?"

"Because you'll drive yourself crazy thinking about all of this bad stuff. Life's too short."

"But I can't stop thinking about it."

"This is not your concern. You need to move on in life and enjoy your time here, and let all the negative stuff go."

"I hope that when you're ready, you'll tell me about it."

He sighs warily. "That's probably not going to happen."

"It will, Dalton. It has to, or I'll find out myself."

"I don't get it. What's with this crazy obsession of yours?"

"I don't know!"

I climb back in the truck, knowing I can't tell him about the voices in my head or the girl from the fruit market. Or how her tragic death caused me to lash out in anger the day before I lost my legs. It's why I need to come to terms with my own hidden truths. I turn the ignition only to realize that Dalton is standing at my window.

"You okay to make it back to your cousin's house?"

"Don't worry about me," I snap.

"But I do," he says tenderly. "I certainly hope you feel better, Lucy."

"Thanks so much for your concern."

"I'll see you around," he says, stepping back from the truck. "And slow down. I don't want you crashing into anything and ending up like Angus Gibbons."

"No chance of that happening. Plenty of fuel left in this old pickup."

This makes me laugh. Good old Angus Gibbons and his infamous plane crash. I wave good-bye and then head back to the house, my lead foot pressing mightily against the gas pedal.

17

I PULL UP TO THE HOUSE AND SEE RUSS HOBBLING down the path and toward the sidewalk. He's using an ornate wooden cane and moving slowly. What's this about? He rarely moves from his chair and hardly ever leaves the house. He makes his way slowly down the stairs leading to the sidewalk. I pull up to the curb and roll down the passenger window.

"Need a lift, Russ?"

"Nah, I'm good."

"Where you heading?"

"The sun came out today, so I thought I'd get some fresh air. Care to join me, young lady?"

"A walk sounds nice," I say, as much as I don't want to go for a walk.

"It'll just be us two cripples."

This line strikes me as odd, seeing how I'd never mentioned my injuries or prosthetics to him. Of course how could he not know? He's Wendy's husband. Russ probably knows all the dirty secrets about our messed-up family.

I park the truck at the curb and join up with him. The rays of the sun work their way through the clouds and filter nicely through the dying leaves. Russ leans on his cane, and for a second I think it might snap from the weight of his immense body. He's a big man approaching three hundred pounds. At over six feet, he's got at least six inches on me. Everything is quiet in this leafy neighborhood, and the afternoon sun throws long shades over the sidewalk. It's days like this when I find myself waxing nostalgic about my hometown, wishing it could always be this way. It strikes me as odd how memory alters perception.

"Truth is, I needed badly to get out of that house," Russ says as we turn onto another street. "I was getting a bit stir crazy in there."

"You must be an expert on military history by now, all those documentaries you watch."

"Beats watching those awful sitcoms. At least I'm learning something about the world."

"It must suck being laid up all the time."

"You, better than anyone, should know how that feels."

"I did at one time."

"How long were you hospitalized after the bombing?"

"Two full years at Walter Reed. But I always believed the day would come when I'd walk out of there like I once did. Not one hundred percent, mind you, but enough to live a normal life." I realize how funny this line sounds, knowing that I could never be the same person as I once was. Losing my legs, in some ways, came to be a blessing in disguise.

"Unfortunately, I'll never live a normal life again. The doctors said my spinal degeneration will only get progressively worse with time. It's similar to Wendy's MS."

"What happened to you in that mill?"

"I got caught in a high-speed conveyor belt. My coworker forgot to shut off the power before I started working on it. Fortunately, I was able to break free before it crushed me. Sunbitch threw me against the floor like I was a rag doll. Shattered two vertebrae in the process."

"Misery loves company, right?"

"Don't you just hate listening to people's sympathy? It's one of the reasons I stay inside all the time." He stops to catch his breath before moving on. "It's like I'm carrying a contagious disease and everyone's afraid of catching it."

"Know how you feel. I hated having to explain the same things over and over to people. It gets old."

"At least your injuries aren't as obvious to the world as mine. Being like this makes me never want to go out in public again."

"I know, right? It feels like *everyone's* staring at you," I say. "It's like people can see the pain inside your head."

"Your mother took it awfully hard when she heard about your injuries. It plunged her into a deep depression, and in my opinion led to her death. Messed your dad up pretty good too."

"My mother paid me a visit when I was recovering at Walter Reed. I didn't want her to see me like that, but she wouldn't take no for an answer."

"Your mother loved you kids. Maybe she loved you all too much, to the detriment of her own health."

"It's one of the reasons I stayed away from her for so long. I couldn't bear the pain of seeing her grieve for me. Or for Jaxon."

"I think she came to terms with Jaxon before she died."

"I certainly hope so."

"You didn't come to your mother's funeral, and Wendy wasn't happy about that. And you didn't come visit us afterward or even call to keep us updated on your progress. Brynn would have loved to have met you when she was a little girl," he says.

"You don't know how much my life changed in those two days."

"I totally understand that, but what about Wendy and Brynn? They're your own flesh and blood and deserved better."

"I know that I screwed up, Russ. I'm trying to make it up to them now, if that's even possible this late in the game."

"Are you going to tell Brynn the truth about your injury?"

"When the time's right, I will."

"I haven't seen Wendy this happy in a long time. She's really missed you, despite everything that's gone down. Brynn's the one who's been most affected by everything these last few years."

"How so?"

"She was extremely close to your mother before she died. Then both of her parents come down with these debilitating medical conditions, making it impossible for us to be the kind of parents we wanted to be for her. Let's just say that she's had her issues."

"But it's not your fault you got injured," I say.

"Doesn't matter whose fault it is. A kid doesn't understand that stuff growing up. They don't care about whose fault it is. All they know is what's real and what's not."

"She seems like a great kid." Then I recall her smoking cigarettes with Stefania in the school lot and telling me about her partying ways.

"She's a good kid, but she's going through some growing pains, and now you coming here on short notice has complicated matters."

"I certainly hope I haven't made things worse," I say, suddenly alarmed by what I might have done.

"Not for the worse, just different. And different can be good in many ways too. Your coming home was inevitable, Lucy."

"Yes, I suppose it was."

"Do you plan on visiting your dad while you're here?"

"Not sure." How many times had I told myself that my father was dead to me? And yet a small part of me still wants to see him.

"You really should go over there. He's still your dad, despite all that's happened."

"The way he treated my mother was terrible."

"Of course it was."

"He's a jerk and a selfish ass. Why should I go see him?"

"I'm just saying. You might regret it if something happens to Neal before you say your piece," he says as we turn the corner.

"Like what?"

"He's not going to live forever. Just tell me you'll think about it."

"Okay, but only because you asked."

"Good," he says, tapping the bottom of his cane on the pavement. "So tell me the real reason you're so interested in this dead girl."

"It's not just a dead girl, Russ. It's a dead boy now too." I watch as two squirrels chase each other around the trunk of an elm tree. How long has it been since I've seen a squirrel? Only when I walked through Washington Square did I ever see them mucking about, and I rarely walked through that part of town.

"You're treading on dangerous waters."

"I might as well tell you the truth, Russ," I say, committing myself to partial disclosure. "I hear voices at night, and they've been plaguing me ever since the time of that bombing."

"A symptom of your concussion?"

"No, because what caused them occurred the day before that roadside bomb. They're partly responsible for my obsession with these murders."

"Care to explain how this came about?"

"I can't right now. It's still too raw."

"Have you talked to a mental health counselor about this? Therapy really seems to have helped Brynn."

"It's not those kind of voices. I'm not schizophrenic or anything like that. And no, I haven't spoken to anyone since I left Walter Reed."

"Might be good for you. They say the VA has help for combat vets like you."

"Jesus, Russ. Do we have to talk about this while you and I are out for a nice walk?"

"You were the one who brought it up."

I laugh. "So I did."

"But no, we don't need to talk about it if you don't want to."

"It's not that I don't want to. It's just that I'm not ready to discuss it yet. I wanted you to know why I'm so taken with these murders."

"I only ask because you're looking into things that have been lightning rods in town. Fawn Grove is definitely not the same place you left."

"I can see that," I say, "but since when is looking into two murders a bad thing?"

"Never said it was. But maybe that's a job best left to the professionals."

"The 'professionals' don't seem to be doing their job very well."

"Be that as it may, you're still playing with fire."

"It's hard to believe that my hometown has become such a dangerous place."

"This immigrant issue has created a lot of resentment and division. And that resentment has pissed people off. It's probably why the refugees yearn for the traditions and customs of their homeland."

"Like killing kids who disobey their laws?"

"Seems barbaric for sure, assuming they're the ones who did it. But then again, how many people in this country are shot to death over drugs or money? Or overdose on heroin? Every society has their problems, Lucy."

"You must have an opinion about these murders."

"Wish it were so. Just don't want to see you sticking your nose into something that could put you in harm's way."

"Thanks for the advice."

"Can't say I didn't warn you about the minefield you're entering." He stops and stares at me as if mortified by his own words.

"What?"

"Oh Jesus, Lucy. I'm so sorry for my poor choice of words. That minefield comment was totally uncalled for."

I laugh and backhand his arm. "Don't sweat it, Russ. There's not much that offends me these days after everything I've been through."

"I often speak without thinking."

"Join the club." We walk a ways before I say, "So what do you hear about this upcoming protest rally?"

"Where'd you hear about that?"

"One of Fawn Grove's finest told me about it."

"I'm scared about what might happen, and that's all I'm going to say on the subject."

We arrive full circle back at the house. I hold the front door open for him, and he goes inside and collapses in his easy chair. His face is red and chafed from exhaustion, and he looks to be in some measure of pain. I grab his jacket and cane and hang them up. He asks for some water, so I go in the kitchen and pour him a tall glass from the tap. Wendy is sitting at the kitchen table and peeling potatoes for dinner, her stiff hands doing an awkward job of it. Tattered brown potato peels lie over the kitchen table like discarded playing cards.

"How was your stroll around the neighborhood?"

"How did you know I went for a walk?"

"I was watching out the window to make sure he got

down the steps okay. That's when I saw you get out of the truck and join up with him."

"It was fine. We had a nice chat."

"It's so good seeing the two of you getting along after all these years," she says. "The exercise is good for him, and he needs more of it. I keep telling him to get the blood moving, but he never listens to me."

"He seems to be in a lot of pain."

"When isn't he in pain?" She stops peeling and sighs. "What I wouldn't give to walk around the block again."

"Sorry."

"Not your fault. I'm just glad you and Russ are getting along."

"I didn't really know him when I was younger, our age difference and all."

"That's understandable. Maybe you two can catch up on things later."

"We'll see." I scoop some peels in my hand and throw them in the trash. "You married a good guy, sis."

"Think I'd marry a jerk?" She grabs another spud. "Will you be eating dinner with us tonight?"

"If I'm feeling better." I hold up the glass and nod toward the living room.

"Go give him his water before he dies of thirst."

I hand Russ his glass, and he leans sideways in his chair. It takes me a second to realize that I'm blocking his view of the TV. He's watching as a pride of lions gang up on a water buffalo and struggle to bring it down. One lion rides atop the beast's back, gnawing horribly into his bloody hide. The others move in and attack the buffalo until it's brought down and becomes dinner.

I can't watch these grisly nature shows, because they depress me. Is nature really a battle of survival where the fittest always win? Like kitchen work? I hobble up the stairs until I'm safely ensconced in my room. The silence both frightens and calms me, and I know I won't sleep tonight. I'm not the least bit hungry, and yet I know I have to eat dinner with them or risk hurting my sister's feelings. Surprisingly, the walk with Russ has helped me in ways I can't quite comprehend. He seems to get me in a way that all the others don't. I felt at ease talking to him, despite not telling him the full extent of my history, or my problems.

The potential for violence in this town is something I'd intuited long before I returned home. It's always been there, waiting for the right moment to rear its ugly face. There's a primal urge subsisting below Fawn Grove's surface that's borne out of hardship, familiarity, and benign neglect. I've always known that it's been lying dormant all these years.

I head upstairs to get some rest and am surprised to see Brynn standing in the middle of the hallway. There's an odd expression on her face that puzzles me. I walk toward her, but she doesn't move out of my way.

"You don't look so good, Lucy. Have you been drinking?"

"Of course not. Why would you even say something like that?"

"You've been acting strange lately."

"I could say the same thing about you."

"What do you mean by that?" She folds her arms tightly around her chest.

"I drove by the school today and saw you smoking cigarettes with some classmates."

"How dare you spy on me like that," she snaps, her face turning bright red. "How would you like it if I followed you around town. Bet you wouldn't think it was so cool."

"I wasn't following you, Brynn. I just happened to be driving by your school when I saw you."

"Please, Lucy. Do you think I'm that dumb?"

"I swear I wasn't keeping tabs on you," I say, hoping she buys it. "Of course I'll never mention it to your parents. It's just that I care about you and want you to grow up to be a healthy young woman."

"That's priceless, Lucy," she says, rolling her eyes. "You're gone from my life all those years and suddenly you care about me?"

"I'm so sorry about that, Brynn. There's no excuse for what I did. But believe me when I say that I do care about you."

Her body appears to relax. "I know you do. And I'm sorry for snapping at you like that."

"No worries. And you have plenty of reasons to be upset right now. Two of your classmates have been murdered and the killer is still out there."

"I know smoking is bad for me, but sometimes I do it just to fit in. And right now, with everything that's happened, I need to be with my friends more than ever."

"I completely understand," I say.

"I can't promise you I'll quit right away, but after this ordeal is over, I'll make it my goal to stop smoking."

"Thank you."

"No, thank you for caring so much about me," she says, moving in for a hug. "And again, sorry for yelling at you like that. That was totally my bad."

"I've forgotten about it already," I say, releasing her from my grip. "Can you see it in your heart to forgive me?"

"I've already forgiven you."

"I love you, Brynn."

"Luv you too, Lucy. Got to get back to my homework." She slips back into her room and closes the door.

That was a close call, I think, as I barricade myself in my room. Brynn's short fuse is something new. But why shouldn't she be upset? No teenager wants to be spied on and then lectured by an adult. I'm at least glad I was able to repair our relationship.

I need to go to that cornfield tonight and see where that boy was killed. If Dalton and the police won't let me inside, I'll sneak in and observe it myself. The army taught us covert methods of travel. Maybe it's time to make use of that training.

Everything is bearing down on me in ways I'd never expected. Cooking in that East Village restaurant kept me from thinking about my own problems, and then finding a solution to them. By working all the time, I avoided the inevitable pitfalls that would arise from self-reflection, and I knew that it would catch up with me eventually.

I lay my head down on the pillow and close my eyes. It doesn't take long before I hear the voices again. It's hard to be mad at them, as much as I've resented them in the past. They're children's voices and they need my help. They're calling out for me. Beseeching me to come to them when I can't even help myself. Come for them in a way I couldn't help that poor girl from the fruit market. Do I experience regret for what I did? Was it worth having these voices plague me? No, I don't regret my impulsive actions at all. I only wish I'd done it sooner for the girl's sake.

18

*T*HE DUTY OF ALL CHILDREN IS TO CARE FOR THEIR parents. My mother is dead, most likely caused by a broken heart. She suffered from both the loss of a son and a husband who didn't care for her. Or else was too selfish to care for anyone but himself. She was forced to lay eyes on a scarred and disfigured child suffering in debilitating pain and with an expressed desire to die. It was all too much for a sensitive woman such as my mother, for whom life in Fawn Grove represented the epitome of a happy existence. It's a good thing she didn't live to see this day. It would have broken her heart to witness such economic hardship, heartache, and sense-less death. Most of the mills have closed or are near bankruptcy, leaving cancer and illness in their wake. She would have been mortified to see her daughter and son-in-law in such bad health. And it would have caused her much sadness to learn that two kids in this town had been brutally murdered. It would have shattered her illusion of a perfectly lived life. That's all my mother really wanted. That's all any of us really wants, when you come right down to it.

The headlights illuminate the dark road ahead. Do I even want to visit my father? I know I said I didn't want to see him, but I lied in spite of myself. I want closure more than anything—to forgive and be forgiven so that I can start to deal with my problems. The thought of seeing him makes my stomach wobble like a water balloon being squeezed in the middle. My father and I need to have an honest talk. To be real with each other and get everything out in the open. It feels as if that's the only way we can move on in our relationship.

In the short time since I've been residing in Fawn Grove, Wendy and Russ have been the closest thing to parents I've had in life. It makes me sad that I'd neglected calling them all those years. I thought I had valid reasons, but they seem inconsequential now. I'd been a selfish fool like my father. But being selfish was the only way I knew how to exist back then. Selfishness was my sole survival mechanism and the only way I knew how to protect myself from all that threatened to destroy me. I wanted to smash all memory of the past and start anew.

The walk with Russ put me at ease. I never really got to know Russ before I left town. I was too young at the time, sixteen when they married. Wendy was twenty-six, and Russ was three years older than Wendy. He had two years under his belt working at the paper mill and was earning a nice living. Wendy became pregnant with Brynn before I left. They looked to have a bright future together—until tragedy struck at almost the same time.

I park the truck alongside the road, roughly a quarter mile from the Garrison Farm. I wonder if the entrance is still being guarded by that stuttering, racist police officer. But why take a chance? I reach down and make sure my boning knife is secure in my pocket.

The night is crisp and cold. A legion of galaxies sparkle above. After grabbing my flashlight, I push my way slowly through the dead stalks of corn, barely able to see in front of me. The darkness out here is stifling and completely blankets everything. I turn on the flashlight, but it struggles to project a strong-enough beam into the matrix of molasses. The ground rises up and down, slowing my progress. Roots and rocks jut out of the ground and nearly trip me.

Is something burning? My nose detects smoke, although it could be from one of the many wood-burning stoves that everyone in these parts uses. I put one foot in front of the other, trying to mentally calculate the distance in my head, which is based on the aerial photograph published in the paper. By my best estimate, it should be three hundred yards east of the main road. That's roughly one hundred fifty yards south of the barn. If my internal compass is correct, I'm heading straight in that direction.

Yet the scent of smoke becomes stronger the deeper into the corn maze I travel. My mind wanders, and for a brief second I think I'm hallucinating and am back in Afghanistan. I stop and compose myself, debating whether I should turn back. Maybe the owners of the farm are burning harvested stalks. But at this hour?

No, that doesn't make sense. It has to be something else.

I stop to catch my breath, realizing that I'm not in the same shape I used to be, traveling back and forth to battlefields to collect and heal the wounded, working days on end through stress and strife, the charred smell of artillery fire strafing my nostrils, blood on my hands and caked under my fingernails along with the dirt and sand.

I hear a faint noise. Voices? But they're not the voices I'm accustomed to hearing at night. I'm not even sure they're voices as much as low murmurings. I move forward, cautious, curious, gently spreading the dead stalks out of my way, careful to move in the direction of the feeble beam of flashlight illuminating my narrow path.

The smell of smoke gets stronger the farther I travel. The hushed voices become more evident as well. Someone else is out here in this cornfield with me. But who? A clearing appears up ahead lit up by a small fire. I see a group of people sitting and standing around the faint glow. I shut off the flashlight and move closer, crouching to keep hidden. It takes a few seconds to realize that they're kids and not adults and that they've gathered around the spot where the boy was murdered. I must have passed the downed stalks without even realizing it.

The kids pass a joint among them. Each takes a long hit before giving it to the next person. Someone lifts a bottle and takes a swig. I'm twenty yards from them and fearful of moving, not wanting to alert them to my presence. Knee to the ground, I remain perfectly still,

struggling to see in the dark. The kids take turns tossing cornstalks into the fire. The flame flashes bright orange before fading, creating a smoky scene that only
further obfuscates my view.

I take out my phone and begin to record them. But
why would they have a party here? Why in the spot
where their classmate was murdered? Are they memo-
rializing him, this being the way kids pay their respects
these days?

A tall boy wearing a wool cap stands and walks toward me, blocking my view of the others. Panic
flushes through my veins. Has he seen me? Or suspects that someone's spying on them? I drop to the
ground and watch as he unzips his fly and begins to
piss on the caked dirt. He totters drunkenly where he
stands, smiling like a goofy teenager. Typical high
school boy. When he's done, he zips up and staggers
drunkenly back to the group. Before he reaches the
fire, he trips on something and collapses face-first to
the ground. The others laugh hysterically at his clumsi-
ness.

Then I see her and it surprises me, although it
shouldn't. Brynn sits on the dirt, near the fire, opposite
from where the boy had been perched. She's laughing,
cross-legged and a can of beer in hand. Someone
passes her the bottle, and she takes a long swig. Her
faces mashes up from the harsh taste before conform-
ing to its natural beauty. From the shape and label of
the bottle, it looks to be peppermint schnapps. A girl
with raven black hair stands three feet away from her
and snatches the bottle out of her hand. She passes
Brynn the joint, and Brynn takes a hit off it before

passing it over. When the girl turns around, I notice that it's Stefania. This is the second time I've seen the two of them together. Apparently, they're closer than they're letting on.

This friendship surprises me, as they seem to be two temperamentally different kids. Both are beauties but on opposite sides of the spectrum. Funny how certain people end up in the same crowd.

The drinking and smoking is not that unusual for anyone who grew up in this town. During our walk, Russ hinted at his daughter's various troubles, but I never really took notice of it until now, despite Brynn admitting as much. But this is what kids in Fawn Grove do: party. It's in our genes. Parents pray that someday they'll outgrow it and become productive citizens, and get a job at the mill like they did. But since there are no more mills . . . I like to think I survived my juvenile antics. As did Dalton. Kids here party for lack of anything more constructive to do, and I hope Brynn will one day grow up and move on to better things.

There's no sense checking in on the crime scene. Besides, there's probably nothing much left to see after they've trampled everything around it. The police won't know or care at this point. All the evidence has been likely gathered, recorded, and entered into the record. This farm is so big that they can't possibly block access to it forever, and the Garrisons will eventually need to clear the withering stalks before winter hits so they can replant come spring.

I want to head back home, having seen all I need to see. But something prevents me from moving. Maybe

I'm afraid of making a noise and being discovered for the creepy adult I am. What if Brynn suspects I'm watching her? She'd never trust me again. It could forever ruin whatever relationship we've been trying to nurture. And because of that I remain deathly still while continuing to film her and her friends on my phone. Something about these drunken kids intrigues me, and I don't know why.

A few moments pass in silent observation before another girl stands and comes into view. She turns, and I'm so struck by the familiarity of her face that I almost let out an audible gasp. Her hair is long and black, and it cascades down over her shoulders, practically covering her face. It's Nasreen, the girl from the Afghani grocery. In the dark, and without her hijab, she looks totally different now. She looks like every other American teen girl who likes to smoke weed, drink booze, and flirt with boys.

The sight of her shocks me. I try to reconcile her face with the image of that quiet girl wearing the headscarf and stocking shelves at the market. Is she trying to fit in with the popular kids at Fawn Grove High, and in the process break away from the cultural restrictions holding her down? It strikes me as odd that she could be so easily accepted into their clique, especially after all the scuttlebutt around town about the Afghani refugees.

Is this diversity at its best? Or worst?

While I'm trying to process this, a man's voice cries out somewhere in the distance. The kids rise to their feet as if trying to discern where this voice is coming from. Brynn stares in my direction, and for a brief second I think she sees me hiding among these decayed stalks. But that's impossible. There's no way she can see me in this pitch-black field. The kids empty their bottles into the pit, and the fire sizzles and flickers out. Darkness falls over the land. One moment the kids are standing like statues. The next moment they're scattering into the black void, calling out to one another as they sprint through the cornstalks.

I crouch low as the voices become louder. Should I stay or go? In my condition, running is not always the best option. Two powerful beams of light flash against a row of cornstalks, and I realize that I'm in danger of being discovered. Is it the police? I picture myself being arrested and hauled into jail, my name and photograph plastered over the front page of the local newspaper. Having my identity revealed in this manner seems unthinkable, especially now that I've made a connection with Dalton.

This is the motivation I need to start moving. I turn and make my way out of the field, careful not to cause any sudden sound. I walk blindly, praying that I'm heading in the right direction, afraid to shine my light for fear of giving myself away. The voices sound menacing and right on top of me. Could they be the ones who murdered that boy? I pick up my pace, grabbing on to the wispy stalks for support as much as for guidance. I trip and fall, trying not to groan in pain. Someone hears my fall and shouts for me to stop. I get up and walk as fast as my rebuilt legs will take me. My stumps feel bruised and sore from the constant pounding of the terrain, but I need to keep moving or else my life might be in danger. Errant bands of flashlight illuminate the harvested brush, and I half expect police dogs to come snarling after me. Or men speaking in foreign tongues, ready with knives to slit my throat.

The darkness combined with my adrenaline rush quickly makes me disoriented. I have no idea where I am or in which direction I'm going, and yet I keep moving, breathless, scared, and in a near-panicked state. Where had those damn kids gone? They're light-years faster than me, their young legs fresh with energy.

At some point the voices fade into the distance. I fall to one knee and catch my breath, praying that the nausea in my gut will go away. I fight the urge to vomit, my face cold and clammy. I kneel quietly for more than fifteen minutes before I feel better. Whoever was chasing me has lost interest or gone in another direction. But could they be waiting for me out there, once I emerge from this field? What if it's Dalton and that stuttering, young racist cop? What would I say to them then?

I thumb the flashlight and navigate my way through the maze, my pace even and steady. Despite having no idea where I'm going, I keep moving, sore legs and all. After an hour of clomping around in the hard dirt, I see a clearing up ahead. Relieved, I emerge from the field and climb over a split rail fence. The backside of a steep hill separates me from the street, which in my state will prove to be quite an obstacle. I descend sideways to keep from falling until I arrive on the hard pavement. Looking around in the dark, I realize I have no idea where I am. The back of the farm? Best to keep walking, close to the shoulder of the road where I can't be seen. Soon enough something will look familiar and I'll discover where I parked the truck.

I walk around the perimeter for well over an hour before I find the main road leading into Garrison's Farm. My thighs are burning, and I can barely walk by the time I reach the pickup. But I'm so happy to have arrived that I want to cry. Tears run down my cheeks as I settle behind the wheel, the weight now off my battered knees. The engine roars to life, and the heat from the blower begins to melt away the chill from my bones. It rushes into my rouged face, smashing the tears against my cheeks and forming them into gray water stains along my skin. It blows my damp hair back as I hug the steering wheel to my chest and clutch it in gratitude.

I need to find out the connection between these teens and the secrets they're keeping from everyone. Brynn will be a tough nut to crack. If only I could speak with Nasreen and ask her about the things that make me most curious. But that's a dangerous proposition now that she's dangled her feet into two distinct cultures.

Was returning to Fawn Grove a mistake? Everything about this town screams messed up, and it's affecting me in the worst possible way. Maybe I should have never come back here in the first place. I had an inkling that returning home might prove to be a bad idea. But I never thought it would be this bad.

Yet despite it all, I know I can't stop searching. It's more about my own selfish needs than anything else. My own secret obsession, my own obsessive secretiveness. Something tells me that I must face these matters head-on to exorcise the demons from my psyche.

* * *

The house is quiet. I go straight up to my room and collapse on the bed, trying to ignore the intense pain darting through my legs. I ring Nadia and ask if she'll come over to the house and stay with me for a while. She's at the diner when I call, helping clean up the place. It was another slow day and Yanni's in a bad mood. When isn't he in a bad mood? She's eager to get out of there, especially if it means being with me.

I need to talk to someone about what I saw tonight. But who can I turn to? I certainly can't tell Nadia about her daughter. Do I tell Wendy and Russ what I saw out in that cornfield? That Brynn was eulogizing her dead classmate by getting drunk and smoking pot in Garrison's cornfield? On the exact spot where the boy was murdered?

I was a rebellious kid back in the day, so I'm one to talk. That was before I joined the military and straightened my life out, to the degree that was even possible. Had someone told my parents about my unruly behavior, I too would have been furious. I would have lashed out and never spoken to them again. Is that what I want to happen with Brynn?

The darkness in my room hypnotizes me. I think about Nasreen and her nebulous ties to both cultures, wondering if she's conflicted about where her loyalties lie. Is this what happened to her cousin? Her drinking and smoking is in sharp contrast to the rigid beliefs her people adhere to. The image I've formed in my head is of her stocking shelves in that Afghani market, her obedience to faith represented by the sacred hijab. The fact that she wasn't wearing it this evening both frightens and endears me to her. Now that's true rebellion. But rebelling against her strict Muslim culture may have dire consequences, especially if the murderer is living among her own people. Strafing the cultures of two distinct worlds could put her in the same danger as her dead cousin.

Nadia knocks on the door and then walks into the bedroom. Russ and Wendy allow her to come up whenever she wants. They've known Nadia since she and her family moved here, and they have witnessed the positive influence she's had trying to make Fawn Grove a better place. But I doubt they know the true extent of our friendship or that we were once a couple back in our high school days.

"I'm here," she says, closing the door behind her.

"Thanks so much for coming."

"It makes me so happy to see you." She climbs under the covers and lies down next to me. "Poor thing. You're shivering like a scared puppy. Do you feel all right?"

I shake my head like a feverish child.

"Would you like me to get you another blanket?"

"I'm fine," I say, wondering if I should tell her what I saw tonight. "How's your father doing?"

"Not so good."

"I'm sorry. I really wish I could help him."

"You could if you wanted. I know you think you flopped in there, but I overheard some of the regulars saying what a great breakfast you made for them."

"They said that about me?"

"Yes. I know there weren't many customers that day, but the ones who came loved that you used fresh eggs and a better grade of meat."

"I did make everything from scratch, even the dishes from your father's menu."

"And it showed. Some asked when you'd be cooking there again."

I turn and see the silhouette of her pretty face. "Maybe there is hope for that place after all."

"I don't know how much longer my father can go on like this. The stress of running that diner is killing him."

"He's impossible to deal with, and he doesn't listen to a word I say."

"We had a long talk tonight. I told him that if things don't change he'll lose everything, including his house, which he's refinanced in order to keep the diner afloat."

"I don't know if I can help him in such a short time."

"You could try. Of course I'll certainly understand if you can't." She kisses my forehead. "Tomorrow will be an interesting day, so get some rest."

"What's going on tomorrow?"

"There's a memorial ceremony to be held in town. The dead boy's parents are planning on speaking at it, and I pray there won't be any anti-immigrant violence."

"I still can't understand who would want to kill these kids."

"I wish I knew the answer to that as well," she says. "I only pray that one of the immigrants didn't radicalize and kill those two, but it wouldn't surprise me either."

"The alternate theory is that someone from town killed them."

"I don't know what to believe anymore," she says. "And as much as I've been advocating for the Afghanis, I'm not blind to the fact that one of them might have turned bad."

"Every religion has their fanatics."

"That's why it's unfair to demonize these people because of one bad apple."

"Assuming it is one of the Afghanis, why would they kill the boy?"

"Best not to make assumptions right now," she says, running her hand through my hair. "Do you know how much I've missed you?"

"I've missed you too."

"Regardless of all the time that has passed between us, you're still the same person as before," she says, caressing my cheek. "Legs or no legs, you're no less beautiful to me than the day you left."

"Thanks, Nadia, but it's obvious that I'm not the same person as I was back then."

"Yes, I suppose you're right. Then again who is the same person they were in high school?"

"I used to have great legs back then, remember?" I laugh.

"You still do. Only they're half as nice now."

"Way to get a leg up on me."

"I don't know much about your life since you left town, or what you experienced in the years afterward, but you're still beautiful to me."

"I've changed in other not so subtle ways."

"Change can be a good thing. It can mean growth and maturity, and the emergence of the authentic self. But enough of that for now. Close your eyes and go to sleep, sweetie. Because when you wake up I'll not be here."

"Where're you going?"

"I have to go home to be with Stef."

"Yes, I forgot about that." I can't believe how selfish I've been, taking her away from her only daughter. "Thanks for coming over when I needed you."

"Shhh," she whispers. "He wants you to cook for him tomorrow. Can you do it?"

"I'll certainly do my best."

"That's all anyone can ask for. I'll leave the diner key for you on the nightstand. Then I'll stay until you fall asleep."

It feels nice to be cared for and looked after. This hasn't happened to me in a long time. It's obvious that Nadia still has feelings for me. It's hard to be loved when you know you can't return such love in full. When you're so screwed up in the head that it takes everything you have just to try to love yourself. Or what's left of your old self.

Her body presses up against mine and feels quite natural. It reminds me of sleeping in my mother's bed and feeling safe and protected. I'm glad I didn't tell her what I saw out in that cornfield. She must have her hands full trying to keep tabs on that wild daughter of hers. I understand the hazards completely because I've been that rebellious child. This town can ruin a certain kind of kid. A kid given no discipline and allowed to run free without consequence or restriction. And yet I sense a deep hostility in Stefania that's borne out of angst and dread, and something else I can't quite pinpoint. Despair? She's the daughter of immigrant parents in a tight-knit town exploding with resentment against immigrants. Then there's the stress of her grandfather's failing diner, and the fact that she's being pressured to work there to help make ends meet. Two of her classmates have been brutally murdered in a manner consistent with Islamic beliefs. It's no wonder she's copping a serious attitude with me, an outsider impinging on the only turf she's ever known. Considering all that she's dealing with in life, I'd be surprised if she didn't drink or get stoned on a regular basis.

19

*N*ADIA'S NOT NEXT TO ME WHEN MY ALARM GOES off. I look at the clock and see that it's three A.M. Despite her reassuring presence last night, I'm glad she's gone. I can't bear to hurt her feelings more than I already have. Nor do I want to lead her on and have her believe that we might once again be a couple. I'm not ruling anything out these days, not when confusion seems to be the norm in my life. My feelings for her are complicated by a warped sense of nostalgia. It's a weird feeling, because all I've been doing for the last decade is trying to forget the past. In the days leading up to my return home, I'd been reinventing Fawn Grove in my mind's eye, and for some strange reason trying to spin it in a better light. Not surprisingly, it didn't live up to my expectations, but then again I really didn't think it would.

I shower and feel significantly better once I put on

my chef whites. It's similar to when Barbara Gordon transforms herself into Batgirl. The uniform gives me a newfound confidence in myself, reminding me that I'm competent in at least one thing in life. My trusty knives wait for me in the canvas bag, and I feel invigorated by my chosen profession. It's the one true talent that I can call my own.

The key to the diner sits on top of the nightstand, where Nadia left it. I pocket it and then swallow a handful of random pills. Grab the syringe, load it, and then stab myself in the thigh.

It's dark and cold outside when I pull up to the diner. Before I can even get out of the truck, I see a car pulling into the lot beside me. An alarm goes off in my head. Could this be the same person who scrawled that message on my windshield? But when I look out the driver's window I see that it's Dalton. His breath dissipates in the frigid Maine air as he gets out of his police car.

"Here to give me another ticket?"

"Saw your truck pull in and thought I'd say hello."

I get out and head silently toward the entrance, and he follows me. I unlock the door and then turn to face him.

"I could keep you company in exchange for a cup of coffee. It's been an awfully slow night."

"Don't really want company when I'm working."

"You're all business in the kitchen, huh?"

"You say that like it's a bad thing."

"Not at all," he says. "Could I at least beg you for a cup, then? I can't stomach the sludge they sell down at the all-night convenience store."

"We don't open for another thirty minutes."

"I won't be a bother. I'll sit quietly and leave you alone."

I debate for a few seconds before nodding for him to come in. After turning on all the lights, I make a pot of coffee using the grounds I purchased at Pam's coffee shop. There's only enough left for a few cups, so I use it all. Dalton takes a stool at the counter, placing his cap next to the sugar dispenser. I go back to the kitchen and pull some items out of the walk-in, readying myself for all the prep work that'll need to get done before opening the doors. When the coffee finishes brewing, I return to the dining room and pour two cups.

"I had a nice time the other night," he says, pouring cream and sugar into his mug.

"Yeah, me too."

"We should do it again sometime."

"Should we?"

He laughs. "Why are you so hard to get along with, Lucy Abbott?"

"Am I? I didn't think I was being that difficult at all."

"You are, but I like that about you."

"You do?"

"Sure. It's refreshing. You're like no other lady I know in this town."

"What is it you want from me, Dalton?"

"I'd like to get to know you better."

"How many times have I told you that my stay here is only temporary?"

"We'll see about that." He smiles.

I laugh at this because he does know me, probably better than even he realizes.

"So what is it you'd like to know about me?" I ask.

He seems to think it over. "How come a pretty girl like you isn't married with kids?"

"I never wanted kids, not that it's any of your business."

"Sorry, I didn't mean to intrude."

"The truth is, I can't have kids even if I wanted them. I suppose I could adopt if I wanted, but I don't think I'd be a very good mother." I sip my coffee.

"I beg to differ," he says. "What about a boyfriend back in New York?"

"Inquiring minds really want to know, huh?" I laugh. "Let's just say that I haven't met the right 'one' yet."

"I see."

"So what are you hearing about this dead boy?"

"It's always business with you."

"Let's play that game where I tell you something if you tell me something."

He sips his coffee. "What could you possibly know about this case that I don't?"

"You might be surprised." I lean over the counter. "Care to indulge a girl?"

He sighs as if to mull it over. "You can't breathe a word of this to anyone."

"Scout's honor."

He takes another sip of coffee. "This kid in the cornfield tested positive for drugs."

"Really?"

"The medical examiner doesn't lie."

"I should think not." It shouldn't surprise me after what I witnessed last night. I recall watching those kids drinking and smoking over that sizzling fire.

"Okay, your turn." He smiles in a patronizing manner.

"I saw the missing Afghani girl."

"That's all you've got?"

"She wasn't wearing her hijab, and she was hanging out with some of the kids in town."

"What were they doing?"

"Partying."

"Drinking?"

"And smoking weed."

"Is that so? Where'd you see them?"

"Over by the train tracks," I lie, not wanting to admit that I snuck onto that cornfield to see the crime scene.

"Maybe she just wants to fit in and be accepted at school."

"You don't find it odd that the cousin of the first murder victim, a Muslim girl, is out partying with some of the kids in town?"

"Not unless you have more information to tell me. We're still operating under the assumption that this is an honor killing."

"What kind of a detective are you, anyway?"

He shrugs and sips his coffee. "An extremely handsome one."

"Modesty alone won't solve these murders."

"Maybe her cousin was partying too, and maybe her parents found out about it and felt that she'd somehow disrespected them. Did you ever consider that?"

"Of course I have. Anything's possible."

"As I've told you, getting these Afghanis to talk has proved extremely difficult." He stands to leave. "Thanks for the coffee. It was delicious as usual."

"Don't expect it on a regular basis. I'm not going to be around forever."

"None of us gets out of here alive," he says. "How about joining me for dinner tonight?"

"What's the occasion?"

"I'll indulge the detective in you. Tickle your brain some more, Sherlock. That way we can talk in greater detail."

"Sure. What time?"

"How about around seven tonight?"

"That'll work. I won't get out of here, anyway, until after the mad lunch rush."

He laughs. "What mad rush?"

"The rush I'm hoping my presence here will soon create."

"Love the confidence, Chef."

"Confidence is my middle name."

"This town could really use a talented chef like you. You should seriously consider relocating here and doing it full time."

"I'm sure there are plenty of cooks in Fawn Grove who could turn this place around. Diner fare isn't exactly my calling."

"If that's true, then I'd certainly love to meet these other chefs." His radio blurts. "Duty calls. I'll pick you up at seven?"

"Seven it is," I say, as I head back to the kitchen.

I realize I'll need to play along with him a bit longer. Not that I particularly minded having dinner with him the other night, despite the atrocious meal served to us. Being with him is not as unpleasant as I often lead myself to believe. It's actually nice to hang out with a familiar face in this shitty town. Someone who pays attention to me and treats me like a lady. I have to admit, the years have been good to him, and he certainly appears to have mellowed out in his old age. He's one of the few people in town who genuinely seems to enjoy my company. Also, it gives me a distinct thrill to go out with him, knowing he has no idea who I am. But the biggest reason to stay friends with him is the privileged access he affords me to these investigations.

I can't help myself when it comes to this business. Despite my better judgment, I devise a menu ten times more ambitious than what's needed. The specials of the day I post on a discarded whiteboard that I find in the back. There's five types of omelettes, as well as buckwheat pancakes and French toast battered in Corn Flakes, filled with sweetened cream cheese and preserves and then pressed together like a sandwich. But then the regulars come in and order the same boring shit. Why won't these people step out of their comfort zone and try something different?

It's slow during breakfast service, and the pace makes me jittery. Thank God it's Stef's morning off and she's not here to insult and mock me. I'm used to cooking five dishes at once while people are cussing me out at the top of their lungs. To keep from being bored, I find myself working a crossword puzzle between orders. Anything to stay busy and keep my mind from reminding me how badly I'm failing here. I bake a blueberry pie for lunch and prepare a dozen fresh ground lamb patties for burgers. By the time Yanni comes in just before noon, I can't wait to get the hell out of here. I rip off my apron as he counts what little money sits in the till. I keep telling myself that it's not my fault and that it's going to take a small miracle to revive The Galaxy. But the pall of failure definitely hangs over me.

"I thought you were going to turn this place around?" Yanni snaps.

"Athens wasn't built in a day."

"Maybe you're not as good as you think you are."

"Oh, I'm pretty damn good all right, but I'm not superwoman."

"Bah! You're all talk," he says, disappearing into the kitchen.

Yanni expects instantaneous results on a pauper's budget. It's as if my sudden presence here is supposed to make customers magically appear. Wolfgang Puck and Thomas Keller working in unison couldn't resurrect this shithole under his thumb. Returning this diner to its former glory will be an uphill battle. The Galaxy's good name has been dragged through the mud for so long now that it may never fully recover.

Yanni shouts at me in Greek as I gather up my knives and place them gently into their respective pouches. Why do I even waste my time here when there are two unsolved murders in town? When I need to work on my own myriad issues? When there's hundreds of restaurant owners back in New York who'd love to have a battle-tested chef like me running their kitchen? Do I stay because Nadia pleaded with me to help her father? Maybe. She has no idea how badly this place is being run. Or what it will take to restore it. The more I try to make a difference here, the more futile my efforts seem.

I toss on my sweater and head out to the dining room, ignoring Yanni's running stream of complaints. Billie leans against the counter wearing a resigned expression on her haggard face, which reveals years of hard living despite the fact that we're roughly the same age. I notice the homemade tattoos scrawled over her skinny arms and hands. To lose this crappy job would cause her serious hardship. Jobs are scarce in this town, even pathetic jobs like this. It's the reason Yanni gets away with being such an asshole to her and everyone else. His family is depending on him and he's letting them all down.

I slam the diner door shut, then jump in my truck and head toward the center of town, where the memorial is to be held. Parking is at a premium today because of this rally. I find a space three blocks from the center of town and then hobble past all the abandoned storefronts and weedy lots. Standing on my feet all morning has taken a toll on my stumps, especially since I haven't worked a regular shift in over a month.

A large crowd stands in front of city hall. Growing up in Fawn Grove, I can understand the pain and suffering these citizens are experiencing. Change in small towns like this is often difficult to swallow, especially for a proud people who remember a Fawn Grove from better times.

Then I see a large group of Afghanis gathered, and it breaks my heart. They've come to pay their respects and show solidarity with the townspeople. It takes a lot of courage and heart for them to come here, and I find myself moved to tears by this display of compassion.

The first speaker heads up to the podium, then begins to speak about the dead boy. Cops appear everywhere, keeping order in case things get out of hand. It's not just Fawn Grove cops, either, but officers from nearby towns. Dalton stands at parade rest just off-stage, dressed in his crisp blues, his eyes scanning the crowd for any potential troublemakers. Cheers go up as the woman at the podium introduces the next two speakers. A man wearing a baseball cap walks up to the podium, holding the hand of a bleached blonde. It takes me a second to realize that these are the parents of the dead boy. Their eyes are red, and it's obvious they've been grieving. The father, I recall, is a minister with anti-immigrant views. I wonder what he thinks of the Afghanis who've come here in support of them. The applause dies down as the woman speaks into the microphone, struggling to tell the crowd what a great kid her boy was.

I turn and head back. This is too painful to watch. A grief-stricken mother talking about her dead son reminds me too much of Jaxon. I make my way back to the truck, an emotional wreck, mascara running down my cheeks. All those years spent in New York and I can barely recall shedding a tear for anyone. Now, back in Fawn Grove, I seem to cry at the drop of a hat.

Emotion overwhelms me as I duck into a doorway. I wait for the wave of sadness to pass. Taking a few deep breaths, I try to compose myself. I think of poor Jaxon and the fact that I'll never see him again. Not a day passes that I don't think about that poor kid. My mother grieved for him as well. She couldn't understand why such a terrible thing happened to her own child. I miss my mother. Both of them are such an integral part of my life that it upsets me when I realize they're gone forever.

Someone opens the door to the storefront, and I scamper onto the sidewalk. Once inside the truck, I have this sudden desire to pack all my bags and head back to Manhattan. Leave Fawn Grove before it destroys me for the last time.

I park across the street from Fawn Grove High. As soon as the school bell rings, I walk across the street to where the school buses are parked. Kids begin to pour out the doors and file past me. Four Muslim girls ramble down the path to their bus. I look for Nasreen but notice she's not among them.

A large gang of townie kids pass me like a river of adolescents. I search around, but there's no sign of her. Then I see two Afghani girls headed toward me. They're talking and laughing like normal kids. It takes me a few seconds to realize that she is one of them. As she approaches the bus, she looks up and sees me standing in her path. Her smile quickly dissipates, and she looks nervous as I begin to edge in her direction.

"You're a hard girl to track down."

"I need to get on my bus."

"We need to talk about your cousin."

"I must get on my bus or it will leave without me." Clutched to her chest is a rumpled copy of *To Kill a Mockingbird*.

"You should listen to what I have to say."

She turns and tells her friend to save a seat for her.

"You need to stop harassing me, or I'll go to the police."

I laugh. "That's hilarious, Nasreen. You won't talk to the police about your dead cousin, but now you're going to tell them that I'm harassing you?"

"Yes." She glances around nervously.

"Maybe you could tell them how you were smoking weed and drinking alcohol out in the cornfield where the boy was murdered. Oh, and that you were not wearing your hijab. I take it your parents wouldn't be too happy about that."

"Why are you making up lies about me?" She looks scared.

"Really?" I laugh. "We both know it's true."

"Look, I beg you not to tell anyone about this. I'd be in big trouble if my parents knew."

"Then talk to me."

"What do you want to know?"

"Tell me what was going on with you and those other kids."

She glances around before ripping a slip of paper out of her notebook. She pulls out a pen and scribbles something on the sheet. The bus driver honks his horn for her to get inside, and she turns to him and holds up a finger.

"What's this?"

"Meet me here this afternoon at four. It's dangerous for me to talk to you in public like this."

"You're certain you'll meet me there?"

"Yes. Then I'll tell you everything I know."

She turns and sprints inside the bus without looking back. The doors wheeze and shut. The engine roars loudly in my ears. Nasreen stares down at me as the bus pulls away, fear evident in her eyes.

I stare at the piece of paper. She wants to meet me at Settlers Burial Ground inside Robinson Woods. I know that place all too well. As kids, we used to play along that well-worn path. There's a smattering of old gravestones surrounded by a measly chain link.

Had I gone too far by coming here to speak with her? She's only a kid. Meeting her in public might have put the girl's life in jeopardy. The thought of her suffering the same fate as her cousin worries me, and now I wonder if I've made another bad decision. And yet I'm desperate for answers.

I turn to leave, and when I look up I see Brynn standing with a group of girls. Stefania is pointing at me and laughing. It's obvious that Brynn's embarrassed. They follow me as I make my way back to the pickup. Stefania lights a cigarette, and the pack of jackals follow, toward the lot where my truck is parked. Someone shouts something, and they all begin to laugh uncontrollably.

"Want a ride home, Brynn?" I say, quickly wishing I hadn't.

"She doesn't need a ride from you, Miss Fancy-Pants," Stefania says. "She's hanging out with her homeys."

"I'm not talking to you, Stefania," I say, which embarrasses her.

"Brynn doesn't want to go anywhere with you. Why don't you go back to where you came from? Busybodies like you don't belong here in Fawn Grove," Stefania says.

"What are you doing here, Lucy? Why are you embarrassing me in front of all my friends?" Brynn says, a look of horror over her face.

Her words sting me.

"I can't believe you'd violate my privacy like this," Brynn says. "You swore that you wouldn't keep tabs on me."

"It's not what you think."

"How can I ever trust you again? You lied to me."

I jump in my truck and speed off, my feelings hurt. I think how embarrassed I'd have been if my mother showed up when I was hanging out with my friends. What right do I have to interfere in her life? And yet I can't shake the humiliation of hearing those girls laugh at me. It made me feel as if I were back in high school all over again.

I park in the driveway, go inside the house, and limp past Russ. It's good that he's napping, because I don't feel like dealing with him right now. I need to rest before I meet up with that girl. Maybe she'll tell me something that'll prove useful in solving these murders.

20

I PULL UP ALONGSIDE THE ROAD AND MAKE MY WAY down to the entrance to Robinson Woods. It's startling how many memories come rushing back as I approach it. I feel like a kid again, getting ready to run for hours on end, searching for frogs and playing tag and Relievio with my friends. But this time there'll be no fun and games.

A sign at the entrance to the trail indicates that these woods are now part of a land trust and can't be developed. I make my way past the sign and see the familiar rocks and trees that once framed our youthful activities. On one of these trunks I'd carved a heart with Nadia's and my initials in it, but I'll be damned if I could find it now. The deeper I travel into these woods, the more thankful I am that I put on my long-sleeved cardigan sweater and knee-high leather boots with the steel toes. The terrain gets rockier, gnarled with tree roots and vines. For a normal thirty-three-year-old, walking along this trail would be of no consequence. But I'm not normal in any sense of the word.

Jaxon used to dart in and out of these woods, jumping off boulders and leaping over puddles of mud, running all day without losing his breath. I remember how he and his friends would pick up large branches and then engage in furious sword fights, pretending to slay dragons and evil demons until someone pretended to die.

The light nearly disappears on account of the canopy of leaves swaying gently above. The leaves are just starting to change color, and soon the purples and reds will dominate the landscape.

I'm sore and out of breath by the time I reach the dozen or so gravestones scattered between the trees. They're flaked, thin wafers sticking up out of the ground at odd angles. Even after all these years they seem out of place in this wooded setting. I park myself on a large boulder and wait. In my pocket sits the trusty boning knife for good measure. Although its effectiveness is limited in many ways, I feel safer knowing it's with me.

I'd forgotten how far into the trail these tombstones are located. The girl must really be frightened if she wants to meet me here, where no one will see or hear us. Maybe she really does know something about these murders, and maybe that information might break these cases wide open. The thought that I might be able to learn new facts about them gives me hope.

But a strange feeling comes over me after ten minutes pass. Is it intuition? A foreboding that I'm in imminent danger and was directed here for a distinct reason? I can't seem to shrug it off. I stand, the pain in my lower legs leaving me momentarily immobile. In agony, I fall back on the boulder, my legs throbbing. This is the cruel joke my body sometimes likes to play on me. In moments of extreme stress, a menacing phantom pain strikes capriciously and without reason.

The afternoon light begins to transition. It's ten past the hour and there's still no sign of her. Why has she stood me up like this? Did she have second thoughts? Did the idea of revealing certain truths about people in her community scare her off? I start to head back to the parking lot, my legs slow and lethargic, the pain fierce in my absent limbs.

But then I hear something and stop. Is it the wind? Or is someone following me? I grab the handle of the boning knife. Maybe I'm being paranoid. Ever since that threat was scrawled on my windshield, I've become more vigilant.

Was it a mistake coming here? I glance around as a gust of wind ruffles the leaves. About two hundred yards separates me from the entrance to the woods. I latch on to my knife. My head fills with conspiracies as I hobble along the bumpy terrain, mindful of the vague, lurking danger. All I want is to return home and climb back into bed where it's safe and sound.

The opening of the trail appears off in the distance. Despite the intense pain in my lower legs, I improve to a steady clip, one step at a time. It's about twenty feet to the parking lot when I hear someone call out. I turn to see if it's Nasreen when something comes crashing down against my head. Everything begins to spin as I collapse to the ground. Someone grabs my wrists, and another person lifts me up by the heels of my boots.

I'm vaguely aware of the throbbing in my head as they carry me away, my arms falling limp by my side. A whistling pierces my ears, and I can hear the crunch of twigs underfoot. Saliva dribbles down my chin. I gaze upward and see the kaleidoscopic treetops. I want to scream for help, but nothing comes out. My vision is blurred, as if I'm seeing things through a Coke bottle. Finally, they let go of me and I fall hard to the dirt. It's the last thing I remember.

When I come to, all I can feel is my head pounding. My eyelids lie thick and heavy over my eyes. I try to move my arms and legs, but nothing happens. Oh my God! Am I paralyzed? I open my eyes and peer into the pitch blackness, panicking. A cool breeze chills my skin and fluffs my hair. For some reason, the insides of my upper arms itch like crazy.

It takes a few seconds before I realize I can't wiggle my fingers. I'm horrified to see that someone has buried me up to my chest. I look around in the dark, wondering if a rock will come smashing into my face. Just the thought of it causes me to thrash about. I struggle to free myself, but my efforts are futile. I twist my head, dodging an imaginary projectile headed toward me. A black blanket engulfs me as I scream for help. After a few minutes I realize that no one can hear me, my voice now hoarse. No one will be able to save me from this terrible predicament.

Everything remains deathly still. A stiff wind whistles through the branches and makes a hushing sound. Trees sway and creak around me. An owl hoots off in the distance. I'm still alive, and this is a good thing. I hope that someone discovers me come morning and calls for help.

Or will the people who did this come back to finish me off? But why haven't they already? There are plenty of sticks and stones in these woods.

The solitude of the night exacerbates the sound of blood pumping through my temples. I take a deep breath and try to relax. Being imprisoned in this ditch is enough to drive a person insane. A sudden thought occurs to me. What if a fox or coyote wanders by and decides to nibble on my face? My monkey brain can't stop thinking about all the worst-case scenarios. Anticipating what's out there is the most terrifying aspect of this imprisonment, especially when I can't see anything.

There was a doctor at Walter Reed who tried to teach me how to meditate. She claimed that meditation could help ward off pain and said that there were monks so skilled at meditating that they could lower their pulse to within an inch of their life. Proper meditation, she explained, could cleanse the mind of harmful thoughts and allow the individual to enter into another realm of consciousness. I never quite mastered the technique, or bought into the notion that meditation could ease my pain, but her words always stayed with me. I suppose I was too stubborn at the time to believe that my mind played a role in my physical recovery.

I close my eyes and try to empty my head of all the negative thoughts taking place. I focus on the mantra she taught me to say whenever I needed to enter into that state. Om Namah Shivaya. Translation: I bow to Shiva, the supreme deity of transformation who represents the truest, highest self.

I begin to say it over and over, and before long I lose

track of time, the mantra being the only thing I'm aware of in these dark woods. My past and present come together, and the person I am, and hope to one day become, merge into a vague spiritual entity that I can't quite explain. The phantom pain in my legs begins to slowly melt away, as do all my fears. I forget about my itching arms. For a brief moment—and I know this sounds crazy—I feel one with everything around me. One with the universe and whoever lords over it. A tranquility settles over my being, and I know that whatever happens, in the end, everything will be okay. If I'm fated to die here in these woods, it will not be the end of my journey.

I open my eyes after God knows how many hours repeating the same mantra and see that the sun has started to rise. A few glints of light begin to illuminate the landscape beyond. The arrival of the sun provides a glimmer of hope that I might soon be discovered by an early morning hiker. A gentle mist lies suspended over the landscape. Ferns and brush are reflective from the dew. When I look up I can just make out the treetops swaying gently in the wind, and I realize with certainty that I've been buried in Robinson Woods.

Now that I'm bathed in light, I'm not as fearful as I once was. Why did the perpetrators leave me here? Why didn't they kill me as they did those other two kids? Were they sending me another message, warning me to stop digging? For a brief moment I experience pangs of survivor's guilt. Life is precious, and I'm thankful mine was spared. But why me? Is it because killing me would cast light on the real killers?

I try to shout out a few words, but my voice is still hoarse from shouting last night. My skin feels moist, and when I shake my head my red hair falls damp around my face. Being buried up to my chest has caused my body to stiffen up and become numb. I'd give anything to be able to free myself and stretch out these vexed limbs of mine.

What if no one finds me here? I think of Wendy and Russ. I think of Brynn. Having handicapped parents must have been difficult for her these last few years. She might soon be forced to chart her own path in life. If I make it out of this ditch alive, should I play some sort of role in her life? Will she even let me after what I've done? If only she knew the truth about me and all that I've overcome just to be here today. How I escaped Fawn Grove those many years ago in an attempt to escape from myself.

Someone buried me for a reason. They want me to stop digging around in this murder investigation and return to New York. Where do I go from here? Resume my vapid life in the city as a lowly sous-chef lacking in ambition and without the courage to face my demons? Return to a life denying certain truths that enslaved me in fear? A life that wasn't so much a life but a way to avoid the past by cooking and drinking, and then repeating the cycle. No, I can't let this happen again. This personal attack will only harden my resolve to track down these killers. Assuming I make it out of these woods alive, I'll make it my mission to find them. I owe it to that lovely fruit vendor I failed to help.

I watch as the sun rises higher in the sky. Birds chirp and sing these long, elaborate songs of incomparable beauty. Despite all the trees rising majestically above, I can see that it's a clear autumn morning. This is a good thing. It means there'll be plenty of hikers and joggers making their way along these trails. I wait a few minutes for my throat to recover. Then I begin to shout again for help.

My voice begins to get raspy. I'm not sure how much time has passed before I finally hear footsteps approaching. I shout again, as loud as I can, until a man's boots appear in front of me. He's carrying a walking stick, and his golden retriever rushes up and begins to lick my face with his warm tongue. The man kneels to my level and asks if I'm all right, and I beg him to help free me from this pit. My throat is parched, and I ask if he has any water. He pulls out a plastic bottle and holds it up to my lips, and I gulp it down greedily while he calls 911.

I close my eyes and fight back the tears, grateful that I've been found. For whatever reason, my life has been spared. Whoever did this thinks they can frighten me off and send me scrambling back to Manhattan. Thank God for that Indian doctor who taught me how to meditate. It shepherded me safely through the night. For once in my life, the universe is looking out for me.

The medics arrive soon after and work furiously to unearth me from this hole. Once they dig out enough dirt, they grab me by the arms and lift me out, laying me on a blanket that had been spread out over the ground. My sweater and clothes are covered in dirt. It feels as if I've been snatched from a fresh grave. It takes a few minutes before I'm able to stand, stretch out, and get the blood flowing through my limbs. Everything in my body hurts, and I'm light-headed. Pins and needles tingle up my arms. For some reason, the skin on my inner biceps still itch like crazy. Bug bites?

The medics tell me to sit and rest, but my body wants movement, space, freedom. My body feels wholly independent from my mind, and I know I must listen to it. I remember experiencing the same sensation at Walter Reed all those years ago, enduring constant pain and suffering, battling through rehab and endless surgeries. The random bouts of phantom pain never made any sense to me. It felt as if my body were playing a cruel trick on the mind. The doctors explained that my mind and body were not properly aligned and that the mind could not comprehend the fact that my legs were no longer part of the total equation. They used mirror therapy to train my mind to the fact that I no longer had legs below my knees, and after a while my mind began to understand that my body was irreparably broken. Although my lower limbs were gone, their respective pain receptors in the cortex were still alive and well. My mind, at times, wanted to break free from the form and experience what it would be like to go out-of-body, floating above the fray of constant pain and suffering.

Surprisingly, I feel more alive now than I have in some time. The medics want to rush me to the hospital, but I tell them that I'm fine and just in need of some rest. I don't even allow them to check me out. No way am I going to allow some faceless doctor to prod and examine me and to expose my body to their inquiry. Or ask stupid questions that I have no intention of answering. I insist on driving myself home, and I promise the medics that I'll check with my doctor as soon as possible.

But then the police arrive and they have their own investigation to conduct. Dalton walks over and gives me a big hug. Oddly, I find myself clinging to him. It's the first time I've felt this way, and it embarrasses me. His face is the only familiar one in the crowd. Tears stream down my cheeks and spill onto his uniform. The medics insist on carrying me out of these woods on a stretcher, but I won't hear of it. Instead I slowly make my way back to the trail, allowing the blood to return to my arms and lower extremities. The insides of my arms itch like crazy. I emerge into the light and feel the pavement underfoot. A sense of relief overwhelms me. My pickup is still where I left it. Fire trucks and police cars are parked everywhere, lights flashing. Dalton escorts me to my pickup and tells me to relax and take a few deep breaths. He's gone from being a cruel bully to my personal savior.

"Jesus, Lucy! What the hell happened in those woods?"

"I was out for a walk when someone attacked me. This time they made good on their threat."

"I'm so glad you're all right," he says, and he looks as if he really means it.

"That makes two of us."

"Why didn't they . . . ?"

"Kill me? Throw stones at my face?"

"I don't even want to think about that."

"Someone in this town obviously wants me to stop looking into those kids' deaths."

"Maybe you should take this warning to heart and let the police do their jobs."

"And give whoever did this the satisfaction of winning? No way!"

"They won't win, Lucy, I promise you that. We'll catch the bastards responsible for this."

"This is insane," I say, appearing contrite. "Maybe you're right, Dalton. Maybe I should just quit all this foolishness and get on with my life."

"I am right about this," he says. "Are you okay to give a statement?"

"There's not much to tell. I went for a walk to clear my head, and the next thing I knew I was buried up to my chest." I can't tell him the whole truth.

"Did you get a good look at them?"

"No. Whoever did this attacked me from behind."

"You must have been terrified being out there all alone at night."

"What do you think?"

"I can't even begin to imagine how scared you must have been, wondering if they were coming back for you."

"The entire time I was in that hole, I kept thinking that a rock might smash into my face at any moment."

"You're a very lucky girl."

"I shouted all night, but no one could hear me. Not until that hiker came along this morning could I breathe a sigh of relief."

"I care about you, Lucy. I don't want to see you hurt again."

"That makes two of us."

"I can protect you and keep you safe. Just let me do my job."

"Thanks, Dalton, but I don't need you or anyone else to protect me."

He laughs a little too confidently. "Didn't look that way to me."

"Despite what happened in those woods, I assure you I can take care of myself."

"The next time this happens, you might end up dead."

"There'll be no next time," I say. "I need to go home and rest. Then I'll decide what to do."

"Let me at least drive you."

"Thanks, but I can drive myself."

"Come on, now. You're in no condition to get behind the wheel."

I laugh and hold out my arms, which are still covered over by my long-sleeved sweater. "Then handcuff me and take me away, Detective."

"Don't be silly," he says, looking sheepish. "Just promise me you'll stop looking into these murders."

I pretend to mull it over. "Sure, if you promise to catch the bastards who did this to me."

"Don't worry, Lucy, I will," he says, walking away. "And be careful driving home."

I rush inside the house, past Wendy, who's calling out my name and asking me where I've been all night. Past Big Russ, who's reclined in his chair and watching a documentary about Angus Gibbons and the plane crash that took his life. Up the stairs I go, past all the family photographs on the wall. Past Wendy's mechanical chair lift. I breathe a sigh of relief once I reach the sanctity of my room.

I turn on the lights and claw at the undersides of my irritated arms. It's as if someone set my skin on fire. I pull off my dirt-encrusted clothes until I'm sitting naked on the bed. My breasts feel raw and chafed, and when I stare down at my arms, I see the cause of my pain. Scrawled over my left bicep are the words GO BACK HOME! On my right arm they wrote B4 UR NEXT! And they're written in red fingernail polish.

Two days have passed and I've barely left my room except to go to the bathroom and take meals. But my decision has been made. My bags are packed and I'm ready to try something bold and different. Lucy Abbott is done meddling around in this town and trying to make a difference. I sit on the edge of the bed, staring down at the pale words outlined on my chafed skin. It took hours of scrubbing before the fingernail polish washed off, but it left these irritated rashes, as well as a distinct imprint. At least no one else knows about this warning scrawled over my arms. If the killer wants Lucy Abbott to disappear, then disappear is what Lucy Abbott will do.

I see that Dalton texted me last night and wants to reschedule our dinner, but I'm done with him for now. I return his text and inform him that I'm heading back to Manhattan, and would he mind giving me a lift to the bus station.

I go over to the bureau and check myself out in the mirror. It heartens me to realize how beautiful I am, even after the trauma of two days ago. My red hair is done up nicely, and my face is properly brushed and rouged. The lipstick is hot pink, and I've added a few curls to my hair. The lashes are long and luxurious. My fingernails are manicured and painted blood red.

The hour has arrived. I grab my three bags and make my way into the hallway. The floorboards squeak as I approach Brynn's room. I notice that her door is open. She spins around in her leather chair and waves to me like one of those beauty pageant contestants. I smile halfheartedly, knowing that this attack must have really frightened her. Part of me regrets embarrassing her in front of her friends that day. I hadn't meant to do it. She spins back to her laptop as I move down the hallway. Will she be okay in the days ahead, now that two of her classmates are dead and buried? Will she ever speak to me again?

As I walk down the stairs, I take in each photograph on the wall. The memories from days past linger longer than I would have expected. Photos from when everyone was robust and healthy. I touch Jaxon's framed face. And baby Brynn in pigtails and smiling, her two front teeth missing. I move past the vacant easy chair and make my way into the kitchen. Wendy is sitting at the table, her eyes red from crying. I go over and hug her. After all that has happened, she knows that this move is in the best interests of everyone involved.

"You really don't have to leave," she says.

"I'm sorry, sis, but I really do. I'm not going to jeopardize my health, or my family's well-being, because I've become this crazy woman obsessed with these murders. That's what the police are for."

"Can we at least get together every now and then?"

"Of course we can, although it might be best to wait until this all blows over."

"You're probably right. I pray they catch the person doing these terrible crimes so we can be a family again."

"Of course we'll be a family again."

I kiss the top of her head and make my way outside, where Russ is standing next to Dalton and Nadia. I give Nadia a big hug and then watch as she scampers down the driveway in tears. Dalton takes my bags and tosses them in the back of his pickup. Then Russ turns to face me.

"Thanks for everything, Russ."

"Wish it could have been under better circumstances."

"Me too."

"What will you do now?"

"Probably return to my former life. I'm sure my old boss will be more than happy to have me back in place."

"Sounds like a plan."

I give him a big hug before kissing his whiskered cheek. His walrus mustache tickles my lips as I pull back. He's like a big, immobile block of wood encasing a teddy bear soul. He gives me his own halfhearted smile as I climb inside the truck.

"Call your sister from time to time."

"I will." I wave good-bye.

"And make sure you eat all your vegetables, Lucy."

"You can count on it, Russ. You too."

Dalton jumps in next to me, and almost immediately I hear the sound of some gangster rapper going on about bitches and hoes and shooting cops in cold blood.

"Jesus, I'm sorry about that, Lucy. I let Brandy borrow the truck and she pays me back by listening to this crap." He pulls out the CD, tosses it in the back, and puts in another.

"Teenagers, right?"

"Just kick those fast-food wrappers out of your way while you're at it."

"We were kids once."

"She's a good girl, despite all the shit her mother feeds her about me."

"Does she know what she wants to do after high school?"

"She loves animals and she's smart as a whip. I keep telling her she'd make a great veterinarian if she could ever buckle down and study, but she doesn't want any advice from her father."

"I really wish I could have met her."

"Maybe you can when you come back."

"If I come back."

"Oh, you will."

I need to change the subject. "Does Brandy play sports or have any hobbies?"

"I used to coach her softball and basketball teams. Too bad she quit, because she was a good athlete. Complained that she didn't like the competitive nature of team sports. Maybe I pushed her too hard when she was a kid."

"Did you?"

"Only because I believed I was helping her."

"Every kid handles pressure differently."

"She's a sweet, sensitive girl. It's a shame her mother drove a wedge between us and created such bitterness."

"I suppose the only thing you can do is keep trying."

"I remember this one time when I was coaching her

T-ball team. She was on second base and this boy hit the ball through the gap. I told her to run home, and she turned and started running toward center field. I caught up to her and asked her where she was going. You know what she said? She told me she was doing what I told her. She was running home." He laughs at this memory, and yet I sense a deep sadness in him.

"That's too funny."

"That's Brandy for you—before her mother messed her up."

Except for the Willie Nelson CD playing, we drive in silence to the bus station. He parks in the station's lot and gets out to take my bags from the bed. Then he places them down next to my feet.

"Are you sure you can't stay longer?"

"No. You were right all along. It's far too dangerous for me to be here right now."

"You could stay with me," he whispers. "My place isn't the greatest, but it's big enough for two people."

I laugh. "I'm an old-fashioned girl, Dalton. That's not going to happen."

"I figured you might say that, and I respect you for it."

"Besides, you knew my stay here was only temporary."

"Seemed as if you'd been getting more comfortable in Fawn Grove and were thinking about staying longer."

"I admit it crossed my mind. Then this happened."

"So you're going to return to New York and slave over a hot stove all day serving the beautiful people?"

"Those beautiful people pay my bills. Besides, I'd never make it in this town as a chef."

"You could save that diner if you really wanted."

"That would mean time and money, two things I'm in short supply of right now."

"Can I visit you? I've got some vacation time coming and have always wanted to see New York."

"Let's just see what happens here first." I playfully punch him in the arm. "You've got a big job to do."

"I've not done much good in my life, but that's going to change when I catch these assholes."

"I have faith in you, Dalton."

"I'll miss you more than you'll know, Lucy Abbott."

"I'm sure you will."

Dalton wraps one arm around my back and then, to my surprise, pulls me in to him. He stares deeply into my eyes, which momentarily causes my knees to weaken. His embrace feels warm and inviting, and I can feel his hot breath against the bridge of my nose. His hand is now pressed against the base of my spine. The other cups my cheek. He lowers his head until our lips brush lightly against each other. I badly want to push him away, but I realize that I've lost all resistance. Our moist tongues taste and explore each other. I close my eyes and lose myself in this sensual kiss delivered by my former adversary. My heart sizzles in my chest, and I suddenly feel as if I'm floating up and away. Time seems to stop, and I realize that I don't want this kiss to end. But then Dalton's lips slowly move away from mine. He releases his hand from my back and the other from my cheek. I remain frozen, fearful that if I open my eyes I'll be forced to watch him leave.

But I do open them. And I see him walking back to his pickup. My entire body feels weak and tingly. I shuffle backward in a daze until I reach the bus station. Dalton's truck accelerates down the road before disappearing from sight. I stagger inside the station, set my bags down on the cold tile floor, and collapse breathlessly into one of the chairs.

Never in my life have I been kissed like that.

BOOK TWO

21

"JAXON?"

That's the first thing my father says to me when I show up at his doorstep. I'm standing in my best outfit, all made up, and nervous to see him. How long has it been since we've laid eyes on each other? He pauses to process everything, staring me up and down as if I'm a marble statue delivered to his door. His hair's all gray, and he's sporting a fuzzy, speckled beard that makes him look like a street person. His tattered clothes have holes in them and appear soiled. It looks to me as if he weighs no more than 120 pounds. Back in my youth he used to be muscled and weigh more than 180.

"How did you recognize me?" I ask in amazement.

"Knew the second I laid eyes on you that you was Jaxon."

"You're the first person in town to recognize me."

"A father never forgets what his own kid looks like."

"What do you think of me now?" I say, spinning around in nervous anticipation.

"Speechless. Had no idea you went this way, but you sure are pretty."

"Thanks, Dad. That's sweet of you."

"Don't just stand there, son. Come on inside," he says. I'm so happy about this reception that I overlook him calling me son.

I'd taken a cab back to Fawn Grove, instructing the driver to drop me off at my father's house. No way I was going to step aside while these murdering cretins got away with threatening me. The meditation I'd done while trapped in that pit had convinced me that I had nothing to fear. If I lost my nerve now, I didn't deserve to go on living. I'd been given a reprieve, and I was hell-bent on making good on it.

My father's house is more a cabin in the woods than a house. I gaze up at it and see that it's in disrepair. Shingles lie broken, and the roof is partially covered over with a grimy blue tarp. Some of the windows are poorly insulated, and the bricks on the chimney are in serious need of repointing. I can only imagine what the inside looks like.

"It's been a long time, Dad," I say.

"Too long," he says as I walk across the threshold. I set my bags down. "So you a gal, or is this some sort of practical joke you're playing on your old man?"

"It's no joke. I go by the name Lucy now."

"I have to admit, this is a bit weird for me."

"I understand. You going to be able to handle it?"

"Why the hell not? You're my flesh and blood," he

says. "Besides, I've been dealing with a lot worse problems than finding out I have another daughter."

"I'm still the same person on the inside."

"You always had a good heart, as wild as you were as a kid."

"So it doesn't matter to you that I'm now a woman?"

"What I thought once mattered to me don't seem so important no more."

"I just want you to accept me for who I am."

"I'll certainly try my best." He looks me over again. "Boy, you really turned into a beauty. Most of those trannies look nothing like you."

"Thanks, but tranny is probably not the nicest way to refer to us."

He sits down in his recliner. "Word is you got hurt over in the Middle East. Most people thought you died."

"Roadside IED. Both legs blown off below the knee."

"Damn! Guess you could say I been out of the loop for a while."

"You could have at least come and paid me a visit while I was recuperating," I say, knowing full well that I would have refused to see him.

"No excuse." He shrugs. "Can't take back the past."

"I returned home in part because I want to forgive you, Dad, and because I want to move on in our relationship."

"I know I haven't been the best husband and father to all of you."

"You should be apologizing to Mom, if she were still alive today."

"I regret what I put that poor woman through."

I sit across from him. Despite the drab exterior, the cabin is neat and tidy inside, and I'm surprised. A massive wood stove sits on the far end of the room. There's a bookcase and a couple of old couches that have seen better days. The most striking and memorable objects are the weathered guitars from my youth, a vestige of his rock 'n' roll days.

"Still play?"

"Every now and then," he says. "Been a long time since I seen you. Not since you left for the military."

"A lot has changed in my life. I'm a very different person than when I left."

"Now there's an understatement," he says. "You were quite the hell-raiser as a kid. Always getting into trouble and giving your mother and I grief."

I smile. "Old habits die hard."

"To what do I owe the pleasure?"

"Would you mind if I stayed for a while?"

He grabs his chin and seems to mull it over. "It's on short notice, but I don't see why not. There's only one bedroom, and I can't sleep anywhere else because of my bad back."

"The couch will be fine."

"Then the couch is all yours."

I remove my jacket and rope my long hair off into a ponytail.

"Them real?" he asks, making weighing motions beneath his chest.

The forwardness of his question causes me to break out laughing. "Of course they're real."

"Could have at least splurged for some bigger ones."

"Ewwwwww, Dad! That's gross."

"Just saying, if you want to go the full monty, the big Ds are the way to go."

"I take hormones for that. They're responsible for this gorgeous body, not surgery."

"Your *entire* body?"

"Can we talk about something else?"

"So how long you think you'll be staying?"

"Not sure yet," I say. "Why? You need me to leave by a certain date?"

"Nope. Just wondering." He glances around as if confused about what to say next. "What was that name you go by now?"

"Lucy."

"Lucy it is, then."

"I'm glad you're taking this so well."

"Not really sure how I'm taking it, so I guess I'll just roll with the punches."

"I appreciate that."

"I suppose you're gonna wanna talk about stuff. Like why I left your mom."

"We'll have time to catch up on all that later. Right now I have some things I need to do."

The first thing I do after speaking with my father is snip off all my hair using a pair of scissors, making sure to cut as close to the scalp as possible. Although it pains me to get rid of my beautiful red hair, I know this is what's needed. Since it's obvious that my father doesn't bother to shave, I grab one of my leg razors, and, with much sadness and regret, scrape off the remaining bits of dyed hair until my dome shines under the light. I'm fortunate that I've never been able to grow hair on my face, so that's no problem. Then I snip off my naturally long eyelashes, which have been a key feature of mine since I was a kid.

I put away all my dresses, stockings, and tapered jeans. My father lends me a pair of his overalls, at least until I can make a run to Goodwill and buy myself some used men's clothes. Although it pains me greatly, I put away my makeup kit, lipstick, and fingernail polish, careful to cut my long nails until they're rounded and more masculine. It feels like an act of self-mutilation, but it's my only option at this point.

I'm fortunate to have packed my spare set of prosthetics. They're the legs I often used in my apartment, and they're much more comfortable than the newer ones. They don't chafe and irritate my stumps as much as the more advanced model. They were the first prosthetics made for me after the attack, and I used them routinely during those two arduous years rehabbing at Walter Reed. The problem with the old prosthetics is that they were manufactured to match my actual height of five foot three. It's why I asked if they could make me some newer ones, legs that would make me a bit taller and more glamorous. Surprisingly, the VA granted my request, elevating me to a more respectable five foot six. Then, dressed in three-inch high heels, I transformed into a statuesque goddess.

My father goes outside and rambles around the grounds. After searching around the cabin, I locate two tattered Ace bandages in one of the lower cabinets. I take them back to his room and close the door behind me. Standing in front of the mirror, I remove my shirt and bra. I'm thrilled the way my body has developed after years of hormone therapy, and so doing this pains me more than anything else. I wrap the first bandage around my upper torso until it fits snugly. Then I repeat this with the second bandage until both are secure. I stand sideways in the mirror and check myself out. Not bad at all. I'd seen plenty of dudes with man boobs bigger than mine.

Except this costume isn't perfect. This is not who I am or who I want to be. Far from it. It's a temporary disguise that I need in order to disassociate myself from my authentic self. A disfigurement that affects my dysmorphia and various body issues. My true self has always been wrapped up in Lucy Abbott even before I knew who she was. She's lived inside me since birth, waiting for her own birthing. Jaxon Ford was a ghost from the past who has, for all intents and purposes, been dead to me. The poor boy died soon after that roadside bombing, after body and mind had been mutilated beyond repair. All that remained was hope: hope that I could reinvent and rebuild myself, and be the person I was always meant to be but never quite had the courage to pull off.

It takes all afternoon to change into this new person. Oddly enough, it surprises me to discover that the Jaxon Ford from my youth looks nothing like this adult version. Thank God! Those years working as a combat medic and then recuperating in Walter Reed irrevocably changed me. I'm now the avuncular version of my old self: bald, crippled, and world weary without the insult of sarcasm. Without makeup to hide all the blemishes, I in no way resemble the Lucy Abbott who gets wolf whistles on the street. I stare at my bare earlobes. Now *that* will have to be rectified. A pair of black-framed glasses and some heavy metal skull earrings will complete my transformation. And a black concert T-shirt, preferably something heavy metal. This will be my new look in Fawn Grove until these murders are solved. I'll observe and keep my eye on things without fear of detection. Then, once everything goes back to normal, I'll return to being Lucy.

Now I have to think about how I'll alter my voice. I've always possessed a perfectly neutral vocal range, which made it easy for me when it came time to speak like a woman. I'd mastered my feminine pitch, and can enunciate with just the right tone. But now I have to swing back the other way. It will take time and lots of work. Smoking cigarettes will help my voice grow raspier and low. I'll gargle with whiskey each day and shout into the dense woods until my voice changes. Then I'll practice speaking until my new voice becomes unrecognizable from Lucy's.

I go outside and find my father.

"Well I'll be damned," he says. "Where'd that beautiful gal go?"

"I'm still that beautiful girl."

"I'm confused. Mind telling me the reason for all this?"

"I'm going undercover in order to learn a few things in town. I'll explain it to you later."

"Thought you already were undercover."

"That wasn't a cover, Dad. Lucy is the real me."

"I'm trying to understand everything, I really am, but it's hard."

"I know all this is confusing to you, but please bear with me."

"If you say," he says as he slips on some soiled gloves. "While you're living here with me, would you mind giving me a hand?"

"Sure." We then proceed to cut wood and pull weeds for the next two hours.

I spend the next few days helping my father around the house: painting, replacing roof shingles, cleaning up the yard, and painting the inside of the house. We don't really talk about anything meaningful, which is fine by me. Before dinner one evening, we settle on the couch with cups of tea. A thick joint sits on the coffee table between us, waiting for my father to light it. Most nights he puts classical music on the stereo before rolling a joint. The choice of music surprises me, since my father had always been a hard-core rock 'n' roll kind of guy. Thirty minutes pass in silence before he clears his throat and looks at me.

"You still haven't told me why you're doing all this."

"Am I bothering you?"

"Not at all. I'm enjoying having you around and keeping me company."

"I'll help you out with all the household chores while I'm here."

"I'm still wondering why you came back to this godforsaken town after all those years away. If I remember correctly, you couldn't wait to get out of here."

"If you think this town's so bad, why are you still here?"

"It's too late for me to leave. I was born and raised in Fawn Grove. Now I'm an old man with no future, just a sorry past."

"I came home because I was suffering from PTSD and needed a break from the city. Wendy agreed to take me in. When I found out about these murders, I just couldn't go back home until I found out who committed them."

"Why do you care?"

"It's a long story."

"Why don't you just go back to New York and be the girl you've always wanted to be?"

"In due time."

"What's the holdup?"

I laugh. "You trying to get rid of me, Dad?"

"Hell, no. You do good work, and good workers are hard to come by." He stares at me in an odd manner. "You gone all the way?"

"Excuse me?"

He strokes his scruffy beard and then makes a chopping motion with his hand. "Excuse my French, but I'm talking about downstairs. The full transition to becoming a gal."

It takes me a few seconds before I realize what he's talking about, and I break out laughing. I roll up my pant leg and show him one of my prosthetic legs as a way of avoiding the topic.

"Damn!" He leans over and examines it.

"Had both of them blown off below the knee. But I'm sure that doesn't answer your real question."

"No, but probably better than having that *other* thing blowed off."

"Says you."

"Says me is right. The only thing I use mine for these days is to go to the john three times a night."

"A dangling appendage of no real worth?"

"It is at this stage in my life," he says. "I still don't understand why you care so much about these dead kids."

"Something happened to me while I was serving overseas, and it had a huge impact on my life."

"Of course it did. You lost both of your legs."

"No, something else."

"I would have thought losing two legs was enough to mess you up."

"In many ways that bombing saved my life. It helped me realize that my body can be irreparably broken but then rebuilt and changed for the better. It was an incident that happened the day before the bombing that caused me to hear these voices."

"Voices? That attack make you crazy?"

"No, I'm not crazy. At least not that I'm aware of," I say, laughing. "I hear them only at night when I'm sleeping."

"And you can't tell me what happened?"

"It's not that I can't tell you. It's just that I'm not ready to talk about it yet."

"I'm all ears when you're up to it."

"Thanks."

"What about those two dead kids?"

"When I learned that that Afghani girl had been murdered, it felt as if I'd been brought back to Fawn Grove for a specific reason."

"To find out who killed her?"

"It sounds crazy, I know."

"That's because it is crazy. It's not your job to track down a murderer."

"Maybe not. Then again, maybe fate has made it my job." I stand and peer past the curtain and out into the woods. A doe and a mother prance through some bramble. "Does the VW van still run?"

"What do you think?" After spending many years

working on mill machinery, my father taught himself to become a skilled mechanic. He could fix most any engine, whether it be a lawn mower, car, or snowblower.

"Can I borrow it to go into town from time to time?"

"What for?"

I walk over and pick up the weekly newspaper, open it to the classified section, and point to an ad.

"You wanna be a line cook at The Galaxy?"

"Just until the time comes when I can return home."

"No offense, but what the hell do you know about cooking?"

I laugh. "Enough to be dangerous."

"If that's what floats your boat, then you can use the van whenever you like. I rarely leave home these days, anyway."

"I'll fill it with gas and pick up your groceries whenever you need me to."

"Did you always know you wanted to be a gal?"

"Let's just say that I've always known that I wanted to be something other than Jaxon. But I didn't really understand these feelings when I was a kid."

"The Jaxon I remember was a little hellion on wheels who skipped school and got himself into loads of trouble. Had himself a little cutie back then too. The Greek goddess, I used to call her."

"You knew about Nadia?"

"I saw you out with her one night but never said anything about it. She probably tried to keep you in line, like most everyone else in town."

"Looking back, I think I got into so much trouble because I was unhappy with myself. I didn't know it at the time, but I was miserable and lashing out."

"I remember how some of the kids used to pick on you, especially that cop. Called you a sissy and a pretty boy. You used to come home practically in tears every day. I'd try to teach you how to defend yourself, but you wanted no part of it," he says.

"I knew how to fight, but Dalton was bigger and stronger than most of the other kids. I could never figure out why he always had it out for me. Maybe he sensed that I wanted to be a girl before even I realized it."

"Probably made him insecure, which is why he took advantage of the situation."

"Thanks for the analysis, Dr. Phil."

"And now to think he's a cop in town. Go figure."

"People change, Dad," I say, recalling that amazing kiss at the bus station. "Did you know that Dalton's the assisting detective in charge of these murders?"

"Nope. But if you ask me, I think one of them immigrants killed those kids," he says.

"I bet you think you're Columbo as well?"

"Just seems to be the thing these people do to their own. The only difference is, now they want to do it in our country."

"But what if, hypothetically, someone wanted to make it look like one of the immigrants did it? Wouldn't you stage it that way?"

"Why would anyone do that?"

"I don't know. I'm just playing devil's advocate."

"The devil's smart enough on his own, Lucy. He don't need you or anyone else advocating for him." He tugs down on his beard and appears to mull it over. "I suppose if someone wanted to use these murders as an excuse to get rid of someone, they'd make it look like a Muslim did it. But killing innocent kids?"

"Now you're thinking like a detective."

"What about that girl you used to go with? You gonna see her while you're in town?"

"I already have. Her father owns The Galaxy."

"Heard that place has gone to the dogs."

"It has. Only dogs wouldn't dare eat there nowadays."

"Speaking of food, I got to get dinner started," he says, pushing himself off the chair.

"Sit down, Dad. I'll do the cooking tonight."

"Huh! That's a laugh coming from someone who couldn't even boil an egg growing up. I taught your mother everything she knew in the kitchen."

"Those must have been on the nights you weren't out drinking or screwing around," I say, trying not to sound spiteful. "Relax, Dad, I'll make dinner this evening."

"Knock yourself out, then," he says, falling back on to his chair.

I grab my trusty boning knife and take over the kitchen. My father has no idea the mad culinary skills I possess. There's a freshly plucked chicken waiting in the sink and some sad-looking vegetables harvested from his tiny garden. I prefer sad vegetables to those GMO monstrosities they sell at the supermarket. In my experience, the uglier the better tasting.

I remember when I was a little boy, watching my father butcher one of the hogs he used to raise in the back pen. Once a year he slaughtered the fattest pig for a big backyard barbecue we used to hold for friends and family. The squeal of that frightened pig still haunts me to this day. And yet I happily noshed on the delicious, moist flesh. The crispy skin was the most sought-after part of the hog. Killing was the price we paid for our food, but as a young kid it scared the hell out of me. The spray of blood as the knife cut through the pig's artery. There was a steel basin underneath to catch the blood, which he used to make sausages. The pig would be hung and then broken down into its respective cuts: ribs, shoulder, butt. The head he'd use to make headcheese. Then after that my father and his merry band would drink and play music all night over a roaring bonfire. Sometimes I can still hear that banjo in my dreams.

That moment of death has always fascinated me. I'd seen it up close and personal while tending to the severely wounded returning from battle. I saw it in the eyes of my fellow soldiers moments after that IED went off. I remember the toxic smoke clouds given off by the paper mills and the greenish foam that collected along the river. And all I could ever think about was that this town was dying a slow death. I had no rationale or clue as to why. Everyone was so happy back then that we never believed these mills might stop producing paper and leave destitution and sadness in their wake. They were our pride and joy, but they were also our downfall.

I've been thinking a lot about death lately. I've had nightmares about being stoned since they buried me in that pit. It's unimaginable what those two kids must have experienced in their final moments. I keep telling myself that death is not the end of this journey but just the beginning, and that their souls are in a much happier place. But that sounds more like a justification for their senseless deaths. A cop-out to appease the living.

I prepare a simple dish of herb-crusted chicken, pan

fried under a brick and then finished off in the oven with some lemon and garlic-infused butter. I whip up a batch of buttermilk bacon biscuits, and I sauté fresh vegetables in the pan juices. Dad seems happy when I present the dish to him. He eats in silence, which I can tell is a sign that he likes it. For dessert, I make a simple blueberry tart using the Maine berries he picked out back. After polishing off his plate, he thanks me and settles back with a thick joint. I can tell he's pleasantly surprised by the meal I've prepared, but he won't come right out and say it. That's the way he's been his entire life. He looks tired from the excitement of my visit, and I wonder about his health. Wendy had expressed concern about it, but I'm not bringing the subject up unless he wants to talk about it.

Once he's safely in his room, I take out my phone and check on a website that markets fake mustaches and beards. I discover that they're made out of real human hair, which is perfect for the way I'm planning to disguise myself. After perusing the site for a few minutes, I order a walrus mustache with accompanying soul patch. I also order some dark brown contact lenses. Delivery in two days and charged to the account of Lucy Abbott.

This way I'll be able to walk into town and not be recognized. Just like when I returned here as Lucy. Only then can I find out for sure who murdered those two innocent teens—before I return to being the girl who returned to Fawn Grove.

22

Two Weeks Later

I REMEMBER APPROACHING THE GIRL'S STALL ONE DAY when I saw an older man leering at her while she was arranging the fruit to be sold that day. Although I couldn't understand what he was saying, I could tell by the look on the girl's face that she was extremely uncomfortable by his presence. She was young and beautiful, and I could see how she'd be the object of many men's desires. Still, it didn't give the leech the right to harass this poor girl.

Upon reaching her stall, I recognized the older man as he slunk away. He sold vegetables in a stall three removed from the girl's. She looked up nervously as I checked out some of her produce. When I looked over, I saw him smiling in a lewd manner, and I knew his harassment of the girl was not an isolated event. Furious, I walked over to his stall and stood in front of his vegetables, glaring at him.

"Give good deal to American soldier," he said, his fake smile making me dislike him even more.

"Keep to your vegetables, pal, or we'll have a problem." I picked up an unwashed potato, nodded toward the girl, and pointed it at him. "Do you understand me?"

The man looked furious that I'd reproached him, but he nodded grudgingly.

I returned to the girl's stall, noticing that she'd witnessed our confrontation. I smiled at her as I looked over her selection of fruits. When I told her what I wanted, the girl picked out my apples and dates before handing the bag to me.

"Thank you," she said, giving me a sly smile of appreciation.

I shrugged and took the bag from her.

She poked her head out of the stall and glanced around before saying, "I feel safe with U.S. soldiers here."

I smiled at her again and turned to leave.

"It's Zarafshan," she said, which caused me to turn back to face her. "That is my name." Then she quickly averted her gaze and returned to organizing the fruit on her stall.

I wish I could say that I slept comfortably on my father's couch, or that I didn't hear the voices, but the truth is that my sleep habits grew progressively worse as D-day arrived. And today, finally, the day has come to debut my new persona in town. For the time being, I'll be known as Iggy. Why that name? Because my favorite song is "Five Foot One" by Iggy Pop.

My mind is having a difficult time processing these

three distinct identities, and this is causing me significant angst. My dreams tend to ramble all over the place. Iggy overcompensates for the ghost of Jaxon, who's trying to inhabit Lucy's mind and body and take control of her. Then there's the little voices crying out for my attention. All of this adds up to one confused individual.

I sit on the couch after a night of tossing and turning and make my way into the shower. I pull off the prosthetics and gently lay them down on the lid of the toilet. Dragging myself into the shower, I let the warm water wash over me. After dressing in my ratty Goodwill clothes and black Metallica T-shirt, I glue on my mustache and soul patch using the water-resistant adhesive. I put in my brown contact lenses, don the black-rimmed glasses, and tie a red do-rag around my shaved head. In this new incarceration, I don't in the least resemble that gorgeous, slender boy from my youth. Nor do I resemble the attractive woman I'd been upon returning to Fawn Grove. I am the prodigal *transgender* son.

The problem is, I feel terrible about the way I look. I know in my heart that it's not the real me. It's not about gender as much as it is about identity. It's about who and what I am, and where I want to be in life. I so badly want to return to the real me that Lucy is ready to burst out of this cocoon of my own making.

I called yesterday about the job, and Yanni told me to come in for an interview. I could hear the desperation in his voice. The key will be for me to show him I'm worthy of cooking his shitty food. Prepare it exactly the way he wants. Only in that way will I be able to blend seamlessly into the background of Fawn Grove society. I'll listen to everything that's being said. Speak only when spoken to. I'll do whatever needs to be done so I can do what I came here for.

Yanni takes one look at my getup, and I can tell right away that he'll hire me. It's not like there's a gang of cooks in line with résumé in hand, waiting to toil at this diner for near minimum wage. Working here is the culinary equivalent of hitting rock bottom. After The Galaxy, there's nowhere left for a cook to go in this town. I doubt I could get a job at Denny's with this place on my résumé. The only demand I make is that he pay me under the table. He steps aside to mull it over. When I tell him I'm willing to take a pay cut in order to make it happen, he waves a greasy spatula in the air and laughs. I'm hired.

"What's your name?"

"Iggy," I say in the most masculine, raspy voice I can muster.

"When can you start?" he asks while manhandling a neon orange mess of scrambled eggs.

"Soon as you need me."

"Grab an apron and start peeling potatoes, then."

"Can I check out the dining room first?"

"Hurry up and be quick about it. We're busy this morning."

Busy?

I make my way through the galley and arrive into the diner, and I am stunned to see that the dining room is nearly full. To my surprise, Stefania is busy at the counter pouring coffees and taking orders. Billie is busing a table in the far corner of the restaurant and seems flustered because she has so many tables to cover. Sitting at the counter is Dalton, and he doesn't look well. Dark bags sit under his eyes. Is he daydreaming about Lucy? Is he heartbroken that she's gone from his life? Was that kiss as amazing for him as it was for me? Stefania turns and stares at me with barely veiled disgust. She rests a long, slender hand on her hip as she takes me in.

"Who the hell are you?" she asks.

"The new line cook," I say goofily, flashing a hook 'em horns hand sign made famous by metalhead rockers. "Iggy."

"Iggy?" She laughs hysterically. "Now there's a messed-up name if I've ever heard one."

"Short for Ignatius."

"My grandfather must have really hit rock bottom if he's hired a guy named Ignatius," she announces to the people sitting at the counter, drawing a big laugh. Dalton manages a tortured smile. "Of course, you're probably way better than the last cook he hired. She was a total loser."

"For real?"

"Miss Fancy-Pants, I used to call her. Thought she was so much better than everyone else in town because she was from New York City."

"Watch your mouth," Dalton says, eying her fiercely. "Lucy was a good person and a helluva chef."

"Oh, please, get a room," Stefania says, rolling her eyes. She crosses her arms over her chest and stares at me. "Poor Detective Dalton fell madly in love with her and he's been sulking ever since she left."

"You're pushing your luck, Stef," Dalton says, pointing his utensil at her.

"What are you going to do? Stab me with your fork?"

"Why'd she leave?" I ask.

"Because she couldn't keep her nose out of everyone else's business," Stefania says. "Then again, I suppose you'd leave too if you'd been buried up to your chest and left overnight in Robinson Woods."

"Damn," I say. "Who buried her and why?"

"You heard about those two murders in town?"

"Sure, who hasn't?"

"She thought she was Nancy Drew and could solve them by herself. That way she could return to New York City a big hero. Only someone buried her first and scared her half to death. That's why she couldn't wait to get out of here."

"I'm not going to sit here and listen to you badmouth Lucy," Dalton says, grabbing his cap. "Especially when she's not here to defend herself."

"Love is blind, Iggy. It's why I'll never fall in love and end up a heartbroken loser like poor Dalton over there," Stefania says, heading over to cash out a customer.

Yanni shouts for me in the kitchen. I ignore his entreaties and follow Dalton out the door and into the parking lot. He opens his car door angrily and is about to get in when he sees me standing there. Does he recognize me, despite the fact that Iggy is three inches shorter than Lucy?

"What the hell do you want?"

"Iggy," I say, holding out my hand. "Just wanted to introduce myself."

Dalton stares down at my hand as if I'm holding a grenade.

"Stef told me about your girlfriend. I'm real sorry, man."

"That smart-ass kid should learn to keep her big mouth shut."

"Is it true what happened to that cook who was here before me?"

"Where the hell you been living? A cave?"

"Up near Bolton Ridge. Don't watch much news."

"There's a lot of meth heads living up in Bolton Ridge. Caught a guy cooking up there last year."

"Not me. I'm just a regular, old-fashioned cook."

"How long you been working at The Galaxy?"

"Today's my first day on the job," I say. "Better be getting back before the boss gets pissed."

"You obviously don't know Yanni. He'll be pissed no matter what you do."

"That bad, huh?"

"Look, don't take this personally, but you'll never be as good as Lucy. That girl was a gifted chef."

"Just trying to earn a living and pay some bills, Officer."

"It's Detective."

"Excuse me?"

"It's Detective Dalton, not Officer."

"Okay, I'll remember that."

"You better, Iggy, if you want to stay on my good side."

I go back inside and see Stefania staring at me as if I'm a child molester, arms crossed and shifting her weight in nervous anticipation of my arrival. Yanni shouts something from the kitchen just as two more customers walk into the diner.

"This place always so busy?" I ask, incredulous at the size of the crowd.

"Hell, no. Denny's caught fire last night and the place burnt down."

"It did?"

Stefania laughs. "Are you for real? It's been all over the news."

"I don't listen to the news. Too depressing." I make a mental note to stay abreast of current events. "Shouldn't you be in school?"

"Teacher conference," she says. "So what else you like to do, *Iggy?*"

I lean over and whisper in her ear, "I like to toke."

"Excuse me?"

"I got some nice herb we can smoke after breakfast, if you like."

"You could get fired if I told my grandfather about this," she whispers.

I know for a fact that she'll not tell the old man. "Just trying to be friendly."

"Meet me by the Dumpster at ten. It usually slows down around that time."

"Sure."

"And bring the weed."

Yanni barks out my name so that all the customers in the dining room can hear. It's so unprofessional that it makes me cringe. What must this look like to diners trying to enjoy their breakfast? I shrug it off and let his comments roll off my back. *Keep calm*, I tell myself. Don't let his cruel words or terrible cooking methods get to you.

"Where you been?" Yanni shouts as soon as I walk into the kitchen. Sweat drips off his lined forehead and onto the sheet of phyllo dough he's rolling out for baklava.

"Sorry, boss. That detective wanted to talk to me."

"What about?"

"Told him I lived up on Bolton Ridge, and he said there's been a lot of drug activity up there. Maybe he thought I was dealing or something."

"Are you?" Yanni slaps his hand down on the moist dough.

"Not on your life, boss! I'm clean as a whistle."

"I better not catch you doing drugs around here. My young granddaughter works in this diner."

"Aye, aye, Captain."

"Now get to work."

I tie an apron around my waist and grab a ticket. Scrambled eggs, bacon, and toast. What a surprise. Against all my culinary training, I pour a dabble of liquid eggs on the flattop and try not to vomit. I'm still Lucy Abbott underneath it all, I have to keep reminding myself, despite the bald pate and stoner dude disguise. It wounds my pride to cook like this. And to talk in this raspy, undignified manner. As the day progresses, I repeat my mantra that I'm a highly qualified chef who's trained for many years. I slow my pace and purposefully make mistake after mistake, which gives Yanni plenty reason to shout at me. He calls me a "fucking moron" and a "redneck hick" and "the worst goddamn chef I've ever hired." Calling me these names, I can tell, makes him happy. Happier than a dining room full of paying customers.

I flip two buttermilk pancakes that I mixed out of a box. A funny thought comes to mind, and I picture Yanni splashing gasoline against the walls of Denny's and then lighting it on fire. The result: Now all their customers are migrating here.

"Dude," Stefania says as we smoke a blunt behind the Dumpster. "Where'd you get this shit? It's totally amazing."

"There's plenty more where this came from," I say with newfound confidence. "How old are you anyways? Eighteen?"

Stefania blows out a cloud of smoke and laughs. "Sure. Whatever you say."

"I could get in big trouble if you were any younger than that."

"Chillax, Iggy," she says, staring at me in an odd manner. "You look familiar for some reason. Have we met before?"

"Don't think so." The thought of her recognizing Lucy Abbott makes me nervous.

She shrugs and takes another hit off the joint, staring at me closely.

"How come they didn't kill that other cook like they did those two kids?" I ask.

"How do I know? Why don't you go track down the killer and ask him yourself."

"Not me. I don't want nothing to do with any of that." I take another hit.

"Hurry up and pass that shit over." She grabs it out of my hand and inhales.

"What do you think happened?"

"Don't you think I'd tell the cops if I knew?"

The glare she gives me tells me I've gone too far. I need to play it cool if I'm to be accepted here.

"Some of us are planning on having a little party soon. Why don't you join us, Iggy?"

"Not sure that's a good idea."

"You wanna keep your job, don't you? I wouldn't want my grandfather to learn that you've been smoking weed out back with his granddaughter."

"When you put it that way, I guess I could swing by for a few minutes."

"Cool. Bring some of that killer weed when you come. And a bottle of booze while you're at it."

I pinch the roach. "Where do you want me to meet you?"

"I'll let you know when the time comes."

"Your mother doesn't care if you go out and party?"

"My parents don't give a shit about me. As long as I stay out of their hair, I can do whatever I want. All my mother cares about are those dumb immigrants."

"What's she do?"

"She's a social worker, and her clients are those Afghani refugees. She cares more about them than she does her own kid."

"Sounds to me like she's only trying to help them settle in."

"What the hell does a stoner like you know about helping anyone?"

I shrug helplessly.

"I bet she never even wanted me. Same with my deadbeat dad."

Stefania heads back to the kitchen and disappears inside. I follow behind and see tickets lined up for lunch service. The difficulty here is cooking down to a level I'm not accustomed to. It's like an Olympic runner slowing her pace in order to accommodate a much slower partner, but deep down the runner's burning desire is to *take off*.

Lunch is busier than I've ever seen it. If only they'd patronized this place when Lucy was here, she might have made a difference. That fire at Denny's has proven to be a real boon for The Galaxy, but it won't take long before these new customers become disillusioned with the crappy food here and drift someplace else.

I purposefully screw up the first few tickets in order to make Yanni happy. Although he grumbles incoherently, I can tell it gives him purpose. It makes him feel superior and needed. I try not to scream when he places an order of spanakopita in the microwave and sets it out for pickup. His Greek meatballs, shaped like miniature footballs, aren't half bad. If only he used a better grade of meat, they might even be exceptional. But he won't, and I can't help but think that an opportunity is being lost to win over these new customers, especially now that his competition has been temporarily vanquished.

I go out to the parking lot for a smoke after lunch service slows down. The half-smoked joint I shared with Stefania sits in my pocket. I had to pocket a couple from my father's stash, and I feel guilty about stealing from him. Because of his condition, he's allowed to possess a certain amount for medical purposes only. He's even started to cultivate his own crop in a hidden patch behind the house. He claims it eases his pain and helps boost his appetite.

I'm halfway through my first cigarette when a car pulls up and parks in front of me. Dalton gets out of the vehicle and strides toward me.

"Got an extra one of those?" he asks.

My knees go weak as I pull out the box, slap it against my palm like a short-order cook, and watch as he picks the smoke out with the tip of his fingers. I pass him mine, which he uses to light his, and stare at his handsome profile.

"You got a cold?" he asks, squeezing his throat. "Your voice."

"Nope," I say, holding up my cigarette. "Too many of these."

"Sorry about before. Being a dick like that."

"It's cool."

"I have a lot on my mind these days." He inhales the cigarette and studies me closely. "Women, right?"

I laugh. "Can't live with 'em. Can't live without 'em."

"You too?"

I laugh again because he has no idea.

"You got a girl, Iggy?"

"Guess you could say that."

"These broads really know how to break a guy's heart."

"Tell me about it."

"Look at you, man. Rocking the concert tee, the do-rag, and skull earrings. Guy like you must be popular with the heavy metal babes."

"Don't I wish?"

He takes another hit on his smoke. "There was no one like Lucy. That was one special girl."

"The one they buried in the woods?"

"That's the one."

"She was hot, huh?"

"Being hot has nothing to do with it. There was something different about her. She had class and wasn't like all the other women around here."

"Wonder who buried her?"

"Whoever it was, we'll find them."

"You really liked this chick, huh?"

"Yeah."

"Thinking about her is driving you crazy."

"Is it that obvious?"

"Big time."

"Trying to solve these two murders is also stressing me out. The chief and the state police have been on my ass, and none of these Afghani assholes will talk to me." He takes another long drag on his cigarette. "You can't believe how much it sucked interviewing that dead kid's mother and trying not to convince her that one of these immigrant fucks did it."

I shake my head and stare at him, feigning sympathy.

"I can't even imagine what that girl went through, being buried and then stoned. Then with that kid having his throat slit like an animal. What kind of person does that to another human being?"

"People sure can be cruel to one another," I say, wanting to let him talk on.

"Tell me about it," he says. "I was certainly no angel growing up."

"I remember this one dude who bullied the hell out of me in grade school. Made my life miserable twenty-four seven."

"Hate to admit it, Iggy, but I was that bully growing up. Makes me sick thinking about it now."

"It should. That kinda bullying scars people for life." It surprises me that he's expressing such remorse. I want to hug him and extend an olive branch of forgiveness. "Why didn't you just convince your girl to stay?"

"That's the thing. I don't even know if she liked me or not."

"Then you should call her and find out."

"Too late. I doubt she'll ever come back to Fawn Grove after what they did to her."

"I certainly wouldn't if I were her."

"Fucking savages!"

"And she's the lucky one."

"How so?"

"She didn't end up dead like those two poor kids." I slide my hand across my throat.

Dalton flicks his cigarette to the ground and stomps on it. "So how you like working here?"

"Beats a stick in the eye."

"Yanni can be a real prick at times." He smiles knowingly.

"At times?"

"You're all right, Iggy," he says, patting my shoulder. "Hey, you wanna grab a beer with me later?"

"Love to, but I'm a little low on funds." I pull out my pockets so that lint falls out.

He laughs at the sight of my rabbit ears. "No worries. The beers are on me tonight. It'll be good for us guys to get acquainted and let our hair down."

"Why not? I got no hair to let down anyway."

This is too good to be true. Does this guy really have no other friends? And yet I realize this could be my way in with him. A way of getting information without getting too close, and without any fear of another one of those crazy passionate kisses.

Before he disappears into the diner, he tells me where and when to meet him. I head to my father's van, parked two streets over so no one will see it, and climb inside.

As soon as I get home, my father welcomes me by passing over his bong. Against my better judgment, I take a hit and am soon feeling relaxed. As much as I'm enjoying the occasional blast of weed, it's a habit I don't want to cultivate. It's bad for my health and could trigger a whole host of problems dealing with addiction, mental health, and weight gain. I tell myself that I'll quit once all this is over. But for the time being it helps make my voice raspy. It also puts me in a better place and helps me forget that I'm this pathetic loser named Iggy. I close my eyes until the memory of being buried alive returns in full force. Then I sit up and catch my breath, and pray for the girl I'd once been. And the woman I hope to become.

23

*M*Y FATHER DROPS ME OFF A BLOCK FROM THE BAR so that the two of us won't be spotted. He offers to pick me up afterward, but I tell him I'll take a cab home instead. I look into his eyes and can see he's mildly stoned. In a few hours he'll be in no condition to drive. Then again, neither will I. The combination of hormones and pills limits my tolerance for everything, including alcohol and weed.

Dalton is sitting at the long bar when I enter. He looks as if he's been on that stool for some time. Overcome by nerves, I want to rush into the ladies' room and check myself out in the mirror. Powder my face and reapply my makeup. It often took me over an hour before I went out in public to face the world. But this is not a date. Just two dudes getting together for a couple of beers. Crotch grabbing, backslapping, and knocking back shots while talking about chicks, cars, and guns. The thought depresses me as I sit down next to him, my nerves still rattled from that ground-shaking kiss. The sensation of being this close to Dalton strikes me as odd, considering that I've been pushing him away since I arrived here as Lucy Abbott. It's the story of my life.

I remember Dalton back in middle school, constantly shoving me to the dirt and taunting me while the other kids stood around and laughed. He'd call me a sissy and a queer, although I never came across as overly effeminate. I would get up and try to tackle him, only to watch as he pushed me back down. Sometimes I tried to run away, but he'd eventually catch up to me and double down on the punishment. Then he'd pull my ears and give me a nasty tit twister or stinging wedgie. I was a stubborn kid. I kept getting up until I couldn't get up anymore, or until one of the teachers or an adult came out and rescued me from his endless cruelty.

Did he detect my inner turmoil back then and exploit it to make himself look good? Or was I merely just a pretty boy with fine-boned features and a slim waist? Could he see into my conflicted adolescent mind and know that I was different from all the other kids? Is that why he bullied me? Because he knew that I stole into my mother's bedroom whenever she was out and put on her lipstick and makeup? Or begged to go with her to the hairdresser so I could watch as they made her look beautiful, wishing more than anything that it was me sitting under that hair dryer? Wishing it was me getting my nails painted and my long, lustrous hair shampooed, cut, and blown dry? At that young age I didn't consciously wish to become a girl. I just knew that certain feminine things that most women enjoyed doing were things I also desired.

Dalton turns and shakes my hand. I squeeze back firmly, projecting masculinity and strength. He's in a good mood, thanks to the drinks he's already consumed, and he appears happy to see me. He orders two beers and two shots of Jack Daniels, and once they arrive we toast. I must monitor how much I drink so that I don't slip up, become intoxicated, and say something stupid. Part of me doesn't understand his motive for wanting a guy like me here. Maybe he's just lonely and has no friends to blow off steam with him. There are lots of these friend-challenged souls in Manhattan seeking out the company of others, people who will tolerate you as long as you'll sit and listen to their long list of drunken complaints.

In some ways I feel sorry for Dalton. He's lived his entire life in Fawn Grove, knowing he's hurt many people. Maybe that's why he became a cop, and why I joined the military. Perhaps he's turned his life around and wants to make amends for the bad things he did as a kid. I'm sure many of his victims will never forgive him for the cruel way he treated them, no matter how drastically he's turned his life around.

"You want another?" he asks, holding up his empty shot glass.

"I'm good for now."

"So how long you been living here, Iggy?"

"Long enough to know the score."

"I know what you mean." He laughs at this. "A lot of people in this town actually like living here. It's like they view their shame as a virtue. Hell, even I'm ashamed to be still living in this dump."

"Misery loves company, right?"

"Exactly, except these people mistake misery for civic pride," he says. "You ever think of leaving this place?"

"And miss out on all these wonderful winters?"

He laughs and takes his fresh shot glass from the bartender.

"Think about it all the time. Guess I'm too chicken-shit to split to warmer climes."

"I had high hopes of leaving at one time. Then I got married and had a kid, and that ended that pipe dream. This town has a way of wearing a guy down."

I sip my beer and think of his conflicted relationship with his daughter. "Girls too."

"Especially the girls. The women here in Fawn Grove age fast once they graduate from high school."

I nod knowingly.

"First come the babies. After the babies comes the weight gain and welfare checks. Then repeat the cycle."

"A lot of them turn to drugs."

"That's because they lost all hope that they can make a life in this town," he says. "Then these immigrants arrive and start demanding free this and free that, and before you know it two kids are dead." He downs his shot and orders another. "If I had any balls, I'd go chase after Lucy in New York City."

"Girl has you by the balls, dude."

"Why you say that?" he asks.

"That line cook's all you can think about."

"No offense, pal, but you're a line cook. Lucy was a *chef*. There's a big difference."

"Whatever. Cooking's just a means to pay my bills."

"Part of me was hoping she'd stick around and take over The Galaxy. Return it to its former glory."

"If you don't like the diner so much, then why do you still eat there?"

"Creature of habit, I guess. At one time The Galaxy was *the* place to go in this town. It meant something to people living here. People went there after the prom, for an anniversary, or after getting laid."

"Hate to break it to you, but Denny's serves way better food than The Galaxy."

"Maybe so, but back in the day you were lucky if you could grab a seat at the counter there."

"Yanni's too set in his ways to change."

"Lucy constantly bitched about that old bastard. Said he used liquid eggs because he was too cheap to buy fresh ones. He thought people couldn't taste the difference."

"Dude's not fooling anyone," I say, trying not to laugh. "Those liquid eggs are nasty."

"You haven't seen nasty till you've seen a kid buried up to her chest and with her face smashed in."

"Thanks, but I don't *ever* want to see that."

"What about you, Iggy?" He sips his beer. "Got a girl?"

"Besides Mary Palmer and her five sisters?"

He nearly spits out his beer laughing. "I'm going to try to forget you said that, especially now that I'm picturing you in that kitchen making burgers."

"Yeah, I got a girl." And her name is Lucy, I want to say.

"She know how to cook?"

"Hell, no. But then again neither do I." I lift my drink to toast. "Not that you'll ever know about my girl's cooking."

"You never know, I might steal her away from you when you're not looking."

"She'll never leave me with a package like this." I grab my crotch in an exaggerated manner, and it makes me want to barf.

"That's a postcard, not a package."

"How would you know? You been checking out my mailbox?"

"I'd never do that to a guy like you, Iggy. Besides, there's only one girl I'm interested in, and she's a long ways from home." He slides off the stool and staggers to the john.

I stand, dreading this moment ever since I walked into this pub, knowing it's necessary to my disguise. I pass the bartender a twenty and ask him to fill my glass with nonalcoholic beer for the remainder of the evening. The alcohol I've consumed to this point has already gone to my head.

The bathroom has three urinals. I pull up to the one on the far right, leaving a free one between us. Pissing while standing feels unfamiliar and takes all my strength. It defies the identity I've strived so hard to create and feels like a betrayal of my true self. It reminds me that I'm still broken, and not yet the woman I hope to become. Time, money, and fear once prevented me from making the full transition to Lucy Abbott. But I've promised myself that one day I'll save up enough money and take that final leap into womanhood.

I turn and glance at him, the strong scent of urinal cake blasting my nostrils. His forehead is resting against the tiled wall, and tears are running down his cheeks. He's not even trying to hide the fact that he's crying.

"Dude."

"I'm sorry," he says, wiping his eyes while he pees. "It's just that my life is so fucked up right now."

"At least you have a life."

"Lucy found an earring at the site of the first crime scene. She showed it to me."

This admission alarms me.

"I didn't want to say anything at the time, but I saw that same earring on the dead girl."

I zip up my fly.

He moves drunkenly to the sink to wash his hands. "We have videos of the dead girl that she made in her apartment."

I wash my hands, ashamed by my excessively shorn nails. "What was she doing?"

"I'm not supposed to say anything."

"That's cool." I walk out the door and park on the stool. Dalton sits next to me and orders two more beers.

"The thing is, I could get in big trouble with the state police if this gets out."

"Then keep it under your hat, bro."

He downs most of his beer and orders another. "You got to promise me that you won't breathe a word of this to anyone."

"Who am I going to tell? I live like a hermit."

"The dead girl was talking to some of the other girls in her class. She mentioned Stef's name. And a girl named Brynn."

Brynn! "Girls will be girls, right?"

"I have a daughter that age. She barely talks to me unless she needs money."

"What's her name?"

"Brandy. She's such a great girl. I just wish her mother would stop bad-mouthing me."

"Sorry to hear that," I say. "So who you think killed those kids?"

He grabs his new beer and looks around the bar as if paranoid.

"You telling me that you don't think it's an honor killing?"

"Yes. No. I don't know what the hell I'm thinking. I'm pretty drunk right now."

"Which one is it?"

"They messed up. I asked Stef what those earrings meant, and she said it was a Greek symbol for 'eternal friendship.'"

"That don't mean shit, Dalton."

He turns angrily and jabs a finger into my shoulder. "It's Detective to you, pal. Show some respect for the law."

"Okay," I wince. "Chill out."

"You chill out." He takes a few seconds to calm down. "We also found a set of footprints that match a popular brand of girls' shoes."

"You said those kids go down there to party."

He looks tormented by all this. "Both of these dead kids had drugs in their system. How else could that happen?"

"So what do you think?"

"I think someone in that refugee community found out about her extracurricular activities and decided that she should be punished."

"Makes perfect sense."

"I shouldn't even be talking to you about this," he mutters, staring at me as if I'm scum.

"I said I won't say anything."

He orders two more beers. "You have kids, Iggy?"

"Hell, no!"

Dalton shakes his head and smiles. "That's what Lucy used to say. Hell, no. Said she couldn't have kids even if she wanted them."

"Barren?"

"Didn't say."

"Who needs the headache?"

"These kids in Fawn Grove are such spoiled little shits," he slurs. "It's this goddamn town that's responsible. For everything bad that's happened here."

"Why do you say that?"

"Lucy would make a great mother, I just know it."

"You have to get over this girl, man. She's driving you crazy."

"She's all I've been thinking about after we kissed that day."

"You kissed her?"

"Yeah, and it was the best kiss ever. But I fucked everything up."

I can't quite believe I'm hearing this. It's both flattering and unnerving to hear it come out of his mouth. Part of me wants to hug this guy, and the other part of me wants to punch him in the face for treating me so badly when I was a kid. Another part of me wants to forgive him. And yet another part doesn't. Shouldn't living one's entire life in Fawn Grove be punishment enough?

We drink up. Or I should say, Dalton drinks. He's drunk beyond caring at this point. My nonalcoholic beer tastes like shit as the night wears on, but it allows me to stay levelheaded and calm. There's nothing I want more right now than a shot of Jack Daniels to numb the pain.

But I know that transgender people have some of the highest rates of alcoholism, drug use, and suicide, and my history with the bottle is not a proud one. Besides being the best chef in the restaurant, I could drink every line cook under the table. I was the girl who couldn't stop partying. I was the girl who couldn't stop the voices in her head from telling her what a phony bitch she'd become and that no one would believe her act. I drank to forget that I was not the woman I was fated to be but a monster slapped together like Frankenstein's creation. I was a monster of my own making, vilified and mocked by that alter ego whispering in my ear. Only intense therapy and Dr. Frankenstein could transition me from monster to Lucy Abbott.

Dalton babbles aimlessly as the night progresses. And yet somewhere deep inside me, I sympathize with his pain. He needs to be forgiven for his sins, but mostly he needs to forgive himself. I want to tell him that we're all sinners to some degree, waiting for forgiveness and a loving embrace. And yet if I give in to temptation, I'm afraid what might happen, or what I might say. I could accidentally reveal my true self and ruin everything. Then I'd be forced to leave Fawn Grove forever without discovering the truth.

"I'd love to get married again and have another kid, one who loves and appreciates her dad," Dalton slurs. "Not a spoiled daughter who never speaks to me and treats me like shit. I'm only thirty-five. I'm still a young guy, right?"

"Of course you are."

"Brandy used to love me when she was a little girl.

Now all she calls me for is money or to use my truck," he says, pulling out his wallet and opening it to a photo of a girl on a horse. "Look at this picture of her. She was eight when I took it. How cute is that?"

"She's a doll. Where was that photo taken?"

"Fryeburg Fair. I used to take her every year and we'd have an amazing time together. We'd get cotton candy and then I'd give her piggyback rides all over the grounds."

"A girl doesn't forget stuff like that, Dalton. She'll remember the good times she had with you, and then she'll eventually come around."

"I really hope you're right, because I love that girl to death."

"Another drink?"

"Jesus, Iggy, I've never met anyone who can drink like you." He laughs and slaps me on the back. "You got a hollow leg or what?"

"Two hollow legs, actually."

He laughs hysterically at this. "Where's my car keys? I gotta get home." He slips off the stool, but I manage to catch him before he falls.

"Oh no, Dalton, you're not driving anywhere."

"I've got a confession to make, Iggy. I was a real asshole growing up."

"I know," I say as I help him stagger out the door.

"You do?" He looks at me suspiciously.

"You told me that story earlier. Don't you remember?"

"I did? What'd I say?"

"You said there was a particular kid you used to pick on when you were younger. Said his name was Jaxon and that you treated him badly."

"That little fucker! I'd punch Jaxon in the face if I ever saw him again."

This pisses me off. "You said you used to beat him up and treat him like shit in front of all the other kids."

"I wish I could go back and apologize to that little fag." He turns to me, anguish over his face. "The kid would never stay down, no matter how many times I told him. It was like he was asking me to beat his sorry ass."

"Why did you feel compelled to pick on him?"

"The kid was weird. Different. Things weren't like that back then."

"Like what?"

"Jaxon was a tough little bastard, but he was also a soft kid. What we used to call a sissy. A pretty boy."

"He's not a kid anymore."

"I'm not proud of what I done to him. But you can't go back and change the past, right?"

"Give me your keys." He reaches into his pocket and fishes them out. Angrily, I press the unlock button and his pickup beeps.

"Never saw Jaxon after he left town. Heard he enlisted in the army and died overseas," he says, tears falling from his eyes.

"Kid was obviously no sissy, then."

"No, he was a hero. Wish I could say sorry for the way I treated him."

"Maybe you already have and you don't even know it."

"You sure you're okay to drive, Iggy?"

"Never been finer."

He collapses into the backseat. I lift his legs and then stuff them inside before slamming the door shut.

I ask where he lives, and he mutters an address. It's been a long time since I've lived in Fawn Grove, and I've forgotten many of the street names. I plug the address into my phone's GPS and let it guide me to his apartment. It brings me to a shitty part of town elevated just off the railroad yard. Down below, I see boxcars lined up on the tracks, ready to be loaded or serviced. I park in the weedy lot alongside a row of dented cars.

"Come on, Dalton," I say, rousing him out of the backseat.

"Detective," he mutters.

I help him inside and up the stairs to his apartment. I can't believe how small and crappy this place is. The first thing I notice are all the framed photographs of Dalton's daughter on the walls, mantle, and coffee table. In every one of them she's smiling at the camera. Some are baby photos, and others were taken before she became a teenager, and before her mother turned her against him. It's obvious that he loves her and is desperate for her to return his love. The sight of all these photos makes me feel sad for Dalton.

This is not exactly the neatest apartment I've ever been in, and I've seen a lot of messy ones. Clothes and fast-food wrappers lie everywhere. My shoulder hurts from helping him upstairs, and my stumps hammer with pain. It's been a long time since I carried an additional 180 pounds over my shoulder. I lower him onto the tattered sofa and gather his feet up onto the cushion. He's already snoring by the time I stand back and take him in. I go into his bedroom and grab his faded Bruins blanket and wrinkled pillow. Lifting his head, I stuff the pillow beneath it and cover him with the blanket. I'm about to leave when I hear him stir.

"Thanks, Lucy," he mumbles.

"If you only knew," I whisper.

"I love you, girl. Didn't mean to hurt you."

"Go to sleep."

"I loved her to death." He turns onto his right side.

"Loved who to death? Lucy?"

"That boy didn't do nothing."

"What are you talking about?"

"She should have never trusted a cop," he says as the horn of a train blares outside.

"Who should have never trusted a cop?"

He adjusts himself on the couch. "The girl."

"Lucy or the dead girl?" I shake his shoulder. "Which girl are you talking about?"

"Lucy?" His eyes briefly open. "Is that you?"

I realize he's been thinking about me. "Go to sleep, Dalton." I kiss his forehead and then he's back to snoring.

I climb inside his pickup and head back to the bar. I'm exhausted from everything. The bar is closed, and all the lights are off. I park in the back lot, then place his keys under the mat. I call for a cab, hoping I don't have to wait too long this time of night.

24

*T*HE DINER IS ONCE AGAIN BALLS TO THE WALLS THIS morning, thanks to the fire that destroyed Denny's. They estimate that it'll be two months before they can rebuild it. Despite the blaze, it's amazing that people have decided to come here to eat. Can they be that desperate? If it were me, I'd rather stay home and make my own breakfast than eat this shit. Pour myself a bowl of Cap'n Crunch with cold milk.

From the kitchen, I can hear the dissatisfied customers grumbling and complaining about the food. The eggs are too rubbery. The bacon's greasy with little to no meat. Too salty. Too peppery. Too bland. Too this and too that. Yanni yells at me for one thing or another, and I feel like grabbing him by the collar and shaking some sense into him. If only I could take charge of this shit show and advise him how to turn it around. Because for the second time since I've worked here I see young faces in the dining room. But then, for the sake of my own narrow interests, I ruin another order of pancakes or French toast. This place is a lost cause and so there's no sense cooking like a pro and revealing my true identity. Yanni likes that I cook down to his standards and that he can pay me dirt. Despite every culinary truth I hold near and dear, I keep my head down and put out plate after plate of garbage.

Then again, it's not too hard to do, considering all that happened last night. Dalton got so drunk that he never made it in this morning. He must have been too hungover or embarrassed to show his face in here. I keep peeking into the dining room, hoping he'll be sitting at the counter, but he's nowhere to be seen. Will he act like nothing happened the next time I see him? Does he not realize what he said to me about these murders? Or that he confessed his love for Lucy Abbott? Me!

My heart beats faster thinking about him, and that kiss, and part of me hopes he'll make an appearance this morning. Have I forgiven him for his youthful indiscretions? Has the bully come full circle? No, because I know that he occasionally spouts off about these immigrants and displays bigoted tendencies. So why can't I understand my own thoughts? And why am I still attracted to him, knowing all I do about him?

Nadia comes back with another half-eaten omelette. It's runny and cooked only partway through. It's odd the way she treats me; it's as if I don't exist. I suppose I'm one in a long line of losers whom her father has hired throughout the years and will soon be fired. So why try to develop a friendship? I chalk it up to the ingenuity of my disguise and the low growl of my voice. I've turned myself into persona non grata in this diner. Those missing three inches seem to have done the trick.

"Jesus! Will you cook it right this time?" she snaps, dumping the omelette in the trash.

"Sorry," I say, watching as she scrapes the plate clean. "Where's Detective Dalton this morning?"

"How do I know?"

"He's usually the first one through the door."

"Dalton's a jerk, so forget about him and focus on your job."

"I don't know, he strikes me as a decent guy."

She tosses the soiled dish into a plastic tub and turns angrily to me. "How would you know about him? You didn't grow up with that asshole like I did. You have no idea what he's really like."

"I suppose you're right."

"Of course I'm right. He's been a bully his whole life, and he hasn't changed a bit. Even his own daughter can't stand him."

I pour liquid eggs on the flattop and watch as it bubbles up into an orange, plasticky flubber.

"Look, Iggy, you seem like a nice guy, but maybe you should just concentrate on your cooking instead of judging others."

"He told me he's a changed man and is sorry for what he's done in the past."

"Is that so?" She laughs bitterly. "If Dalton had his way, he'd kick all of these poor immigrants out of town. Does that sound like someone who's changed for the better?"

"But he's a good cop, right? He's trying to catch the killer of these two kids."

"Have you looked into his job performance? He's had more complaints than any other officer on the force and has been suspended twice."

"For what?"

"Excessive force. It's all on the public record."

I add shredded cheese, ham, and shallots. "I heard he was in love with the cook before me." I fold the omelette over, plate it, and then hand it to her.

"Where'd you hear that?"

"He pretty much told me so himself."

"He said that?"

"We had a few beers last night. Said he really misses her."

She laughs. "Trust me, he'd be the last person on earth she'd fall in love with. She's been in love with someone else for a long time now."

"Who?"

"That's none of your business," she snaps, disappearing into the dining room with the omelette.

Billie comes in with a stack of pancakes that I purposefully forgot to put chocolate chips in. I quickly whip up a new batch.

The day continues in this crazy fashion until my shift ends and I have the afternoon to myself. I know what I need to do. The key to these murder cases is the girl who works at the Afghani market. The same girl I was supposed to meet in Robinson Woods the day I got buried up to my chest. She was the only person who knew I'd be there. I've spent the past few weeks following her every movement. Now I've got to make her talk.

* * *

I've observed that she works Saturdays until three. Then she usually gets a ride to Robinson Woods for her weekend walk. She thinks she's so smart setting me up like that. Does she honestly think I'd let her get away with it? No one assaults Lucy Abbott and walks away scot-free.

I go inside the store and pretend to shop. The chef inside me can't help but to be in awe of all the exotic goodies on the shelves. But I must keep my head down and concentrate on the task at hand. The girl is kneeling on the floor and stocking boxes in an orderly fashion. A blue hijab covers her head. Is this the same wild girl who was drinking and smoking in that cornfield? She's so focused on what she's doing that she doesn't even bother to look up as I pass. This despite the fact that I'm the only American in the store.

I purchase some flatbreads, jars of red tahini, and figs, and I head out to the van. Then I speed over and park in the lot of Robinson Woods before she arrives. While I wait for her, I take out my red wig, jeans, and a sweatshirt from my backpack. In the backseat are the newer, longer prosthetics I use when I'm in my real skin. Next to that is a stun gun and some nylon restraints I'd purchased in a shop a couple of towns over. I switch everything out as best I can, adjust the wig over my scalp so that it is taped and secure, and then apply my makeup while staring at myself in the rearview mirror. I take out the brown contact lenses and reveal my blue eyes. Last, I put on false eyelashes for the first time in my life. It's not perfect by any means, but it's a hundred times better than being a dude. More than anything, it makes me incredibly happy to be

Lucy again, even if only temporarily. For the first time in over a month, I feel at ease with myself despite what I'm about to do.

Satisfied with my appearance, I throw a scarf over my head and make my way into the woods. It feels much like heading into battle and tending to the wounded, gunfire rattling all around me, my nerves on edge. The trail is quiet and peaceful. After fifteen minutes, I arrive at the tiny frog pond that I once frequented as a young boy. I distinctly remember Jimmy Adams catching a bullfrog and then blowing it to smithereens by lighting a firecracker in its mouth. That's Fawn Grove youth in a nutshell. To my right there's a large mossy boulder next to the makeshift trail where the medics carried me out.

I make my way behind the rock and wait for the girl to arrive. With the stun gun in hand, I'm eager to find out what she will say to me, even if I have to resort to force to get it.

When she comes into view I notice that she's walking with Stefania. I hadn't expected her to have company, but I can't back out of my plan now. Nasreen's not wearing her hijab, and her black hair is tied neatly into a ponytail. She looks like any other normal American kid out for a stroll. It's clear to me what a beauty she is, and I can see how popular she'd be at school. Her skin shimmers with a caramel-colored hue, and her green eyes sparkle like a wild Irish field. Why am I now only noticing this? Am I envious of her natural beauty? Does she remind me of that tragic girl from the market?

I slip behind the boulder as they approach, gripping the stun gun in my pocket. As soon as they take the turn, I leap out from behind the rock and stick the stun gun into Stefania's back. It troubles me what I'm doing, that I'm inflicting pain on an innocent teenage girl. I pull the trigger, and she collapses to the ground, letting out a feral scream. I take out the nylon restraints and secure her hands and ankles. Nasreen sees me doing this and freezes. Our eyes meet for a brief second before she takes off down the trail.

"Don't move, or I'll come back for you," I whisper in Stefania's ear.

"Please don't kill me," she groans.

"I think you know who I am and how badly you've treated me."

"Lucy?"

"That's right," I say. "Miss Fancy-Pants."

Nasreen trips over a root and falls headfirst. It allows me to make up considerable ground. She jumps to her feet and turns to face me, slowly backing away in fear. By the look in her eyes, I can tell she recognizes me. I thrust my gun hand forward and zap her in the ribs. She screams and staggers backward, her leg muscles barely able to support her thin frame. I move forward despite the intense pain shooting through my stumps, hoping that she won't be able to get too far. But then she stumbles on a rock and lies sprawled over the dirt. I pounce on her, asking God to forgive me for what I'm about to do. Then I jab the stun gun into her side until she's shuddering in pain. I turn her onto her stomach and stick my elbow into her spine so that she can't move.

I secure her wrists behind her back with the nylon

restraints and pull her to her feet. She's dazed and sobbing in hyperventilating gasps. I drag her into the woods, through a thicket of shrubs. Sweat drips off my scalp and into my eyes. When we're out of view from the main trail, I take out another restraint and secure her to a thin birch tree located just off the trail. All this has taken the wind out of me, and I must stop and catch my breath. I crouch to her level so she can see my strained face.

"It's you. The devil," she says.

"Yes, I'm back."

"Stef said you left Fawn Grove for good."

"You shouldn't believe everything you hear."

"You won't get away with this," the girl says rather bravely, which impresses me.

"Oh, I think I will."

"They should have stoned your ugly face when they buried you in that hole."

"Who buried me? And why did you set me up like that?"

Tears dribble from her eyes.

"You better talk or else."

"What if I don't? Are you going to kill me?"

"No, but I'll make sure that everyone in your community sees this." I take out my phone and show her the clip of her and her friends in that cornfield. There's even a close-up of her smoking weed and kissing one of the boys. Nasreen watches it for a few seconds before turning away.

"Shut it off. I don't want to see anymore."

"If I show them this, you could be the next one buried up to your chest."

She laughs through a veil of tears.

"What's so funny?"

"You and everyone else in this town are so stupid. You have no idea about my people or what they're really like."

"What are you talking about?"

She begins to hyperventilate, and I wait for her to calm down. "It's the racist people in this town who have created these lies about my community."

"You expect me to believe that?"

"Not all Muslims are killers and terrorists, you know. The Afghanis are good people."

"I also know that Muslims are not supposed to drink alcohol or smoke pot."

"So I screwed up." She regains her bravery. "Yes, my parents would be upset if they saw that video, but so would any parent."

"What are you saying?"

"Do you really believe an immigrant killed those two kids?"

"I don't know what to believe anymore." I hear Stefania in the background calling out for help. I position the stun gun to Nasreen's neck. "If you say anything, I'll do it."

"Go ahead. It'll only hurt for a short time."

"Yes, but it will hurt really bad. So don't make me do it."

"I don't care."

"I have a feeling you know what happened to those kids."

"You have no proof of anything," she says. "Besides, I'll end up like Sulafi if I say anything."

"It might be worse if you don't talk."

She smiles bravely in defiance. "So are you going to hurt me or not?"

"Who buried me in that hole?"

"You should have never come to our neighborhood and attacked Tarek in front of his wife. Do you know how humiliating that is for a Muslim man? To be struck by a woman in front of his own wife? Everyone there is angry with you, and at all the racists in this town who want to kick us out simply because we left our war-torn country."

"Where were you on the day I was attacked?"

"I came here but you never showed. So I left."

"You never saw me?"

"No."

"I don't believe you."

"Believe what you want," she says. "So go ahead and show that video if you like. If they end up killing me like you believe they will, then my blood will be on your hands."

Her words frighten me because I know she's right.

I walk briskly out of the woods and toward the entrance to the park. As soon as I hit the trail I hear both girls shouting for help. The trail snakes back around until it ends up at the parking lot. By the time I reach my van, I realize that I'm sweating profusely. An elderly couple wanders past me before disappearing into the entrance to the woods. I climb inside the van and move to the rear, where I rip off the wig. Using a wet tissue, I wipe the makeup from my face and remove the false eyelashes. It pains me to leave Lucy behind, but I must act quickly before anyone sees her. I tie the do-rag around my head, change back into my brown contact lenses, put on my glasses, and then switch prosthetics so that I'm once again Iggy.

I arrive at my father's house more confused than ever about the state of affairs in Fawn Grove. Disappointment sets in upon realizing that I extracted nothing useful from the girl. My legs sear as I hobble through the front door. Maybe Nasreen is right and her community has been falsely demonized. Then who killed those two kids?

My father comes in after stacking wood. He sits across from me and lights up a joint. When it's lit he inhales deeply. He looks emaciated, and I wish he'd tell me what's wrong with him. After a few more hits, he leans over and offers me a toke, but I decline. I don't want to get high and lose my train of thought. I need my wits about me if I'm to figure out who killed these kids.

I turn on the radio I'd purchased and hear "Girl of My Dreams" by Angus Gibbons. Turning the knob, I find the news station and lie back on the couch.

"You okay, son? You don't look so good."

"I'm not your son anymore, Dad. Get it through your thick skull."

"Sorry," he says, taken aback by my reply. "It's going to take some time before I get used to all your changes."

"Jaxon's gone and he's never coming back. My name is Lucy now, no matter how I look to you."

"Okay, take it easy," he says. "Care to talk about what's bothering you?"

"No."

"Better time than any."

"If you'd bothered to return my calls all those years

ago, then maybe you'd know something about me," I snap.

"I was hitting the bottle pretty hard after I split from your mother. Lost my job at the mill and was down on my luck. I didn't talk to your sister for years."

"But you do now."

"We get together every so often. It's not the best of circumstances, mind you, but it works for us. In fact, I'm supposed to pick up her and Russ today. But since you got home so late, I'm clearly in no condition to drive."

"Maybe you should lay off the weed then and try to stay sober."

"Weed's the only thing keeping me going." He laughs. "Your sister and Russ have been looking to hire someone to drive them around to doctors' appointments and help them run errands. I've been doing it until they can find someone, but it's getting harder for me."

"Harder in what way?"

"Harder in that I'm not getting any younger."

"Care to tell me the real reason you left Mom after she was diagnosed with cancer?"

"It freaked me out when she came down sick. I couldn't handle the responsibility of taking over all the household duties and then dealing with her illness. I'd always wanted to play in a band. Then I lost my job at the mill and everything went to hell." He shrugs. "By the time I realized I'd screwed up, she didn't want nothing to do with me."

"You were hoping to get back with Mom?"

"Of course. Your mother was a wonderful woman who didn't deserve a hound dog like me. But it was too late for second chances." He takes another hit off the joint. "Never said I was a good father or husband. At least I was able to apologize to her before she died."

"I was only sixteen when you left. Did you have any idea how that affected me?"

"There are things I wish I could take back. Saying I'm sorry will never make it right with you, Lucy. I know that."

"You hurt me bad."

"Is that why you wanted to be a woman? Because I abandoned you and your mother?"

I break out laughing. "Hell, no, Dad. Your shitty behavior had nothing to do with my wanting to be a woman. I would have been this way no matter what you did."

"That makes me feel a little better," he says, looking relieved. "All the same, I'm sorry for the way I treated you."

"I want to forgive you, I really do."

He laughs and takes another hit.

"Maybe if you didn't smoke so much weed, you'd be more productive."

"Why don't you drive over there and help your sister out?"

"Me?"

"She pays ten bucks an hour and it's easy money. I told her she didn't need to pay me, but she insists."

"But I'd be lying to her if I went over there dressed like this."

"You're lying to everyone anyway wearing that disguise. Might as well be of some use while you're at it."

"She can't know who I am."

"Then don't tell her. I'll call and tell her I found someone to drive them around. A guy down at the diner looking to earn a few extra bucks."

"I can't believe I'm doing this."

"She's your sister and she needs you. God knows that spoiled child of hers doesn't lift a finger to help them."

"You think Brynn's spoiled?"

"Is the Pope Catholic? That girl's worse than a banana left out in the sun. She does whatever she damn well pleases and has no respect for anyone or anything. You should see the way she looks down at me whenever she comes over here. Like I'm scum of the earth."

"That's because you've never played any role in her life."

"That's no reason to be rude."

"Wendy told me she's been seeing a therapist."

"Lot of good that seems to be doing," he says. "You'd think with two disabled parents she'd try to be more understanding."

"Okay, call Wendy and tell her I'll come over."

"Iggy, right?"

"Yeah, Iggy from the diner." I watch as he takes another hit off the joint. "You should really take it easy with that stuff."

"It helps with the pain."

"What's the problem?"

"What isn't the problem?" He places the roach in the ashtray and lets it smolder. "I'll make a deal with you. You don't talk to me about smoking weed and I'll stop asking about your various issues."

"You got a deal."

25

R USS AND WENDY ARE EXPECTING ME WHEN I SHOW up at their door. Russ instructs me how to position the ramp to the van. I slide the door open and watch as Wendy guides her wheelchair up and into the van. Once inside, she secures herself using the seat belt until she's resting comfortably. Russ sits in the passenger seat, groaning painfully until all his thick limbs are stuffed inside. As soon as everyone is settled, I climb into the driver's seat and take off.

It feels odd being in this van with my sister and her husband, knowing that they have no idea who I am. I feel like Lucy dressed in a bizarre outfit that identifies me as Iggy. My normally low voice has been made even raspier from smoking pot and hacking up morning phlegm.

I turn on the radio and wait for the news to come on,

expecting to hear about the two girls attacked in the woods. I imagine that a hiker happened upon them and called the police. But no sooner do I turn it on than Russ switches the station to country music.

"Sorry, but the news depresses my wife," Russ says.

"No worries," I say, listening to a singer named Kenny Chesney.

"What'd you say your name was, fella?"

"Iggy."

"That short for Ignatius?"

I laugh. "Yeah, but no one calls me that."

"Did you know that Ignatius was a student of the Apostle John and was born in Syria?"

I shake my head.

"Don't mind my husband," Wendy says from the backseat. "He's a vessel of useless information."

"I like to keep my mind active and fully function-ing," Russ says.

"I told him he should try out for one of those trivia shows," Wendy says.

"Like *Jeopardy*," I say. "I love Alex Trebek."

"Watched this documentary last year about Ignatius. Did you know that he later became a bishop and then was martyred? Odd how some things parallel our cur-rent times."

"How so?" I ask.

"With these immigrants and the murder of those two kids."

"Now that you mention it, I suppose there are some similarities."

"How do you know my father?" Wendy asks.

"He came into the diner one day and we got talking. Asked if I wanted to make some extra money."

"That's odd," Wendy says. "My father hardly ever goes out to eat."

"That's because he spends most of his money on Mary Juwanna," Russ says, pretending to smoke a joint.

"Stop it, Russ. You know it helps with the pain," Wendy says, slapping her husband on the arm.

"What's the matter with him?" I ask.

"Cancer. Doctors say it's gotten into his bones," Russ says.

The word *cancer* sends a shudder up my spine. I suppose I should have guessed as much, but I didn't want to admit to myself how dire the situation was. The fact that it's in his bones is definitely not a good thing. I wonder how much time he has left. Do I dare ask?

"How you like working at The Galaxy?" Russ asks, thankfully changing the subject.

"Pays the bills," I say.

"My wife's sister cooked there a few times. She found it frustrating to work for that miserable Greek."

"That was your sister?" I say, glancing at Wendy in the rearview.

"I suppose you could say that."

"Damn! I got some tough shoes to fill then. Everyone at the diner tells me what an amazing chef she was. They also said she was beautiful beyond words."

"Lucy was one of the top chefs in New York City," Russ says proudly. "And she was also quite a looker."

"Can't really blame her for leaving the diner. Yanni breathes down my neck all day, cursing me out for the smallest of things. Hell, I'd leave too if someone buried me up to my chest," I say.

I park in the lot and then move Wendy down the

ramp. Russ walks with a cane and moves at the speed of an eighty-year-old. We make our way inside the supermarket and take our time shopping for the items they need. An hour later, and with the cart full, we make our way to the register. Russ explains that they like to shop every week, which is why they need someone to drive them around. Soon enough we're back in the van and heading home.

I move Wendy down the ramp and then carry all the bags inside. She tells me to rest them on the table, which I do. I stand alone in the kitchen, waiting for her to return from the living room. Am I supposed to put away the groceries? I stand awkwardly for what seems like a long time before venturing in to see if she's okay. Part of me wants to run upstairs and reclaim my old childhood bedroom. Lie down on that familiar mattress and take a long, restful nap. But instead I see Russ and Wendy huddled over Brynn, trying to comfort her. What's wrong? She's sobbing in exaggerated gasps, but as soon as she sees me standing there she stops crying and glares at me. She looks angry, as if I'm the one to blame for whatever's ailing her. I feel like slinking back into the kitchen and escaping out the back door. The TV is turned on to the news.

"Who's that?" she asks in a hostile tone.

"That's Iggy, dear. We hired him to help us run a few errands."

"Where's Grampa?"

"He wasn't feeling too well today," Russ says.

"What's wrong, sugar?" Wendy asks, cradling her daughter's head in her hands. "Why are you crying?"

"Jesus! Haven't you been listening to the news? Someone attacked my friends in Robinson Woods and left them there to die," she says, her eyes still glued to me. "What if they come after me next?"

"You know we wouldn't let anything bad happen to you," Wendy says.

Brynn laughs in a sarcastic manner. "How would you ever stop them? You're in a wheelchair. And Dad's a goddamn cripple who can barely get out of his own way."

"Don't talk like that about your father, Brynn."

"It's the truth, and you know it."

"Trust me, baby," Russ says, "we'd never let anything bad like that happen to you."

"Why is that creepy little man staring at me?" she snaps, sniffing back the tears. "Please make him go away."

"Maybe I should head out," I say, hitching my thumb over my shoulder. "Need help putting the groceries away?"

"Don't worry yourself with that," Russ says. "There should be two twenties on the table, Iggy. Thanks for all your help."

I wobble into the kitchen and see two twenty-dollar bills where he left them. Knowing that Wendy and Russ need this money more than I do, I stuff the bills into one of the utility drawers in the hope they'll find them later and forget they ever paid me. It's the least I can do for the kindness they've shown me. I slip out the back door and drive home.

All I can think about is that snotty little niece of mine and how rudely she treated her parents. Maybe Dad's right and Brynn's the one who needs to be taught a lesson.

I wonder about Brandy. Is she as spoiled as Brynn?

Has she developed an attitude problem like Stefania? I wonder if she's as pretty as those two. It must be tough to grow up with a father like Dalton and a stuck-up mother like Debbie. It's no wonder these kids drink, smoke, and act like such little jerks. Their parents are all screwed up.

Everything is quiet as my dad and I sit in his living room, listening to the fire crackle. I lie sprawled over the sofa, thinking about what my sister had said about our father. It's hard to believe that cancer has gotten into his bones and is worming its way through his frail body. It's why he spends so much time hanging around this dilapidated camp and getting stoned all day. He's preparing to die. But how much time does he have left? Months? Weeks?

Warmth emanates from the fireplace as he gets up and throws another log in the blaze. Do I dare broach the subject with him? It occurs to me that he's not been making regular visits to the hospital for chemo or radiation, or whatever they must do to fight such an illness. It tells me he's given up hope and is preparing for the worst, hoping to spend the remainder of his days in quiet solitude.

I realize that my coming home is a blessing in disguise. At least I'll be able to make peace with my father before he dies.

"Sympathy for the Devil" gives way to the news. My ears perk up as the reporter announces that two teen girls were attacked in Robinson Woods. The girls were shaken up but otherwise in good condition. The perpetrator secured the victims with nylon restraints and then used a stun gun to subdue them. The motive for the crime is not known, the reporter states, but neither girl was sexually assaulted. The police are curious if these crimes are related to the deaths of those two kids.

My cell phone rings after the news is over. "Back in Black" by AC/DC begins to play. But it's Lucy's phone that's ringing and not the cheap Tracfone I purchased for Iggy.

I wonder if I should answer it so soon after the attack. But on the third ring, I snatch it off the coffee table and stare at the caller ID in surprise. Almost immediately, my heart begins to thump.

"Lucy? It's Rick Dalton."

"Please tell me you've caught the murderer."

"Unfortunately, that's not the reason I'm calling," he says. "You sound strange, Lucy. You all right?"

"I've come down with laryngitis," I say, quick on my feet.

"Sorry to hear that."

"Look, Dalton, I'm here in New York City and you're in Maine. We both know it can't possibly work between us."

"This isn't a personal call, as much as I'd like it to be."

"What's up?"

"I don't know how to tell you this."

"Then just spit it out."

"Two girls were attacked in Robinson Woods, and both of them are saying that you were the one who assaulted them."

I burst out laughing. "That's the most absurd thing I've ever heard. How in the world could I attack them when I'm sitting here in Manhattan?"

"I don't know, but it's my duty to inform you of the accusation and follow up on it."

"What would you like me to do?"

"The chief ordered me to go down there as soon as possible and ask you a few questions. Basically, he wants me to confirm that you've been in Manhattan the entire time."

"Fine, but can't we just do this over the phone?" I say, slightly panicked.

"He'd like me to meet with you in person."

"I suppose we could do that." This is a disaster.

"Did you do it, Lucy?"

I laugh. "Do you really think I'd fly up to Maine in order to attack two teenage girls I don't even know?"

"But you do know them."

"Who are the girls?"

"I'm not at liberty to say. They're minors is all I can tell you right now."

"You're not at liberty to say, but you can call me up and accuse me of attacking them?"

"I didn't accuse you, Lucy, these two girls did. I suppose it's theoretically possible that you flew or took a bus up to Maine and then returned home. I'm not saying you did, I'm just trying to do my job."

"Then do your homework, Dalton. Check the airlines and bus lines to see if my name is on any of their passenger lists. I can assure you it isn't. I don't own a car, so you can rule that out. And you'll discover that I haven't rented one."

"There are people checking on that right now."

"Did you ever consider that these girls are lying in order to set me up?"

"We're considering every possibility."

"I can't believe this is happening." I try to sound visibly upset.

"It's merely a formality. I'm certain you'll be cleared of any wrongdoing."

"I'm the victim here. I'm the one being falsely accused," I say, raising my voice. "I was the one buried in those woods and left to die."

"The people who attacked you didn't intend for you to die. If they did, you wouldn't be here right now."

"I'm not there in Fawn Grove, which is exactly my point."

"We can meet for coffee if you like. It doesn't have to be for very long."

"I have nothing to hide. You can even talk to the guy I was hanging out with yesterday."

"A guy?"

"Take it easy, Dalton. He's just a friend."

"Okay," he says, sounding relieved. "I plan on driving down there tonight."

"Call me when you get in and we'll set up a time and place to meet."

I drop the phone in a state of panic and head for the door. I look back at my father and see that he's asleep in his chair. After finding a blank piece of paper, I scribble a note for him when he wakes up.

I need to return to Manhattan as soon as possible. But how? Dad's old van might break down along the way. It's too late to fly, and even if I could fly, I'd have to use my real ID. Then an idea comes to me that's so brilliant that I sit back and laugh. I can't believe this will be so easy.

I hop in Dad's van and drive as fast as I can over to Dalton's shitty little apartment next to the train tracks.

I stagger up to his apartment and knock three times in succession, trying to catch my breath. After a few seconds the door opens and Dalton stands there staring at me as if I pushed his mother down a flight of stairs.

"What the hell do you want?"

"It's me. Your old pal Iggy."

"I know who the fuck you are. I asked what you wanted."

"Can I come in?"

"Not a good idea right now. I'm packing for a trip." He doesn't step aside to let me in.

"Where you going?"

"New York City, not that it's any of your business," he says. "Look, I don't have time to stand around and bullshit with you. So if you don't mind, Iggy, how about taking a hike."

"I came over to see if you were okay. You drank up quite a storm the other night."

He laughs bitterly. "You my mother now?"

"No, but I was worried when I didn't see you at the diner."

"I took the day off from that shithole and ate a decent breakfast for once."

"You said some pretty crazy things to me that night."

"Get the hell inside," he says, dragging me in by the collar. He stands over his sports bag and places a folded shirt inside. "Whatever I said to you that night was in complete confidence. Understand?"

"Sure."

"Is that the only reason you came over here? To check up on me?"

"Yeah. I thought you and I kind of bonded that night."

"So we had a few laughs. Big deal."

"Hey, I really enjoyed hanging out with you."

"No offense, Iggy, but I needed a shoulder to cry on and it happened to be you that day."

I collapse on the couch, feeling the scarred tissue along my thighs burning in pain. "So, why you going away?"

"Police business."

"I bet you're going to see that girl, right?"

"Ever try minding your own business for once?"

"Never been to New York City."

"Me neither, but there's a first time for everything."

"Would you mind if I tagged along? I have money and can pay my own way."

He looks at me and laughs. "Are you for real?"

"I've hardly ever been out of Maine and always wanted to see the Big Apple, especially now that they built that 9/11 memorial."

He laughs again as if it's a stupid idea.

"I can keep you company during the long drive, and I'll pay for my own hotel and gas fare."

"We won't get in until later tonight."

"Got the day off tomorrow and nothing else to do."

He stops packing and stares at me. "Suppose I could use the company in case I get tired."

"What time you leaving?"

"Shortly."

"Mind if I go home and grab a suitcase?"

"We're only going for the day."

"That's all the time I need," I say. "Might bring back some souvenirs too. One of those 'I Love New York' T-shirts."

"Better hurry, or I'm gonna leave without you."

"Where should we meet?"

"In The Galaxy parking lot in fifteen. If you're not there, I'm gone."

"I'll be there all right. See you in a few."

I race home and grab a suitcase, then pack my wig, my makeup kit, a colorful cable-knit sweater, my black leather boots, a Ralph Lauren wool wrap coat, and my favorite square green ankle pants. Oh, and the new, taller prosthetics made specifically for Lucy. Dalton's waiting in the car, the engine running, when I get to the diner. I park the van in the back and then slip into the passenger seat next to him.

"Road trip," I say cheerfully, placing my oversized bag in the backseat.

"Hold on to your do-rag, Iggy, because I'm about to go all Indianapolis 500 on this cruiser."

"Very cool," I say. "Being a cop lets you break the speed limit, right?"

"And a license to kill when the circumstance calls for it." He laughs. "So don't tempt me."

"No way I'm gonna piss you off. Not when I got a bucket list of things to cross off in the next twenty-four hours."

*   *   *

The Maine landscape speeds past us as we barrel toward New York City. At one point I notice the speedometer hitting 100, and I fear the prospect of a moose jumping out in front of our car and smashing through the windshield. I picture our mangled bodies torn to pieces, blood spattering over the leather seats. Then the medics arrive and find my battered body, and everyone in town will learn Iggy's true identity.

Dalton drives with a grim determination, making me wonder if he's curious about the attack on those girls or merely excited to see Lucy. What will he say to her once they're sitting across from one another and staring into each other's eyes? Will he bring up that kiss?

It isn't until Connecticut that he speaks. I have to admit that I'm half asleep when he pipes up, my head leaning against the cold passenger window. I didn't want to sleep, too afraid of what I might say if I slipped into a dream state. I raise my head and blink, noticing that we're zipping along quite nicely in the left lane. It's a miracle that we haven't gotten pulled over by a state trooper.

"I have to admit, Iggy, I was shocked by how much you drank the other night."

"I told you, it's these hollow legs of mine."

"Jesus! How'd you manage to get home from the bar?"

"I crashed at your place after I drove you home and then drove your truck back to the bar the next morning."

"Really? I never even noticed you were there."

"No offense, but you didn't notice much after a certain hour."

"My head reminded me of that the next morning."

"So you going to tell me the real reason we're headed to New York City?"

"Two girls were attacked in Robinson Woods yesterday. One of them is claiming that Lucy Abbott assaulted her."

"*The* Lucy Abbott?"

"Yeah, the chef at The Galaxy you replaced."

"The same girl they found buried in those woods?"

"One and the same."

"The girl you have a major thing for?"

"What the hell are you talking about?"

I laugh. "You were drunk that night and told me how much you loved her."

"That was the booze talking."

"So you don't love her?"

"Love is a strong word." He looks sheepish. "Okay, so I like her some. There was definitely chemistry between us."

"You get lucky?" I elbow him in the arm.

"Don't be crude, asshole," he says, pointing a finger at me. "And don't even think about coming with me to meet her. This is strictly police business."

"Sure, I get it, you're all business."

"I'm serious. Go see a movie or something until it's time to go home."

"Relax. I'm getting my own hotel room. Then I'm gonna pig out at one those delis that sell those big-ass sandwiches."

"Katz."

"No Broadway shows for me. They're too expensive."

Dalton laughs. "You're a real piece of work, Iggy.

Katz is the name of the deli that serves those sandwiches. I saw it on one of those cooking shows. Corned beef and pastrami."

"That's the one."

"You can crash on the floor of my room if you like. Save a few bucks."

"No, thanks. I'm getting my own pad with a big, comfy bed."

"It'll cost you an arm and a leg in that city."

"Might never get there again, so I figure I'll treat myself."

It's eleven o'clock by the time we arrive in the city. The vitality of Manhattan still amazes me as we drive down Park Avenue. New Yorkers are out and about, hitting the bars and restaurants, waving down taxis, and walking arm-in-arm down the street. It makes me realize how much I both love and loathe this town. In my current incarnation as Iggy, I feel completely out of my element here, and it embarrasses me. I feel like a tourist in my own city, which is essentially what I am. Lucy Abbott, as sophisticated and worldly as she deigns to be, is in reality a country bumpkin from Maine.

I know Manhattan like the back of my hand, having partied in nearly every club and bar on the island. But tonight it feels foreign to me after living in Fawn Grove. It takes living outside of New York to realize how hard it is to actually survive in this crazy city. It's ridiculously expensive and overcrowded. The pace is so competitive that even the rats have stopped racing.

But then I remember the energy and the explosion of ethnic foods, the intellectual vigor of the bookshops and cafés, the driving ambition of the A-type personalities who handle the reins of finance and industry, especially the ones who work in the culinary realm. There's no better place in the world to make one's reputation than in New York.

Dalton parks alongside a hotel in midtown. A valet resembling a tin soldier comes out and takes the wheel of the unmarked cruiser. I can't imagine how much the town of Fawn Grove will be charged for the luxury of Dalton staying here for the night. Five hundred bucks? And fifty bucks for the use of valet parking? Food and drink as well? I stand warily on the sidewalk next to him as the valet driver zips down the boulevard and disappears from sight. It takes a few seconds for me to realize how much Dalton towers over me, and how tiny these prosthetics make me appear.

"You wanna go grab a drink before we hit the hay?" he asks, holding up his credit card. "Courtesy of the Fawn Grove PD."

"Nah, I read that that deli is open twenty-four seven. Enjoy your fifteen-dollar cocktail, Detective."

"Some drinking pal you are. Meet me back here tomorrow at one sharp."

"Aye, aye, Captain." I start off down the boulevard, looking for a taxi to flag down.

"Oh, and Iggy?"

I turn to face him.

"Enjoy your corned beef sandwich."

I give him two thumbs-up, throw my suitcase over my shoulder, and then wave down a cab. When I look over at the hotel, I notice that Dalton's gone.

The driver asks where I want to go, and I give him an address on the Upper East Side—a one-bedroom on Second Avenue that a good friend of mine sublets for cheap money. I met Ethan when he was Jessica at a support group for transgender people. We hit it off immediately and became best buds. When he lost his apartment, I let him crash at my pad until he found something more reasonable. I figure he owes me a favor, although I know he'll be more than happy to put me up for the night. I text him, and he agrees to leave work early and meet me in front of his apartment.

I dig into my bag with frenzied economy as the cab cruises toward the Upper East Side. I remove my brown contact lenses, put on the wig, and then make my face up in the compact mirror, knowing how disappointed Ethan would be to see me like this—a sad little man who is a throwback from a sad little mill town.

By the time we reach the ornate brownstone on Second Avenue, I'm done up as good as I'll be. Ethan's sitting on the stoop and looks amazing as he rises to greet me. He's been lifting weights and now sports a rugged beard that puts the final cap on his path to masculinity. Because of our busy lives, it's been six months since we've seen each other.

"Lucy, it's so wonderful to see you."

"Thanks for bailing me out, Ethan," I say as we embrace. Looking up at my friend, I realize that I forgot something important.

"Damn, girl! Did you shrink while living up there with the polar bears?"

"You know there's no polar bears in Maine, smartass." I laugh at this. "I'm wearing my old prosthetics."

"Shortness looks cute on you," Ethan says. "But what happened to your voice?"

"Fighting off a cold."

"Does that mean you can't join me for a beer?"

"I really wish I could, but I have to get up early and meet someone for coffee tomorrow."

"Ooooooh! Anyone special?"

"I'm sure he'd like it to be."

"But you don't like him in that way and so you're letting him down easy."

"That's the problem with me. I have no idea what I like or dislike these days. I'm still a work in progress."

"Fortunately for me, I was never confused about my preference for hot babes."

"That's the advantage to being a butch lesbian."

"Besides short haircuts and having good taste in flannel shirts?" He laughs.

"You'd fit right in in Maine wearing flannel," I say. "Are you seeing anyone new?"

"Little hottie at the gym named Caitlyn. Works at Goldman Sachs."

"A fit Wall Street girl who's good with money? Nice!"

"Wish we could catch up, Luce. I have the day off tomorrow."

"How about when I get back from Maine we'll go out and get drinks at Earl's? My treat."

"Sounds like a plan. Come on upstairs and make yourself at home. And whatever you do, don't wake me up while you're making yourself pretty."

"Creating this stunning appearance takes focus and a steady hand. Quietly is the only way I can do it."

"You know I'd do anything for you, girl."

"I know," I say, kissing his cheek. "Would you do me another big fave? If anyone calls you asking about me, would you mind telling them that I've been staying with you for the last few weeks? Oh, and that we were hanging out yesterday."

"You in trouble?"

"Not with the law. But it will be a cop who contacts you."

"Of course, Luce. I'll always vouch for a girl like you."

I push myself up off the couch two full hours before I'm to meet Dalton. He texted me late last night with the name of a coffee shop where I should meet him. I know exactly where it is. I stagger into the bathroom and stare at my tired, frazzled face. The sight of a wrinkle often sends me into a tizzy, reminding me of my age. I reach for the anti-aging cream in an attempt to stave off mortality. It's going to take at least an hour to get rid of the teabags under my eyes and the creases around my mouth. Being gorgeous doesn't come naturally to me, nor does it come quickly, although once I'm fully made up and dressed to the nines, I know I'll feel beautiful again.

I think back to my time serving in Afghanistan and how the children would run up to us on the streets, begging for a coin or a sweet treat. Many of them were homeless, their parents either killed in the war or imprisoned by warlords. They would plead for us to take them back to America whenever we left that godforsaken land. Recalling those days, it makes me feel fortunate to have been born in such a great country and to have survived that disastrous war mostly intact. Survival, to me, has always meant pursuing the life I was meant to live and being the best woman I can be. I think of all the injured and dying soldiers I tended to on the battlefield, and how it pained me to know that many would never come home to fulfill their own hopes and dreams.

Tears threaten my mascara, and I must wipe away what I've painted and start again. Lipstick. Eyeshadow. Eyelashes. Rouge applied carefully along the high cheekbones like Michelangelo painting the Sistine Chapel. Doing this makes them look more elongated and prominent. False eyelashes that equaled my own. Then the red wig gets applied meticulously so that it will stay in place in the event of a midtown gust. I attach the prosthetics, and like that I'm tall and graceful once again. Square green ankle pants that fit me to a T and accentuate my lean figure. Leather boots with three-inch heels that, with the aid of my prosthetics, lift me to a stately height of five foot nine. Last, I adorn myself with a black Ralph Lauren wool wrap coat. Once I'm done, I check myself in the full-length mirror tacked to the back of Ethan's bathroom door. Drop-dead gorgeous! I actually feel sorry for Dalton. Poor lovestruck Dalton having to deal with me on *my* turf. It must hurt to be pitted against a woman like me, knowing that he's doomed to live the rest of his life in Fawn Grove.

I move quietly throughout the apartment, trying not to make any noise that might wake Ethan. Chefs don't get much sleep, so when we're allowed the opportunity, we take it to the hilt. I scrawl a thank-you note for him, brand it with a kiss, and then tiptoe down the stairs.

New York is alive at this hour, and the burst of early morning energy lends itself to optimism and endless possibilities. I move to the curb, luxuriating in my gorgeous identity but knowing that I'll hardly stand out in this town of beauty queens and supermodels. Making myself up in such a startling manner compensates for my many insecurities in life. The weight of those two dead kids falls easily from my shoulders like a distant memory. I know this feeling is fleeting, and that I will eventually return to Fawn Grove and grieve for them, but for now fabulous feels liberating.

The physical act of hailing down a taxi never fails to enthrall me. I snag one almost immediately and park myself in the backseat, drawing frantic looks in the rearview mirror from the obese immigrant sitting behind the wheel. He's Indian or Pakistani and happy to oblige my starved ego by ogling me. I give him directions to the coffee shop, and we arrive in less than five minutes. I stride nervously toward the cafe after leaving the cabbie a ridiculous tip. A quick glance in the compact assures me of my exquisiteness. I practice speaking so that I'll sound more like Lucy, although with a slight case of laryngitis. My heels click loudly on the pavement as I approach the front door.

As soon as I enter, I see Dalton sitting off in the corner, looking like a lost soul in a faraway land. I take a deep breath to keep my heartbeat steady. He stands as soon as he sees me, his mouth agape, his black hair plastered in *Mad Men* style to one side. I have to admit that he looks rather dashing today, and in the right clothes he might actually appear fashionable. I walk over and sit across from him, my heart pounding, remembering that amazing kiss we shared at the bus station. A confident smile is etched over my caked face. Dalton asks what I'd like to drink, and I order the priciest coffee on the menu. A few minutes later he returns clutching two mugs, his eyes glued to me.

"Compliments of Fawn Grove's finest," he says, placing the cup down in front of me.

"Salud," I say, toasting him.

"I must say, Lucy, you look stunning. This town seems to bring out the best in you."

"Why, thank you, Dalton," I say rather sweetly. "But I thought you said this visit was all business."

"Am I not allowed to compliment you?"

"Knock yourself out, then." I laugh and cross my legs.

"I know this is awkward, me coming all the way to interview you about this silly allegation."

"Not in the least. Okay, maybe it's a little weird, but it's still nice to see you. The fact that you don't trust me has nothing to do with our friendship."

"Trusting you is not the issue. The chief ordered me to come down here and confirm your physical presence. This case is so messed up that we have to follow every lead possible."

"So these idiotic teenage girls claimed that I attacked them in Robinson Woods?" I make a show of laughing. "That's so bizarre, Dalton, that I don't even know where to begin."

"Kids, right?"

"But why make up something so outlandish?"

"That's what I want to know. These two seemed convinced that you were the one who attacked them."

"I bet they did, despite the fact everyone in town knows that I've been living in Manhattan the entire time."

"Please don't be offended at the questions I'm about to ask."

"I'll certainly try not to."

"Where were you yesterday?"

"Hanging out at Ethan's apartment on the Upper East Side."

"Ethan a close friend of yours?"

"If you're asking if he's my boyfriend, the answer is no."

He appears relieved at this answer. "Would you mind giving me his contact information so I can check everything out?"

"Of course." I scribble Ethan's name and number down. "How are you holding up, Dalton? You don't look so well."

"I've had better days."

"Sorry to hear that."

"You, on the other hand, sound like shit."

"Laryngitis, so don't get too close to me unless you want a souvenir to bring home."

He shrugs and then stares at his notebook.

"What's new in Fawn Grove? Yanni find another cook?"

He glances up at me and laughs. "You're not going to believe this, but he hired this little troll named Iggy. You should see this chump."

"Is he a decent chef?"

"The worst ever. But beggars can't be choosy. Ever since the Denny's burnt down, The Galaxy's been busier than it has been in years."

"The Denny's burnt down?"

"They think it's arson."

"The crowds won't stay long once they get a taste of Yanni's food."

"Not once Denny's is rebuilt."

"Damn shame they're wasting such a golden opportunity to win over new customers."

"So tell me how you're doing."

"I'm not going to lie to you, Dalton. Being buried in those woods really messed me up. There's been more than a few sleepless nights. I've actually been thinking about seeing a therapist."

"That's funny you say that, because I've been thinking about doing the same thing. Seeing a therapist, I mean."

"Because you're so depressed that I'm gone?"

He laughs. "Don't flatter yourself. I've got my own issues to deal with."

"You? The great Detective Dalton from the Fawn Grove PD?" I say. "What issues could you possibly have?"

"For starters, my life's a mess. I've got a delinquent daughter who's been brainwashed by her mother and refuses to have anything to do with me unless she needs money. Then there's the image of these two dead kids that keeps replaying in my head. One with her face smashed in and the other with his head nearly decapitated. I've also been hitting the bottle more than I should."

"Self-medicating." I recall all the wounded and depressed vets I'd encountered who'd sought solace in the bottle. "So tell me, why would these girls make up such a blatant lie about me?"

"No idea. Maybe they want to get you in trouble, for whatever reason."

I sip my coffee. "Any developments with these murders?"

"No, but I'm fairly certain that one of those immigrants is responsible for those kids' deaths. Now I just have to prove it."

"Based on what?"

"They formed the sign of Islam in that cornfield, the same sign that was scrawled over your windshield. Isn't that enough evidence?"

I shrug. "So who were the girls that fingered me?"

"I told you over the phone, Lucy, I'm not at liberty to say."

"Come on, Dalton. I could make a phone call right now and find out their names."

"Okay, but you didn't hear it from me."

"Of course."

"It was the girl from the Afghani market and Stef. The two of them were strolling in the woods that afternoon when the attack happened."

"Stefania?" I act shocked. "What did she say?"

"Said she didn't get a good look at her attacker but that she recognized your voice. Said you identified yourself as Miss Fancy-Pants. Then claimed you used a stun gun on her before securing her wrists and ankles with nylon restraints."

"That's nuts!"

"I know. Same with the immigrant girl. Only she swore that she looked you in the eye and spoke with you."

"What's wrong with these kids?" I glance around the café. "Think it could have been someone made up to look like me?"

He smiles.

"What?"

"Take this however you want, Lucy, but there's no one in Fawn Grove who looks quite like you."

"I'll take that as a compliment."

"You should."

"So you drove all this way by your lonesome just to ask about my whereabouts?"

"I actually drove here with that new line cook I was telling you about. Said he's never been to New York before and begged to take him with me. Figure it was better than driving all this way by myself."

"I'd love to meet him and catch up on all the diner gossip."

"Sorry, but he took off on his own. Said he wants to explore the city."

"Can't you call him back?"

He shakes his head.

"Too bad. That might have been fun chatting with him," I say. "Yanni will eventually run him off the line too."

"No great loss. He isn't the best or brightest cook Yanni's ever hired, that I can tell you."

"How's Nadia doing?"

He shrugs. "Nadia and I, as you might already know, have never seen eye to eye on matters. I guess we ran in different circles growing up."

"Still, she's a good person, right?"

"Yeah, I suppose. But if you ask me, she seems more concerned about helping these damn freeloaders than she is about raising that smart-ass daughter of hers."

I bite my tongue at this racist remark and wonder how I ever could have been so attracted to him. "What about her husband?"

"She should have kicked Niko to the curb years ago. I never liked that guy, going all the way back to high school. I had to teach that punk a lesson one day out in the school parking lot."

"You and Niko fought?"

"Wasn't much of a fight."

"Poor Nadia."

"Nadia's made her own bed," he says. "I still don't know why those girls would make up such a lie if they knew you were living in New York."

"We both know that Stefania hates my guts."

He laughs. "It's not just you she hates. That girl hates most people she comes in contact with."

"But she seemed especially hostile to me. I think it was because I don't live in Fawn Grove."

"Assuming you're right, what would they stand to gain by such a lie?"

"No idea," I say. "Who else is close to Stefania?"

"Her mother and maybe some of her friends at school."

"You said Nadia works with the immigrants?"

"These immigrants have given her not only prominence in town but job security."

"Not when two kids end up dead in what is believed to be a pair of honor killings. I imagine that people in town are angry with her."

"Maybe so, but have you seen her agency's coffers since that first murder? They've increased their federal grants and donations threefold."

"How do you know that?"

"It was reported in the local newspaper," he says. "The rest of the people in town are hurting and losing jobs, and yet they keep giving more money to these ingrates."

"Are you implying that Nadia's in it for the money?"

"No, that's not what I'm saying. We may not be friends, but right or wrong, Nadia believes that what she's doing is right. I'm just explaining how her agency benefitted from these immigrants coming here."

"So that brings us full circle."

"I have to assume that Stef and that Afghani girl were lying about you. But for what reason, I don't know. Maybe someone they know at school attacked them and they're fearful of turning them in."

"Or they set it up to make me look like the culprit."

"Another possibility."

"So where does that leave us?"

"Right back where we started."

I drink the rest of my coffee and stand to leave. My mission here has been accomplished. Little does he know that I hitched a ride with him and then convinced him that I was in New York City the entire time. I can't help but think how brilliant I am. As much as it pains me, I need to quickly clean myself up and return to being Iggy so I can catch a ride with him back to Fawn Grove.

"Do you have to leave so soon?" Dalton says, standing like the gentleman he believes himself to be.

"I have a busy day in front of me. I'm still looking for work, and to the best of my knowledge, I believe I sufficiently answered all your questions about my whereabouts."

"You passed with flying colors," he says. "Can I at least walk you to the sidewalk?"

I shrug noncommittally. "I don't see why not."

"It really warms my heart when you say it with such passion."

"We're living hundreds of miles apart, Dalton. It's not like anything will ever happen between us."

"I know, but a little enthusiasm never hurts, especially after the way we parted back in Fawn Grove."

"We both know that kiss was a mistake."

"If it was, it was a mistake I wouldn't mind repeating."

We move outside, standing on the sidewalk as the river of Manhattanites streams past us. New York has transformed yet again into a swirling mass of humanity where people are born, live, and die on this overpopulated island purchased for pennies on the dollar. I flip my hair over my shoulder, stare at all the tall buildings down the street, and demonstrate my cosmopolitan flair.

"I've never met anyone quite like you, Lucy."

I laugh and glance briefly at one of the shawarma street carts. "Honestly, I never know whether you're teasing or paying me a compliment."

"Oh, it's a compliment all right," he says. "I've really missed you."

"What about all those desperate housewives back in Fawn Grove? I'm sure one of them would love to hook up with an officer in uniform."

"But none of them like you."

"Come on, Dalton. Don't make this any harder on me."

He smiles. "It's Detective, remember?"

"Maybe you'll be promoted to police chief in a few years, assuming you solve these murders."

"Tell me what I can do to get you back there."

"I'll not even consider returning to Fawn Grove until those two murders are solved."

"Then I promise you I'll crack them," he says. "And when I do, you should come home and take over The Galaxy."

"With what? My good looks?" I laugh at such nonsense.

"I'm sure some sort of financing deal could be arranged, seeing how that place has such historic significance."

"Nice to see you, Dalton. I really must be going."

I turn and stride purposefully down the sidewalk until I disappear into the crowd. I can barely breathe I'm so flustered. Good thing I told him I had laryngitis, because I don't think I could handle another kiss of that magnitude.

26

*T*HEN I'M BACK TO BEING IGGY JUST LIKE THAT, THE transition not as carefree and breezy as I expected. I feel like an actor playing multiple roles while trying to keep everything in check.

Dalton picks me up on the agreed-upon street corner just after one in the afternoon. I climb in next to him, and we drive back to Maine in relative silence. Prior to meeting him, I'd dashed over to Katz's and ordered the biggest sandwich on the menu, half of which I gave to a homeless guy on the street. The other half I stashed in my bag as proof of having been there. I glance over at Dalton as we drive out of the city. The look on his face is tortured, as if someone wearing stilettos had stomped on his heart and pierced a hole through it.

In many ways the silence between us is a good thing. I find it bizarre to be sitting in this police car next to him after how we parted ways. He still loves me. Or I should say he loves Lucy Abbott. And yet he thinks this Iggy character I've inhabited is a total chump worthy of laughter and derision. It almost makes me feel sorry for both Dalton and this sad fictional person I've created. This dorky, lovable loser named Iggy.

In many ways, Dalton remains a complete mystery to me. Has he changed for the better, or is this version merely a continuation of his sorry past? A bully in a cop's uniform? Or a cop who was once a bully? What's a bully after all but an insecure person who's been wounded by the people closest to him? That could apply to just about anyone, myself included. My sense of insecurity comes from a deep misunderstanding of who I was growing up. No, who I was meant to be. It's like the phantom pain I occasionally experience in my legs; the real me was never there to begin with, but merely a ghost inhabiting the role of Lucy. Jaxon was the closest to my true self, and he hurt me. Not intentionally, but his mere existence hurt me in more ways than I care to admit. More than Dalton and my deadbeat dad combined. More than the jihadists who blew my legs off and killed that innocent girl from the fruit stand. Only when I finally became Lucy Abbott did Jaxon cease to cause me any pain. He vanished, and yet somehow I couldn't totally extricate him from my being.

Knowing what I know now, Jaxon's actions were those of a confused, angry boy lashing out at others. He inflicted pain on himself and those around him as a cry for help. Then he joined the army to try to right his wrongs, all under the guise of serving his country, when in reality he was fighting an all-out war with himself.

Despite the intensity of his conflicted feelings toward his gender, Jaxon found a girlfriend and thought that might solve his issues. Only it made everything worse, because it felt unnatural, and by making it worse he increasingly sought refuge in his hidden desires. Every time he walked past the beauty parlor, he felt envy mixed with guilt. Every time he locked himself into his room with his sister's makeup kit and one of her party dresses, he experienced tremendous bouts of self-loathing. And yet Jaxon would stare at the girl in the mirror and know that this was who she was supposed to be. Then he mistakenly believed that by joining the army and leaving town, his masculinity would be restored and his life saved. But when that didn't work he was out of options, save death. He could help others but not himself. At first he wished that roadside bomb had killed him. It took some time before he realized that the bomb that killed and maimed him and his fellow soldiers had actually saved his life.

Dalton drops me off in front of The Galaxy just after ten. All the lights are off and it's eerily quiet. So different from the big city I call home. The disparity between Fawn Grove and Manhattan suddenly hits me like the weight of a dropped anvil. The city fostered my anonymity. It nurtured my gender transition and allowed me the space to breathe while I fit into my new skin. On this most recent visit, the city told something else: It released me into the air and told me to fly. Fly, Lucy, fly.

Oddly enough, Fawn Grove seems the place I should be right now. Like the recently arrived Afghanis, I too am an immigrant in this town. A sexual refugee from a hostile land. Death seems an apt metaphor in many ways, because if I go back from where I came

I most certainly will die. I hope I can finally shed the remaining bits of my past so that Lucy can prosper and bloom. This body is only big enough for one person.

"Thanks for the lift. Crossed another item off my bucket list."

"Glad you enjoyed yourself, Iggy."

"Hope you had a little fun too," I say with a wink and a smile.

"Like I said, strictly police business."

"Which means it's none of my business whether you got lucky or not," I say.

"Damn straight it's none of your business."

"Think I'll go home and polish off the rest of my sandwich."

"How was it, by the way?"

"Amazing! You shoulda seen that place."

"Maybe I'll go back there someday and try one."

"The pastrami was so pink and juicy."

"Get your mind out of the gutter, Iggy," he says, before driving away.

I toss the remainder of my sandwich in the Dumpster. Salty smoked meat piled four inches high is not my idea of fine dining.

All the lights are off in my father's place by the time I arrive at his cabin. I pull into the dirt driveway and make my way inside, but my father's nowhere to be seen. I go into his room and see him lying on the bed. His bong sits on the nightstand next to him, and he waves when he sees me.

"You okay, Dad?"

"Don't feel so hot tonight."

"Anything I can do for you?"

"A prayer'd be nice, although I never did believe in God."

"You need me to take you to the ER?"

"Probably just a little indigestion," he lies. "You're a good daughter, Lucy. Now close the door and let me rest."

It touches me that he thinks of me as his daughter, despite the clown outfit I'm wearing. I shut the door to his room, knowing full well that his days on this earth are numbered. But referring to me as Lucy will be something I'll always remember. The fact that he called me his daughter not only is touching but also feels as if progress is being made. It makes me want to stay in this town and nurture that kind of tolerance in others. The kind of tolerance that the God-fearing and the godless will share and respect in kind. Respect for one another and our freedom to love the way we've always desired to love. And be loved in return.

I lie down on the couch, completely exhausted from that road trip with Dalton, and consider all that's happened. I fall asleep with these thoughts swirling around in my brain, hoping that tonight they might crowd out the voices that have long taken hold of it.

My father is fast asleep when I wake up the next morning. I put the back of my hand to his forehead and check his temperature. Normal. On the nightstand sits his battalion of orange pill bottles. Most of them are full, which tells me he's abandoned all hope and is self-medicating with weed until the time comes for him to exit this life. At this stage in the game, does it really matter?

I work a full shift at the diner, pumping out meal after shitty meal until the misery comes to an end. Dalton didn't come in this morning, and I can't say I blame him. It was a long journey to and from New York City, and I bet he slept in, having heard what he needed to from Lucy. I try to talk to Nadia when she comes in, if only to hear the sound of her familiar voice, but she has no patience for me, a short-order cook from the sticks who struggles to make a simple omelette. Nadia's refusal to pay me any attention hurts more than anything else, although I know why she's doing it. I keep thinking she loves me, but then I have to remind myself who I'm disguised as.

I have no doubt that Dalton was tossing around theories and considering every possibility. Nadia would be the last person I'd ever suspect of hurting someone. In many ways, I still love her. Maybe not romantic love, but surely the love one has for a sister or close friend. She knows more about me than anyone. We made awkward love as teenagers, unfulfilling as it was unsatisfying. We learned about sex as we went along, without a video or manual, the secrecy of our flawed intimacy its own private reward.

I go home that afternoon to find my father sitting in his recliner and looking pale and sickly. I shudder to think that he might be closer to death than expected. Death seems to be the motif in my life. Everything in my vicinity is dropping off into that black spiral where nothing returns in its original form.

He assures me he's all right and that I should go about my normal business. Wendy called the diner earlier and asked if I'd take her to the hairdresser this afternoon. So I drive over and pick her up, watch as she motors up the ramp and into the van. She talks on and on about the most inane matters, and I try hard to listen, obliging her by nodding my head nonstop while she rambles on. She rewards me with an extra five-dollar tip at the end of the day.

Three boring days of this when I should be out doing something more useful. It's driving me crazy. Dalton comes into the diner on the third day but pays no attention to me. I take Russ to Buck's Comics that afternoon and wait patiently in the van as he spends over an hour scanning comic books. I sit with the key in the ignition, listening to music, my head resting on my numb hand. The news comes on and a reporter says something that stuns me. An unnamed immigrant has been charged with the murder of those two kids. What's this? I lay on the horn for Russ to come out.

"Jesus, Iggy, what's your damn rush? I wasn't finished searching through all the *Spawn* comics," he says after settling in his seat.

"Sorry, boss, but something's come up." I turn off the radio so as not to upset him.

"Everything okay?"

"Not sure."

I pick up speed through the center of town when I see something that jars me. I slow the van down and watch as four college students walk over the crosswalk, their hands moving rapidly in quick bursts of energy: American Sign Language! It gets me thinking, and my brain starts to process the myriad thoughts running through my head. I wonder if that Afghani man I encountered on Blueberry Hill murdered those two kids. He seemed radical enough to commit such a crime. Something in my gut tells me that he lacks the calm temperament to bury and stone a person to death. Or execute a crop circle after killing that boy. I could be wrong. I probably *am* wrong. But I think I've figured out a way to learn more about these murders, thanks to these deaf students walking across the street.

"Why the hell you slowing down, son? There's a line of cars behind you beeping up a storm."

"Sorry."

"You act like you've never seen a bunch of deaf kids before."

"It got me thinking about something."

"Care to divulge?"

"Not really." I step on the gas.

"You're a strange fellow, Iggy."

"Tell me something I don't already know."

"Despite all your quirks, you're kind of growing on me."

"Thanks. I guess."

"Don't ever guess, son, when you can use your brain. It's always best to use inductive and deductive reason like Sherlock Holmes did."

"I'll certainly remember that the next time I'm solving a murder."

"One never knows, Iggy."

I drop him off at his house and speed off before he can say good-bye or offer up any more of his long-winded theories. I glance in the rearview mirror and watch as he clutches his collection of comic books and hobbles up the steps.

My father is outside and carrying some logs when I pull up to the cabin. In his condition, I know he shouldn't be exerting himself too strenuously. I go over and help him. He says not a word to me as we carry the logs back and forth from the yard and to the side of the house. Despite being exhausted, I continue to work until we have a healthy stack of wood piled high for the winter. But will he make it that long?

He collapses into his recliner once we're inside and asks if I'll make him some herbal tea. I can barely contain my excitement at what I've uncovered. A sense of empowerment sweeps over me as I pour boiling water over the green tea bag. I hand him the cup, grab my cell phone, and settle onto the couch.

It amazes me that I didn't think of it before. I turn on my phone and find the video I recorded in that darkened cornfield. It's been waiting all this time to be examined and interpreted. I press play and begin to watch as the kids drink and smoke pot at the scene of the crime. The fire burns between them, providing just enough light to reveal their youthful faces.

I replay the video over and over, trying to accustom myself to everything that occurred. At one point during the party, Stefania stands in front of the fire, bottle in hand, and speaks to the others. It's mesmerizing to watch her in action, especially with her gorgeous face lit up by the flames. I wonder what she's saying to those other kids or whether she's merely rambling on in drunken fashion.

I'm not sure how I had the wherewithal to zoom in on them, but I'm glad I did. There's no sound because I was too far away, but that's beside the point. Their conversation would not have been picked up anyway. After ten minutes of watching the video, I shut off my phone and lie back on the couch. I feel dizzy, but confident, and completely ready for what I need to do come morning.

The muscles in my arm ache from carrying all that firewood. I haven't done that much exercise since I was in the army, when I used to jog five miles a day and do push-ups and sit-ups. Back when I could perform medical tasks tirelessly and for long periods of time.

I need to have one last conversation before I lay my head down and fall asleep. I grab my phone and make my way into the bedroom. Calling Dalton is a pretty rotten thing to do, but I need to stay on his good side if I'm to learn the truth about these matters. And if that means Lucy Abbott must sweet-talk him every so often, then so be it. I punch his number into my phone, and he picks up after the third ring.

"Lucy?"

"Congrats, Dalton. I heard you've arrested a suspect. Tell me it's true."

"How did you find out so soon?" He sounds like he's been drinking.

"My cousin told me. So it's true?"

"Nothing's certain yet, but it looks like we have a strong case against this guy."

"Innocent until proven guilty, I thought."

"He's not even a citizen. What we should really do is treat him as if he's a foreign enemy."

"Is he talking?"

Dalton laughs. "You know I can't tell you that."

Do I hear a trace of doubt creeping into his voice? "You don't sound overly confident."

"We found a knife in his trunk with dried blood on

it. The state police lab is testing it right now to see if the blood belongs to the dead boy."

"Case closed if it does, right?"

"Proceed with caution is about the best advice an old detective ever gave me," he says. "Hey, it was nice seeing you the other day."

"Likewise."

"Once these murders get cleared up, maybe you can come back to town and pay us a visit."

"Who knows, Dalton, you might be seeing me sooner than you think."

"If only I could be so lucky."

But you are.

I hang up the phone and return to the couch. Upon looking up, I notice that my father has fallen asleep with a doobie in hand. I stick the joint in the ashtray before he burns the cabin down. The vision of him consumed in a pyre of his own making passes through my mind. Maybe it wouldn't be such a bad thing for him to go out in a blaze of glory. There's certainly worse ways to die, and cancer is at the top of most people's list. As is being buried up to your neck and watching as the stones start to fly.

27

I CAN BARELY LOOK AT STEFANIA THIS MORNING WHEN she brings back the first ruined plate of scrambled eggs. I left them on the flattop too long so that brown spots appeared through and through. She cusses me out before flinging the plate across the room. It smashes against the far wall and all the food spills off the plate, making a mess everywhere, which I'll later be forced to clean up. Instead of leaving, she approaches me with two fists clenched by her side. Her lips are a fierce two-inch slit of nubile pinkness. For a brief second I fear she's going to strike me. With or without Yanni here to run things, this vessel called The Galaxy is a rudderless shipwreck waiting to capsize.

Stefania stands in my way, blocking my path to the refrigerator. When I move to the side, she moves along with me. She's many inches taller than me and intimidating for a fifteen-year-old girl. When she stares down, it's as if she really wants to pummel me into submission.

"What the hell do you think you're doing?"

"I need to scramble more eggs for that order. So if you'll excuse me."

"Screw the eggs. You're the worst cook I've ever seen."

"Thanks for the vote of confidence," I say. "Now I really need to get back to work."

"I get the feeling you're screwing these orders up on purpose, Iggy. No one can be that dumb."

"Why would I do that? I need this job."

"You tell me, jerk-off."

"Swear to God I'm doing my best."

"Are you trying to ruin my grandfather's diner on purpose?" She puts her face close to mine.

"No! How could you even think that?"

"There's something weird about you, Iggy, if that's even your real name. How is it you suddenly appear out of nowhere, acting all chill and offering me weed and in need of a job?"

"I have no idea what you're talking about."

"Brynn says you're driving her parents around town and helping them run errands. What's that all about?"

"Earning some extra cash on the side."

"Bull! I might just tell Dalton about all the joints you've been smoking out back. And that you offered me some."

"You gonna narc on me? Especially after I shared my weed with you?"

"No, I'm going to narc on you for trying to ruin my papou's diner."

I work the rest of my shift in relative silence, careful

to stay out of Stefania's way. Why is she suddenly being so mean to me? I need to hold my tongue for fear of being uncovered. What I'd really like to do is drag that girl out back and teach her a lesson she won't soon forget. It's obvious that Nadia has lost control of her daughter. Or maybe she never asserted control over her in the first place. I wonder if Nadia has any idea how badly she behaves when she's not around.

Once the lunch rush is over, and I've finished scrubbing the kitchen clean, I grab the envelope of cash that Yanni has left for me and head out. Dalton is sitting in his police car with the engine running when I emerge. It'd be rude to walk past him without saying hello. For some strange reason, I get the distinct impression that he's been waiting all this time for me to show up.

"Hey," I say, looking into his window.

"Get in the back, Iggy."

"Am I in trouble?"

"We need to talk."

I open the door and sit nervously in the backseat while Dalton finishes typing something into his computer. A police report? Summons? All of this fresh animosity worries me.

"You a junkie?"

I laugh. "Don't you have more important things to worry about?"

"Just answer my question."

"Hell, no, I'm no junkie."

"Stef said she saw you smoking pot by the Dumpster and that you offered her some. Is that true?"

"Just the part about me smoking by the Dumpster. Helps calm my nerves after dealing with Yanni all morning."

"Just because we had a few beers the other night doesn't make us friends."

"I know that. I just figured you were being nice to me."

"You think I'm going to look the other way when you're doing something illegal?"

"I thought weed was legal in Maine."

He sighs impatiently. "The point is, just because I'm a nice guy doesn't mean I'm a pushover. I'm not going to let you get away with anything just because you and I had a few beers. Understand?"

"Of course."

"Better not hear you're offering weed to minors or else you'll regret it. Smoke that shit at home, because if I catch you with it here I'm going to bust your ass."

I nod.

He sits staring at me in the rearview for longer than I'd like. "She called last night."

"Who called?"

"Lucy. Said she might consider coming back now that we've got a suspect."

"That's great news, Detective. But are you sure you got the right guy?"

He shakes his head in disgust. "Of course I have the right guy."

"How do you know for sure?"

"Didn't you watch the news? We got an anonymous call, and when we got there we found him pushing his female cousin around. She works at the Afghani grocery and was one of the two girls attacked in Robinson Woods."

"So you believe he was the one who attacked Stefania and her friend, and they were too afraid to finger him?" I say.

"Exactly. When we searched his car we found the knife in his trunk with the victim's blood on it. And we also found some boots we're testing for cornstalk residue."

"Maybe someone planted the knife on him."

"What the hell are you talking about, Iggy?" he shouts angrily. "Maybe you should try working on your damn cooking skills before you start lecturing me on police work. Now get out of my car."

I jump out and head toward my van parked in the back lot. But before I can make my way to it, Stefania stands in my path, blocking me from reaching it. Her wiry arms are crossed and she's smiling so sweetly that it worries me. This can only be bad news. She holds her hand out as if to shake. I take it and let my palm go limp in hers.

"I'm really sorry about what I said to you in there, Iggy. I was just upset."

"Why'd you tell Dalton I was smoking pot?"

"Can never be too careful in this town. Wanted to see if you were one of those perverts who gives kids weed and then molests them."

"You think I'd do something like that?"

"Like, duh! Two of my classmates are dead and I was just attacked in Robinson Woods. Think I want to end up like them?"

"Why don't you just leave me alone and let me live my life," I say.

"You and Dalton seem pretty tight."

I continue toward the van but she runs out in front of me.

"Seems weird considering that no one has ever seen you in town before. How long have you two been friends?"

"What do you know about friendship? You're just a kid."

"I know a lot more about friendship than you think," she says, tugging down on her friendship earring. "And I also know most everything that goes on in this town."

"Enough to ruin a guy like me." I walk past her.

"I said I'm sorry, Iggy," she says, grabbing my elbow.

"Empty words."

"I want to make it up to you. Remember that party I told you about? Well, a few of us are getting together tonight. Will you swing by and join us?"

"Why should I do that after what you told Dalton?"

"I've already apologized. What more do you want from me?"

"To leave me alone."

"I'd hate to make up some lame story about how you tried to cop a feel from me in the kitchen. Who do you think they're going to believe?"

I turn and glare at her. "You wouldn't?"

"Oh, I most certainly would," she says. "Come on, dude. We just want to have a little fun. I bet you liked to party back in the day."

"Still do."

"So you'll come?"

"Do I have a choice?"

"Not really," she says, smiling. "Oh, and Iggy?"

"What?"

"Bring a bottle of booze with you. And a bag of that killer weed too."

She tells me where to meet her before I jump in the van and pull away. When I look in the rearview mirror, I see Stefania standing in the middle of the parking lot with her wiry arms crossed and a big smile over her face.

These deaf students suddenly appear everywhere in town, walking around and gesturing with their hands. Is it because I'm only now noticing them? The school has always been like an invisible beacon up on that hill, but when I was a kid most of the students kept to themselves and hardly ever ventured into town. There was nothing much for them to do down here except mingle with townsfolk and be ignored. Different times, I suppose. The hearing impaired back then were about as welcome in Fawn Grove as a beauty queen from Manhattan. It's nice to know that some things in this town have changed for the better. Everything being equal, I'd like to think that a person such as Lucy Abbott would be welcomed back with open arms.

I walk into the coffee shop and wave to my two old classmates. Of course they have no idea who I am, but they wave back in a friendly manner, as if I'm one of their regulars. Surprisingly, the place is empty. But I'm sure that will soon change.

After ordering a coffee and croissant, I sit in the corner thinking about how I'll pose my question. Thirty minutes pass in silence before three students from Dunham College walk in and sit by the window. Two girls and a guy. To my untrained eyes, it looks as if they're swatting flies out of their faces. Their hands move so rapidly from one sign to the next that it boggles the mind that they can understand one another. Barb walks over and takes their order, and I hear their overly strained voices. They speak in that strange manner of deaf people—loud and with a noticeable lisp.

Approaching these students will require tact and diplomacy. I considered going directly to the college but didn't think it a good idea in my current disguise. There's no way they'd take a guy like Iggy seriously. Not to mention that I didn't want to get any college officials involved in the case, which could further complicate matters. I need to do this the right way, quietly and under the radar.

After a few nerve-racking minutes, I head over to their table. The students freeze when they see me approaching. It's not quite a look of fear in their eyes as it is the cautionary gaze one gives another when an outsider tries to infiltrate the tribe. As a person who's lived most of her life as an outsider, I know this feeling all too well. It's a circling-the-wagons mentality. I'm an interloper into the exclusionary world of the hearing impaired, and I'm definitely not welcome.

The students stare up at me, waiting to see what I have to say. I stand awkwardly, wondering how to broach the subject. I have no knowledge of sign language and can only hope that one of them reads lips.

"Can anyone help me?" I say.

The students glance at me before signing to one another. I have no idea what they're saying and wait patiently until they're through. It feels odd being the subject of their conversation and yet knowing nothing about what they're saying. I'm not your average Fawn

Grove citizen. When they look at me, they likely see a diminutive, doe-eyed gimp wearing a red do-rag, black-rimmed glasses, a Metallica concert T-shirt, and skull earrings.

"What's up?" the guy says in that muted way.

"I was wondering if maybe you could help me with something," I overarticulate.

"With what?" he says, his eyes staring at me with a puzzled expression.

"I'm assuming you read lips?"

"You're sharp." He turns to the others and signs, and they laugh at my expense.

"I was wondering if you could translate something for me. I'll pay you."

"Depends on what it is and how much."

I pull out my phone and show him the video I took of the kids in the cornfield. It's thirteen minutes and twenty-three seconds. He doesn't hit the play button, but instead hands it back to me.

"That's a lot of work," he says.

"I'll give you fifty bucks."

He signs to the others, and they sign something back in reply. "Where do you want me to do it?"

I point to my table.

"Payment up front."

I hand him two twenties and a ten, and he leaves the others and walks back with me to my table. Once we're seated, I take out a notebook and pass him my phone. I tell him to write it all down. Before he watches, I make him promise to keep this information to himself. After a few seconds reflecting on what he's about to do, he agrees to my terms. Then he presses play.

He begins to scribble down what's being said, occasionally stopping to look up at me. When the video finishes playing, he stares at me in a strange fashion. Three pages of scrawled notes lie in front of him.

"Thank you," I say, taking the phone off the table.

"This is messed up, dude."

"I know, but you promised to keep this to yourself."

"You need to do something."

"Why do you think I hired you?" I take out another twenty and hand it to him. He pockets it and then heads back to his friends. Soon enough they're signing and laughing and drinking from their mugs of coffee.

I grab his notes and start to read them.

28

I DON'T WANT TO LEAVE MY FATHER TONIGHT. HE'S gotten a second wind and his complexion seems healthier and more robust than before. But I can tell it's only a temporary stay of execution, because otherwise he appears to be going downhill. We sit together in the living room eating a simple supper of elbow macaroni with black pepper, butter, and shaved parmigiana cheese. The news is on, and they show footage of the accused Afghani man being led to the station for questioning. Not surprisingly, it's the same guy I encountered that day on Blueberry Hill.

I'm fairly certain he's innocent, although I can't fully articulate why.

Dad falls asleep in his chair just after eight. I grab one of his comforters and cover him until he looks sufficiently warm. As much as I hate to do it, I sneak into his room and pocket some of his herb for this house party I'm being forced to attend. Stefania is a clever, nasty girl who shouldn't be messed with. Despite her age, she's mastered the art of blackmail. She'd already narced me out to Dalton for smoking pot, and I have no doubt she'd tell the cops that Iggy tried to feel her up. I can't afford an accusation of inappropriately touching a minor, and then all the questioning and bad blood such a terrible accusation would carry with it.

I slip out the door while my father's asleep and jump into his van. The nearest liquor store is three miles down the road, and as much as I detest buying booze for minors, I walk in and scan the shelves. What kind of booze do fifteen-year-olds prefer these days? When I was a kid, we drank mostly beer. I snatch a bottle of Smirnoff off the shelf and stick it under my arm. Can never go wrong with vodka; it's a rule that's always done good by me when attending a party.

Then I'm back in the van and heading toward the address she gave me.

The neighborhood I enter is one of the most affluent in Fawn Grove. It's where the executives, high-level managers, and bankers purchased homes when Fawn Grove was in its heyday. The houses are large Victorian and brick estates. Not quite mansions, but not your average homes either. This neighborhood is located on a hill overlooking the valley, and at one time, before the trees grew tall, it gave the affluent citizens here the most beautiful view of the Alamoosa River.

I drive slowly down the street, staring up at all the homes. Some are still in decent condition. Many more are a far cry from their former glory days and in need of much repair. I keep driving until I see a group of cars parked along the road and lined up in the driveway. It matches the address Stefania gave me. Something tells me that going up there is a bad idea. But what's the alternative? Getting picked up for being a child molester and having my cover blown?

Another car pulls up ahead of me, and three teenage girls pile out and run happily up the stairs, each with a six-pack of wine coolers in hand. I grab the bottle of vodka, hidden in its paper sheath, and slowly make my way up toward the house. The hint of a thumping bass indicates that the music tonight will be played at ear-deafening levels. I walk up the stairs and onto the porch. It takes me a few seconds to work up the courage to ring the bell. After a few seconds, a pretty blond girl appears holding a red cup. She laughs drunkenly when she sees me, as if a thirty-something doofus like me had been expected to show up at this party.

"Can I help you?" Another girl runs over and starts giggling drunkenly over her friend's shoulder.

"Stefania asked me here."

"You mean Stef?"

"Yeah, Stef. She asked me to bring this too." I show her the bottle of vodka, certain that it will usher me through the door.

The girl turns and yells for Stef at the top of her lungs. Then the two girls disappear inside the house. Stefania arrives a few seconds later. Her hair is down, and there's a far-off stare to her eyes that tells me she's high. Otherwise she looks gorgeous, and I can't help but be jealous that nature's been so kind to this brat.

"You made it, Iggy. And you brought a bottle of booze like I asked. Well done."

"Did I have a choice?"

"Not if you wanted to keep working at the diner."

"I really need that job."

"Which is why I asked you to come," she says too cheerfully. "Did you bring the weed?"

I take the baggie out and show her.

"You're the bomb, dude." She snatches the bottle and bag out of my hand. "Come on in and meet everyone."

She opens the screen door for me, and I head inside. The music blares in my ears and instantly makes me dizzy. It's gangsta rap, and the bass is turned to full volume. The walls and floorboards seem to vibrate around me like Jell-O molds. Every room in this house is filled with teenagers drinking and smoking pot, and I can't believe I have to stay and endure this misery. I'm the smallest person in the room, and it makes me feel as if I'm back in high school all over again.

We move into the living room at the far end of the house. A group of kids are sitting on the couches and passing a joint between them. I can't say that I'm unfamiliar with this scene, having attended many house parties in my youth. A few of these kids I recognize from that night in the cornfield. The sight of Nasreen sitting across the coffee table surprises me. I was under the impression that her cousin—the murder suspect—was the one who pushed her around, but I don't see any sign that she's injured. She's gripping a red cup and sitting casually. On the other end of the couch sits Brynn, and she too is partaking in the joint being passed around the room. The sight of her makes me nervous, and for a brief second I wonder if she'll recognize me. I freeze momentarily as Stefania gestures for me to sit between the two girls. I debate turning around and heading home, but where will that get me?

Maybe if I play my cards right they'll confide in me and talk about their two dead friends.

The song on the speakers changes, and a more aggressive gangsta rap song starts to play. I feel confused and dispirited as I sit next to my stoned niece. Stefania sits across from me and rests her long, tanned legs on the ornate coffee table. Another pretty girl sits across from me, and it makes me wonder where all these beauties are being spawned. I don't recall this many gorgeous girls here when I was growing up. This new girl is bouncing her knee over her leg and staring at me with a look of hidden despair. I've seen this look on girls many times before, recognizing it for what it is: a girl who's dying to speak her mind and spill some long-held secrets. If my recollection serves me right, she's the girl in the video wearing the blue hoodie. Her intense glare starts to freak me out, and I look away so as not to crack under the pressure of her scrutiny.

So why does this girl look so familiar to me? It seems as if I've seen her before, in another time and context, and yet I can't recall having ever met her. Is my mind playing tricks on me? There's no way I could have come in contact with her, and yet as I stare at her, that face calls out to me. They are features I most assuredly know.

I don't know what's going on here, but I don't plan to stay for long. Someone passes me a joint, and I take a modest hit. I turn to pass it on to someone else, but Brynn orders me to take another, and so I do as instructed. A red cup is placed in my hand, and a purple concoction is poured sloppily into it. Someone calls for a toast, and our cups meet in the middle, plastic crashing against plastic. A boozy liquid splashes out and onto the coffee table. Then we all drink. It's a sugary punch of some kind and tastes strongly of alcohol. Another toke, another toast, and I'm off to the races.

I stand to leave, but someone pushes me back down on the couch.

"Where do you think you're going, dude?" says a handsome boy wearing a knit cap.

"I have to get going," I say.

"Why? The party's just getting started," Stefania says.

"I have to be at the diner early or your grandfather will have my ass," I say.

"Forget about my miserable old grandfather tonight." Stefania laughs. "Drink up and have some fun."

"Yeah, because her grandfather won't have to worry about that shithole for much longer," Knit Cap says.

"Why's that?" I say.

"Didn't you see what happened to Denny's?" a preppy-looking boy says.

"It burned to the ground," I say.

"Stupid line cooks," Brynn says, laughing. "I heard they didn't clean their grease traps. Do you clean your grease trap, Iggy?" she asks too innocently.

"I try my best to keep them clean."

"Fuck Denny's," Knit Cap says, punching his fist down onto the coffee table. "Greedy corporate fucks. Serves them right burning to the ground like that."

"Have some more punch, Iggy," Stefania says, lifting the pitcher to fill my cup. I raise my hand to block it, but she pours it over my fingers. "Dude!"

"Sorry."

"Why you stressing out on us, man?" Knit Cap complains. "Now drink up and chill with your homeys."

I drink and smoke until I realize I'm somewhat wasted. No way did I plan on this happening, especially since I have to drive home tonight. But what choice did I have? Before I realize it, the house is wall to wall with kids, but only six of us sit in this living room, separated from the rest of the house. Is this where the coolest of the cool kids hang? The misfits and future criminals? The music blares loudly in my ears, thumping beats and angry rap lines. Why haven't the police arrived and broken up this party? Sometime later I'm ushered drunkenly through the back door, which is accessible only from this room. I stagger down the concrete stairs and am led by the arm to an oversized SUV parked in front of a garage. Is Knit Cap in any shape to drive?

He turns the volume up full blast until it pulsates in my ears. "All Apologies" by Nirvana. Then after that it's gangsta rap followed by a raucous live version of "A Girl Like You" by Angus Gibbons. At least these kids respect their roots. I ask where we're going, but my voice is drowned out by the wall of music. Someone passes me a joint. I decline, but they insist, holding it out until I take a hit. When I turn to see who it is, I'm surprised to see Brynn sitting next to me and smiling deviously. She looks as wasted as I am as she holds the joint aloft in her slender fingers. Her nails are painted bright pink, and the dark eyeliner gives her eyes a smoky appearance, making her look older and more sensual. I take a quick hit and pass it to the girl next to me, noticing that it's the girl from the party who sat glaring at me. Who is she, and what deep secret does she need to confess?

My mind is spinning, and it's a good thing I didn't

eat, or else I might have thrown up in this SUV. We speed through the dark streets, and as we do, I have this crazy notion that our wild joyride is not going to end well. My entire body is numb and achy, and the hint of phantom pain begins to form at the base of my feet. At one point during this frenetic drive, I feel the girl next to me squeezing my hand. Or maybe not and maybe my mind is playing tricks on me.

The SUV jerks to a stop and the kids stagger out, laughing and joking. Someone grabs my hand and pulls me along. I shuffle into the dark and fall to my tortured knees, my vision blurred from all the booze and weed. Two of the kids help me up and then lead me over to a structure that I can't quite see. I'm helped through a door and left to stumble around in the dark. I latch on to something for support before tripping and falling against the floor. Something crashes, and I hear metal clanging against metal. A slimy object hits my face as I reach around on the floor for something to hold. The kids are shouting at one another and throwing things across the darkened room. What in the world are they doing?

The lights flicker on, blinding me. I slowly stand and bury my head on a table covered in slime. Everything is spinning, so I lean over to keep myself from falling. I want badly to go lie down somewhere and sleep off this drug-induced haze. Something seems familiar about this table I'm leaning on. I raise my head up and vaguely recognize the sight of The Galaxy's cluttered kitchen. It's spinning madly around me. The kids bang pots and pans together like some drunken marching band. Why is Stefania destroying her grandfather's kitchen? Knit Cap grabs food out of the walk-in and begins to throw it around the room. A slimy chicken breast lands on my forehead before falling to the table.

I rise up to complain but fall backward along the slippery floor, which is now covered with meat, vegetables, and quantities of unknown salad dressing. I try to stand, but on these prosthetics, and in my drunken state, standing will not be an option.

The smell of smoke hits my nostrils first. Then the screeching sound of a fire alarm blares in my ears. It takes me a second to realize that these delinquents have set the diner ablaze. I thrash along the floor like Michael Phelps in a breaststroke for gold. I fling my body around on a sea of Thousand Island dressing, propelling my body toward the door. Two black boots stop in front of me, keeping me from moving. I arch my neck to see who it is but can't make out the person's face because everything is spinning. Did one of them slip me a Mickey? The handle of a wooden roller dangles like a pendulum in front of my eyes. It's the one Yanni uses to roll out his prepackaged phyllo dough. I arch my head only to feel the barrel come crashing down over the back of my skull. My cheek smacks against the wet floor, and my eyes roll back in my head. The roller falls against the tiles in front of me. All I can hear is laughter as these kids sprint out the door. Someone lifts me up by the collar and orders me to smile. I open my eyes briefly before realizing that I can't move my arms or legs. There's a cell phone in front of me. Then my body falls back to the floor. Before I pass out, I realize that I'm going to die in The Galaxy.

* * *

I wake to the sounds of sirens going off and flames snapping in my ear. In front of me is the massive green Dumpster separating me from the diner, which is now totally engulfed in flames. How did I end up here? Did I walk out of The Galaxy on my own volition? Or did someone drag me out of that burning caboose?

As I stand dizzily to leave, I realize that my head is also on fire. Bolts of lightning strike in my vision, and apocalyptic claps of thunder resound in my eardrums. The memory of that wild house party returns in full force. It's no wonder I have such a brutal headache. But I'm also still drunk and high. I bring my hand up to my shaved scalp and feel the bloody lump that has formed along it. Then I vaguely remember being struck over the head with Yanni's rolling pin. Those bastards wanted me dead. Obviously, one of them kept me alive. But for what reason?

I back away from the parking lot as a fire truck pulls up in front of the burning diner. My clothes are wet and completely drenched in Thousand Island dressing. Slipping into a nearby street, I hobble along the dark-ened sidewalk, trying to blend into the night. What time is it? I reach into my pocket and pull out the Trac-fone. It's 12:27 A.M. There's a text message on my phone that was left just before midnight. Someone wants me to text them back.

It's roughly four miles back to the van, and about seven miles back to my father's place. It's crucial that no one sees me lest they think I set fire to the diner. I'm a strange-looking dude staggering around late at night and slathered in orange salad dressing. It'd be comical if it wasn't so tragic. Despite the fact that I'm still drunk, I decide to hike all the way back to the van. If I can make it, I'll drive over to the next street and sleep off my hangover.

About two miles into my trek I begin to experience an agonizing fatigue. My stumps radiate with pain, and I'm sweating profusely. Smoking all that weed has sapped my lung capacity, and I must stop every now and then to catch my breath. My headache has been reduced to a dull hammering in the temples. A light flashes off in the distance, and when I stare down the country road, I see two headlights approaching. I duck into the nearby woods and wait for the car to pass. To my surprise, it's a police car, and it's barreling straight toward The Galaxy. But it's way too early for Dalton to be on shift.

I continue on my way, my stumps in such pain that I must stop momentarily to rest. There'll be hell to pay once I return to my father's place. I have no doubt that they're raw and infected, and in need of much medicated cream. The last mile will be a bitch. I stare up at the expensive houses located high above town. Sweat pours down my face as I rest my hands on my knees and take a series of deep breaths.

The climb is slow and arduous, and my back begins to ache. It seems like forever before I'll make it back to the van. Thankfully, it's parked in the same spot where I left it. My body rejoices at the idea of rest. Finally, I open the door and collapse inside. I wait a few minutes before turning the ignition, relieved to hear it purr to life. I guide the van away from the curb and cruise slowly down the quiet street. My skin feels clammy, despite the rivulets of sweat pouring down my forehead. I glance in the rearview mirror and see a ghost staring back at me. Far from the glamorous woman I was back in Manhattan, this is the worst I've looked in ages.

I turn the corner and head up the street where the party was being held. I look up at the house as I pass. The lights are still on, and a few cars are parked along the sidewalk. It's not quite the full-on rave it had been when I arrived, but there's still some activity going on up there. Are those murderous arsonists celebrating my death? The death of The Galaxy? I pick up speed until I'm turning off the street.

Glancing toward the rear of the van, I see that it's littered with tools, plywood, and junk. No way I'll be able to sleep back there. And my back will be much worse in the morning if I do. The long hike back to the van has sobered me up and convinced me that I'm okay to drive to my father's house. The streets will be deserted at this hour. Most of the police officers will be down at the diner, examining the scene of the crime. Arson and attempted murder, no doubt, although only a few people will know about the latter.

Not a single vehicle passes me on my way home. I breathe a sigh of relief once I park in the dirt driveway and begin hobbling toward the door. It's dark and warm inside, and the embers in the wood stove are still glowing. I check in on my father and see that he's sound asleep. I remove my wet clothes and head to the couch. The wounds along the bottom of my stumps badly need to be cleaned and massaged with ointment, but I'm too tired to do it right now. I'll save that until morning. Instead, I remove my prosthetics, lay them gently down on the floor, and then fall back along the seat cushions. Resting my bruised head on the pillow, I fall asleep almost immediately.

For some strange reason, the girl from the fruit market comes back to me, and I suddenly remember what her name means. Zarafshan—spreader of good things. And with shame and much guilt, I remember her telling me how safe she felt because American troops were stationed nearby and keeping order on things. Keeping her safe.

It's as much motivation as anything for me to get to the bottom of these two murders.

29

MY FATHER'S SHAKING MY SHOULDERS WHEN I WAKE up. The sun filters in through the flimsy curtains and seems to burn my retina. How long have I been out?

"Wake up, Lucy," he says. He's dressed in boots, jeans, and his winter coat despite it not being winter yet. His cheekbones appear sunken, and his skin has that papery look of onion skin.

"What time is it?"

"Just past noon."

"I slept that long?"

"You certainly did," he says. He turns and points to the old television, which he hardly ever watches.

I sit up and rub my bleary eyes. The news is on, and the top story is about The Galaxy burning to the ground. The bottom of my thighs are molten lava as I keep my eyes glued to the set. My father goes over to his recliner and sits.

The reporter interviews a tearful Yanni. He's overcome with emotion and speaks about the diner as if he's lost a beloved family member. Behind Yanni are a slew of firefighters dousing the pile of rubble, hoping to cool down the smoldering remains so they can search through the rubble. An important piece of Fawn Grove's history is now gone, the reporter says.

What do I do now? I'm out of a job. It's bad enough that I have nothing left to do, but now I have zero access to Dalton and these two murder investigations. The diner was my last conduit to the town's activity, and to Stefania and her gang of malicious teens.

The screen transitions to the news desk. Fire investigators strongly believe that the fire had been intentionally set. The burn pattern leads investigators to conclude that an accelerant had been used to ignite the front section of the diner. Further sampling tests will be needed before they can determine what caused it.

Police are searching for an itinerant cook who worked briefly at the diner, believing him to be a person of interest. A photograph is put on-screen showing a dazed-looking Iggy taking a selfie of himself inside The Galaxy's kitchen. His eyes are glazed, and he appears to be stoned. Behind him the place is a mess. Pots and pans lie everywhere. Food has been tossed all over the floor. Iggy's face is contorted and staring up at the camera as if surprised. Off in the distance, flames can be seen rising up.

The screen transitions and a reporter stands in front of a modest bungalow. I recognize it immediately. A mother stands with her arm around her grieving teenager. It's Nadia and her daughter, and Stefania's crocodile tears make me sick to my stomach. She looks like an Athenian goddess after losing the Miss Universe title to Miss Sparta.

"What was the suspect like?" the reporter asks her.

"He was so gross, always making dirty jokes and commenting on my body," Stefania says. "And he smoked a lot of pot."

"Why didn't you tell anyone when it happened?"

"Because my grandfather's an elderly man who has a hard time finding cooks. Maybe if I'd reported him earlier, the diner would still be here. But I didn't want my papou to lose his business because of me."

Lying little bitch!

"Did he ever put his hands on you?"

"No, but that's because I stayed as far away from him as possible. Sometimes I'd see him smoking pot out by the Dumpster. I told him he shouldn't be doing that, and that my grandfather would be angry if he knew he was getting high on the job."

"How did he respond to that?"

"He warned me that he would burn this place to the ground if I ever told anyone."

"So you didn't say anything?"

"I was scared at first." She shakes her head and starts to cry again. "I eventually reported him to a Fawn Grove police officer, and that's probably why he set my grandfather's diner on fire."

My mind can barely process this sensory overload, and it takes a moment for me to realize how rotten these kids are. They set me up to take the fall, but more important, they tried to kill me. No, they tried to kill Iggy. Thank God I managed to escape, although I can no longer use my Iggy persona to snoop around town. They succeeded in killing off both Iggy and Jaxon in one fell swoop, and I'll be damned if they lay a finger on Lucy Abbott. I'll do anything to protect her.

But how do I make my way back into Fawn Grove's good graces? When Lucy left, she claimed she left for good unless these two murders were solved. I look over at my father and notice that he's staring intently at me. I forgot about him. After shutting off the news, I sit back on the couch and think about what to say.

"It's not what you think."

"Looks like you've got some explaining to do," he says.

"That girl they interviewed is a rotten liar."

"So what's the truth?"

"Her name is Stefania." I neglect to mention Brynn for fear of angering him. "She told me to meet her last night at a house party her friends were having."

"That's asking for trouble. Why'd you go?"

"Because she said she'd tell the cops I tried to feel her up in The Galaxy's kitchen if I didn't show up. I couldn't allow her to get me in trouble."

"So you went to the party?"

"I figured, what's the worst that could happen?" I say, taking out my Tracfone and turning it on. "They got me drunk and then drove me down to the diner. Those kids were the ones who torched it."

"Miserable little tykes," he says, shaking his head. "Where are all the parents these days?" Is he being ironic? Does he not remember abandoning his own family years ago?

"They poured gasoline over the dining room and then lit it on fire. Someone hit me over the head and then left me there to die."

"How'd you get out?"

"That's a good question."

"What about that photograph they put up of you—
or Iggy—on television?"

"I don't remember taking it," I say, holding up my
Tracfone. "Someone must have taken it after they knocked
me out and then e-mailed it around town. That's how it
ended up on social media."

"What's social media?"

"Facebook and Instagram." I realize he has no idea
what I'm talking about. "They sent that photo out to
everyone they could. That's how the news station got
hold of it."

"Sneaky little bastards." He starts to cough. It takes
over a minute before he's calm enough to hear me.

"They probably burned the diner down for the insurance money and then tried to put the blame on me."
I stare out the window. "But what would a fifteen-year-
old girl know about insurance policies and arson? And
why would she even care about her grandfather's diner?
She's not getting any of the money."

"You better change your outfit. The police will be
scouring this town looking for you." He gets up slowly
and begins to walk toward his bedroom.

"Where you going?"

"Not feeling too good, especially after seeing that
news report. Think I'm going to lie down for a spell."

"Shout if you need anything."

He waves his bony hand in the air before disappearing inside the room.

I take off my pants and see the bloodied acrylic
socks pulled up over my stumps. I gently pull them off
until I see the assortment of cuts and bruises over the
scarred surface. A box of wet wipes sits on the coffee

table. I pull a few out and begin to carefully clean the wounds. It's extremely painful to the touch, and I wonder how I'm ever going to walk in these prosthetics again. After they're wiped clean, I toss the bloody wipes on the table and pick up the tube of medicated ointment. I squeeze lines into my palms and then massage them into the chafed folds of skin. I unroll some gauze, which I always keep in my bag, and wrap it around both stumps until they're adequately covered. Then I take two fresh acrylic socks out of my bag and pull them tightly over the bandages.

Something from last night comes back to me. I grab my Tracfone and open the message. Someone wants me to text them. Whoever pulled Iggy out of that burning diner obviously has something important to tell me. I wonder if it's safe to call them. But then why would they save my life?

The prosthetics lie on the floor below me. I'm not ready to put them on just yet. I remove the brown contacts from my eyes, allowing them to return to their natural blue color. What now? I can't go out into the world as Iggy, and I certainly can't walk around town as Lucy. And creating another persona is totally out of the question. I've used up my personality quotas for a lifetime. Best thing to do now is sit back and rest, and try to think of a way out of this crazy mess.

The message on my phone intrigues me. I'll call this person later and find out what they want. And then I'll ask them why they saved my life.

Sometime later I hear the sound of my phone ringing. I jolt upright on the sofa and pick it up. But it's my other phone that's ringing. The one registered to Lucy Abbott.

"Hello?"

"You're not going to believe what I'm about to tell you, Lucy."

"Who is this?" My head is spinning cobwebs of barbed wire around my brain.

"It's Dalton," he says. "Brace yourself, because The Galaxy's gone."

Dalton? "What do you mean gone?" I act surprised.

"It burned to the ground last night." He sounds almost happy when he says it.

"Oh my God!" I say. "Let me guess. Yanni didn't clean the grease trap and it caught on fire?"

"Nope. Someone torched it. The fire investigators are almost sure of it. Of course they have to do an investigation first, but they found evidence that an accelerant was used."

"An accelerant?" I play stupid. "What's that?"

"Someone poured gasoline in the dining room and set a match to it."

"They think Yanni's trying to collect on the insurance?"

"No. The main suspect is the cook who worked there. Iggy."

"Why do they think it's him?"

"Seems he was a disgruntled employee. Yanni was hard on that poor slob, and it looks like Iggy was trying to get back at him."

"By burning down the diner?"

"Apparently so. He must have been drunk, because this idiot actually took a selfie of himself inside the place just after he torched it."

I laugh. "He must be the world's dumbest criminal."

"They think he also might have burned down the Denny's. That's why The Galaxy has been so busy as of late."

"Have the police found him yet?"

"No, but we will. A guy like that won't get very far in this town."

"Good work, Dalton. You're really hitting your stride."

"Maybe you should think about moving back, Lucy."

"Why in the world would I return now?"

"Because we captured the killer of those two kids, and the people here badly want The Galaxy replaced in its original form. A few of us think you're the one to do it. It's as much a historical landmark in this town as is the monument they built for Angus Gibbons."

"Do you have any idea how much it would cost to find a similar caboose and then make it look like the original? You know I don't have that kind of money."

"I've talked to a few of the bankers, and they're willing to give the new owner a generous business loan well below market rate. Someone in town has already set up a GoFundMe page for The Galaxy, and it's managed to raise over two thousand dollars since the fire. The town council is talking about applying for the historic registry, meaning you'd get additional federal grants as well."

"This all too much for me to think about right now."

"This is your big chance, Lucy. You'd be a returning hero if you came back to Fawn Grove and resurrected The Galaxy."

I hang up and lie back against the armrest. A returning hero in more ways than one. The thought of running that diner swirls curiously in my head. Am I really considering it? It's not the worst idea in the world, but attitudes here would have to change first before I'd take on that challenge. The thought of operating my own establishment has always intrigued me. I envision a stainless steel exterior and a retro bar with a sleek dining room. The menu would be reinvented to incorporate classic diner fare from around the country. I picture people from all over traveling here to eat my food. Maybe even the *Diners, Drive-Ins and Dives* crew.

While I'm getting lost in this silly daydream, my phone buzzes, jolting me back to reality. It's a text message. The person leaves a number and time of day for me to get back to them. Three-thirty this afternoon. The time on my phone tells me it's six minutes until two. Roughly an hour and a half until then. I type *OK* and then lie back on the sofa, wondering what crazy thing will happen next.

I punch in the numbers and listen to the ringing. A few seconds pass before the phone picks up. There's no hello or answer. Just an awkward pause.

"Thank you for saving my life," I say.

"Don't thank me." Her voice sounds young and jittery.

"I assume it was you who dragged me out of that burning diner."

Another long pause.

"Why did you save my life?"

"Because I'm tired of everything going on in this crappy town. Things need to change, or someone else is going to die."

"Why did they torch the diner?"

"Why do you think?"

"I don't know, that's why I'm asking."

"Look, I can't talk for long, but you're in a lot of danger if they find out that you're still alive."

"Think I don't know that? My face has been plastered all over the news."

"I'll also be in a world of trouble when they dig through that rubble and discover that there's no body beneath it."

"Will they know it's you?"

"It's possible, seeing I didn't leave with them. That's why we must act right away."

I pause to consider her words. "What should I do?"

"You're going to have to prove your innocence if you hope to live a normal life in this town. Otherwise you better move to Alaska."

"How do I do that?"

"That's why I called."

"Mind if I ask who you are?"

"I was with you last night, but I can't give you my name. If any of the others find out what I'm doing, I'll end up like those two dead kids."

"Are you telling me that all of this is related?"

"Of course it's related. And it's not what you think."

"In what way?"

"It's worse. Much worse." Another awkward pause passes between us. "I had no idea they were going to try to kill you, or I never would have gone along with it. I only thought they were planning to set you up to take the blame."

"And you were okay with that?"

"No, but it's better than being an accomplice to murder."

"Why didn't they kill that woman before me? The one who worked at the diner?"

"I don't know anything about that. Someone wanted her to live and I'm not sure why. You, on the other hand, were totally expendable. And I think you know why."

"Because I'm a redneck loser in people's eyes? A nerdy pothead who cooks at the diner?"

"Yes. And because you're easy to blame. Don't take this the wrong way, Iggy, but hardly anyone would miss a guy like you, or ask why you'd torch a dump like The Galaxy, especially after Stef made all those nasty accusations against you."

"All of them false, by the way."

She laughs. "Of course they're false. That's just Stef being Stef."

"I take it she's the leader of your little ring of juvenile delinquents?"

Another laugh. "Oh no. Stef's an angel compared to that one."

"Mind telling me who 'that one' might be?"

"Keep that selfie on your phone, Iggy. It's going to save your skin."

"Why?"

"I downloaded photo-imaging software on to my computer, thanks to my dad's credit card. He once showed me how to do it. It allowed me to blow up that selfie to three thousand times the original. It's not easy to see, but if you look closely you can make out who took that photo of you."

"How could I see who took it if the person was behind me?"

"This person wasn't behind you. The person who

snapped that photo lifted you up and positioned themselves in front of you so they wouldn't be seen. In the blown-up version, you can make them out in the reflection in your eyes. It's the same person who hit you with that rolling pin and left you for dead."

I remember the dangling rolling pin and the black boots. I assume they belonged to one of the boys in the group. Either Knit Cap or Preppy.

"I have to go now, but I'll send it to you."

"Wait!"

"No, I have to go. When you see the person in the photo, then we'll talk. You may be surprised. Or maybe you'll have figured it out by then."

The call ends. I wonder who this girl might be. It must have been that pretty girl glaring at me from the opposite sofa. Who is she, and why is she helping me? Are those out-of-control kids responsible for all the mayhem and death that has occurred in this town? The notes from that cornfield bonfire seem to indicate that this is the case.

My phone beeps, and it's another text message. This one is a .jpg file. I open it and see the glassy reflection of a person. It takes me a few minutes before realizing that I'm staring into someone's pupil—Iggy's pupil through the brown contact lens. The person's identity is hard to discern, but after studying it closely, I can finally make out who it is. Their identity shocks me. It's certifiable proof of arson and attempted murder. Possibly two murders.

Now I need to figure out why.

30

*I*T WILL COME AS A REAL SURPRISE TO SOME PEOPLE when they clean that rubble up only to discover that there's no burnt corpse buried beneath it. The firefighters and investigators will have no idea that someone was supposed to die in that blaze, which means that they're not expecting to find Iggy's body. Only those involved in the crime will be shocked when this is revealed. They'll want to know how Iggy escaped and who helped him out of that burning diner.

A long time has passed since my father disappeared into his room. I wonder if he's all right. The prosthetics lie on the floor beneath me, but I'm hesitant to put them on. But then an hour passes and I have to use the bathroom. I slip them on and walk gingerly to the toilet. After relieving myself, I hobble to my father's bedroom and check up on him. It's dark inside and smells oddly medicinal. I stick my head in the door and hear him moaning.

"Are you okay, Dad?" I kneel next to his bed.

He opens his glazed eyes and looks at me, then nods his head imperceptibly.

"What's wrong?"

"I think it's time, Lucy."

It can't be. I don't want to consider the possibility that he's leaving me so soon after we've been reunited. I fight back the tears.

"Would you like me to call an ambulance?"

"There's nothing they can do for me."

"They must be able to do something."

"What? Extend my life for a few more miserable months? No, I won't stand for it."

"Tell me, what can I do?"

"Just stay by my side and hold my hand."

"I will, Dad, and for as long as you need."

"Please forgive me for all I've done."

"I've already forgiven you."

"Good. I just wanted to make sure we're all right."

"We definitely are."

"I'm scared, Lucy."

"I know, Dad. I'm scared too."

I stay by my father's side as he slips in and out of consciousness. At times he seems like he's getting better. He sits up and eats a little soup. He asks if I'll light a joint for him, and I do. The weed seems to ease his pain and make him more comfortable. It's only delaying the inevitable, but at least it keeps his mind off the fact that he's dying. Or maybe he's already made peace with this.

Two days pass in this oscillating state between recovery and near death. I'd brought the radio in his room so he could listen to the music he likes. We talk a little, but not much and not too deeply. He's not in a talkative mood. Our conversations tend to the banal: weather, time, things that need to be done around the house before another brutal winter hits. By the third day things take a turn for the worse. The pain intensifies, and he begins to slip in and out of consciousness.

"Hold my hand, Dad. It'll be over soon," I whisper.

"Take my van and get out of here before they find you. Promise me you'll do that."

"Don't worry about me."

"You've been good to me, Lucy. I don't deserve a daughter like you."

"Shhh," I say. Because no one deserves a daughter like me.

"In my bottom drawer there's a shoebox with some money in it. Share it with your sister."

He smiles and lifts his forefinger and thumb up to his mouth as if smoking a joint. Had my father been dealing weed all these years to support his lifestyle? He closes his eyes and falls asleep. I hold his hand and watch as his breathing becomes labored. After an hour of watching him fade away, he gasps and takes his last breath. I kiss his cheek, pull the sheet up over his head, then cry for my father for the last time. The father I barely knew.

I set myself up in a hotel near the bus station. I'd ditched my father's van in a dilapidated lot a few blocks away. Using the Tracfone, I call the medics and tell them where to find him. I expect Wendy to call soon after and deliver the bad news. When that happens, it will be time for Lucy Abbott to return to Fawn Grove and tie all these disparate ends together.

Lying in bed, I open up the shoebox and am shocked at what I see. There's more than fifteen thousand dollars in neatly banded twenties.

Drug money?

The church is half full of mourners. Dalton is sitting in the third row and Nadia in the second. Wendy sits next to me alongside Big Russ and Brynn. I can barely make eye contact with this duplicitous niece of mine after what happened the other night. Did she know what was planned for Iggy? For that diner? Or was she in it just for the kicks? Someone obviously convinced those kids that Iggy could be a conventional scapegoat for the torched Galaxy. There's something evil lurking beneath the surface of this mill town that has the feel of rot and disease.

The grieving moves to the cemetery. The weather is typical of a Maine autumn, overcast and blustery. The wind rushes through the uncut lawn and rustles the roses that my sister laid next to the grave. I can feel Dalton's eyes on me throughout the service, and it gives me the creeps. When it finishes, we walk as a family back to the pickup. Dalton approaches me before I have chance to escape.

"I'm so sorry about your uncle, Lucy."

"No big deal. I wasn't that close to him anyway," I say, despite the shame I feel after saying it.

"He was a good man."

"No need to lie," I say. "We both know that he abandoned his family and sold dope to make ends meet."

"You knew he was a dealer?"

"Didn't everyone in town?"

He nods sympathetically. "Have you given any thought to the diner?"

"Haven't had much time, considering all that's happened." I open the door to the pickup. "You find the guy responsible for torching it? That cook?"

"Not yet, but we will. This Iggy character couldn't have gone too far."

"You knew him better than anyone, Dalton. Did you have any idea he was capable of such a crime?"

"No. He seemed like a lovable loser to me. They're now saying that dirtbag was responsible for burning down the Denny's as well."

"I still don't understand how someone could be so stupid as to take a selfie while the place was burning."

"Who knows why criminals do what they do?"

"How about the Afghani guy you booked for murder? Still convinced he's the one?"

"Says he has an alibi for the days those kids were murdered. Wouldn't you know it's his wife. Of course the freeloader's on the dole and probably gets housing and medical for nothing, so he had all the time in the world to do it."

This statement infuriates me, but I try to keep my composure. "But you found the knife with the boy's blood on it. That should be enough evidence to convict him, right?"

"One can only hope. I'm fairly certain he killed that kid, but you can never have enough evidence in this day and age. We also found a pamphlet about jihad in the trunk of his car."

I climb into the pickup and roll down the window. "Good luck with the investigation, Dalton."

"Can I see you again? Maybe grab a cup of coffee while you're in town?"

"Sure."

"I hope you can stick around now that we've got a suspect."

"Everything in my life is so crazy right now. How about we wait and see what happens?"

"Sure, but you should seriously consider bringing back The Galaxy. The bank is willing to make the new owner a deal they can't refuse."

"Give me some time to think about it."

"Take all the time you need." He rests his hand on the door. I place mine over his and let it linger a few seconds longer than I should.

"It'll be some time before they clean up that rubble."

"Maybe burning to the ground is the best thing that could have happened to that dump."

"Easy for you to say."

I text the mysterious girl and set up a place and time for us to meet. She seems eager to get things off her chest, operating under the deluded notion that she's dealing with this fictional character named Iggy. She tells me to meet her tomorrow afternoon down by the riverbank where the immigrant girl was killed. It's an unusual place to meet, but what choice do I have? For all I know, it could be a setup for something else. But why would she save Iggy's skin only to kill him again?

I've agreed to meet Nadia tonight for a drink in one of the downtown lounges. Should I tell her what Stefania's been up to? No, best to remain quiet and let events unravel as they will. Maybe she already knows about Stefania's wild ways and is purposefully ignoring this behavior, choosing to live her life in a bubble. After what Stefania has done, she deserves to be punished— and severely. It would upset Nadia greatly to learn that her daughter runs with a group of wild kids who drink, do drugs, and are responsible for torching her father's beloved diner.

What about Wendy and Big Russ? Do they have any idea the extent of Brynn's true nature? It pains me to think how clueless they are as parents, too caught up in their own health issues to see the truth about their only child. Wendy and Russ seem to be operating under the misguided belief that Brynn is a good kid merely going through a difficult phase in life. Do they have any idea she smokes weed, gets drunk with her friends, and is an accessory to attempted murder?

I walk downstairs and see Russ in his chair watching television. Suddenly his parental shortcomings appear all too obvious and it pisses me off. I want to grab him by the collar and shout for him to get out of that chair and pay attention to his daughter. He nods at me as if nothing out of the ordinary has happened, then returns his attention to the show. Maybe this is his way of escaping his parental responsibilities, his chronic pain, and my father's death. I wander into the kitchen and see Wendy chopping vegetables and then palming them awkwardly into a large ceramic bowl. An un-cooked chicken sits nearby, waiting to be rubbed with oil and seasoning. I sit down across from her and watch as she performs the prep work.

"What are you making?"

"Chicken pot pie. It was Dad's favorite."

"Never knew that."

"There's a lot of things about him you didn't know, especially being away all those years."

"Like that he sold drugs to support himself?"

She stops cutting. "How did you know about that?"

"Wasn't it obvious?"

"I guess if you lived in this town long enough you knew that about him. But he'd stopped dealing years ago."

"I hope his weed never made its way into the hands of kids."

"No one ever said our father was an angel."

"No, he was never accused of that," I say. "Where's Brynn?"

"She's out with some friends. I think it's good for her to be with others in her time of grief. The death of her grandfather has affected her more than anyone realized."

"Do you think she loved him?"

"What kind of question is that?"

"Take it easy, Wendy. I was just asking."

"She's young and has experienced a lot of hardship in her short life. Those two dead kids were her class-mates, and I would imagine it's a difficult thing for a teenager to deal with."

"Would you say that Brynn's a bit wild herself?"

She looks up at me as if taken aback by my comment. "No more than any other kid in this town. And if I remember correctly, you weren't exactly a saint either."

"No, not even close."

"You gave Mom so many ulcers that she had chronic stomach pains. You were often the *wildest* kid in your group."

"But I was never malicious or mean-spirited."

"No, you were never that."

"Would you say that Brynn has issues?"

"Don't we all?"

"Issues that concern you?"

"What's this about, Lucy?"

"I'm just concerned about her."

"Brynn's issues are nothing like the ones you or I have." She holds my gaze. "Why are you asking me all this? Did Brynn say or do something?"

"No." I try to keep a straight face.

"I told you she sees a therapist from time to time. It's not like we're ignoring her problems."

"That's good," I say. "I just have this gut feeling that she may need more help than she's getting."

Wendy glares at me for longer than I'd like. "How dare you! You think you can just waltz into my home and tell me how to raise my daughter?" She slaps her stiff hand down over the table. "You're the last person in the world who should be lecturing me on how to raise my child, especially after what you put our mother through."

"You're right."

"Maybe that's why Dad left. Because he didn't know how to handle an out-of-control kid like you. A kid who refused to listen to authority or obey rules, and who would break his school's windows and steal cars with his friends just to go out on joy rides."

"I've changed, Wendy. I'm a better person now."

"That doesn't change what you've done."

"Look, I'm sorry about what I said before."

"You were way out of line."

"I don't know what it is, but this town has a strange effect on people."

"Then maybe you shouldn't stay here. Maybe this town just isn't right for you anymore."

"Maybe you're right."

"This might be hard for you to believe, but I actually like living here. So did Mom. She thought this was the best place on earth to live and raise a family."

"But she grew up here when people had jobs and nice homes and everyone was happy."

"True, but her love for this town was unconditional. To the day she died, she could never understand why you wanted to leave Fawn Grove so badly."

"I'm sorry, sis." I stand to leave. "I shouldn't have said what I did."

"Where're you going?"

"To meet Nadia."

"Are you planning on staying with us for long?" she asks coldly.

I shrug.

"Could you at least help us out with some of the chores while you're staying here? Dad used to drive us around before his health got worse. Then he handed the job off to that firebug. Guess you never really know people, right?" Is she referring to me or Iggy?

"Dalton tells me they haven't found him yet."

She laughs. "No, but they will. The funny thing is, he seemed like a decent little guy."

"Must not have been too smart if he's taking selfies at the crime scene."

"I feel bad about The Galaxy burning down. As bad as that place was, it's an important part of our history."

"Some people believe this Iggy character didn't do it."

"He took his picture inside while it was burning. Who else could have done it?"

I shrug before saying good-bye and then leave out the kitchen door. Discussing Brynn with her was a bad idea. She'll find out the truth soon enough. Because when Wendy gets mad like that, she's someone I'd rather not be around.

"My father's really depressed about what happened," Nadia says to me as we sip sweet margaritas at one of the chain Mexican restaurants. A pile of greasy yellow chips and bowl of processed salsa sit on the table between us. "He was really hoping he could turn The Galaxy around after all these new customers started coming in."

"He had to know it was only temporary until Denny's was rebuilt."

"Not really. He felt that he could win them over with the new menu he was developing, thanks to you, using real eggs and fresher ingredients. If only he didn't hire that creepy line cook."

"Iggy?"

"Yes. He applied for the job a few weeks after you

left. Didn't even catch his last name because he insisted on being paid in cash. Who knew he'd resort to burning the place down in a drunken rage?"

"Did your father have insurance on the place?"

"Not enough to rebuild. Even if he did, I'm not sure he has the energy to go through with such a project. He refinanced his house to cover the diner's losses, and the insurance will barely allow him to break even."

"That's too bad," I say. "Do the police believe this Iggy torched the Denny's too?"

"That's what I heard, but who knows?" She sips her drink. "What a mistake it was to hire that guy. It was just so hard for my father to find good help. If only you'd stayed on, things might have been different. As it is, you at least managed to convince my father to change his menu, although it may be too late now."

I sip this disgusting mess of syrup and alcohol, the rim topped with a sea of chipotle rock salt. "I've seen the selfie that guy took. He looks to me like he's so stoned he can't even stand, never mind light a fire."

"That idiot screwed himself royally when he snapped that selfie." She reaches out to hold my hand. "I'm so sorry about your father. How you doing with that?"

"We'd been estranged for some time now, so it's no big deal."

"Still, it's your father. I'd be heartbroken if I lost mine." She sips her drink. "What will you do now? Go back to New York City?"

"I have no idea." I laugh at something I just remembered.

"What's so funny?"

"Dalton has this crazy idea that I'll stay in town and

take over The Galaxy. He thinks that your father will sell it to me on the cheap."

"He might consider it," she says. "He really wants The Galaxy to live on."

"Dalton has no idea what it would take to return that place to its former glory. Probably well into the six figures."

"I think Dalton has eyes for you, Lucy. Isn't that disgusting?"

"You really think?"

"Unfortunately, I believe it's true," she says, squeezing my hand. "Of course he doesn't know the real you like I do. He doesn't know who you were and where you've been. Only I'm privy to that information."

"He might rethink things if he did."

"Oh, he most definitely would," she says, laughing. "He'd freak out if he knew you were that beautiful boy he used to pick on."

"Bully is more like it."

She shakes her head. "I wish he was the one who moved away instead of you."

"I can't even imagine what he would do if he found out the truth about me."

"No matter what happens, he'll never love you like I do," she says, and I can tell she means it. "I know you like no one else, Lucy, and I'm totally comfortable with your past, as well as the beautiful woman you've transitioned into."

"Thanks."

"We could finally be together again. Like old times, but without the shame or stigma attached to us. Niko and I have been over for a long time now. With your skills as a chef and my connections in town, you could make a real go of returning The Galaxy to its former glory."

"It's too much to think about right now, especially so soon after my father's passing."

"I understand," she says. "The Galaxy has been a real drain on my family. I've been spending way too many days behind the counter when I should have been out servicing my clientele. Now that they've arrested this individual for murder, maybe everyone can breathe a sigh of relief."

"What about Stefania?"

"What about her?"

"Shouldn't you be spending more time with her?"

"Stef and I have a wonderful relationship," she says, regarding me oddly. "In a few years she'll be off to college. Then I'll have an empty nest."

"So Stef's a good student?"

"Her teachers tell me she's extremely bright and tests off the chart but that she could put more effort into her work. She studies most nights at a friend's house. Life is so hectic, the only time I ever see her these days is when we're working together at the diner."

"It must have been hard for her, getting up so early and working alongside her grandfather. He's not exactly the most cheerful guy in the world."

"My father's a difficult man to work for, especially if you're a teenage girl trying to fit in and be popular. And with the deaths of these two kids, it's been very hard on her. But Stef's a resilient girl. She'll bounce back."

"The paper is calling this suspect a lone wolf."

"The Afghanis are a wonderful people who work hard and are family oriented. We shouldn't blame the lot of them for the actions of one religious fanatic."

I down the remnants of my drink. A hint of phantom pain begins to develop in my lower calves. Despite Nadia's insistence that we have another, I tell her my sister needs help back at the house, and she buys the excuse. Then we embrace before I head out.

31

*A*FTER PARKING THE TRUCK, I MAKE MY WAY THROUGH the woods and down to the river's edge. My wounds have not healed completely and so the going is slow. In my pocket is the stun gun and can of pepper spray that I'd used on those kids, as well as my trusty boning knife. With everything going on in this town, I fear for my safety now more than ever. I'd been buried in those woods and then left to die in that burning diner. The underbelly of this small town has proved too dangerous for me to walk around without protection.

The last time I came to this spot I was with Dalton to look over the crime scene. I remember how he tried to kiss me as I leaned back against that rock, and then how he fled in anger when I rebuffed his advance. I'm hoping this meeting will help me connect the dots to these two cases and establish a clear motive.

I sit atop the boulder and stare down at the spot

where the girl was killed. It seems strange that an Afghani refugee would hike all the way down here in order to bury and then stone a girl to death. Why do it here as opposed to all the other places he could have done it? The man I encountered on Blueberry Hill was a hothead with a volatile temper. Someone like that tends to act out of impulse rather than thoughtful deliberation. Burying that girl and then throwing stones at her face was a calculated act that was carried out in methodical fashion. A typical stoning is attended to by the entire community, each offended member ready to inflict their personal dose of punishment with rock in hand.

This river's edge is now a place of recreational activities and fun. Light-years from when its waters carried the mill's toxic sludge downstream. Kids have always come here to party—away from adults and responsibility. They come here to forget that they live in this isolated town, which is covered in ice and snow six months out of the year. Then there are the people who come here to fish and swim when the river runs low in the oppressive heat of summer. Death isn't supposed to happen in a beautiful spot like this. But it did.

The river gurgles and bubbles upward, moving toward the center of town at an impressive clip. It widens as it heads north. The rocks that crop up come summer are now buried beneath the river's robust currents. Back when I was younger, when this river was polluted, no one dared dip their toe in it for fear it might dissolve. Green foam would form along the banks and cling there for weeks. But in the last few years, as technology has increased and the mill's production has slowed, this river has been making a comeback.

When I look over I see someone walking through the woods and heading toward me. I presume it's the girl. She hops easily down the first set of banks and makes her way to me. Her gait is youthful and robust, that of a healthy and vibrant teen. The closer she gets, the more I recognize her from the other night. She's the girl who was staring desperately at Iggy at the house party, dying to tell him her ugly little secret. She seems surprised to see me. But why? Then I remember why. I'm not Iggy. I'm Lucy Abbott.

"Who are you?"

"I'm a good friend of Iggy's. He was too scared to show his face around here, so he asked me to come and meet with you."

"No way." She turns and starts back.

"I wouldn't leave if I were you."

"Well, you're not me now, are you?" she says as she walks away.

"I have enough evidence to go to the police. If you talk now, you might be able to save yourself."

She stops and turns to face me. "You don't have shit, lady. If you did, you would have gone to the police a long time ago."

"Oh, but I do. And I think you know why I haven't gone to the police."

She turns to me. Despite the fear on her face, she's a lovely looking thing with reddish blond hair that falls lightly over her delicate shoulders. She walks over and stops near the boulder, gazing at me with scared eyes.

"You're bluffing."

"I swear to you I'm not."

"Where's Iggy? Is he okay?"

"He's fine, but you'll need to deal with me from now on. Iggy's too frightened."

"I feel sorry for that guy. One of the boys spiked his drink that night."

I don't respond, but it confirms my suspicions.

"Like I said, lady, you'd have gone to the police long ago if you're so damn sure of yourself."

"We both know why I can't."

"And why's that?"

"Because you were at the diner the night it was torched. You're one of the few people who knows the truth about what really happened."

"Of course I know what happened. I was the one who went back and saved your loser friend from burning in that diner."

"You were also the one who sent him that photograph, which tells me you know who took that selfie. It's the reason I can't go to the cops."

"Iggy showed you that photograph?"

"Yes, and only someone who was there would know that Iggy didn't take it."

"How do you know Iggy, anyway?"

"That's not your concern. What you should be concerned about is who took that photo."

"So you recognized the person?"

"Yes."

"Which means you can't go to the police, because you know that my father was the one who took it?"

Her words shock me. "Dalton's your father?"

"Lucky me, right?"

"I had no idea." All those photos in Dalton's apartment suddenly return to me. She was that cute little girl he'd been so proud of. She was that same sullen teen who'd turned on him and refused to return his love. Staring at her, I begin to see the strong resemblance to her father.

"How could you?" she says. "So what other evidence do you have that's so damning?"

"I was in that cornfield the night you and your friends were 'grieving' your dead friend."

She laughs and crosses her arms.

"What's so funny?"

"That you thought we were grieving. Maybe I was the only one doing that, but the rest of them weren't. For them, it was more like a celebration."

"Celebrating what?" I say, even though I now know what it was.

"What do you think?"

"I made a recording of you and your friends that night. You were all making jokes and laughing at the expense of those two dead kids."

"I can't believe you were spying on us."

"The police will be quite interested when I hand my phone over to them and they see that you're involved in all this."

She paces nervously back and forth, unsure of whether to proceed with this discussion. I need her to stay and talk to me. I need her to explain what happened that night and then repeat it to the cops before her father hears about it.

"You have to help get me a deal with the state police. I didn't want any of this to happen, and I certainly don't want to go to jail."

"Then tell me what you know and we'll go to the

police together. I'm sure they'll go easy on you if you cooperate."

"You probably think Stef's the leader of our gang. Well, she's not."

"Is it the kid wearing the knit cap?"

"Jamie?" She laughs. "God, no. Jamie's so lame it's pathetic."

"Then who?"

She looks around as if nervous to say the person's name. "Brynn Petersen."

"Brynn?" The sound of my niece's name sends a shock through my system. "Are you sure? She seems so quiet and unassuming."

"Which is why everyone's scared shitless of her."

"So what happened the night the girl was killed?"

"Sulafi was beautiful but naive. Thought she was going to be famous when she grew up, and bragged about it constantly until we were all sick to death of hearing how great she was. Then she started seeing Taylor behind everyone's backs. Of course Brynn wasn't happy when she found out. Maybe she liked Taylor herself. Or maybe she felt slighted because Sulafi was an immigrant and dating the boy without telling anyone. Most likely it was because Sulafi was always boasting about herself and looked down on the rest of us, saying how horrible Fawn Grove was compared to her own country. Who was she to put us down when we took her people in and paid for their food and housing? Because of that, Brynn arranged for all of us to come down here one night so we could watch as she taught Sulafi a lesson."

"A lesson about what?"

"That she was no better than any of us townies."

"Brynn was planning to kill her?"

"Oh no, I don't think she ever planned on that. Brynn can be mean when she wants to. She's one of those emotional bullies with a terrible temper. And nothing frightens her. It's the only reason I joined that clique, because she threatened to make my life miserable if I didn't."

"She made you join?"

"In so many words. I was popular in school, and my father was a cop. Because of that, I suppose I was expected to join."

"Or else she would have bullied you mercilessly?"

"Exactly. I was more scared of what she might do to my reputation if I turned her down. Brynn was known to spread vicious rumors about you if you pissed her off. She could make your life miserable if she wanted."

"Brynn Petersen?" I say incredulously. "You've seen her do this?"

"Oh yeah, more than once. For whatever reason, her behavior started to get worse in middle school. One girl even tried to kill herself after Brynn spread a nasty rumor that she was sleeping with one of the teachers. They found the girl in her bathtub with her wrists cut."

"That's horrible. I've never known Brynn to be so cruel."

"Then you obviously don't know her that well."

"No, I suppose not."

"How do you even know Brynn?"

"She's my niece."

The girl laughs. "She's your niece? God, I'd be scared to sleep in the same house with her."

"So what happened to Sulafi?"

"We were all drinking and smoking weed and having a good time. Then Brynn started in on her as we all stood around and watched. To be honest, it made me queasy the way she was harassing and insulting her, but what was I to do? She kept at it until Sulafi fell back and hit her head on the boulder. A huge knot grew on her temple, and we all thought she was dead."

"What happened next?"

"We were scared that Brynn might have killed her—except for Brynn. I remember looking over at her and seeing a big smile on her face. After a few minutes had gone by, Sulafi sat up and started crying. I remember feeling relieved that she was still alive."

"I'm sure you were."

"Sulafi starts screaming hysterically at Brynn. She threatened to go back and tell her brother what she did. She claimed that he was crazy and had served in the military back in Afghanistan. She said he'd come storming down to the river and kill us all once she told him what Brynn had done. I was drunk and scared, but I couldn't leave for fear of pissing Brynn off. Besides, we all knew we'd be in big trouble if word got out that a group of us townie kids beat up an immigrant girl."

"So then what happened?"

"Brynn flipped a switch, just like that, and lost it. It was insane. Before I knew it, she was banging Sulafi's head against the rock until the girl passed out."

"And you think that killed her?"

"I'm not really sure what happened after we left."

"You all took off running?"

"No. We were wasted and didn't know what to do. I was scared what Brynn might say or do next. Or that she might turn on me for whatever reason. We didn't want to just leave the girl there."

"So you buried her and made it look like she'd been pelted with stones."

"Are you crazy? None of us had even heard of stoning before this happened." She climbs the rock opposite me and sits down cross-legged. "Stef said she would call her mom and that she would know what to do. Supposedly, she worked with the immigrants. At the time, I figured her mom would get the girl some medical help and then convince her not to say anything to anyone. We thought everything would be all right."

"So Nadia came down?"

"Eventually. We tried to talk Stef out of calling her mom, but she swore to us that her mom was cool and would do anything to protect her—protect us. No way she would turn us in to the cops, Stef claimed."

"So Nadia came down here with a shovel and helped you bury her?"

"Jesus, lady, let me tell the story, okay?" she says. "Her mother arrives and tells us not to worry, that she'll take care of everything. She escorts us into the van she used to transport the Afghanis around town. Then she drove us all home. But before dropping us off, she made each of us swear to never tell anyone about what happened down here, or we would all go to prison."

"Why would Stefania's mother agree to do this?"

"I don't know. Stef says her mother feels crazy guilty about the way she raised her. I guess she had a crappy father, too, but she didn't get into that part of her life. Maybe it was because her mother made her work in that awful diner three days a week. Whatever the reason, Stef said her mom would do virtually anything to protect her, and boy was she ever right."

"What about Taylor, the boy who had his throat slit?"

"He was heartbroken over Sulafi's death. It messed him up so bad that we were all worried he might go to the police. He broke down one night when he was drunk and threatened to spill his guts and tell the cops what Brynn had done. You can imagine how Brynn reacted to this."

"She was obviously not happy?"

"Would you be? She was furious and made Stef call her mother and warn her what Taylor was about to do, and what would happen to all of us if he talked. I woke up the next morning to the news that they'd found him with his throat slit. Not sure who did it, but it scared the heck out of me. That night you saw us in that cornfield, they were celebrating his death."

"Jesus!" I say. "What I don't get is your father's involvement in all this. Why the selfie with Iggy?"

"My father's an asshole, if you must know the truth."

"There's being an asshole and then there's murder."

"How do you think we got away with drinking and smoking so much weed? As long as we kept a low profile, my father always looked the other way."

"But why was he involved in that fire, and why leave Iggy in the diner to die?"

"I'm not sure. Maybe he was trying to frame that loser for everything bad that had happened in this town."

I was afraid to ask the next question. "Where did you get the weed?"

"I have no idea. Brynn took care of that," she says, sliding down the boulder. "Said she had a source."

Had my father been selling it to his granddaughter

all along? Or had she been stealing it from him when he wasn't looking? Maybe that's what I want to believe. Either way, it reflects poorly on both of them. He'd kept bags of it around the house, ready at his disposal and easy to find. I couldn't open a drawer or cabinet without discovering a bag of it stashed somewhere.

"I need to get back home," she says.

"Can I give you a lift?"

"No, I 'borrowed' my mother's car," she says, making quotation marks with her fingers. "My dad's busted me a few times already for driving without a license, but he never follows through with it."

"He doesn't care?"

"It's not that he doesn't care. It's that he cares too much. He'll do anything if I'll agree to be his princess once again, including bailing me out of trouble. Of course I'll never love that jerk."

"Why not?"

"He left my mother when I was a little girl and then hardly ever visited me. My mother's told me all the shitty things he's done to us throughout the years, including not sending her child support and harassing her over the phone."

"Have you ever talked to your dad about this?"

"Why should I? He makes up these lies that my mom shut him out of our lives and that she poisoned me against him, but he's lying," she says. "Look, I gotta go."

I watch as she walks toward the bank. I'm about to follow when I see someone coming out of the woods. The girl freezes when she sees who it is. Then she looks back at me with a frightened expression—as if I'm the one who should be afraid.

32

I SLIDE DOWN THE ROCK TO SEE WHO'S WALKING TO-
ward us. It's a man, and he's wearing a blue uniform
and cap. Normally, I'd be happy to see a police officer
in this situation, but considering that it's Dalton, I move
behind the boulder and grip the pepper spray in my
pocket. The pregnant river laps a few inches from my
feet as I try to keep myself between Dalton and this rock.

"Come out from behind there, Lucy. Everything's
going to be all right," Dalton shouts in his friendliest Officer Joe voice. "What are you doing down here with my
daughter?" Upon reaching her, he places his hand around
the girl's neck and squeezes until she winces in pain.

"Stay away from me, Dalton." I pull the pepper
spray out of my pocket, careful to keep it hidden behind the rock. Although it won't protect me against his
gun, it might be my only hope of surviving this ordeal.

"I thought you and I were going to have coffee together and talk about reopening the diner?"

"I'm not having anything with you after what you've done."

"What did you do?" He turns to his daughter. "Did you open your big mouth?"

"I swear I didn't say anything. She threatened to go to the police if I didn't meet her here."

"Leave her out of this, Dalton. I know you took that selfie of Iggy and set The Galaxy on fire."

"Oh, Lucy." He shakes his head sadly. "I did it all for you. For us, actually. Part of the reason I arranged for The Galaxy to burn down was so that you'd come back to Fawn Grove and then take over the diner. That way we could be together."

"There was never an us."

"Burning that failing diner solved a lot of problems for a lot of people in this town. The fact that Iggy had to take the fall for everything was an unfortunate consequence, because he seemed like a decent guy."

"So you admit that you snapped that photograph?"

"Even if I did take that loser's picture, there's no evidence to prove that I did it, other than my daughter's word, and she's not going to say anything. Right, honey?"

"Whatever," the girl says, rolling her eyes.

"Did you know that when you blow a photograph up many times over you can see objects in the victim's pupil? Objects that were right in front of the victim at the time it was taken."

"It wasn't supposed to be like this, Lucy. These kids were supposed to just lay low and party like when I was a kid. Harmless fun, right? Be like every other dumb-ass teen who grew up in this depressing armpit of a town. Instead, it turned them into little monsters."

"Speak for yourself," his daughter says.

"I am speaking for myself," he replies.

"That's right, because your father was one of the most feared bullies in this town when he was a kid," I say. "It's no wonder your daughter is scared of you, Dalton."

"My wife poisoned Brandy against me until she believed I was the devil. She fed her lies upon lies with her toxic personality. This was the only way I knew how to gain my daughter's trust and prove that I still loved her." He stares down at Brandy. "Isn't that right, hon?"

"That's not real love," Brandy says, tears flowing down her cheeks. "Love is being there for me when I needed you most—and you never were."

"Why don't you go back to the car and wait for me. I'll be right up." He releases her neck and pushes her firmly toward the path leading to the woods. "And don't try to get away in your mother's car, baby doll. I disabled the battery."

Brandy sprints up the steep bank and then disappears into the woods. Dalton watches for a few seconds. When he's certain she's out of sight, he walks toward me. With practiced ease, he pulls out his service revolver and holds it down by his side. Only the boulder separates the two of us. Behind me the river roils and bubbles.

"We had to do it, Lucy. To protect our kids and make sure they didn't get into trouble. God knows it was the least I could do for my daughter after all I've put her through with that mother of hers."

"Who's we?"

"We. Us. We made it look like one of the Afghanis did it. I had no idea about stoning until she explained how these Afghani savages punished their women."

"Maybe the real savages have been right here in Fawn Grove all along," I say, holding the pepper spray below the rock so he can't see it.

"How would you even know, never having children yourself? You don't know what it's like to be a parent and have to deal with all their messy issues."

"Just because I don't have kids doesn't mean I condone what you've done."

"I really like you, Lucy. I never intended for you to get involved in all this."

"Ha! I would have never settled for a creep like you, anyway."

"You liked me well enough to kiss me that day at the bus station." He rests his arms on top of the boulder. In his right hand sits the revolver. "If you'd just minded your own business, we could have been good for each other."

"You would have treated me just like you treated all the other kids you bullied growing up, including Jaxon."

"Jaxon?" He laughs. "How do you know about him?"

"I know you treated him like dirt."

"Sure, but Jaxon deserved most of the beatings he got. The kid never knew when to stay down. It was like that sissy wanted me to keep pounding on him."

"Jaxon was no sissy," I say, fiercely defending that innocent boy. "It was Nadia who told you about the practice of stoning. She called you when that girl got hurt, and you took care of the situation. Then you made it look like something else."

"Bravo, Lucy, you figured it all out. You're a genius detective," he says. "The truth is, Nadia and I can't stand each other, and never could, but we acted in the best interest of our kids."

"The boy was going to tell everyone what happened, but then you took action before he could say anything."

"What did you expect me to do? Taylor was going to rat those kids out, including my daughter, and I couldn't let that happen." He looks genuinely pained. "I admit that everything spiraled out of control, but we had no other choice."

"Makes me glad I never had kids," I say, trying to delay the inevitable.

He shakes his head wistfully. "It's amazing what we'll do for these spoiled brats of ours. As they say, blood really is thicker than water." He rests his chin on his gun-toting hand, which is resting on the boulder. "You're so damned beautiful, Lucy. It pains me to have to do this to you."

"But there's more fish in the sea, right?"

"Not in this town. Fawn Grove's like a pond that no one stocks, and then the water keeps getting more polluted with each passing day." He lifts the gun and steadies it on top of the rock. "It's too bad. I'll never again meet anyone quite like you."

"I take it you planted evidence on that Afghani hothead to make it look as if he killed the boy?"

"That scumbag's probably a terrorist anyway. And that confrontation you had with him helped convince my chief that he was a danger to the community," he says. "Staging those two deaths helped Nadia as much as it helped me."

"And how is that?"

"Her agency got additional funding from the feds. And the deaths of those two kids helped convince more townspeople to join our anti-immigrant crusade."

"You wanted to drive them out of Fawn Grove?"

"Ideally, but once they settled here, that proved harder than expected. We hoped to at least cut back on all the welfare and benefits these leeches received. We have people in our own community who are hurting and can't find work. It makes me sick to my stomach that we're helping these freeloaders over our own citizens."

"So you two were working both sides of the coin?"

"It didn't start out that way. But that's how the world works, Lucy. And burning down that failing diner was a way to close down that dump and prevent her father from having another heart attack. Then I figured I could persuade you to move back to Fawn Grove and resurrect The Galaxy."

"I'm going to the state police with this information and turn you in, Dalton."

"Is that so?" He shakes his head as if amused. "I'm afraid I can't let that happen."

"I thought you cared about me?"

"I do care about you. That's the shame in all this. I let you live when I directed those kids to bury you in that hole. I thought that by scaring you like that, you'd come to your senses and stop snooping around in this case. I thought that might scare you enough to come running back into my arms."

"So it was you who wrote that message on my windshield?"

"Actually, it was Brynn who came up with the idea. That girl's as cold as they come."

"And you ordered those kids to scrawl threatening messages on my inner biceps."

"Don't you see? I cared about you. I was trying to protect you from all this nasty business."

I gaze over his shoulder as if someone is coming. The expression on his face changes, but he doesn't bite until I jump up and down and start waving my free hand around. He looks confused as I shout for this imaginary person to come over. Dalton turns his head to see who's approaching, and when he does I take out the pepper spray. Once he turns back to me, I shoot it into his face. His gun goes off, and a bullet whizzes over my head. Dalton cries out in pain, staggering back from the rock while frantically rubbing his burning eyes. He holds out the gun and points it at an undefined target in front of him.

"Where are you, Lucy Abbott? Don't try to run from me, or you'll make it worse." He fires off another round, and the bullet ricochets off the boulder. "You can't escape from me. I'll find you one way or another."

I duck behind the rock, realizing that I stand no chance of sprinting past him. Not with these flimsy legs of mine. The pepper spray will soon wear off and he'll be able to see me trying to get away. I'm too far removed to disable him using the stun gun. I turn and see the fast-moving river, and I realize that it's my only hope. But can I survive in those frigid waters?

I rip off my jacket and then remove my boots. Wading in, I can't tell how cold the water is because of the prosthetics. I take a deep breath, say a quick prayer, and dive in. The temperature of the water hits me like a sack of bricks, and I can feel all my muscles tightening up. I struggle to breathe as the current pulls me downstream. Having spent many hours rehabbing in the pool at Walter Reed, I'm a very good swimmer. But swimming in a fast, ice-cold river is altogether different from swimming in a warm pool with physical therapists all around you.

My muscles struggle to cope as I get swept downstream. The thought of drowning terrifies me, and I start to flail about. I cry out for help, but no one is there to hear me. I somehow manage to move my arms and legs, barely keeping myself afloat. Gunshots go off in the distance, but I keep treading water, mindless of what's to come. My body's shivering, and I know I don't have much time before hypothermia sets in. I need to find a way out of this river before it kills me.

Trees and bushes stream past my outstretched arms. Suddenly I hear someone calling out my name. When I turn, I see Dalton in the water fifty yards behind me. My head goes under, and when it pops back up, I realize that my wig is still clinging to my head. A tree branch extends out over the riverbank. Desperate and running out of energy, I paddle frantically toward it and raise my right arm. The branch smacks into my palm as my lower body propels downriver, threatening to take the rest of me with it. I somehow manage to hold on until I pull myself up. Then I inch toward land, making my way forward until my feet touch down on the muddy bank.

"Lucy!" Dalton shouts as he sweeps past me.

My entire body is shivering in an attempt to keep warm, but at least Dalton's no longer a threat. I drag myself up the steep bank until I'm standing in an empty meadow. I'm trembling uncontrollably as I trudge forward on false legs. Off in the distance, I see a sprawling new housing development. Dalton shouts out my name, and when I turn back, I see that he's hanging from a branch fifty feet downstream. He slides his hand along the slender limb, working his way toward shore, desperate to catch up to me.

I walk as fast as I can toward the row of town houses, trying not to panic. Soaked to the bone, and without footwear, it's a slow and arduous march. Dalton continues to call out my name, a note of desperation in his voice. I turn and to my horror see him limping in my direction. He's wet and exhausted but determined to get his hands on me before I reach someone and spill my guts about what happened.

I pick up the pace, but he's quickly gaining ground. Unfortunately, my legs won't move any faster, and I realize that he's going to catch up with me. Then he'll try to kill me in this open field, where no one will bear witness to my death. He shouts my name, now only a few feet behind. I'm out of breath, cold, and exhausted, but I keep churning these tired legs as best I can. I feel his arms wrap around my waist and his shoulder ram into my back. He tackles me to the ground until he's sitting on my stomach. River water drips onto my face as he pins my wrists to the grass and holds them there. I struggle but remain helpless beneath his weight.

"I loved you, Lucy." He's sobbing as he places his unshaven wet cheek against mine. "I'm so sorry."

"Please don't do this."

"Why, Lucy? Especially when you knew how much I cared about you?"

"We can work it out, Dalton. You don't have to kill me."

"I have no other choice," he sobs.

"I swear I won't tell anyone. I'll go back to New York City and you'll never hear from me again."

"It's too late for that," he says. "It's either you or me now."

He lets go of my wrists and wrings his hands around my throat. Turning his face, his cold lips press lightly against mine. I reach down with my free hand, grab the handle of the boning knife in my pocket, and pull it out. His hands tighten around my throat as he continues to shower me with kisses.

"Good-bye, Lucy."

"I wasn't always Lucy," I manage to say.

"You'll always be Lucy Abbott to me."

"I have something to tell you," I gasp. "I was once Jaxon Ford."

"Jaxon?" His hands ease up, and he lifts his face to study me. "What are you saying?"

"I was once Jaxon, that little boy you used to bully," I croak, gripping the knife. "But I'm Lucy now. A woman, Dalton."

"No! That can't be." He looks shocked, his face inches from mine, his hands still wrapped around my neck. "Jaxon died overseas in combat."

"No, he didn't die. He lost his legs in a roadside bombing and then became Lucy Abbott." With all my might, I thrust the knife into his back below the collarbone.

His face contorts in horror and he howls, his hands tightening around my throat. I struggle to pull the knife out as I gasp for air.

"You're lying!" he wails.

"I swear to you I'm not. Iggy rode with you to Manhattan and then changed back into Lucy."

"No."

"Yes, Dalton. I played you."

I rear back and stab him again, this time closer to his heart. Dalton screams in agony, his hands locked in a death grip around my throat. I can barely breathe now and am close to passing out. Kicking my legs, I manage to pull the knife out of his back and stab him one last time near the neck. My vision fades to black as I feel his hands begin to loosen around my windpipe. A few seconds pass before his body topples over my face. I turn my head and cough violently, pushing Dalton's convulsing body off me. Then I lie on the grass for what seems like forever, gasping for air, until someone comes over and kneels by my side.

"He tried to kill me," I say, my entire body trembling.

"I know," the woman says. "I see everything out kitchen window and call police."

"Thank you."

"Come, let's get wet clothes off you. Police should be here any minute." The woman helps me to my feet, and to my surprise I realize that she's wearing a hijab and burka.

"Please call my sister and tell her to come get me."

"Come. Let's get you inside."

I stare down at Dalton's lifeless body before we leave. His eyes are open, and he's staring up at the autumn blue sky. A rivulet of blood trickles out of his mouth. The woman helps me inside her house and instructs me to go into the bathroom and dry off. She runs upstairs and returns a few minutes later with some fresh clothes to wear. Then she opens the bathroom door and hands them to me. It's a black burka and headscarf, loose fitting but it'll do. Her kindness and generosity astound me after all the turmoil her people have gone through in this town.

The police arrive as I lie on the sofa in a daze. A detective sits across from me and begins to ask me a series of questions. In my throaty voice, I tell him all that has happened in Fawn Grove and what the guilty parties have done. He looks confused at first, but when he sees Dalton's lifeless body out in the field, he begins to take me more seriously. I tell him to interview each kid separately and pit one against the other. He sighs, telling me that he knows what he's doing.

After I've answered all the detective's questions, two cops escort me out to Big Russ's truck, advising me not to leave town. I turn back and smile at this kind woman as she waves good-bye. Standing in front of every door are Afghani women and children, watching the police lead me down the stone path. What are the odds that an immigrant would help me through this ordeal, then hand me a fresh, clean burka to wear home?

Russ doesn't say a word as he drives me back to the house. I wonder what he's thinking. Was I suffering a nervous breakdown? Drunk? He'll no doubt want to know how I ended up in an Afghani woman's home wearing a burka and headscarf. He doesn't know yet about Dalton, but he will by this evening. He has enough sense not to ask me anything while I'm in this dazed state.

I'm unsure whether to tell him the truth about his daughter. He'll find out soon enough the kind of monster he's raised. I'm betting that a police car is already at the house, waiting to take Brynn down to the station for questioning. I imagine that police cars are now pulling up to each kid's home, ready to ask them what they know about these crimes. What will Russ and Wendy think of me when that happens? What will they think of their daughter? Will they defend Brynn? Will they say that her behavior was that of a frightened young girl? A girl who was forced to do the bidding of two adults, one of whom was a cop?

"Is this as awkward for you as it is for me?" Russ finally says as we pass through the center of town. "I'm not even supposed to be driving."

I look over at him and say nothing.

"Feel like you need to tell me something?"

I do but say nothing.

"Come on, now. Say your piece."

I turn and stare out the window. "Brynn's not the girl you think she is."

"What right do you have to lecture me about my daughter when you've never had kids of your own?"

The town of Fawn Grove flies past, and it looks sadder than ever.

"We've been good to you, Lucy. Took you in when you were sick and had nowhere else to go."

I see Pam's coffee shop and the mill's steaming smokestack.

"I didn't want to say this, Lucy, but you're a train wreck waiting to happen. You act like everything's all a game to you. Now I find you in an immigrant woman's house doing God knows what, dressed in a burka, the police surrounding the place. You hear voices at night and suffer from PTSD. Maybe you should worry more about your own mental health rather than questioning my parenting skills."

I continue to stare out the window because a response is not warranted. They'll soon learn who Lucy Abbott is and what she's made of. Never again will I be bullied or pushed around. Or let innocent kids get hurt for no reason. For the first time in my life, I feel like I'm completely free from Jaxon's long shadow. May that poor boy rest in peace.

Epilogue

*I*N MANY WAYS IT'S BEEN DIFFICULT TO RETURN TO New York City. The transition has been hard, the fall-out in Fawn Grove even worse. Initially I thought that's where I belonged. Home is where the heart is, and all that corny bullshit. In the end I realized it was never meant to be. Jaxon left that place for a specific reason—to be free from the scrutiny of small-town minds. It was these same small-town minds that made life miserable for Jaxon, and he knew this far before Lucy arrived at the same conclusion. Like anywhere else, most of the people in Fawn Grove are kind and hardworking folks. It's always the assholes who make up a tiny percentage of the population. But as they say, a few bad apples can spoil the barrel. And it's those bad apples one tends to remember in life.

So from Jaxon's ashes Lucy Abbott was spawned.

I haven't talked to Wendy and Russ since leaving. It's understandable. This has been a difficult time for them as well. I don't think they blame me for their daughter's actions, and let's face it, how could they? But it's still hard for them to accept that their only child is a murderer without conscience. It's hard for everyone in town to accept. These children were born and raised in Fawn Grove. What these kids did was so horrible that the only option for many people is to deny it ever happened. Put it out of mind. Who would have thought kids could be so cruel? But they are. And they were.

And yet the adults were worse. These kids learned this behavior from their parents. Or, to be more specific, in their parents' absence. Now Nadia is serving time in prison and Dalton's dead.

We were a broken family before all this occurred. Now we are nothing, because you can't break what doesn't exist. Both of my parents are gone and buried. Brynn is now serving time in a juvenile correction facility until the age of eighteen. Me, I'm living in New York City where I belong. Wendy and Big Russ still live in that old creaking Victorian, their health deteriorating with each passing day, spirits broken, never to recover. And that's just in my own messed-up family. Imagine how many families have been ruined by this depraved cycle of abuse.

I remember driving back with Russ and seeing the horrified look on his face when he saw all those cop cars parked in front of his house. He drove slowly up the driveway before hobbling inside. I trailed behind him, sensing what I was about to see once I walked into that living room.

Brynn was sitting on the couch and talking to one of the detectives in a calm and cutesy manner. Her arms had been cuffed behind her back and she spoke in a low voice, as if she was speaking to a three-year-old. Despite the grim circumstance, she looked beautiful. I've always thought she looked that way because her true self was finally revealed to the world. I remember at the time wondering how she could look so lovely after all that had happened. How could she maintain her composure and act so damn calm? It made me slightly jealous. That she didn't have a care in the world.

My problem had always been that I cared too much.

Brynn was telling the cops everything she knew, or at least her version of events. I distinctly remember her glancing up at me and smiling. I'll never quite forget how sweet she looked at that moment. She seemed extremely confident of her powers of persuasion, as if she could talk her way out of all the terrible things she'd done.

She blamed everyone but herself. She blamed Dalton and Nadia. No surprise. She blamed her own parents for not adequately supervising her during her formative years. She blamed Fawn Grove and the effects small-town life had on her development. She blamed the Afghani girl for falling against that boulder and hitting her head. She blamed boredom, drugs, and alcohol. She claimed she'd gone along with everything only because she was scared for her life. Dalton was an influential detective in town who held a lot of power. And Sulafi had threatened to send her Muslim brother back to that river and kill her and all her friends. Nadia threatened any of them who opened their mouths, which was how Taylor ended up in that lonely cornfield with his throat slit.

Please! I wanted to run out of that room screaming. But I had to admit she was good. A natural.

I knew immediately she would receive a light sentence once convicted. Brynn had a lot of things going for her: She was young, pretty, and a very skilled liar. At the age of fifteen, she had a spotless record and a history of good grades. Her parents were invalids and in declining health, and she claimed that her grandfather's death had greatly affected her. It didn't hurt that she could act sickly sweet on cue. I knew juries typically went easy on teens who'd been used as pawns in the commission of violent crimes, especially when it involved cops and murder.

I feared for a world in which this manipulative psychopath might one day roam free to prey on others. This lying, murderous girl with the addictive blue eyes and dimpled cheek was a menace to society.

I told the police everything I knew. I handed over the video of those kids speaking in the cornfield and told them about Dalton's reflection in the selfie. They sent the original photo to the police lab, blew it up many times over, and confirmed that it was Dalton. When they combined my statement with the testimonies of all those kids, the pieces started to fit together.

Surprisingly, Stefania had no compunction about testifying against her mother. But she adamantly refused to testify against Brynn. Whether it was out of loyalty or fear, no one knows. As much as Nadia tried to protect her daughter and keep her safe, a mother's love will never be reciprocated in full. I know this because my own mother felt the same way. It soon became apparent during the trial that Stefania greatly resented Nadia. Stefania had abandonment issues, a psychologist testified. Her mother focused all her energies on the Afghani immigrants instead of her long-neglected daughter. It came at a steep price. I think this compulsion Nadia had to help these refugees manifested from the shame of her own immigrant past. But at that I'm merely playing dime psychologist.

The more I reflect on things, the less surprised I am that something like this happened in Fawn Grove. Everything that occurred there was the result of an imperfect storm: small-town dynamics, dysfunctional families, cyclical abuse, economic hardship, a clash of cultures pitting two desperate peoples against each other, drugs, alcohol, resentment, boredom, the mill's toxic history. You name it. It makes me wonder why something like this hadn't happened *sooner*.

I returned to Manhattan and found work almost immediately. A chef with my skills will not sit on the sidelines for long. An enterprising young woman I knew opened a fabulous bistro in Brooklyn and, to my surprise, asked if I'd come work for her. I'd gained somewhat of a reputation while slaving away all those years, refusing promotions and lucrative job offers. I interviewed with her, and she hired me on the spot.

The bistro took off, and I found myself once again immersed in kitchen work. Beautiful, glorious kitchen work. It took my mind off all the bad stuff that had happened in the last year. In my spare time, I began to see a therapist, and she helped me through my various issues. We talked about the voices in my head, and I told her about the day before the roadside bomb that rendered my lower legs moot. For the first time in years, I began to sleep at night, and it changed my life. It gave me a newfound hope that I might one day live as a normal woman, and that I might be able to share my life with someone. It provided me with the framework to at least think about making the full transition to womanhood. Cutting the cord, so to speak. In my mind, I'd been a real woman for quite some time, but now the physical transformation would seal the deal. I just needed to pull the trigger when I was ready.

I told her about the girl from the fruit market and how I vowed to never sit idle again. I told her about the night before my legs got blown off and how I couldn't get that young child's voice out of my head. It was a cry for help, and although I'd heard these children's voices many nights in the past, I'd never done anything about it.

It had been a difficult week. Soldiers were dying on the battlefield and in the operating room. I'd been wrestling with my gender identity and confused that it was finally coming to a head. I experienced random bouts of dysmorphia mixed in with a crippling sense of depression. At the time, I didn't think I wanted to be a woman. Or deserved such privilege. It seemed unnatural and perverted, and yet so right. What was wrong with me? Why was I the only soldier in my unit made to feel this way? To want to be something that he was not. It seemed that God had a cruel sense of humor.

My confusion that evening was compounded by the relentless sound of the child's cries. I covered my ears and hummed a tune. But the cries now seemed as if they'd been branded into my brain. After an hour of this torture, I couldn't tell if the voice was real or imagined. I just wanted it out of my head.

That last night before the roadside bomb took my legs had been the worst. I lay in my cot sobbing and cursing all that was wrong with me. Was it really so bad to be a woman when I was a man? Then I heard that child's voice, and it was like a switch had been thrown in my head. Enraged, I thought about how I'd failed to save that beautiful girl from the market. I ran out and made my way down to where the voice was coming from. I stopped when I arrived at the tent, which belonged to an Afghani general we were helping to train. When I pulled up the flap to his tent, I saw a very young boy sitting on a cot. The boy was wearing a heavy gloss of red lipstick and a long dress and was crying. He looked surprised and relieved to see me. For a brief second, I wondered if he was real or just a figment of my imagination. The general, an ugly war hog with a bad case of acne, turned toward me and smiled knowingly. At that moment, a thousand thoughts ran through my mind, and not a single one of them was good.

I snapped. I completely lost it like Brynn did down by the river. Maybe it's in our shared DNA to lose control of ourselves so fully. My vision turned dark. Confusion turned into chaos, which resulted in moral anarchy. I lashed out, that's all I know for certain. After that I don't remember a thing. I only remember waking up the next morning and noticing that my hands were bruised and bloodied. Someone shouted a command, and in minutes we were being ordered to head out to the battlefield to save lives.

During the ride, one of my fellow soldiers explained how he and another soldier had pulled me out of that tent and hustled me back to the compound before anyone noticed. The boy had run off. I'd beaten the general so badly that everyone feared I'd killed him. Good, I thought. I secretly hoped I had, despite the consequences facing me. I only hoped that my fellow soldiers wouldn't have to pay the price for my impulsive actions.

My unit never made it to the battlefield that day.

I never found out what happened to that general,

whether he lived or died, and honestly I don't really care at this point. Because the next memory I had was of lying in that hospital bed and listening as the doctor told me that my lower legs had been blown off.

I'd gone to visit Brynn in the juvenile facility where she was assigned. The institution was located just south of Portland and a two-hour ride from Fawn Grove. A year had passed, and I hadn't been back to Maine since. My contact with Wendy and Russ had been cut off, due to the bad feelings still lingering over all that had happened.

The visiting room was a nondescript rectangle of cinder blocks filled with old tables and rickety chairs. On one side of the room sat a hunkering steam radiator that hissed and knocked. It sounded like an inexperienced xylophone player making soulful music. All the windows were covered over with steel bars. I was nervous as I waited for her. What would she look like? How would she react to seeing me, knowing that I had lied to her about my identity? Anyone looking in might have mistaken me for her fashion-conscious mother.

And I was scared. Scared of facing her.

After ten minutes of waiting, Brynn waltzed in. Even dressed in a hideous orange jumpsuit, she took my breath away. She flashed me an All-American smile one might see in a Gap ad. Her blue eyes shimmered in the cold light, and she'd combed her hair straight back so that it flowed naturally. I was surprised how much she'd grown in such a short time; ironically, at least three inches taller since I'd last seen her. But what I noticed most was that she looked weathered. Or weary.

Maybe a cocktail of the two that struck a subtle note in me at the time. Serving with other juveniles had irrevocably changed her, despite all the cutesy gestures she made trying to persuade me otherwise.

"Look at you," Brynn said, making a show of sitting across from me. "Lucy Abbott, private investigator."

"Hello, Brynn."

"You sure are a sight for sore eyes."

"I'm not here to argue with you."

"Why should you? I'm the victim here. The neglected child who's been taken advantage of and used for others' personal gain. If you had just gone back to New York City, I would have never ended up here."

"You can't blame me for what happened."

"I was a frightened young girl and scared for my life," she said as if she'd really convinced herself of this lie.

"Have you spoken to your parents?"

"Of course I have, and they've forgiven me completely. They know how dangerous Dalton was and what Stef's mom put us through. They'll do anything to help me get back on my feet when I leave this dump."

"What will you do?"

She laughed and flipped her hair back. "Like you really care. You probably wished they'd locked me up and thrown away the key."

I did but would never admit to it. "I know you can't stay in a juvenile facility forever," I said. "Will you go back to Fawn Grove?"

"I was thinking about going to college and getting a degree in veterinary science. I love animals." She stared down at her soft hands and almond-shaped nails. "Whatever happens, I'm getting the hell out of Fawn Grove just like you did."

"Getting a college degree is a smart move. It's a good way to better yourself."

"Do you really believe I was that stupid? I knew all along that you were Jaxon."

I shrugged. At this point, what difference did it make whether she knew? Besides, I couldn't tell if she was lying or just trying to manipulate me.

"I would have never ended up here if you hadn't come along and spoiled everything."

"You want me to apologize for that?"

"I don't believe in apologies. I don't apologize for anything I ever did. Look to the future, my therapist keeps telling me. Put all that negative stuff behind you."

"Good advice."

"You must have thought you were so much better than everyone else," she said, laughing. "Just like Sulafi."

"Actually, quite the opposite. I hated myself for a long time and thought I was a worthless human being."

"Isn't that strange? I've always loved myself. Maybe that's why it was so easy to get those kids to do whatever I wanted."

"You mean bully them?"

"I can't help it if people want to do nice things for me."

"Even bad things?"

She laughed. "You're not half as pretty as you think you are, Lucy. All that ooey-gooey makeup makes you look like a drag queen."

This insult stung, but I didn't want to give her the satisfaction of seeing me upset.

"Did you hear the big news?"

"No."

"Stef's grandfather dropped dead, and someone

bought the rights to the diner. Supposedly, they're going to rebuild and make it bigger and better than ever. Put a rocket ship out front and add a bar."

"Cool," I said. "I have to ask you something, Brynn."

"Isn't that the real reason you came? Not to see how I'm doing but to see if I'll answer your questions?"

That was true. "Were you getting that weed from my father?"

"Oh, God, did you have to ruin my day by mentioning him?" she said. "You knew about the weed?"

"It came to me later, but I didn't want to believe it was true."

"That creep sold lots of it back in the day, but he didn't sell it to me."

Her utter contempt for everything irked me. I wanted to reach across the table and shake some decency into this immoral niece of mine, but I managed to keep my composure.

"Oh, Lucy, he didn't want me to have it. But I went up there with Mom and Russ one day and discovered bags of it everywhere. I swear I wasn't looking for weed, but there it was in his drawers and cabinets. It was like finding a stash of gold. So I thought, why not help myself to it?"

"He was using it because he had cancer."

"Ha! Keep telling yourself that." She started to trace her fingernail over a deep gash along the tabletop.

"It helped him with the pain after being diagnosed with cancer."

"Maybe by then it did, but he'd been smoking and selling it for a long time before I ever found it. Think I didn't hear my parents talking about him when I was a little kid?" She stared down at her long nails. "He didn't want me to have it, if that makes you feel any better."

"If he didn't want you to have it, how did you end up selling it?"

"He caught me stealing a bag one day. I threatened to tell Dalton about it if he didn't give me a bag every now and then. He knew what Dalton would do to him if he found out."

"Dalton knew about it?"

"Of course he knew. His daughter was one of us, and he wanted more than anything to get on her good side. So he looked the other way when we sold it. It paid for our booze and wild parties. Dalton would have done anything for that bitch kid of his."

"Just like Wendy and Big Russ did with you?"

"You know as well as I do that you can't really spoil a kid from Fawn Grove. Living there is punishment enough. It's like Wendy and Russ made up for their physical ailments by allowing me my freedom."

"I call it spoiled."

"Call it whatever you want."

"Did you intend to kill that Afghani girl?"

"Intend is a loaded term, don't you think?"

"Not really. Either you intended to kill her or you didn't."

"I certainly was mad at Sulafi. But then I never know what I'm going to do until after I've done it, and by that time it doesn't really matter," she said. "Does that answer your question?"

Surprisingly, it did. Because I experienced the same dark feelings when I pummeled that general.

"At this stage in the game, what difference does it make what I intended to do?"

"None, I guess."

She was much sicker than I realized, and I feared for society's welfare once the day came when she'd walk out of this place. I couldn't believe she was my own flesh and blood, and yet I'd snapped just like her. Was it nature or nurture that caused her to turn bad? I stood back from the table and prayed that she'd get the help she needed before being released.

"Leaving so soon?"

"I have to get back home. I'm working tomorrow."

"A working girl. Nice! Which street corner?"

"That's not a nice thing to say."

"Whoever said I was nice, Lucy?" she said. "Besides, can't you take a joke?".

"Not ones in bad taste."

"I'm sorry you took offense to that," she said too sweetly. "Are you still living in New York City?"

I nodded.

"I might come and visit you once I get out. Always wanted to see Manhattan. Is it all right if I crash at your place when I get there?"

"I'm not so sure that's a good idea."

"Why?" She laughed. "Don't tell me you're scared of me?"

I didn't want to admit to her that I was.

"You've got nothing to fear, Lucy. I've been rehabilitated and learned the error of my ways." She giggled as I headed for the exit. "You go, girl. Or are you still technically a boy?"

I turned and took one last good look at her.

"Watch out, Lucy Abbott. I'm coming for you one of these days." She laughed hysterically.

I scrambled past every checkpoint until I was finally

outside and gasping for air. My pulse raced, and my skin felt hot and moist. I wanted to lean over and vomit on the pavement. I thought of my poor sister and brother-in-law. As I slipped inside the rental car, I prayed that I would never have to see my niece again.

My life has changed drastically for the better. I sleep through the night. I eat healthy now and practice yoga once a week. I've even been dating as well. I left the bistro months ago and started my own gastropub in Hell's Kitchen, which I've named Trans Am. It's an inside joke, but the people who know me get my unique sense of humor. Trans Am features quality beers and ales paired with classic dishes from around the country: gumbo, lobster rolls, spaghetti with chili, poutine, and Kansas smoked ribs, to name just a few. Food that sticks to the ribs and makes people comfortable and happy. It's why I cook now, to make people happy.

I've even decided to go through with gender reassignment surgery. It's exciting but scary to know that Lucy Abbott will be a completely functioning woman in the near future.

Not a week goes by that I don't think of Fawn Grove and the terrible things that happened there. The memories are slowly fading with each passing day, but they've not all been exorcised. Nearly two years have passed since I spoke to Brynn in that correctional facility. She's out of my life forever. Good riddance.

I'm exhausted when I arrive home late in the afternoon. Ten straight days toiling at my restaurant and I'm badly in need of some rest. Tomorrow I have off. I plan on lounging in my apartment, reading the Sunday

Times, and drinking copious amounts of strong coffee. I change my outfit and put on something more comfortable. The TV comes on, and the first thing I see is a documentary about the plane crash that took Angus Gibbons's life. It reminds me of Big Russ, and so I quickly change it.

I pour myself a glass of wine, settle into my comfortable chair, and click the remote until I find a decent movie. The silk robe feels luxurious against my skin. But then the buzzer to my apartment goes off, and I shoot up out of sleep. I must have dozed off at some point, because the movie I was watching has changed and now Anthony Hopkins glares out from behind that hideous mask. Who could be calling on me at this hour? I walk over and ask who it is. No one answers. I ask again, but there's no reply. Am I imagining things?

Then I remember Brynn. Has she been released from that juvenile facility? Two years have passed since I last saw her. Is she waiting for me downstairs? To crash on my couch? I step away from the door and stare at the speaker in shock. For some reason I can't stop thinking about her. Will she come for me now? Attack me on the street when I least expect it? Maybe I'm just imagining things and it's really not her waiting for me down in the lobby. Will I be ready for her if it is? What will I say to Brynn when the time comes? I grab a steak knife, grip the handle like I did on that fateful day when I killed Dalton, and slip it into my pocket for good measure.

Then I wait for her.

Yes, I know I'll be ready.

Acknowledgments

First, I'd to thank all the booksellers for carrying and selling my novels. Without them, *Pray for the Girl* would have never ended up in your hands and in your minds—or on your eReader. Thanks to all the wonderful readers who've turned their love of books into my life's work. Spreading enthusiasm by word of mouth is still the best way to help an author succeed. I couldn't have done any of this without my terrific agent, Evan Marshall. His guidance and advice have made all the difference in my writing career, and he's never afraid to give it to me straight up. I owe a great deal to my editor at Kensington, John Scognamiglio. His patience and editing brilliance really made this novel sing. Thanks to Lulu Martinez, Robin Cook, Lauren Jernigan, Steven Zacharius, and everyone else at Kensington for assisting me through the publishing process. Your dedication and support are appreciated more than you know. Portland, Maine can be a cold place, but the writing community there is exceptionally warm and inviting. Thanks to all my fellow writers who have helped me along this journey. Finally, I would have never been able to do this without the love and support of Marleigh, Allie, and Danny.

With **The Neighbor** *and* **Pray for the Girl,** *Joseph Souza proved himself a master of twisty and unpredictable psychological suspense. In this riveting new novel, a mother is unwittingly drawn into the dark underbelly of her picture-perfect Maine town . . .*

Shepherd's Bay has been home to generations of lobstermen and their families. Lately, affluent newcomers have been buying up waterfront property and mingling uneasily with the locals. Tensions are high, especially since Blair Pryce—a teenage boy from the wealthier side of town—disappeared weeks ago. But another disturbing incident soon follows.

When high school junior Katie Lee and her friend, Willow Briggs, fail to come home after a night out, Katie's mother, Isla, is frantic. Two agonizing days go by before Katie is found, bruised and bloodied, yet alive. Isla is grateful. But Willow, a wealthy newcomer from Los Angeles, is still missing. And Katie can't remember anything about the night of their disappearance.

Isla tries to help her daughter sort through her hazy recollections, and to recall the truth of her tangled friendship with privileged, beautiful Willow. At the hair salon she owns, Isla hears dark whispers about wild parties, drug deals, and love triangles gone wrong. How much truth is in the gossip? Is Blair's disappearance linked to the others? And what other shocking secrets lie at the heart of Shepherd's Bay—and of the family Isla is struggling to hold together?

Please turn the page for an exciting sneak peek of Joseph Souza's
THE PERFECT DAUGHTER
coming soon wherever print and e-books are sold!

ISLA

*S*HE SHOT UP OFF THE MATTRESS, HER FACE BATHED IN a sheen of sweat. Had she just heard something? Or had she suffered another bad dream? She'd been having a lot of them lately, ever since that rich boy from Harper's Point vanished without a trace. No, something seemed not quite right. She glanced across the bed, registering Ray's absence. It was just like him to disappear when she needed him most.

The alarm clock on her nightstand flashed 3:32 in red digits. She turned toward the large bay window, which Ray had installed last year, despite having no funds to do so. A wonder the bank had even loaned them the money. And yet it really opened the room up and provided them with a beautiful view of the bay and the ocean far below.

She remained perfectly still. Then she heard it again.

A loud crashing noise downstairs. Someone appeared to be mucking about in her kitchen. A jolt of adrenaline spiked through her. She flung off the well-worn quilt, the same quilt her mother had made as a wedding present for them so many years ago. Her mother, God bless her soul, had been one of those quilt-obsessed women who the older she got, the more fanatical about quilts she became.

She walked over to the bay window and noticed that Ray's beat-up truck was not parked in its usual spot. Not like he hadn't disappeared from their bed before, often in the middle of the night. She'd gotten used to waking up and not seeing his long, wiry body next to hers.

Another loud smashing noise came from downstairs.

Terror gripped her as she quietly opened the bottom dresser drawer. Reaching down, she punched the four-digit combination into the electronic keypad on the safe and waited a few seconds. The door to the safe opened and revealed the loaded Glock. The sight of the gun scared her, but she was now glad to have it. She picked it up and let its weight settle in the palm of her hand. Then she pulled out her phone and dialed the Shepherd's Bay Police Department instead of 911, knowing that all 911 calls were directed to a regional dispatcher twenty miles away, and they didn't know their ass from their elbow about the street patterns in this town. Karl Bjornson answered. She'd known that voice since they were high school sweethearts.

"Someone's in my house, Karl," she whispered. "Hurry up and send someone over."

"You sure it's not the wind? It's been blowing pretty

hard tonight, and you have all those trees around your property."

"I know what I'm hearing. The noise is coming from inside my house. Besides, I think I know the sound of wind blowing through the trees." Something else crashed downstairs and jolted her to the reality of the situation.

"Where's Swisher?" Swisher had been Ray's nickname since childhood.

"How the hell should I know? Just send someone— and fast."

"Okay, Isla. Take it easy. I'll be right over."

Holding the gun aloft, Isla tiptoed to the doorway, trying to be as quiet as possible. Her two kids lay asleep in their rooms, hopefully unaware that an intruder was rummaging through their house. She cinched her robe so as not to trip over it and made her way downstairs. Her face grimaced in agony every time one of the worn floorboards creaked underfoot, and she prayed the intruder in her kitchen wouldn't hear her approaching. She gripped the Glock in hand once she reached the landing.

Her heartbeat raced as she leaned against the kitchen doorframe. She took a few deep breaths, psyching herself up, grateful that she'd always been a light sleeper. Would she have the nerve to shoot the bastard if it came to that? Yes, she realized, she would. Hopefully, the mere sight of her would scare the person away. Besides, her house held nothing of value.

Still gripping the gun with two hands, she held it up by her chin so that the barrel pointed toward the ceiling. Her hands trembled at the prospect of shooting another human being. From the sounds of it, the intruder seemed perfectly fine rummaging around in her kitchen. But what were they looking for? She counted down from three, took a couple of deep breaths, and then jumped out, pointing the weapon.

What she saw surprised her.